I0563485

Haunted

Haunted Book One

R.L. Merrill

Haunted
Copyright © 2014, 2016, 2024
Celie Bay Publications LLC

Published By: Celie Bay Publications LLC

Cover design by: Elizabeth Mackey

Edited by: Revisions by Edit Me This, Original by LTE Editing

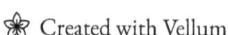 Created with Vellum

I owe all of my success and achievements to my mother, Linda Rae. Thanks, Mom, for always being there for me when I needed you

HAUNTED

This is an updated release for Haunted's 10th Publishversary! This was my first self-published title and I've released more than sixty titles since then. I've done a few rounds of revisions of this book over the years, and though there are parts that I would do differently if I were writing the book today, I love that this book still resonates with new readers, and it still makes me incredibly proud.

There is at least one more story to be told in this world, and I will get to it, but if you can't wait, be sure to check out my release in the Road to Rocktoberfest 2024 shared world, *Feuds and Interludes*, for a little teaser.

The Haunted Series, Teacher: Hollywood Rock 'n' Romance Trilogy, and the *Rock 'n' Romance Series* are some of my favorite stories that I've written, and I look forward to revisiting those worlds in the future, so ***stay tuned for more...***

PROLOGUE

December, 2011

Blood throbbed in time with her heartbeat against her tender skin, making this the most uncomfortable plane ride she'd ever experienced. It was even worse than the red-eye from L.A. to Japan she'd taken a few months ago while getting over a bout of bronchitis.

She'd known it would be painful getting a tattoo, and had heard the aftermath wasn't easy either. She'd followed the artist's directions for aftercare, but she still felt like she had a third-degree burn on her right hip. Thankfully she'd brought a loose skirt for the trip, although it was still clinging to her raw flesh.

The artist had been so patient with her, reassuring her that the pain would be worth it in the end. She was really nice, too. Someone she could have been friends with under different circumstances. They'd talked about many things, and she almost felt like she could have told her anything.

It got her thinking that maybe it was time to get some help.

When the flight attendant announced they could take off their seat belts and deplane, she was thrilled. She grabbed her overnight bag and briefcase and stood in the aisle. It had been a long couple of days, but she was so glad she'd been able to see Mama and get away from the insanity here. Tomorrow night was the big release party the Bones latest album, and she had been planning on flying home just before, figuring the party would take the focus off her little trip. Her husband was having fits, though, which was why she was home a day early.

It was worth it, she told herself. The yelling, the threats... She could take it for a taste of home. For how much longer, though, she had no clue.

She loved him, so very much. But he was dangerous—and the danger was not only emotional. She also didn't know how much longer she could take the pressure of putting on a happy face for everyone without breaking down. She had to make it appear that everything was peachy but inside, she was crumbling.

"Where the hell have you been?"

These were the words that greeted her when she got home.

"What the fuck was I supposed to tell everyone? Who were you with? Were you with someone else?"

These were the usual questions. She'd grown so tired of them.

"You better not even think about leaving me. I won't let you. I won't let some other guy *touch* you, not as long as you're still breathing, do you hear me?"

She was beginning to think the threats were real.

She was so tired. If only she didn't love him so much. If she could just get him to see that there wasn't anyone else...

"Haunted"

Her eyes our lens
   Her smile our light

Her laugh our applause
Her death our tragedy

April 2012

ONE

" I told you not to engage in oral sex right after getting your piercing! It was explicitly written in the directions. If the ball has disappeared into the flesh of your tongue then I suggest you go to the E.R." Mackenzie slammed down the phone with a huff, completely flustered. "I don't care how hot the guy is who wants to get blown, if you just got your tongue pierced the day before, you say *'hells no.'* But they never listen."

I blew my bangs out of my face and chuckled. "How many of those calls have you gotten this month?"

She threw up her hands. "I've lost count. Between this, and the guy who lost his piercing inside his girlfriend's swath of forest...I'm very clear about the fact that I am *not* a medical professional and they shouldn't call me when they have medical emergencies. What will it take for these people to get a lick of sense?"

"Well, she tried to have a lick a something, maybe dat's the problem," laughed my client, Daryl. He was enjoying our exchange. I think he came in so often because he liked our company. The tattoos were just souvenirs.

I smoothed the soapy spray across his arm with a paper towel. A few more passes of my needle and his daughters' portraits would be done.

I reached up with the back of my arm and wiped the sweat from my brow. The air conditioning being on the fritz was not helping matters tonight. The AC was just another thing nagging at me from my endless list of "Shit to Do ASAP." Being a shop owner was far less glamorous than most people assumed. Besides getting to tattoo to my heart's content, I also had the added bonus of having to maintain an old building on the edge of the French Quarter. But this is what I told myself I wanted to do with my life, so bitching about it was not allowed.

"What's a 'swath of forest' anyway, Kenzie Kitten?"

Mackenzie shot Daryl an annoyed look. "Think of a word your less-enlightened sex likes to use to refer to a vagina."

He appeared deep in thought. "I'm stumped," he finally said. "Besides, it's not like I should be using that kind of language around ladies such as yourselves."

I rolled my eyes. "Doesn't stop most of the dudes who come in here," I muttered.

Mackenzie was full of spit and vinegar tonight. "Well it should, dammit. I mean, shit. Don't nobody got any fucking manners anymore?"

She had us in stitches. I could tell she was tired, though. She'd had a busy day today, piercing a few navels and parts farther south, and selling our shop merchandise to a surprisingly large amount of foot traffic. Plus, it took a lot of energy to be her.

"Jay, you got any more appointments tonight?" Mackenzie was up front looking over the books. She was a Jill of all trades; she could pierce, massage, do professional makeup and create masterpieces with hair. Thank the gods she was also much better with numbers and seemed to love handling the business side of this venture, because it was totally frustrating to me.

"Not tonight. I'm calling it quits after I'm done with Daryl here."

The large man grunted and wiped the perspiration off of his bald dome. It was unseasonably warm for an early April afternoon. Soon the humidity would blanket New Orleans like a hot towel at a barbershop and the tourist crowds would thin for the summer.

"Aw, come on now, sugar," he purred in his Cajun drawl. "I wanted to take you out for a drink after dis. You owe me after five hours of my blood, sweat and tears." He gave me a wink and then a grimace as I finished the last of the sky-blue shading. Daryl's piece featured his two daughters dressed up like little angels having a tea party. I based it on a gorgeous candid he'd taken of them a few weeks ago. After he'd had it developed, he'd dashed straight over with it so I could start drawing.

The incongruence of this burly biker with two cherubic princesses in pink popping off his biceps would have been laughable, but A) no one laughed at Daryl; and B) everyone knew how much the president of the local motorcycle club, The Righteous Riders, loved his little girls.

Daryl Doucette was in his mid-fifties and built like a lumberjack on steroids. He shaved his head but had nearly a foot-long reddish beard. He scared the shit out of most people. However, if he chose to let you into his circle, you were treated like royalty.

I'd been lucky enough to meet him shortly after my arrival in town, and through him, I'd acquired most of my now admirably sized client base. It seemed someone who could do traditional-style tattoos as well as color portraits and surreal subject matter was hard to find in the area, so my appointment book filled up quick. I'd met Mackenzie along the way and we'd decided to get a place together. That was a year ago, and our little shop, Pins and Needles, was keeping its head above water.

"You're sweet, Daryl, but I have a long day ahead of me tomorrow and I need to get some shut-eye."

He narrowed his eyes at me and then nodded. "You got visitors tomorrow, yeah? How long dey here for?"

I sighed as I pulled off my gloves and sat back to give his piece a last glance. I was pleased with my work; the girls' tiaras sparkled just the way I wanted and their blue eyes really looked alive. It was almost as if you could reach out and pinch their cheeks. Of course, if you made that mistake, Daryl would knock you on your ass.

"They'll be here two days. They're just flying in to check on me. They're probably convinced I'm selling my body to support myself since 'tattooing will never make you any money'."

My stepmother, Shannon, and my grandma were supposedly flying out from California to celebrate my 26th birthday. In reality, I knew they were coming to make sure I wasn't starving or resorting to illegal activity. It'd been a year and a half since I'd left my home in Northern

California, and I'd never looked back. That didn't mean that family ties disappear, however. It was less painful to just focus on my new life here in N'awlins than to dwell on the circumstances of my leaving.

"And after dat, you'll let me take you for dat drink now, won't ya?"

I gave Daryl a big hug, loving the way he and his papa-bear beard and big belly made me feel appreciated in a way so different from my own father.

"I *will* see you after that, Daryl, but only to come visit those beautiful daughters and that *wife* of yours, to see how they like your new ink and to make sure you're taking good care of it."

He blushed and chuckled his agreement. Working around mostly male artists and clients meant having to dodge come-ons, hands, and whatever was unwelcomely thrown your way.

"Yeah, yeah, just rain on my parade. Can't an old man dream?"

It was my turn to laugh. "Not when those dreams will have you singing soprano. Now get home and go to bed. Drink water and take Ibuprofen."

He waved goodbye and climbed on his Harley. The motor growled to life and shook the windows as he revved it up and pulled out onto the street.

I went about cleaning my station and setting up for the next day. Shannon and Grandma weren't due in until four and were taking a cab from the airport to their hotel, so I'd have time to maybe take a walk-in or two before meeting up with them. Keeping busy was how I was going to make it through their visit in one piece.

A few minutes later, Daryl's Harley pulled up out front again, and I frowned and looked around to see if he'd left anything but came up empty.

"What's up, Daryl? You want your money back already?"

He laughed out loud and stepped up to the counter to give Mackenzie a hard time. "Nah, chère, I figured I'd come back and take Kenzie for a ride."

Mackenzie rolled her eyes. "Don't tease like that; you know I want your bike. You might not make it back, old man. I might dump your ass in the swamp and take your bike for a nice long ride. No one would ever find you."

He pulled a lock of her cotton-candy-pink hair and whispered something to her that resulted in her socking him in his good arm.

"Hey, now. I'm wounded over here." He rubbed at his good arm with mock suffering.

"You're gonna be wounded when I call Katie," Mackenzie warned.

This back and forth was Daryl's favorite pastime, but it was completely innocent and both Mackenzie and I knew it. He loved his wife desperately and just got a kick out of being a dirty old man with his favorite two hot young things.

"Now now, tame yourself, Kenzie Kitten. I remembered I got something to tell Jaylene." He looked over at me, suddenly all business. "My nephews and their band are coming to town for a bit. Dey rented an old place here in the Quarter to work on dey new album. Dey want to get tattooed while dey here, and of course I told dem you'd have to do it."

I narrowed my eyes at him. "You didn't promise my hand in marriage to any of them, did you?"

He chuckled again, his shoulders shaking. "No way, chère. None of dem could make you happy like I could. Dey just boys, you need an experienced man." He waggled his eyebrows at me and it was my turn to roll my eyes.

"Ha ha, funny guy. You better watch out or the next time you ask me for a tattoo, I'm going to let Katie at you with my machine."

He held his hands up in surrender. "No way. She'll tattoo 'Property of' on my man parts and that wouldn't feel none too fine. On my honor, Jaylene, I told my nephews you are the best and to come and see you. Dey seen your work on me and my boys, and dey wanted me to set up an appointment for dem to come in and talk to you."

"Of course I'll meet with them. When did they want to come in?"

He rubbed the back of his head and gave me that boyish smile of his that I could never resist, not when it meant he needed me to babysit, or when he needed me to go check on Katie if he was on the road. I raised an eyebrow and crossed my arms in front of me.

"Well, the thing is...I told dem you could meet tonight. I meant to tell you about it before we started and, well, I was just too excited about my new ink."

He knew I'd never say no to him, so I heaved an exaggerated sigh and said, "What time will they be here?"

At that moment, a black Hummer pulled up out outside, music blaring from partially downed windows.

I looked over at Mackenzie, whose eyes were wide with excitement. We were both currently unattached, and while I was completely satisfied with that arrangement, she was always looking for Mr. Right-for-the-time-being. And rock 'n' roll boys were her weakness.

Mine too, if I was being perfectly honest.

The doors opened and out poured five sunglasses-wearing, denim-clad, tattooed and pierced rock 'n' roll boys.

Mackenzie grabbed for her pink lip gloss without taking her eyes off the men about to enter our shop and applied said gloss expertly, screwed the cap back on and placed it under the counter. I glanced at her outrageous outfit of the day—a light teal bustier decorated with black ribbon, black above-the-knee ruffled skirt, white tights and matching teal four-inch stilettos. With her pink hair, false eyelashes and expertly applied makeup, she was a knockout. Her style decorated most of our shop, and somehow avoided clashing with my black-and-chrome, heavy metal influence.

I smiled and shook my head, hoping none of these men were a walking heartbreak for her.

My appearance of the day consisted of well-worn and torn Levi capris, a black tank and low-top red Chucks. My blonde and black hair was piled on top of my head in a messy, half-pulled ponytail. It was desperately in need of some TLC.

The door opened and our welcome bell chimed. The first one in walked directly over to Daryl, who was in front of me at the counter, and the two embraced warmly. The others shook hands and hugged him. It was obvious they all respected and probably feared him. I saw out of the corner of my eye that a couple of the guys had picked up my portfolio and were glancing through it, exclamations coming out at each page's offerings.

"I gather this is one of your nephews?" I smiled professionally at the man currently hugging Daryl. His black hair was stylishly spiked all over the place and he had pleasant hazel-brown eyes. He was a few inches taller than my height of 5'8", lanky, and wore a white tank undershirt and black denim, tight-fitting jeans over black leather motorcycle boots.

"Jaylene, dis is my nephew, Marcus Lambert, singer for Maggie's Bones. Marcus, this beautiful lady is Jaylene Charles."

Marcus took my hand and leaned in for a kiss on the cheek. I was only sort of used to this typical Doucette greeting. Most of the people Daryl introduced me to greeted folks like this.

"So pleased to meet you, Miss Charles. You do amazing work and my uncle gave you the highest of recommendations." His eyes crinkled when he smiled in a way that probably made most young women lose their panties in a heartbeat. If that didn't completely slay them, his slight Cajun drawl would finish them off.

"Thank you, Mr. Lambert. Daryl is too kind. He tells me that you all would like to get some work done?"

He nodded and immediately he lost some of his playfulness. "Yes, ma'am. A tribute piece. But let me first introduce you to my mates." He gestured to the rest of the ragtag group.

They had been chatting quietly, with the exception of a tall guy who still had his aviator shades on and was looking out the front window. I couldn't see his face but he was imposing even from across the shop. His toned arms were crossed over his chest and both were covered in black and gray sleeves spreading out from under his snug white t-shirt. He was wearing black board shorts with Vans, a chain hanging down from his belt loop.

Marcus introduced his band mates and I had to focus on breathing as I was presented with each one of these otherworldly handsome men.

"This is Mage, our bass player. My brother Jade, our rhythm guitar player. Star, our drummer. And that over there is D, our lead guitarist."

The man looked over and nodded at me. His shoulder was touching the window, giving me a perfect view of his profile once he'd turned away and continued to stare out the window from an angle. My line of sight was immediately drawn to his mouth, perfect lips that were held in a barely perceptible pout. Beneath his tattoos, his skin was very fair, making his black hair that much more dramatic.

I had to tear my gaze away from this D guy to say hello to the others. They all greeted me as Marcus had and I went through the motions, head spinning. Damn. Too much male presence and cologne can make a gal heady.

Mage was around six feet with long, curly brown hair, rich tawny skin and pale green eyes. He and Jade were similarly built, but Jade's jet-black, straight hair hung down to his waist and he had the same hazel eyes as his brother Marcus.

Star was the lone blond in the group, with hair that stuck up all over, tan skin and dark brown eyes. He was a little shorter than the others and leaner. He moved like a boxer, quick and dangerous.

"It's nice to meet you all. Do you have reference material or ideas?"

They all looked at each other uncomfortably. Mage and Jade actually put their heads down. D was rubbing the heel of his palm against his chest. Even the air felt heavy.

Marcus spoke up. "Actually, we had something a little unconventional in mind."

I frowned. The artist in me was intrigued. "How unconventional are we talking?"

Daryl laughed out loud. "Chère, don't you go worrying your pretty little head. These boys are harmless."

Marcus made a show of giving me his most innocent smile, complete with fluttering eyelashes. My eyebrow rose even higher, although why I was surprised this man-child would resort to juvenile gestures is beyond me.

Daryl put his arm around Marcus's neck and pulled him into a headlock. "Let me put it to you dis way—if dey don't behave, I'll tear dem limb from limb. I don't care how many millions dose limbs are worth."

The guys laughed nervously, all except Mr. Mysterious, who was still staring out my window with a thoughtful look on his face.

Double damn.

Daryl pushed Marcus away and Marcus ran a hand through his hair and chuckled. "Now, Uncle Daryl, would I ever be anything other than a gentleman?" Daryl narrowed his eyes at him and the others snickered.

"Alright, would I ever be anything other than a gentleman with a woman you had under your protection? No, absolutely not. I value all my, ahem, body parts."

They all laughed at that, including me. Then I suddenly remembered Mackenzie and turned to see her talking animatedly with Star over at the other counter. He was looking at her trays of body jewelry. It appeared Star was intimately familiar with a piercing needle. He had wide gauges in his ears, a stud through his bottom lip, a ring through his nostril, and one ear was speared with a barbell. As he smiled and spoke to her, I could see light glinting off a tongue stud, something Mackenzie seemed to be studying seriously.

"So what do you think, Miss Charles?" Marcus was smiling at me expectantly. It was obvious he was the voice for the band. "Are you willing to work for us? We'll pay you generously for your time away from the shop."

I started at his words. "Away from the shop? I'm sorry, just where do you expect me to work?"

Marcus looked questioningly at his uncle. Daryl put his hands up. "I hadn't told her yet, son." He turned to me with a serious look on his face. "These boys will be staying at the St. Germaine house for the next few weeks. They'd like you to come and stay with them, hear their stories, and help them design their pieces."

I'd been by the St. Germaine house, it was on one of the haunted tours Mackenzie and I had taken a few months ago. I had been utterly entranced by its beauty and the chilling stories the tour guide had told us. One of my favorite authors was rumored to have tried to buy the house, as it had inspired her writing.

Shaking myself, I questioned Daryl. "And how am I supposed to be gone from my shop for that long?" I'd never denied Daryl anything. How was I supposed to say no? But our shop was only in the black because I worked my ass off five, sometimes six days a week. "I've got appointments scheduled." I looked over at Mackenzie for help, but she was too busy making eyes at Star.

"I had our attorney draw up a contract for you to look over, Miss Charles. Please, if you would be so kind, take tonight to look it over and we'll be in touch tomorrow. I really do hope we can work together. It would mean a lot to us."

I could sense a profound sadness from Marcus when he spoke. He looked over at Mr. Mysterious, who had taken off his sunglasses and was looking at me with the deepest blue eyes I'd ever seen. His beanie covered all but the very front of his black hair, which was pushed back from his forehead. The bottoms of his ears were visible and both were adorned with thick silver hoops.

My breath caught in my chest and I couldn't help but stare as he moved gracefully over to stand next to Marcus. He looked to his band-leader, who he towered over, then to Daryl, who patted him fatherly-like on the back.

He swallowed and spoke in a low, quiet voice. "I understand you're very busy, Miss Charles. But we need the right person if we're going to do this. It's time, and we really need to move on. So please, think about it?"

Such sadness. My mouth went dry as his blue eyes held mine.

"I will. Think about it. I'm sorry; this just isn't something I've ever done." I glanced again over at Mackenzie and this time she was looking at me, nodding excitedly.

"Can I call you tomorrow evening? I just...I need to figure out if it's even possible." I glanced down at my appointment book. I was booked solid this weekend and most of next week. I gulped. That money would get us through the slower months until the weather cooled and the tourists poured back in.

Marcus appeared relieved I wasn't just shutting them down and showing them the door. "That would be just fine, Miss Charles. We're getting settled in over there so here's our manager's card." He handed me a gray card with an embossed black skull taking up the entire left side. It had the name Sherry Jordan on it with a Los Angeles area code.

I looked up at Marcus and then to D, who was looking down and nodding while Daryl talked to him quietly. He glanced up at me and the faintest of smiles lifted his lips. Then he looked back at Daryl, embraced him, put on the sunglasses, and walked out to the car to wait for the others.

Mackenzie batted her glittered lashes at Star, who seemed ensnared and had to be physically removed from the premises by his band mates, one hand dramatically over his heart.

The men filed out and Daryl followed them to the door, shut it, then turned on me as the Hummer blasted to life and pulled out onto Frenchmen Street. He smiled at me, confident he was going to get his way. He might have also noticed my gaze following the men out. They looked as good leaving as they had coming in.

Well, shit. More than my inner artist was intrigued.

"So what do you think of my boys, eh? Their music is a bit screamy for my tastes but their hearts are good. They've had some heartache, them. You can help them heal, Jaylene. You know you can. Working with them might send your business into the big time; these rock stars, they all be comin' to you then."

I smiled at his assurance.

Daryl somehow sensed I had daddy issues and did his best to subtly play the part for me. "What other reservations you got?"

"*Who's* got the Master's degree here? Geesh, I think you make a better therapist than I ever would have."

He laughed deeply. "Dahlin', what do you think my job is? All I deal with is head cases."

He was right. Daryl's club was full of men and women who were all damaged and derelict, but they paid complete allegiance to him. During their time with Daryl, they all worked toward becoming upstanding members of society. He hadn't gotten to be their president by shying away from a challenge.

Not like me. I'd graduated Magna Cum Laude from California State University, Hayward, with a Master's degree in Counseling Psychology, ready to begin my career. Life had other plans for me, and now my place was here. I knew I'd made the right choice for me, but echoes of others' expectations made me question my decision regularly.

Not Daryl, though. He believed the best work was done on the front lines, and he considered my chosen profession as reputable as they come. Gods bless this man.

Again, I was faced with the dilemma of how I could get out of this situation without damaging my relationship with him, a relationship that went beyond professional to more like family.

"Daryl, I can't just walk away from my business for weeks. I'm booked almost solid and I need the money to get through the summer. Not to mention, some of my appointments are friends of *yours*."

He nodded, a smug look on his burly face. "You just be sure to read dat contract. I think dem boys will take care of everything. And if anyone gets upset, you just tell dem to come and see me, y'hear?"

Sigh. Daryl could just snap his fingers and things were taken care of? Okay, he probably could—but I didn't like being beholden to anyone, and as much as I trusted him, I could never ask anyone to bail me out. And it wasn't just me that was a part of this decision.

"What about Mackenzie? I can't just leave her."

Mackenzie put her arm around me. "For that, Jay? You'd *better* leave me. I will never forgive you if you don't leave me for them. You *must* go stay with that fine-looking bundle of male specimens."

Leave it to her to be ruled by her hormones. I shrugged her arm off. "Kenzie, I can't base my business decisions on a bunch of hot guys."

She looked at me as if I were her slower younger sister. "Um, duh. Yes you can, and you'd better!"

I glanced at the contract; it read like legalese blah-blah. Then I peered up at the Metallica clock over my station—7:30. I still needed to clean my flat and do laundry before I could even get to bed, not to mention I needed to clean *myself* up before my family arrived. I needed a haircut, I probably still had yesterday's eyeliner on, and my nails were a mess—and don't even mention my feet.

I pulled back my long blonde and black-streaked hair and blew my bangs out of my face. Then I made my excuses and told Daryl I'd see him soon. He reminded me to read the contract and he stepped out the door.

Mackenzie locked it behind him and then turned on me with a challenging stare. "You're thinking up reasons why you shouldn't do this. Well, unthink them. Do you even know who they are? Maggie's Bones are *huge*. They toured with Avenged Sevenfold. Remember when I went to that show? They totally rock."

Mackenzie and I shared a love of rock music, but mine was

entrenched in music pre-1995 and hers started about that time. I was forever trying to school her, and she would bring stuff in to play for me that was okay, but lacked the soul I found in the older stuff.

"That's great, Mackenzie. Why don't *you* go tattoo them?"

She crossed her arms over her generous cleavage. "Girl, be real. You know this is a great opportunity. Go read that contract and if it's for enough money to get you by, then do it. Even if it's not, hell, it's enough eye candy to get you by for a lifetime. *Damn*, they are fine-looking men."

I shook my head as the number of upcoming appointments swam in front of my eyes. It had been a long day and this proposition had me overwhelmed.

"Go upstairs and get your head together. Read that contract."

Mackenzie was doing her best to wear me down. I shook my head at her again and waved good night, reminding her to set the alarm and turn out the lights after she did her orders and answered shop email.

She and I both had flats upstairs, a perk to this shop space. We were sort of roommates but had our own spaces as well. And I needed my space tonight. I checked the back door, found it locked, and then trudged up the stairs. I had been going since eight this morning, worked through lunch and then ate a protein bar around four. My stomach was growling so I heated up some leftover spaghetti and sat down at my little dinette with the contract.

Contract of Temporary Employment between Jaylene R. Charles and Maggie's Bones, LLC.

Period covered: from April 13, 2012, to May 1, 2012

Place of employment: St. Germaine House, Rue Royale, New Orleans, LA.

Description of Duties:

Embed with members of organization and work with them to design a memorial tattoo to Margaret Boudreaux. Conduct interviews and planning sessions with each member individually and as a group. When design is agreed upon, complete memorial tattoos.

Amenities: Room and board will be provided on the premises. Wi-

Fi, computer, drawing station, table, and all other necessary items for work will be provided.

Restrictions: No visitors allowed. Personal phone calls will be limited by work schedule. Employee may not discuss the nature of this arrangement, nor the memorial, with anyone in the press or anyone not deemed need-to-know status. All drawings will be approved by the members of the LLC and will become the property of the LLC upon completion of the contract. No alcohol or controlled substances will be allowed on the premises, nor is the employee to partake of said substances for the duration of the contract.

Compensation: Employee to be paid a sum of $17,000, with separate payments for each of the completed memorial tattoos, with amounts TBD by employee.

Any questions or issues with the contract may be discussed with LLC representative Sherry Jordan.

What? The? Hell?

Isolation? My art would become the property of the LLC? No controlled substances?

Well, that last one wouldn't be a problem. I didn't drink much, especially not while I was working. Never did drugs; they had no appeal for me. And it sounded like I'd be working 'round the clock.

I picked up the phone and started to call Daryl—then realized I probably shouldn't discuss any of this with him, in case he wasn't on the "need-to-know" list, although he probably was. But how *much* did he know? If he trusted these guys, I assumed I could too, but holed up with them for two and a half weeks?

And $17,000? That was a hell of a lot of money, more than I'd make in the shop. And that wasn't including the actual pieces I tattooed. Damn. That would go a long way towards keeping us afloat. It would be a safety net.

I blew my bangs off my forehead with a huff and read over the contract again. So many things could go wrong with this situation. What if these guys were all assholes and I wasn't inspired to draw anything for them?

And that's exactly when inspiration hit.

Mr. Mysterious, or D, whatever his name was. Something about him spoke to me.

I picked up my pencils and opened a sketchbook lying on the shelf next to me. From memory, I drew him as he was standing in front of the window. It was amazing how I could recall so many details. From my perspective at the counter, I'd seen his profile behind his sunglasses. His lashes curled back against heavy eyelids and deep, furrowed brows. Wasn't there a scar in his left eyebrow?

I stood up quickly and stepped back from my drawing. He was staring up at me. I'd drawn him looking out the window with his shades on, but his reflection faintly showed those sad eyes. I traced my finger over his face and wondered what could have made him exude so much sorrow. The memorial must be for someone he cared deeply about. They had all seemed so uncomfortable talking about it.

"Well, those counseling skills I paid so much for just might come in handy," I said to myself as I walked over to my window. Things were just starting to get moving outside. With the window open, I could hear a guitar playing soulful blues. The music was pouring from the doors of the club across the street and it sounded sweet to my ears, so I left it open while I ran a bath. I figured after I'd soaked for a bit, I could attack the house and get it in decent shape for my visitors. My appearance would never meet their standards but then hey, what about me did?

My stepmom and grandma loved me dearly, but my tastes had always crossed the border of what they found acceptable into completely out-there territory. A lot of folks couldn't understand the draw of tattoos and I gave up trying to explain it to them.

I had them because they were pieces of my life, my experiences, people who were important to me. I'd been into drawing from the time I could remember. I'd shirked art class assignments in favor of doing what I wanted to do, the one area I could be myself and not conform to what others thought I should be doing. I spent so much time trying to please others that my drawings were the one place I could please myself.

The summer after my freshman year at Cal State, I walked into my first tattoo shop and walked out with a sun tattooed on my lower back, to light my way.

Unfortunately, when tattoos went mainstream and every other girl was getting a lower back tattoo, it was dubbed the "tramp stamp" and I was once again trying to dig my way out of others' expectations. Guys thought tattoos meant easy access. A few well-placed punches put an end to that reputation, and I was considered unapproachable from then on. All because I didn't want to be groped. Which was perfect; I didn't need that kind of attention.

That first trip not only branded my skin, it landed me a job that I absolutely loved. I was a shop girl for the rest of college. Eventually I showed my boss Stephen my drawings, which led to him insisting upon me becoming his apprentice.

I was leading two lives: college girl by day, tattoo artist by night and weekend. My coursework was tough but I somehow managed to get through a bachelor's and then a Master's degree. I'd always wanted to help people, loved being a sounding board to others, but I pushed forward with the degree because my family insisted I'd starve if I depended on tattooing for a living.

Never mind that my boss was very well known and respected, and made a comfortable living with his art. The thought that I was letting my family down nagged at me so much that I left the tattoo world and threw myself into an internship. A professor hooked me up with one of his colleagues, who gave me his undesirable clients, and I soon grew to loathe it.

My father was pleased, though, and all I'd ever wanted was his approval.

But then I got the early morning call.

Grandma asking me to come home. Me dropping everything. My father in the ICU with more tubes in him than I could count. A horrific week of watching him, waiting for a sign he would make it. And then saying goodbye.

That was it for me. I couldn't get out of there fast enough. I found a place to rent in New Orleans, a city I'd fallen in love with during a Spring Break trip I'd taken with some folks from the shop, and I bailed.

I hadn't been back since, and didn't plan on it. Shannon and Grandma said they understood, but they'd been shocked and frankly a little pissed I was "running away from my problems."

As far as I was concerned, I was running away from a life I dreaded and running to a new start.

My father's shadow was always there, making me doubt myself, but the longer I was in New Orleans, the easier it was to put those doubts in a lockbox and hide them away. Real healthy for a therapist-in-training.

"Brrrr!" The water had gone completely cold and I had a chill that was only remotely connected to the temperature. I got out and dried off, cursing when I realized I'd forgotten to shave my legs. I threw on a robe and stepped out of my cozy bathroom.

My flat wasn't much, there was one wall separating my teeny bedroom from the tiny living room. You entered into the kitchen, the bathroom was off to the right, and you had to walk through the dining area to get to the bedroom. My apartment and Mackenzie's mirrored each other. They were old but had character, and we had worked for a solid six months trying to make them livable. I owed her a lot. She'd kept me sane when I'd doubted we could pull off the shop.

The blues music was gone and in its place I could hear the thump of hip-hop, so I quickly shut the window. On a whim, I walked over to my computer and Googled Maggie's Bones. Their website had a decent design, lots of skulls, which I dug. They had an audio feature, so I hit play and was immediately bombarded with screeching guitars. I adjusted the volume and then let it play. I was just doing research, not stalking. This is what I told myself.

I grabbed some black nail polish and decided I'd redo my nails and toes. The first song ended and a second one started up, this one with a definite classical influence.

Why do I care? Why do I let it hurt me?
   Your words, like glass, slice me to the bone.
   I'm helpless, you're there in all your glory
   Me here cut to pieces, it's all I've ever known.

Whoa. Whoever the lyricist was, he obviously knew a little about pain.

. . .

Why do you keep me? Why do I stay?
  Your kisses, like acid, burn me to the core
  I'm helpless, you're there in all your glory
  Me here burned to ashes, it's all to settle scores.

I figured it wouldn't hurt to read a little about them while my nails dried; just doing my research.

The bio section just said they were family and friends who had been playing together since high school. They went to L.A. to hit the big time and were discovered by a major label. They stated their influences as metalcore, classic heavy metal, and Cajun and blues artists from New Orleans. Nice. Then I skimmed over some of their song titles...

"Mystikal Stick"? "Sin on My Face"? "Loving a Stranger"?

Those certainly sounded more Spinal Tap than Cajun and blues. What the hell sort of music was this?

Their cover photo was a close-up of Marcus, smiling wickedly with his hands outstretched. The other four were behind him: Star and Jade stood back to back with smirks on their faces, Mage was looking up, and D (the D apparently stood for Devon, according to the site) stood off to the side looking down and to the right like he didn't want to be there. Their most recent album, put out in December, was called *Burns Like Ice.*

O-*kay*. Not the most uplifting stuff I'd seen, but then this was the new age of metal. To be fair, the '90s grunge movement had certainly influenced this pessimism.

Another song started and it was mellower than the first. They weren't bad, actually. No Sabbath or Metallica, but better than a lot of the more current metal bands Mackenzie tried to get me to listen to. Marcus had a nice, clear, melodic voice, when he wasn't growling or screaming. They were good. Especially the guitar solos...

I smacked my forehead. This *wasn't* about Devon. It was about doing a job and getting paid handsomely for it. From what the contract said, I was supposed to help these guys deal with their loss, something to do with Margaret Boudreaux, and hopefully create some meaningful artwork for them.

Definitely this was a request within the scope of my expertise. But why was I feeling apprehensive? Maybe it was the whole "embedded" and "property" and "need-to-know status" that had me feeling a little creeped out.

I left the music playing, did a half-assed job cleaning up my flat, and collapsed on my bed with the weight of my thoughts pulling me under into a deep sleep.

Two

A loud sound woke me with a start the next morning and I practically fell out of bed, trying to remember where the hell I'd left my phone the night before. It was always on my nightstand when I went to bed. Apparently in my stupor, I'd gone to bed without it. I scrambled into the bathroom and found it, still chiming away in my pants pocket.

I was too late to answer and I didn't recognize the number. A few seconds later it buzzed to let me know I had a voice mail.

"Good morning, Miss Charles. This is Sherry Jordan, I represent Maggie's Bones. I wanted to discuss the contract you received yesterday and see if you had any questions for me. The band would like your answer by this evening, if possible. Call me, let's talk. I'll be available off and on this morning. Bye now."

Hmm, professional but friendly. I took a moment to collect myself and looked at the time. Ugh, nine. I needed to open the shop at ten, work until five, and then meet up with Shannon and Grandma at their hotel.

I hit redial and the phone rang twice before she answered. "This is Sherry."

"Hi. Sherry, this is Jaylene Charles. The tattoo artist?"

"Great. Hello, Miss Charles. I'm so sorry I wasn't there in person yesterday to meet with you. I had to fly back to L.A. to handle some business with the band's label. I thought maybe woman to woman, we could discuss the arrangement. I'll admit that as much as I love those guys, they aren't always the best at dealing with folks."

I liked her already. She talked about the band as if they were her bratty little brothers. "They were fine, they had a great negotiator with them."

She laughed heartily. "Do you mean Mr. Doucette? Jeez, he's worse than they are, but I understand you're friends with him, so you must know what I'm talking about."

My turn to laugh. "He's a force to be reckoned with, that's for sure. And they seem to know their place with him."

"Absolutely. So did you have a chance to read over the contract?" I admitted I had and she was quiet for a moment, her tone growing more serious. "And did you have any questions about it?"

I didn't know where to start. "I'm assuming the band wants their privacy and that explains the no-visitors or talking-to-the-press parts. I have no problem with that; I certainly respect the confidentiality of my clients. I guess I don't see why I need to stay with them? It's only a few blocks from my place."

"Part of the privacy is keeping their comings and goings private, including those who work with them. If folks knew they had a tattoo artist working on them, the tabloids would be all over that. Not to mention, they keep odd hours and want you to be available whenever they're ready. This is a personal thing for them. They're trying to get past an extended period of writer's block by coming to New Orleans, coming back home, and Marcus came up with the idea of the memorial as a way to maybe get them past it."

"A memorial for Margaret Boudreaux," I stated, and she confirmed.

"Yes. I'm not at liberty to discuss her with you. The guys want to tell you the story themselves. Can you work around that?"

"Sure. I guess so. This just isn't something I've ever done. I'm also concerned about my clients. I'm not sure what to do with my full schedule. I'd need some time to work that out, perhaps be allowed to leave occasionally?"

"I'm afraid that won't work, there's already quite a crowd hanging out in front of St. Germaine, trying to get an idea of who's staying there. As it is, we've got to come up with a plan to get you over there undetected."

I choked out a laugh. "This is beginning to sound like some cloak-and-dagger operation. Are you sure they're just a rock band and not superspies?"

I bit my tongue, what the hell was I doing, cracking jokes about this with her? Luckily for me, she laughed.

"You'll soon see just how covert our operations have to be some-times. The only reason they could come over yesterday to see you was because Mr. Doucette arranged the car for them, something he borrowed from a member of his club."

That's where I'd seen that damn Hummer before. "Rudy's! Of course. Rudy's been in here a lot lately, trying to decide what to get for his next tattoo. He's a little sweet on my coworker too, but I think she finally told him they wouldn't be dating. He left quite defeated."

Sherry laughed at that. "Men—they are forever little boys. Listen, I've got a meeting in about five minutes, is there anything else I can answer for you? Anything I can say to persuade you? They've got a lot riding on this, Miss Charles. Otherwise, I wouldn't be asking so much of you."

"I understand. Thanks for your time, Miss Jordan—"

She stopped me. "Sherry, please. And you are very welcome. I'd do whatever it takes to keep my boys happy, short of kidnapping you."

I wasn't sure how I felt about the kidnapping remark; hopefully that was off the table.

"It's a very generous offer, Sherry. Let me look at my schedule down in the shop today and I'll let you know my decision."

She thanked me, let me know again how much this would mean to the band and to all involved, and we said goodbye.

Wow, no pressure there. Yikes.

I'm not a miracle worker. I'm an artist—a tattoo artist. Sure, I've got a background in counseling, but if these guys were dealing with some heavy shit, why not go to a therapist? Metallica did it.

When I got downstairs, Mackenzie was playing the same album I had listened to last night by Maggie's Bones.

I shook my head. Definitely no pressure. "What do you think you're doing, turncoat?"

She turned, startled, and held a hand to her chest.

"*Moi*? Turncoat? Surely you jest. I have only your best interests at heart, Jay. And how much more interesting can this job opportunity be?"

I hesitated at what to tell her but I figured I'd need to explain my whereabouts. "Mackenzie, they want me to stay with them, twenty-four/seven, for seventeen days. That means no Jaylene at the shop. How can you be encouraging me to do this?"

She gave me an evil laugh and pointed a long silver nail at me. "Because, sweetie, you'll be with *them* and they are *hot* and it will *rock*."

She was *so* not seeing the big picture. "Do I have to remind you that we have customers? Ones who rely on me to be here? Who pay us so we can keep up our little love nest?"

She just shook her head, grabbed me by the upper arms and plopped me down on the stool in the counter. "Jaylene, for the love of all that's holy, you need to relax. It's only a couple of weeks. Think of it as summer camp—with really good scenery."

I groaned louder and she tried to assuage me by giving me a shoulder rub. In another life, she'd been a massage therapist, and a really good one.

"And I really can handle things," she was saying. "I already called Troy Lewis up in Baton Rouge and he said he'd come down with his apprentice and cover for you."

I jerked around, almost getting gored by a gigantic flower ring on her left hand. "You called *Troy*? Damn, Mackenzie. You could have talked to me about that first." Troy Lewis had sold the shop to us a year ago. He said he was tired of the tourists and wanted to move on and travel for a while. He'd offered his services if we ever got slammed or wanted a little variety. He was a solid artist, good with traditional, well versed in Japanese style. He could certainly cover the walk-ins.

I'd have to reschedule my regular clients, though. I had a couple of large pieces I was working on that the clients were coming in to get finished.

"Fine. I'll make some calls, see if I can free myself up."

I looked up at her. She was positively vibrating with excitement. Why wasn't I that worked up? Oh I know, because I was having some gigantic doubts.

"Kenz, you sure you're okay with this? You won't give the shop back to Troy, will you? I want to come home to our little love nest when this is all over."

"See, this is *exactly* what I'm talking about. You need to be nesting with a really nestworthy cock, not me." I smacked her ass before she was out of reach. "I'll be fine, Jay. Honest. But if you care about me at all, you'll save some for me?" She ran her hands over her breasts and licked her lips.

I threw a pen at her and she turned to help our first walk-in of the day.

I spent the next half hour making calls and was able to reschedule all but two of my clients, both of whom were on the second Saturday I'd be gone, and they had already bought plane tickets to come out here. Maybe I could get a day pass? I thought I'd run it by Sherry, so I called her but got her answering service.

"Hi, Sherry. I'm looking at my schedule and I can't get free on the twenty-first. I don't know what that does for the arrangement. Call me if you'd like to discuss. Thanks."

Unable to do anything else about it, I got to work cleaning up and setting out some new flash I'd done recently. Maggie's Bones was still blaring—Mackenzie was obviously not going to let up—so I gave in and listened, maybe bobbing my head just a little.

You pretend not to notice
  You're breathing faster
  I creep up behind you
  You're breathing faster
  I whisper my intentions
  You're breathing faster

One lick, one bite, one taste of you
I'm moving faster, I'm moving faster

Don't it make you want to scream
  Don't it get you on your knees
  Don't I make it so obscene
  Don't you want it, beg me please

Alrighty then, that's how it is with these guys. I wonder who wrote these tasty little morsels? What would I learn from my time with these guys? If I didn't have Daryl's assurance that they would behave, I'd be freaking out right now. I *was* freaking out, definitely. Mackenzie was right. They were an incredibly good-looking group of guys. Especially Devon.

I looked down and realized I was drawing him again. I wadded up the picture and threw it in the trash.

Okay, mind on the task at hand, Jay. Must focus.

An alarm beeped on my phone and I remembered I needed to check the flights and make sure Shannon and Grandma were on their way. I had an email from Shannon with the flight information, and another one from this morning that said they were getting ready to board the plane, couldn't wait to see me.

"Jay, Troy said that it's fine, he rescheduled some of his clients to come down here. He'll be here on Thursday to meet you and go over the schedule."

So it was a done deal. My schedule had been cleared and a replacement brought in. No sweat.

"Thanks." I looked down at my split ends, and then I looked around at the quiet shop. "Kenz? Think you might want to give me a quick haircut, dahlin'?"

My attempt at a drawl had her rolling her eyes. "You Californians just cannot imitate our sensual way of talking."

Mackenzie had grown up in the Garden District, gone to private schools, participated in Mardi Gras parades and the whole nine. Was a bit of a beauty queen. Then she'd opted out of her scholarship to Tulane and ran off to New York with a boyfriend. When he ran off on *her*, she'd enrolled in the Paul Mitchell Academy to learn the tricks of the beauty trade. She came by it naturally anyway and had decided it was her God-given duty to bring beauty to all who desired it.

She accepted the fact that beauty and I were passing acquaintances and did her best to encourage but not smother me with it.

"Of course, love. But you need more than just a trim. Your color is a mess. Want me to do that, too? You want Surfer Girl or Shop Girl? I can do you however you like."

She kept a station in the shop for the occasional makeover so I let her give me the works. She loved to do it, I loved her, and therefore it wasn't too much of a sacrifice.

When she was finished with me, my natural blonde was back, the black erased with a little help from our friend bleach, and she'd even added some darker blonde highlights. My brows were perfectly shaped and I didn't have to resort to bodily harm when she tried to go lower with the wax stick. I assured her that my grooming down below was up to date.

"Oh, you natural blondes, you just don't know how lucky you've got it. If I don't wax, it looks like dust bunnies are creeping out of my panties."

That was just too much of a gnarly visual for me. Thankfully she was done adding a touch of makeup before I jumped out of the chair.

"Thank you for that parting note." I looked over in our full-length mirror—and gasped when I saw the magic she'd worked on my hair. It looked natural but still edgy. I kept the back all one length, stick straight down to my waist, with just a bit of bangs. The darker highlights brought out my dark brown eyes and the natural-looking makeup added a glow to my face, a glow that had probably been missing for a while.

"Your outfit is a total drag on my makeover, though. Can I dress you, too?" She smiled sweetly.

I took one look at her, in her red leather hot pants with zippers, thigh-high fishnets, white satin blouse...

"Thanks, really. You've spent too much time on me today. And frankly," I gestured to her outfit, "you seem to have a lot going on there yourself."

She looked at me, puzzled—it took her a minute to catch on sometimes—and then she threw her hairbrush at me.

I ducked out of the way and scooted upstairs before she threw something harder or got better aim.

I looked in my wardrobe and decided on plaid board shorts, a black, fitted Metallica t-shirt and my Converse. I figured I'd better not push my luck. Too many changes and people might get strange ideas.

It's not that I didn't take pride in my appearance. I loved my artwork. I had a sleeve on my left arm with the classic movie monsters, skulls and crows, and both calves had large color pieces I had designed and my former boss had inked. I had yet to get my back done, that was going to happen soon, but I was still looking for the right person and thinking of the right design.

I heard the bells chiming as I came back down the stairs and as I emerged in the shop, I saw Katie, Daryl's wife, coming in with flowers.

"Jay! I'm so glad I caught you." She came past the counter and swept me into a huge hug. "Daryl's piece looks amazing. You made them look so beautiful." Joyful tears were pouring down her face, and Mackenzie came over with the tissue.

Katie handed me the bouquet of Gerbera daisies and lavender and dark purple irises. They were lovely and I placed them on the counter.

"Katie, I had great material to work with. That is one of my favorite pieces I've done yet. Your girls are so photogenic. They make good art. How are Grace and Allie?"

"They're perfect, Jay. Really. They are growing up so fast, and now I have them immortalized on that big old lug. My only complaint is that now I have to be careful where I smack the bastard when he pisses me off. Can't be touching my babies in anger."

She sniffled and we all laughed. Katie was in her early thirties with long, bleached-blonde hair. She'd definitely had some cosmetic work done, but not to the extreme, and she made jeans and a tee look like haute couture. She was a tough chick, but was just as welcoming and warm as her husband. I'd eaten many home-cooked meals at their house over the past year. They were especially fond of strays like me, and for some reason kept me around.

I loved their little girls. They were three and five, and were so damn cute and charming that they had all the adults in their lives eating out of their hands. Perhaps that's why they liked me to babysit. I didn't fall for it and the girls loved a challenge.

"Jay really did a great job. And speaking of jobs..."

I gave Mackenzie a warning look and slight shake of my head. Which she ignored.

"Where have you been hiding those nephews of yours and the rest of that holy-hot-as-hell crew? I mean really, we've known each other for how long and you didn't introduce us?"

Katie rolled her eyes and said, "If *you'd* cleaned up their drunken puke so they didn't get busted and been forced to wash their nasty, wet-dream-covered sheets, you wouldn't think they were anything but the snot-nosed brats they are. But I do love those guys. They're like little brothers to me."

She stopped suddenly and the tears threatened to come back, only this time, not out of joy.

"So you've known them a while?"

She nodded. "I met them when they were probably twelve or thirteen. One of their sisters was my best friend. So...your stepmom gets in this afternoon, Jay?"

I nodded, completely aware she was changing the subject and completely willing to do the same.

I looked at the clock and saw it was three already. "Yeah, I should get over to their hotel in a bit. Did Daryl take care of his arm like I told him to?"

"Of course. He listens when *you* tell him to do something. Next time I need him to change the oil in my car, will you tell him for me?"

I giggled. "Is it really that bad?"

She nodded. "Hell yeah, it's that bad. I sometimes think I have to remind him to take a shit."

I loved her foul mouth. It made me feel better about my penchant for profanity.

"I need to go pick up the girls from their gran's. I'll see you in a couple of weeks?"

Okay, guess she was in the need-to-know club. I wasn't sure how to respond to that. "Why, are you guys going away?" I asked her, playing along with her game.

She smiled conspiratorially. "No, but I hope you are. See ya." She winked at me and her sashaying hips swayed her right out the door.

"Well if that wasn't a ringing endorsement, I don't know what is." Mackenzie grabbed my arms and forced me to face her. "What are you afraid of?"

Her tone was concerned, not sarcastic, so I answered her honestly. "It's a lot of pressure, and I don't want to let anyone down. I'm not a miracle worker, and it sounds like that's what they're expecting. I don't know if I can do this, Mackenzie."

She shook her head. "I don't think miracles are part of the deal. What you are is an incredibly talented artist and a trained psychotherapist. You are a beautiful and funny woman who lacks fashion sense but makes up for it with her quick wit. Daryl loves you, and he obviously recommended you because you are the best for the job. Sure, it's out of your comfort zone, but wasn't moving to New Orleans? And you haven't been eaten by a gator or run over by a Mardi Gras float, have you?"

I giggled with her and pulled her into a hug. "And you, my Pink Lady friend, are too good for my ego." I grabbed up my keys and wallet and turned for the door. "I'll think about it on my walk over to the hotel."

She groaned and continued to chastise me as the door slammed shut behind me.

Oh Fates, what do you have in store for me?

THREE

The walk across the French Quarter to the Maison Dupuy Hotel was the perfect length of time for a debate between my internal angel and devil, but not too strenuous that I ended up sticky and sweaty.

I said hello to the bellhop. He'd been by the shop before with his friends, and he opened the door graciously for me.

"I'm still coming to get a tattoo from you, Miss Charles. I'm just a little chicken."

I smiled at him. "I promise I'll be gentle. Come on by anytime...uh, make that in a couple of weeks. I might be out of the shop for a bit."

He nodded, looked surprised, but knew enough not to ask.

I texted Shannon and she said they had been taking a short rest and would be down in a few minutes. I checked my email on my phone and found one from Sherry Jordan.

"Hey Jaylene! Good to hear from you. I talked to the guys and they said we can work something out for that weekend. If anything, we can have Mr. Doucette create a diversion and sneak you out. If that's the only holdup, I hope we have a deal? Please call me tonight and let me know. Thanks."

I blew out a breath, unsure if this was good news. It would have been easier to say no if I had the excuse of my out-of-town clients to use. Now I had no excuse.

I just didn't know whether I could handle all those men. What if they had certain "appetites"? Rock stars were notorious for that kind of thing, and being locked up with them for seventeen nights was totally pushing my luck for sure. I guess all I'd have to do is pull the Daryl card. He definitely seemed to have their respect. Could I really pull this off?

"Well hello, sweetheart." Grandma walked gingerly toward me with a cane in one hand and her other outstretched for a hug. My grandmother had the best hugging skills on the planet. She was soft and warm, smelled sophisticated, and squeezed you 'til you thought you'd burst.

Shannon was right behind her, eyes bright, with another big hug and a kiss on the cheek.

"How are my two favorite Silver Girls?" When they'd moved down to the desert after my father's death, I'd called them the Silver Girls, claiming with their gorgeous locks they'd give the Golden Girls a run for their money. The two ladies were friendly to all walks of life and could keep you in stitches with their stories. I enjoyed their company, even if I *was* perpetually frightened that I'd use the wrong fork or knife. "How was your trip?"

Grandma launched into a litany of her aches and pains, but when she was through, she said how happy she was to be around all the French cooking here in New Orleans, second only to France.

"Are you up for a short walk or would you rather stay here and eat at the Bistreaux?"

Grandma didn't feel up to a walk but wanted to visit so we rounded the corner and went into the restaurant. The Bistreaux was mostly empty on this weekday and it was early yet. Most folks ate late here, a habit I'd had to get used to. We made small talk while we ordered, they asked about the shop and my flat. I asked them about their new house and their activities. We ate quickly—and then the questions started.

"You look well, but are you sure you're alright, sweetheart?"

Grandma sounded very sincere, but then Shannon snapped, "Oh, Mom, she's where she wants to be." She didn't sound even remotely happy for me.

"I *am* happy here, I love this place. An artist can't ask for a more inspiring environment than this."

Shannon smiled at me condescendingly. "Yes, Jaylene, but art alone does not pay the bills. Unless you count that branding you do as 'art'. It's certainly not what your father would have wanted to see you doing with your college education."

I took a deep breath and counted to ten before speaking. "Shannon, I can understand that you don't agree with my choices, but I haven't asked you for anything, have I? I'm not starving. I have a roof over my head. Most importantly, I have friends who appreciate me. I'm doing what I want to do and I'm happy. I co-own my business. I would hope that he might consider that somewhat successful." My voice was a bit quieter than I'd wanted it to come out.

She looked away and drained her water glass. Then said, "You're right. I'm sorry. We all have to make our own choices." She grabbed my hand. "Your father would have wanted to know you were happy, even if he didn't agree with your decisions." She started to cry slightly and we hugged each other. Silently I thanked Mackenzie for the waterproof mascara.

"Thanks, and I'm sorry too. But *you* guys are okay, right? That's what I've been worried about."

Shannon attempted a smile. "It's hard. I still cry every day, but I'm doing what I can to take care of myself. And Mom is getting to play bingo and paint. It's lonely, sure, but we have the dogs and we have each other. We'll be fine."

I leaned over and kissed her cheek. I sucked down the rest of my Diet Coke and prayed for the server to bring us our check.

When he arrived, I stuck my debit card in his hand and waved off their protests. I asked what else they had planned and they said tomorrow morning they were planning to go to the New Orleans School of Cooking. I wished them well with that. The woman who gave the lessons was a kick in the pants. She could even give my grandma a run for her money when it came to storytelling.

We agreed to meet for lunch at my favorite restaurant, The Praline Connection, which was just a couple of blocks from my shop. They would come over after, see my place, and then I would get them a cab back to their hotel. They had an early flight out Friday morning so I would say goodbye tomorrow afternoon.

Then I would pack for seventeen days. Maybe. I still couldn't decide whether this was insane or a great opportunity.

I hugged them both in the lobby and was able to keep the tears at bay until I got outside, but that was the best I could do. The walk back home was tear-soaked. Thoughts of my father had me trembling violently. Luckily not many folks were out on the streets.

When I finally looked up, I was on the corner of Burgundy and Ursulines, just a couple of blocks from the St. Germaine. Which had me curious. I turned in that direction and wiped my face on the inside of my shirt. The buildings on these streets were so lovely and romantic, *anything* could happen and you'd think it was magical.

A group of young men in sailor uniforms walked by on the opposite side of the street, pausing to ogle a group of girls in short-shorts and camis. I smirked to myself, grateful I blended into the woodwork.

I guess I'm not that feminine in my dress, but I do like nice things. I could appreciate a cute dress or a nice pair of shoes with the best of them. I just felt out of place wearing clothes like that, as if someone would recognize me for the fraud I am. I never grew out of my tomboy stage I suppose; I felt more comfortable like that. Besides, getting a guy to notice you was the easy part. It was getting him to see you as more than a nice rack and a piece of ass that was the true test.

I stopped at the Royal Pharmacy to grab a bottle of water and when I stepped outside, I looked across the street at the St. Germaine. I drank deeply from the bottle and looked up at the balcony. I could hear men's voices and guitars being tuned through the open window, but the street was empty. Maybe they truly were getting the privacy they desired here.

I heard someone start laughing loudly and a door on the second-floor balcony swung open. Out stepped one of the guys, lighting a cigarette.

Suddenly I felt like a voyeur, so I turned quickly and headed across the street towards my shop.

I was caught like the not-slick person I am.

"Miss Charles? Is that you?"

I froze in my steps. I could pretend that I didn't hear him, but with the lack of traffic, both human and vehicular, he'd think I was either deaf or trying to be rude. I turned slowly and shaded my eyes from the sun.

"Jade, right?"

He nodded and yelled to the others, and I had to suck back a loud groan.

"Hey, guys, it's Miss Charles, she's right outside. Hey! Are you going to come stay with us?" His question was so innocent, I was suddenly struck by how "Wendy and the Lost Boys" this situation was.

"I, uh, I haven't made a final decision yet."

He *pouted*. Full on stuck-his-lip-out and pouted. "Awww, *hey guys*. Get out here! She says she's not sure she's coming."

I heard a chorus of "What? She has to come!"

The next to emerge was Marcus. He leaned both arms on the railing and looked down at me. "What is it? Don't you like us?"

More pouting. *Geesh*.

"No! I mean, sure. No, of course, you guys are great. I'm just, well... I'm just not sure I can do what you want."

Star pushed Marcus out of the way and said, "Seriously? Your work is *amazing*, Miss Charles. You *have* to come. It won't be right without you. Tell her, D."

My heart dropped as they all started yelling for him to come out. So much for covert operations.

"Guys, really. I'll call Miss Jordan when I get back to my shop."

The four of them leaned down over the railing, their upper bodies almost falling into the street. "But does that mean you're coming? Please?"

They were grown-ass men acting like little boys—and for the life of me, I could not tell you what would be more adorable. They were harmless, right?

They all started in.

"C'mon, please?"

"We'll beg."

"God, no. Do you want the whole world to know you're in there?" I was shouting in a stage whisper. "You guys are supposed to be here in secret."

"They're pretty pathetic when they beg, aren't they?"

A deep voice spoke from directly in front of me. Devon had come out the front door and was leaning against the post with his hands in his pocket, shades low on his nose.

I must have had my jaw close to the ground because I heard a chorus of giggles from the boys up above.

"Bring her up, D. Don't let her get away."

"Will you morons shut your traps? The whole city will know we're here if you keep this up." He turned and gave me that ghost of a smile again and stepped closer. "C'mon, let's get you back to your shop before they hear them all the way in Mississippi."

He gently grasped my left arm and directed me across the street. I glanced back at the guys, who had their chins leaning on the railing, whispering and snickering with each other before they looked around and filed back in the door, crouched down like ninja school rejects.

I covered my mouth with my hand to stifle my laughter.

"It's okay to laugh, they're often this embarrassing. But mostly they're just pains in the ass, nothing dangerous or anything."

I couldn't get over how deep his voice was, and how soft-spoken. He slid his hand down my arm, looked at my hand, and then must have thought better of it because he shoved his hands in his pockets. I did the same, feeling oddly like a teenager out on my first date.

"I was on my way home from seeing my stepmom and grand-mother. They're visiting from California, and I was just walking back to the shop." It sounded oddly like a confession to explain why this wasn't stalking behavior. Nervous, I kept talking. "I really *was* going to call Miss Jordan when I got back to the shop."

He nodded and kept walking, eyes straight ahead and unreadable behind his shades. We walked on in silence until we reached Frenchmen Street and turned right. His outfit today consisted of a pair of worn Levi's and a white shirt with the Ramones logo on it in black. His black hair was combed back and he'd added some product. I tried to sneak looks without being obvious but he seemed really aware of his surroundings.

Like when I was looking at him instead of paying attention and he stopped suddenly, throwing an arm across my stomach—to keep me from stepping in gum.

"Didn't want you to mess up your shoes."

I stepped over it, mumbled my thanks, and felt my cheeks burning. He cracked a smile, maybe even more than a ghost this time, and kept walking.

When we reached my shop, he stepped ahead of me and opened the door. I thanked him again as I walked past and he nodded at me, his eyes following me inside.

"Hey, how was— Dinner," Mackenzie faltered as she came out of the back office. Her eyes flared and she pursed her lips. "Who's your friend, Jay?"

"Mackenzie this is Devon. Devon, this is my shop mate, Mackenzie McGowan."

He shook her hand loosely, murmured, "Pleased to meet you," and stepped back, putting his hands in his pockets again.

"Can I get you something to drink?" Mackenzie walked over to our fridge—well, more like pranced giddily. "Some water? I bet it's hot out there." She grabbed him a bottle, threw me a heated glance over her shoulder, and pranced giddily once more back to the counter to hand it to him.

"Thank you, Miss McGowan," he said in that barely audible voice of his. He cracked the bottle open and wandered over to the counter where my portfolio sat.

Mackenzie reached over, trying to be sneaky, and pinched me hard on the back of the arm.

"Hey!"

I glared at her and she started making "What is going on? How did you end up with him? Did you kiss him yet?" faces at me.

I said loudly, "Mackenzie did my inks get delivered today?"

She took my hint and totally overdid her, "*Yes!* In fact, you *did* get a package today. Let me just go in the back and make sure that everything came in that you ordered." She skipped back to the office, shut the door, and a few seconds later the music came on loudly. She'd put on her current favorite, Black Tide's album *Postmortem*.

I shook my head and closed my eyes, doing the breathing thing before walking over to where Devon was studying my work intently. I watched as he turned the pages slowly with his long fingers. I noticed that he had lettering on them; it looked like LOVE on one hand and... was that PAIN on the other?

"I like this one here." He pointed another long finger at a photo of a portrait of Angus Young from the *Highway to Hell* album cover. It was one of the first portraits I'd done after arriving here.

"Thanks. Love Angus. That was done on one of Daryl's buddies."

He looked over at me for a moment, nodded, and went back to looking.

I studied him and desperately wished my sketchbook was nearby. His movements captivated me, like the way his bottom lip pursed out just a bit farther than the top one. They had me licking my own lips.

Gah. Stop it. He's a client, for goodness sake.

He closed the book and looked around the shop before landing his gaze on me. "Miss Charles, I know this whole situation seems strange. Really, the lawyers insisted on us doing everything so formal. I don't know who they think they're protecting...us or the label." He stepped back from the counter and looked around some more, obviously feeling somewhat uncomfortable.

I leaned against the counter, resting my elbows on top of my portfolio. "Are you guys having some sort of problems or is this the usual level of intensity?" I was kind of joking, trying to make light of the situation, but I was really unsure how to read him. I was very aware that he was standing only two feet away from me. I was also aware of the fact that my head just came up to his shoulder, and I'd thought I was tall. He was sort of freakishly tall.

He looked at me again and I wasn't sure if I wanted him to take the glasses off or not. I thought that maybe his gaze would be too intense for me.

"We've had a difficult year. We're late on our next album. Our contract had us releasing an album a year for four years. We were supposed to be ready to go into the studio this month and we haven't even written anything yet. We've been stuck, writer's block or something. Anyway, yeah. So they're threatening us with financial shit if we don't get our album at least rough recorded by the end of May. So I guess this is kind of our last attempt at making this work."

He looked down at his feet and I could see his brow furrowed. If I had known him better, I would have reached out for him right then. I desperately wanted to ease him somehow. He was visibly upset, but I didn't know how he'd react. Some people really didn't respond well to strangers touching them.

"And you guys really think I can help?"

He nodded and took a deep breath, slipping off his glasses. "Uncle Daryl told us how you tattooed his guys after they lost their friend in Iraq, that somehow they were better after, they could kind of put it behind them and move forward. I don't know if it will work or not for *us*, but the last idea the guys had sure didn't."

I frowned and took a chance by asking, "What was that? If you want to tell me, that is."

He huffed out a laugh. "Well, Mage, you know...he has that name because he claims to, I don't know... Don't laugh, okay? He takes it kind of serious. He claims his ancestors are witches, like voodoo or something, I don't really know. When we were kids, he was always trying to get us to try some shit like Ouija boards, voodoo dolls, crazy stuff."

I couldn't help but notice the change in his voice. It had a really nice tone to it when he was talking about his friend.

"Anyway, he hired some chick to come and do a séance out at my family's place on the bayou. Almost burned the place down. The lady swore we had a vengeful spirit who would haunt us unless we gave her an extra five hundred."

He laughed out loud then, and it sounded like music to my ears. He rubbed his bottom lip between his thumb and forefinger, touching a spot where he had a hint of a soul patch. It was dark like the rest of his hair. His humor changed his posture and he seemed a bit more perked up.

"So did you pay her? Was she able to exorcise the spirit?"

He looked at me to see if I was taking him seriously, and the warm smile he gave me when he saw that I was made my heart drop into my stomach. His eyes crinkled a little on the sides, kind of like Marcus's, but Devon's seemed friendly. Not, you know...*friendly*.

"Actually, we haven't been back out there since that night. The other guys were scared shitless. They claimed they heard noises and swore we'd be possessed by evil spirits if we went back." His humor faded at that. He cleared his throat and ran a hand over his hair. "You'll probably think we're total freaks after that story."

"Not at all. Hey, sometimes you have to think outside the box, right?"

He shrugged and looked back down.

"I'm sorry, Devon." This time I *did* touch him. I placed my fingers lightly on the back of his hand. "That's what you guys want me to do, right? Hear your stories? And just from the little I've learned about you all, I'm guessing there will be more stories like this?"

He looked down at our hands and sucked in his bottom lip. I pulled my hand back and he looked at me, giving me his small smile again.

Wow, I'd just met him and I was classifying his smiles into categories: ghost of a smile, half smile, small smile... He was so beautiful it was almost painful, especially when I looked into those soulful eyes. I felt like I was bathing in his pain. I had to do something to help that.

I stood up straight and leaned a hip against the counter, crossing my arms.

That drew his eyes downwards for a moment. Was he checking me out?

He shook himself. "I don't mean to keep you. The guys just, well, they wanted me to ask you if you'd come. And *I* wanted to ask you to come. Please. If nothing else, it will be a fun couple of weeks, maybe we'll write some songs and you can add some pictures to your book here." The ghost smile was back and he traced my nameplate on the outside of the portfolio.

I was so touched that he had asked me like that. Just from this short time together, I knew he didn't talk much. The few glimpses of laughter I saw from him showed a man who loved his friends and just wanted to see them happy. It was nice to see such camaraderie. I was feeling much less threatened than I'd felt earlier today.

I couldn't let them down. I'd make it work somehow.

"Well, as long as you promise there will be no cutting the heads off chickens or sacrificing virgins, I guess I can make it."

He smiled at me and I just desperately wanted to reach out and touch his lip. I tucked my hands back into my pockets to be safe.

"Of course, Miss Charles. We'll call those rituals our true last resort. Although I can't guarantee there won't be any reading of the tea leaves or tarot decks being shuffled. Is that going to be a problem?"

I shook my head seriously. But then I thought of something and tilted my head to the side. "You guys just do whatever it is you need to and let me know what you need from me. I do have one thing to tell you...I don't want to make anyone uncomfortable, but I have a slight compulsion you should know about."

His brows rose and he looked startled. "Really? What is it?"

Smothering a laugh, I said as seriously as I could, "I need to draw, a lot. I always have a sketchbook with me, so I'll probably do lots of drawings of you guys. Will that be okay? I'll submit everything to you before I go, as per the contract."

It was his turn to smirk. "That's it? I thought it was going to be something much scarier, like organizing the sock drawers or lining up all our guitar picks by size and color. Don't laugh, we had a roadie once who did that and it drove Marcus batshit crazy."

"No, nothing that serious. I just, um...sometimes it makes people uncomfortable. That's all. Nothing creepy."

He shook his head. "You do realize we're all musicians? Damaged musicians? We stop mid-sentence to write down lyrics or explain things in demented sound language. I think you'll find us to be kindred spirits."

I smiled and stood straighter. "Well, then. I guess I'd better go call Sherry."

He smiled back, looking relieved. He grabbed my hand and put it between the two of his much larger ones, cradling it gently. "Thank you, Miss Charles. Really. This means a lot."

His voice cracked at that and I couldn't help myself. I reached my other hand up and touched his mouthwateringly exceptional biceps. "It's fine. It'll be a good time. And please, call me Jay."

He nodded. "Okay. Jaylene. It's a beautiful name."

My cheeks flushed at that. I stumbled back, nearly tripping on my feet. "Great. Okay. So...I need to pack. Um. Anything in particular I need to bring?"

He shook his head. "Just whatever you need to work and whatever you need to be comfortable."

Somehow I didn't think comfy sweats and ducky slippers were what I would be comfortable in surrounded by these guys.

"Okay. I'll just go call Sherry." He stood there smiling at me, looking relieved, and anxious, and pleased. I think. I stepped back and he didn't move. "Thanks for walking me back, Devon."

He smiled and nodded. "We'll see you Friday...around ten? That seems to be an empty time on the street over there. We'll try to be up and presentable." He looked worried.

I shook my head. "Don't change anything for me. I'm there to see you guys in your element, right? Oh, wait. You guys should at least be dressed. That would be good. I don't know what a bunch of guys do when they're staying together."

He laughed at that, his smile growing relaxed again. "You don't have brothers or anything?"

I shook my head. "Nope, just me. I'm an only. Guess I was enough of a nightmare, my parents didn't dare to have more."

He frowned and then narrowed his eyes at me. "Or they just realized they should quit while they were ahead."

Oh. My. Did he just say that?

He put his sunglasses back on and smiled his half smile again. "Good afternoon, Jaylene." He turned and stepped out the door.

I fell onto my stool. I must have been holding my breath because all of a sudden I felt lightheaded.

"OMG was that not the cutest thing *ever*? Jay, he is *adorable*. And hot, and sweet and sexy, and if I were you, I'd pick the bedroom next to his just so you can dream about him next door." Mackenzie had her hand on her throat and looked like she was about to swoon.

"Kenzie! This is work. Remember work? That thing you're going to have to do all by yourself while I'm gone? Aren't you even a little bit peeved I'm going?"

"Of course I'm peeved at you, dammit. You will *so* squander this opportunity you've been given, I know you. You're living the dream,

Jay. Five hot guys—totally unattached, if the Internet can be believed—and you're there to 'work'." What*ever*." She stomped off, cursing me under her breath, so I made my escape.

But as I neared the steps, I panicked. "What the hell am I going to wear?"

I could hear Mackenzie laughing at me from down below. Brat.

I climbed the stairs slowly, my heart pounding in my chest. I wasn't sure what affected me more, the decision I'd made...or Devon. And he was definitely affecting me.

I didn't do well with guys when it wasn't a joking-around situation. I was never sure if they had the right idea about me. A tattooed chick makes some think "for a good time, call." Shit, I even dated one guy who assumed because I had tattoos and some piercings, I was into some other kind of lifestyle, which I'm *not*.

So I've spent most of my potential dating years as "friend material." Guys poured out their hearts to me on a constant basis about the one who got away, or the one who wanted someone else, or even the one who wouldn't give them the time of day. I did my best to help them navigate the feminine mystique.

Perhaps I wasn't the best one to do that, because I never seemed to be able to get past a few dates, often with wrong-for-me kind of guys. So what did I know? What could I bring to the table? I wasn't into games of any kind and had no tolerance for people who were.

I sighed and picked up the phone to call Sherry. I found two missed calls and messages, one from Sherry and one from Daryl.

"Hey, dollface, just wanted to tell you how much the girls love seeing themselves on their daddy's arm. Beautiful work, you did. Beautiful like you. I hope you help dem boys of mine. Marcus, Jade and Devon are my blood, and the rest are like family, and you know what dat means. I put the fear of God into dem if they harm one sweet hair on your head. You call me if they do, now, y'hear? Call that Miss Jordan, now, Jay. This is good for you, too."

For such a tough guy, he sure could be sweet. It meant a lot to me that he was watching out for me and that he thought I could help "dem boys." Boys seemed to be a very fitting description for them after their behavior earlier.

"Hello, Miss Charles. No pressure, I just hadn't heard from you and wanted to make sure you didn't have any other questions for me. I also wanted to tell you that I've been authorized to pay you whatever you ask in order to get you to sign, if money is the issue. The guys were specific, and I am quoting them, 'This is priceless, Sherry! Work your magic!' So this is me, trying to work my magic. I'll fly there and get on my knees if that's what it takes. Call me, or I'm booking the flight."

A weaker person would certainly take advantage of an offer for more money. More money wasn't the issue for me, as they were already being generous. And I wasn't even upset about my drawings becoming their property. Once I got the drawings out of my head, I didn't need them anymore.

Sherry picked up after the first ring. "Miss Charles? Jaylene? Is that you? Do I need to book a flight out there?"

I laughed at her tenacity. "I don't think so. I've called to say I'll accept the job. I'm sorry I've been reticent, it's just not something I've ever done before."

She laughed. "You think I've ever *asked* someone to do this before? Okay, it's true, rock stars sometimes have some strange requests..." Her voice changed, got softer. "But these guys are different. They've been through a horrible ordeal, Jaylene. There's no other way to describe it. I'm afraid if they don't get past this, it will wreck not only the band and their burgeoning career, but it will destroy them personally. Trust me, I've seen a lot of rockers hit bottom, and it ain't pretty. I've never seen anything like this though. I probably shouldn't be telling you this...but you're really their last hope."

Wow. I was worried about just how deep I was getting into this already. "I don't know what to say, Sherry. I really don't. I'll do whatever I can but like I said, I hope you aren't expecting miracles."

"I don't mean to scare you. I love these guys and I don't want to see them hurting anymore, is all. So you'll do it? That's so great. I'm so glad. Now, let me give you the details—"

"Wait, Sherry? I do have two questions for you."

She audibly swallowed a drink of some kind. "Hit me. What do you need?"

"The first one is a little embarrassing, but, uh...what should I bring to wear? I mean, are we talking business casual or formal or anything? If so, I'm totally going to need to go shopping."

She laughed loudly. "Oh, girl, that is a good one. Have you seen them yet? If you showed up in formal wear, they would freak out and think they were going to a funeral or something. Just be yourself, that's who they asked for."

That was so not helpful, and I told her so.

"Really. As far as I know, the only thing on the agenda is hanging out at the St. Germaine. They may have some friends in to play, they may go out in disguise, you never know with them. They're quite the pranksters when they want to be, but I've warned them that you would probably not appreciate that. Be aware, however, that they only *mostly* listen to me when it comes to that stuff."

"I can handle that, I think. I've worked with all guys since I got into tattooing, so I'm sort of prepared. Okay, that's question one. Question two is kind of a big-picture question: Who is, or was, Margaret Boudreaux?"

It had been bugging me from the start but I'd been preoccupied mostly with the details of actually deciding whether to accept.

Sherry was quiet for a minute, her voice solemn when she came back on. "The official answer is that Margaret Boudreaux was formerly the manager of the band. She passed away in December." She was quiet again, probably thinking about what else to tell me. "That's really all I should say. They'll tell what they want you to know when you get there. Okay? I'm sorry, Jaylene, that's the best I can do."

"No, it's fine, thank you. I guess I wanted to be prepared but it'll be better coming from them. I should go pack, uh, some clothes." My heart pounded even harder now that I'd said yes. Maybe I should get my blood pressure checked. Was twenty-six too young to have a heart attack?

"Thank you so, so much, Jaylene. Now, about getting over there. Mr. Doucette has agreed to pick you up and bring you over with your things. It might be a little secret agent-y, but he'll be using his company vehicle. Provides good cover."

Daryl ran a roofing company. Did that mean I would be going in through the roof?

"Yes, it does mean you'll be going up like one of his employees. Another one will be bringing your gear in the front. Just tuck your hair up and he'll give you coveralls. It'll be fine."

I snorted. "Of course, I'm climbing a roof. No problem. All joking aside, is the press really that bad? I mean, are these guys *that* famous?"

Sherry laughed again in disbelief. "Honey, where have you been? Maggie's Bones have topped the *Billboard* rock charts three times, have two gold albums, and have toured with Avenged Sevenfold, Papa Roach, and they've even toured Europe with Megadeth on their Gigantour."

Okay, *those* bands I had heard of, and I knew they were rock's recent torchbearers. This was much bigger than a group of guys from Louisiana.

"I guess I've been under a rock? I don't know…I mainly listen to whatever's on my iPod, mostly older stuff. I did listen to them a little last night and they have a decent sound."

"Some good stuff, for sure. Definitely. I think they'll win you over during your stay. They are completely irresistible. In more ways than one. I should tell you that although you *are* safe from harm, you won't be safe from *charm,* so be careful." She snickered as I thanked her again and we hung up.

Charm? I'm sure they wouldn't waste it on me. I blew my bangs out of my face and grabbed a duffel to pack my things. My wardrobe consisted of shorts, tanks, boxers and tees to sleep in. I even threw in the two sundresses I owned, thinking I might need them. Nothing fancy, because I didn't own anything fancy.

Just then, I heard Mackenzie at the door.

"Jay, you in there?" I opened the door and she pushed past me. "Okay, what did you pack? Tell me there's something in there that a girl would wear, for the love of the gods." She started throwing my clothes out of the bag. "Boring. Boring. *Gross!*" She turned to look at me when the bag was empty. "If I didn't know better, I'd think you were wearing your little brother's clothes. You can't go stay with rock star boys dressed like a teenager. C'mon, love. We're going shopping."

"Mackenzie, it's eight at night. Where the heck do you think you're taking me?"

Her grin was completely evil, mischievous.

Uh-oh.

"I just got off the phone with Sabrina and she's meeting us at her shop."

"Are you nuts? Her stuff is outrageous!"

Mackenzie was shooing me out the door and down the steps to the back of our building. "Oh, nonsense. She's got some great vintage stuff. She's already pulling some for you to try on."

I groaned loudly. "Ugh. What did you tell her, Mackenzie? You're not supposed to say anything about what I'm doing." I stomped down the street next to her, sulking. "Mackenzie." I even tried whining to get out of this. "You know I hate shopping."

"You'll hate it even more if you go over there feeling uncomfortable because you're dressed like a sweaty, prepubescent boy. You have the cutest shape and gorgeous long legs. What if you decide you like one of these guys?"

I looked away before she could see me blush.

"You *do*! Oh, it's D, isn't it? You always go for the stoic types. Oh, he's sooooo hot. Maybe now you'll be able to give those nipple piercings I gave you a test run."

I socked her in the arm. "Hey! You got me drunk. It was on a dare, or else I *never* would have let you do that."

She rubbed her arm but was laughing hysterically. "You're just lucky I didn't dare you to let me pierce your labia," she cackled.

I swung to sock her again but she jumped out of the way, so I just crossed my arms over my chest and sulked even more.

The truth was, I actually kind of liked my piercings. My breasts were fairly average and...I don't know...I guess the tiny barbells I had through each nipple just added a little something. And once they'd healed, they felt kind of nice.

The only other out-of-the-ordinary piercings I had were my upper ears, my tragus, and a tiny diamond stud through my left nostril. I'd seen Mackenzie pierce some interesting things, but never had the desire to take my body modification any further. The nipples never would have happened if I wasn't incapable of backing out on a dare. Luckily that's the most danger I've ever been in. So far.

Mackenzie had me laughing by the time we got to Sabrina's

boutique, French Market Stitch. I loved her style but was always too afraid to try to pull it off myself. Sabrina and Mackenzie had gone to high school together and had quite a collection of stories about their escapades. Sabrina had welcomed me into their circle of friends immediately, making me feel more accepted than I ever had by any girls growing up.

Sabrina was 5'4" and busty, with fire-engine red hair in a pinup 'do. Like Mackenzie, her makeup was always perfect and her clothes, while covering more skin than my shop mate's, were just as flamboyant. Tonight she was a little toned down, wearing a black, knee-length pencil skirt, and white blouse with a sweetheart neckline and red polka dots. She gave me a big hug, took in my "hobo-wear," as Mackenzie called it, and shuddered.

"My Lord. It's about time we cure you of your fashion statement." She ushered us inside, locked the door, and walked me over to her elaborate dressing area, complete with a raised platform surrounded by mirrors.

I was starting to get into this girlie stuff just a smidge, and then Mackenzie put a glass of champagne in my hand. "What's this for?" I was more of a cookies-and-milk kind of partier, but I did like the occasional glass of bubbly.

"A toast. To our lovely Jaylene. May she finally get in touch with her feminine side and finally let a *boy* touch her feminine side." The two of them clinked glasses and high-fived.

I was tired of fighting them so I allowed them to dress and undress me for the next two hours like a very apathetic mannequin, ignoring their continued jabs about my boring cotton undergarments.

Most of the clothes were okay, not too fancy, and were definitely comfortable. Sabrina knew enough about me to choose wisely. There was an adorable red dress that was too good to pass up. I picked out a couple of halter tops and a couple of pairs of capris. Mackenzie was allowed to pick out two outfits for me, and Sabrina chose two sleeveless button-down shirts.

I figured I would work in my "hobo wear" and save these clothes for when I wasn't tattooing. I wasn't trying to impress anyone. However, I guess what Mackenzie said earlier was sinking in. At my age, there was no reason for me to dress like an adolescent boy all the time. I did like feeling girly sometimes. And being around Devon made me want to feel womanly.

We stumbled home, still giggling, around one in the morning. After our shopping binge, we went across the street to see Sabrina's boyfriend Kurt perform in his blues-rock band. I grew a little melancholy when I thought of not seeing my girls for seventeen days. It was strange. I'd never really had close girlfriends growing up, so now that I did, I hated to let them go. I was sure Mackenzie would find a way to text me for hourly updates, and if I wasn't careful, I'd find her climbing in the back window.

I woke up early the next morning and tried to remember just how I'd been talked into all the shopping. Sabrina didn't want money, she wanted to trade work, and so we planned to meet up after my job with the Bones to get started on a design. The barter system was alive and well in the Quarter. It had come in handy when I needed stuff fixed around the building; something Daryl had taken advantage of on more than one instance.

I enjoyed the walk over to The Praline Connection to meet up with Shannon and Grandma. The morning was cool and misty. The break from the heat was nice. I'd cleared my schedule for the day to spend time with them so I didn't have to worry about being gone from the shop.

The ladies thoroughly enjoyed their cooking class. They met me at the restaurant and regaled me with stories from the class. They agreed with me on the quality of the fried chicken and they even tried the alligator sausage.

We walked from there over to my shop and apartment, which they politely admired. I was proud of Shannon for not finding any dusty spots, or at least not sharing if she did. Mackenzie dazzled them both and they became fast friends. I seemed to be surrounded by women who could dazzle. I felt like a fizzle around them.

Grandma started to get tired so I called them a cab to take them back to their hotel. She was going to a bingo hall that night and she needed to take a nap. We hugged goodbye and I promised I'd come home this fall sometime, hoping that would appease them.

Shannon got in the cab last and gave me one more hug. "So you really are okay? You're happy? You certainly look like you're in your element." The last she said with an exaggerated laugh.

"I'm really happy here. I also just got offered a travelling opportunity so I won't be in the shop for a couple of weeks, in case you have trouble getting ahold of me."

She looked surprised. "What will you be doing?"

I wasn't sure how much to tell her, so I said, "Tattooing a group of people in the music business. It's a good opportunity for me and for the shop."

She smiled. "Well, I guess you *are* doing well then. I love you, sweetheart. Happy birthday."

I thanked her and told her I hoped she was taking care of herself. A kiss on the cheek and a slam of the cab door and they were on their way, out of my life for the time being. It had been nice seeing them but now I needed to get my head together for my next adventure.

Troy came in early that evening to go over plans for the shop in my absence. I told him who was coming in and for what. He looked over my drawings and told me numerous times how happy he was with what I'd accomplished, even going so far as to praise my work and to mention the possibility of me tattooing *him* after I was finished.

He was crashing with friends while he was covering for me, but it felt weird to know someone was going to be in my space. I knew Mackenzie would be there, so no funny business would go on, and I'd get Daryl to come by, too. He was a good spy.

I also had to finish packing my gear. Daryl wasn't coming over to pick me up until 10 a.m., so I'd have plenty of time to take Mackenzie out to breakfast at The Old Coffeepot in the morning.

Sleep did not come easily, so I read a horror novel until around 3:00 a.m. before finally shutting out the lights. I dreamt about ghosts and guitars.

FOUR

The next morning, I was tired but wired with excitement and nerves. What if we didn't get along? What if they hated my work? What if this little experiment was a failure and I disappointed the guys? Or even worse, what if I disappointed Daryl? These guys were obviously important to the people around them and, apparently, to millions of fans.

Mackenzie tried to help over breakfast but as someone who'd never failed at anything, she had little to go on.

"I've spent my life disappointing people. How the hell am I supposed to not disappoint the band?"

"Wow, that negativity is doing wonders for your complexion. Jay, you are so talented. So...what? You decided to do what you loved instead of what could have paid you handsomely?" She shook her head and made a sign of the cross. Then she folded her arms on the table and leaned in, giving her perfect cleavage a little lift. "Tell me honestly, Jay. Are you happy here? Doing what you're doing?"

I nodded. "Of course. This last year has been the best. Maybe it was just my stepmom's under-reaction to the shop that has me in a funk, I don't know. I love it here, and I love working with you, Kenz. I don't know what I'd do without you." She reached over to grab for my hand but I covered hers with mine. "I just can't shake the 'what ifs'. Maybe I'm supposed to be doing something else with my life?"

"Maybe you are, and what you are about to do is going to help determine that." She waggled her eyes at me and leaned in even closer. "Yeah, what you're about to do. Have you lost sight of the fact that you're going to be holed up with five—count them—*five* tattooed, pierced, talented, extremely *hot* guys? For seventeen days. I so envy you."

With Mackenzie, it *would* come down to that. I couldn't think of it that way, though, and I told her so. She groaned obnoxiously.

"You are such a party pooper!"

We paid the check and walked back over to the shop, giggling the whole way. She'd had a dating dry spell for quite a while and was trying to decide how much trouble she wanted to get into before I returned.

Daryl was waiting for us in his van at the shop. "I hope you're packed. We gotta jet, chère."

I unlocked the door and gave him an exasperated sigh. I'd chosen one of my new outfits to wear today: a pair of white capris with bright orange and lavender flowers, an orange cami, and tan sandals. Daryl noticed the difference immediately. He complimented me, which made me squirm, and it took a grave look from Mackenzie to keep me from running upstairs to change.

He packed my travel kit with my machines, inks, gloves, paper towels, cleaners, Aquaphor, lamp and a few other tricks of the trade. I carried out my duffel and my folding table, which got me a growl from Daryl. He was chivalrous and couldn't stand seeing a lady lift heavy items. I smiled sweetly at him and he couldn't stay mad for long.

When everything was loaded in the van, he reached in and handed me a set of way-too-big coveralls. "You got a cap you can tuck all that gorgeous hair into?"

Mackenzie handed me one of our shop caps and I wrapped my ponytail up inside. "Well, girl, you go have your adventure and promise to call me every day so I know you're okay."

It was a rare serious moment from my shop mate, and as we hugged, I shivered to think about being away from my main support here in town. Heck, my main support system period.

"Thanks for everything, Kenz. Even if I don't always go along with your crazy schemes, I'm so glad you're in my life. I don't know what I'd do without you."

She sniffled and pulled back. "Shut up, Jay. You're going to smudge both of our makeup." She gave me a playful push towards Daryl, blew us both a kiss and headed back inside.

Daryl and I climbed in the van for the less-than-five-minute drive over to the St. Germaine. The plan was that we would park on the Ursulines Avenue side and set up the ladders to look like we were going up on the roof. We would have to carry my supplies, with the exception of the table, up the ladders to the balcony to look more realistic.

Definitely a plan a dude would come up with. I honestly don't think people would even notice if we just strolled in the front doors, but Daryl insisted stealth was the way to go. Because I looked so like a roofer in these ginormous coveralls that could fit two more of me inside.

After we parked on the side street, Daryl raised his ladder and then motioned for me to go ahead of him. I gave him one last beseeching look, praying he'd decide this was a bad idea. Instead he slung my tote over my shoulder with my equipment in it and stepped around behind the ladder to hold on to it.

I sighed loudly and started to climb, hoping my uncoordinated ways wouldn't cause me complete humiliation. I climbed the ladder looking down at my feet the whole way, to make sure I didn't miss a step, my shoulder killing me from the weight of my bag.

When the street looked really far away, I looked up to see how much progress I'd made.

Marcus's hazel eyes were right in front of my face, on top of his shit-eating grin.

Startled, I slipped down a step on the ladder and he suddenly dropped the grin and reached for me, grabbing my arm and shoulder strap.

"Here, let me get that for you. You alright?"

I nodded and allowed him to take my bag. "I told Daryl this was a bad idea." At the top now, I looked at the railing and tried to figure out how I was going to swing a leg over the side without becoming a splat on the sidewalk. I spoke out loud to myself. "Well, at least if I make a mess, the street sweepers will be by in the morning with their lemony-fresh dish soap."

"Can I give you a hand?" Marcus was back, reaching out for me. I looked up at him like "really?" But he just reached down and plucked me off the ladder and swung me over the rail.

"Marcus! One would think this ain't your first rodeo."

He smirked and looked down at me. He wasn't much taller, maybe four inches, but obviously much stronger. "You insinuating I've helped a girl over a balcony before?" He put his hand to the scruff on his chin. "I might be guilty of something like that." He chuckled and I just rolled my eyes.

"Well, you've probably blown our cover now. Who would believe a roofer had to be lifted over the railing?"

Daryl was coming up behind me and I watched as he effortlessly climbed over the rail. He handed me my duffel and I grabbed my work tote from Marcus. "Where should I put my stuff?"

He led me through an open door onto a gangway and to the right. Inside, the building looked much bigger than from the street. The gangway circled the upstairs, leaving an opening that looked down upon a dance floor and the bar and stage below. Upstairs, there were several doors, probably leading to other rooms, and across from the balcony was a large room with pool tables, couches, and a huge flat screen TV.

I stumbled and dropped my duffel, in complete shock, when I saw the rest of the guys were singing along to the TV, and Star was even dancing.

"You okay?"

Marcus had come up behind me. I turned to look at him, my face must have given away just how completely thrown I was. "Is that..." I started.

And he finished, *"Big Time Rush*? We love that show." I continued to stare. Then he opened his mouth and started to sing a tune dripping with adolescent boy pop musings. The "a-o-a-o" bits had me dropping my jaw in utter confusion.

Weren't these guys supposed to be metal singers?

Mage and Jade hadn't noticed me watching. In unison, they jumped up and started dancing with Star. They were copying the routine from the TV in perfectly synchronized moves. Marcus pushed past me and joined them.

These four tattooed and pierced guys, in their black board shorts and varying degrees of shirtless-ness, were dancing and singing their hearts out to some boy band madness. It was kind of the cutest thing I'd ever seen.

They finished the song and started high-fiving each other.

"You can pick up your jaw now." Daryl laughed behind me. "I told you these boys was harmless." He chuckled as he passed me on the narrow walkway, carrying the rest of my equipment. "Your room's over here, dahlin'."

My room was on the far right at the end of the gangway. When I walked inside the doorway, I was pleased. The natural light in here was amazing at this time of day. There were two windows, one to the back of the building and one looking down on Ursulines. The room was spacious, had a simple queen bed at the back corner, and an elaborate drawing table had been set up for me under the other window. The ceilings were at least nine feet, with large support beams running across and two ceiling fans that kept the air moving nicely.

I heard a loud *thunk* behind me and I turned around to find myself face to chest with Devon, who had been absent from the *BTR* tribute moments before.

"I brought your table. Would you like it set up?"

I shook my head. "No, thank you. I won't need it until we get started with the tattoos." I couldn't stop staring at him and I felt like a complete dork. But then I realized he was kind of staring at me, too.

"Um, there's a bathroom through there." He pointed to a doorway on the left.

I looked inside and there was a claw foot tub with an industrial showerhead rigged up. The bathroom was in a sad state, like someone had started to remodel and quit in the middle. I noticed a door on the other side. "An adjoining room?"

Devon nodded. "That's where I crash. The other guys room on the other side of the rumpus room."

Daryl came in with the rest of my things. "Here you go, chère. You got what you need, yeah?"

I nodded. "Thanks for getting me over here—I think. That was an adventure." He giggled. I swear I even saw the corner of Devon's mouth turn up but I couldn't be sure.

"It was worth it to watch you on that ladder there."

I raised my eyebrow at him, wishing I could look as fierce as I wanted to.

"Here, let me give you back these ridiculous things." I took off my hat and shook out my hair and then I unzipped the coveralls and stepped out of them. I handed them over to Daryl, who was trying really hard to stifle a laugh. I followed his gaze over to Devon—whose eyes were so wide you could see the entire whites.

He made a choking sound and started backing out of the room, his cheeks turning a nice shade of rose. "Um, I'm just going to go let the guys know you're getting settled in and, uh, we'll see you in a few. Uncle Daryl, thanks for bringing her over." They shook hands and Devon hurried out the door, pulling on the collar of his white tee.

"The boys might be harmless, chère, but *you* ain't gonna be if you keep undressing in front of them. You better keep your clothes on, girl, or you be givin' them heart attacks, you."

I socked him in the shoulder and he scooped me up in a big hug.

"I'm teasing you, sugah. I'm outta here. I'll be around but you call me if you need anything." I kissed his cheek even though he was a rascal, and I told him as much.

"Can you swing by the shop a couple times and check on Mackenzie? Make sure Troy isn't getting too comfortable?"

He nodded. "Affirmative. I'll take care of all that. You just take care of my boys here."

I nodded back and waved goodbye.

I looked around my room and decided to unpack my clothes into the chest of drawers and small wardrobe at the foot of the bed, but first I sat down for a minute to collect myself.

I was really here. And I really needed to go out there and face them.

I stepped out onto the gangway and walked over to the rumpus room, where they were all flopped on the huge leather couches, still watching *BTR*. Devon was sitting in a chair in the corner, tuning an acoustic guitar.

"So were you guys just practicing your boy band moves in case this whole rock 'n' roll gig doesn't pan out?"

They all turned around and said hello, shaking my hand again and leaning in to kiss my cheek. Devon remained in the corner, looking up once and catching my eye. He nodded and that slight, slight smile was back. I just smiled back at him, trying not to get lost in his blue eyes again.

"You don't watch this show? You're missing out. They're fun. We actually went to their concert out in California last summer. They put on a good little show, they do." Star was non-apologetic in his *BTR* admiration.

"I've not seen the show before. I really don't watch much TV."

They looked at me like I'd grown a second head.

Mage started in first. "No TV? Man. Well, the show is about these four guys from Minnesota who audition to start a group, and—"

"Mage if you're going to tell the story, tell it right." Star was adamant. "Only James was auditioning for real, the other guys were just along for support but when the producer chose Kendall, he said they all go or none of them go. Then they moved to Hollywood to become superstars." He was quite proud of himself for getting the facts straight.

"I had no idea. Well, the music is okay I guess, for a kids' show."

They started singing again, and I was just thrown by how adorable they were. No pretenses, no trying to act tough or cool. Not at all what I'd thought about a rock band. And they had all the vocal parts down.

"They're kind of like us, I guess," said Jade. "We were all friends growing up and went to California together to make the big time, too." The other guys got that sad smile going on again.

Marcus came in with a basket and a small cooler. "Lunch, people. Come and get it." He set the stuff on the large square ottoman between the couches and the guys all grabbed for sandwiches and drinks. He slapped their hands away. "No way, dudes. The lady goes first." He smiled sweetly at me and gestured for me to take my pick of the spread.

I thanked Marcus and walked around the couch to peer inside the basket. I pulled out a turkey avocado sandwich and grabbed a Diet Coke from the cooler. The guys were watching me with big smiles on their faces, waiting for me to get settled.

I took a spot at the end of one of the couches. "Thanks, guys. I appreciate this."

Marcus nodded at the others and they dove in. The way their limbs were flying and the tangle of their bodies had me thinking about what a mosh pit would look like at one of their shows. Devon waited until they were through before walking over and taking what was left.

With a mouthful of sandwich, Jade said, "There's a thocked thidge an thnackth downthtairth behind the bar if you get hungry. Help your-thelf." He may have spit some of his food on Mage, who was sitting next to him, but I was likely the only one to notice.

"Yeah, and Mr. Daryl told us you like Diet Coke so we got a bunch." Star at least swallowed before talking.

They were finished with their sandwiches before I even came close to eating half. I wrapped the other half and set it down on the table. "I tend to treat my Diet Coke like others treat coffee, I'm afraid. Thanks for taking care of that."

"Anything for you, Miss Charles," said Jade, who had left a cushion's space between us on the couch.

"Please, call me Jay, or Jaylene. The 'Miss' feels kinda funny." They looked to Devon and Marcus, who nodded, and so they agreed.

"Okay, Jaylene," Mage said, trying my name on for size, almost waiting to see if he'd get struck by some natural occurrence for not using the Miss.

I thought it was very respectful how kids were taught in the South to call their elders Miss or Mister. But it felt weird, especially when they weren't that much younger than me. It was almost as creepy as being called ma'am.

Mage leaned forward, resting his forearms on his legs and rubbing his hands together. "So when is your birthday?"

I was startled by his question. "Um, why?"

The other guys mumbled to themselves and Marcus even hung his head in his hands. "Here we go," he muttered.

"Oh, uh, just because I was wondering what your sign is. I was going to do your star charts for you." He looked at the other guys. "What? Is that weird?"

Star slugged him in his thigh. "Dude, she just got here. You want her to bail on us?"

"No, it's okay. It's actually today."

They all looked at me, stunned. Mage especially. "Truly? And Friday the thirteenth, even?" His voice was filled with wonder and I fought the urge to giggle.

Mage was definitely striking. He had a wide smile and full lips. His eyes looked not so much dangerous, more like always on alert, as if he never really relaxed. He made you feel like he was always watching. It didn't unsettle me; rather, it felt like I was being looked after.

"Yes, why? I don't really celebrate birthdays much so I didn't think about it." I hadn't even told Mackenzie, just didn't seem like a big deal.

They were all still looking at me. "So, April thirteenth is your birthday. Okay. Very interesting. Mind if I ask what year?"

Marcus groaned loudly and Devon got up, shaking his head and walking out of the room.

"Guys, this is serious. I'm not... What?" He looked around at them like he was afraid he'd just spilled the beans. "Oh no, am I being rude? Shit. Sorry, I mean shoot! I forgot it's not cool to ask women their age or something."

This time I couldn't help it, I had to giggle. "No worries, Mage. I was born in nineteen eighty-six."

He grabbed the pencil behind his ear and started writing something down and seemed very into whatever he was doing. Jade spoke up next.

"That was a really good year. *Top Gun* came out, *Ferris Bueller's Day Off*. And of course, *Master of Puppets, Peace Sells... but Who's Buying?* Great year."

Boy, he sure knew his pop culture trivia. "Yeah, I'm kind of fond of it, I guess."

They all started buzzing. Marcus grabbed an acoustic guitar and started playing "Sanitarium". Star grabbed his sticks and started banging out the beat on the ottoman. I wondered if they did this often, just burst into song. I admired that ability.

Devon came back into the room with a pack of guitar strings. He leaned over the back of the couch behind me, his breath hitting my neck as he whispered, "Happy Birthday, Jaylene." I smiled up at him and he went back over to the corner and started restringing the guitar he had been working on.

"Wow, it's awesome that it's your birthday. We should totally celebrate. What's your favorite food? We'll order it for dinner. Devon's mom cooks for us, she'd be happy to make you whatever you want." Jade was very insistent.

"Oh, thanks, but no. You don't have to do anything special for me. I'll just have whatever she's making. I'm sure it will be good."

He just looked at me like I'd spoken Swahili for a moment. "Not do anything special? For your *birthday*? What, do they not celebrate birthdays where you're from?"

Star threw a drumstick at him. "Hey, shut up! Maybe she's like Jehovah's Witness or something. Don't be offensive, dickhead."

I giggled. "I'm not Jehovah's Witness. It's no big deal. I just never had much use for birthdays, is all." I had to change the subject fast. Mage was looking at me weird and continuing with his writing.

"So, why don't you guys start telling me a little about yourselves? I have to be upfront and tell you that before the past couple of days, I hadn't really heard much of your music."

They were all looking at me, confused. I tried to recover.

"It's good. I listened to some the day you guys came in. Uh, Mackenzie is a big fan." Still the blank looks. "I don't really listen to the radio or anything." I let out a big breath, blowing my bangs out of my face. Okay, this was going really smooth.

"So which album did you listen to?" Marcus was leaning in, studying me.

"I, ah...whatever was on your website? *Burns Like Fire*, I think?"

He narrowed his eyes. He was sitting on the ottoman and he scooted over until he was right in front of me. I felt myself sinking back into the couch. "It's Ice. *Burns Like Ice*." He cleared his throat and lowered his voice a little, biting on the corner of his lip. "Which song did you listen to?"

Okay, now *I* was feeling the burn. In my cheeks. There was no way I was going to start reciting lyrics. From the way he was leering at me, I was beginning to get the picture that Marcus was the primary songwriter and was trying to use his sexual assertiveness to get to me. I shifted in my seat.

"I don't really remember. It was something smutty." I had to fight back; let him know he wasn't going to get to me that way. Stand up for myself. That was my tactic.

His lips peeled back into a very satisfied male kind of smile. "Smutty. Yeah, boys, I think she heard us. So it will take us a little work to win her over, that's okay." He leaned even closer, putting a hand on the couch next to my thigh, his knees touching mine. "I like a good challenge."

Oh shit.

"Knock it off, Marcus. She's not here to stroke your ego. Or anything else belonging to you." Devon had spoken from the other side of the room but hadn't looked up from his job.

The other guys started to chuckle, hiding their grins behind their hands.

Marcus gave me one last smoldering look and turned to them, standing up. "Hey, I'm only trying to find out what the lady likes. If we aren't her cup of tea, perhaps she'll tell us who is?" He smiled sweetly at me and I hoped I hadn't pissed him off.

"Well, I'm pretty much into older heavy metal and some of the stuff from the nineties. I listened to a lot of Zeppelin and The Doors growing up, my stepmom was a fan. I love AC/DC, with Bon Scott specifically. Metallica I've seen four or five times in concert, Megadeth, Pantera... That kind of stuff. Oh, and I like seventies and eighties punk. Do I pass your test, Mr. Lambert?" I couldn't help issuing a challenge of my own.

"What's your favorite Doors album?" Mage was looking at me intently, tapping his pencil against his chin.

"Has to be *Strange Days*, I guess. I love 'People are Strange'. But their debut was great as well."

He nodded thoughtfully. "That's a good one. I loved the cover Echo and the Bunnymen did for that movie *The Lost Boys*. That was a great flick." Mage obviously knew his '80s trivia as well.

"That's a good movie. I've actually been to a lot of the spots they used to film that movie."

Star and Jade leaned in, interested in our conversation. "Us, too,"

Jade said. "We stayed in Santa Cruz once when we were touring out west. One of our early shows was at The Catalyst. You ever been there?"

I nodded. "Sure, I saw Agent Orange there once."

"No way. I love them." Jade started naming off other California punk bands and we seemed to like a lot of the same stuff.

Marcus cut in then. "Okay. Well, at least you have good taste, even if it's a bit antiquated. Our music is certainly influenced by the early metal but we've tried to step it up a notch."

I caught Devon's smirk out of the corner of my eye but I didn't want to interrupt Marcus. He seemed like he was about to give a serious speech.

"Our first three albums were very edgy for metalcore, which is why expectations are so high for us. We have a lot riding on our next album —and I, for one, don't want to be written off just yet." He had his hands on his hips and almost seemed to be scolding the others. Tension started to build and I was getting a clearer picture of why they needed me.

Devon spoke up next. "We do have a lot riding on our next album, Marcus, and that's why we need to be open to new ideas and influences." He nodded almost imperceptibly at me.

Perhaps he was trying to help me get a feel for the group dynamics. It was already apparent that while Marcus was the most outspoken, Devon was equally in charge, and the other three followed them to varying degrees. I wanted to explore this dynamic more but felt it safer to change the subject.

I leaned forward and took Marcus's arm in my hands, turning it over in the light. "Who's done your tattoos? I'm seeing a lot of similar styles. Did you guys get work done by the same people?" Encouraging people to talk about their artwork could lead in all kinds of directions, and these guys were eager to share.

He looked down at his arm distractedly, like he wasn't happy about the subject change. "I got a few done when I was younger, around here, before going to L.A. But my arms were done at Six Feet Under in Upland. You heard of it?"

"Corey Miller's place, sure. They do good work there. The line work is really good here." He had an intricate sleeve involving Gothic crosses and skulls with angel wings. I grabbed for the other hand and heard an intake of breath from him.

I looked up to see him looking down at me with a sneer. "You want to inspect anything else?" It was obvious that this type of come-on worked for him, but I was so not buying what he was selling.

"Thanks, but I'm just interested in what's been *done* to your skin, not what you like to do with it."

The guys all laughed at that comment and it even got an apprecia-tive smile from Devon. I was simply setting boundaries.

Marcus chuckled but I had the sense that we weren't finished testing each other. Jade slid over next to me and started showing me his tradi-tional work, telling me stories about each of his tattoos. Pretty soon the four guys were all crowded around me, showing me their ink. Troy had done some of their work, as well as a couple of other local artists. They'd also gotten work done in L.A. and the surrounding areas. Most of it looked great, but they each had at least one embarrassing tattoo story.

"Star, show her your pinup." Jade pulled Star's shirt up. On his rib cage, he had a scantily clad pinup done pirate style. But the proportions were way off. "They put six fingers on her right hand."

I giggled but hurried to reassure him. "Unfortunately, it happens. When I was still an apprentice, my mentor caught me before I misspelled 'Independence' on a guy's chest. It was huge. It probably would have been the end for me."

"What about you? Who did your work?" Jade asked. They were looking intently at my arms but seemed hesitant to touch me. They would put their hands out and then pull them back. It was too cute. Even Marcus was looking from afar.

I told them about the shops I'd been to back home. Most of my work, including my arms and a large piece on my thigh (which of course I wasn't disrobing to show them), was done by my mentor Stephen Pierce at Black Heart Tattoo in Hayward. They asked what an appren-ticeship entailed, and I told them I'd worked closely with Stephen for a year and a half before he made me an official artist in the shop.

We'd been chatting for about an hour, I guess, when Marcus looked at his watch and said, "Well, fellas, time to get to work."

They all groaned and stood up. Mage followed them, picking up some leftover trash. I stood to help him.

"It's okay, I got it." He winked, took the trash from me, and carried it over to a small kitchenette I hadn't noticed. He grabbed a bottle of water and gestured to me with a second bottle. I nodded so he tossed it gently to me.

"Thanks, Mage." Marcus was chatting with Devon by the chair where he'd been working on the guitar. I stepped over, a little unsure whether they wanted their space or not. "Hey, I don't mean to interrupt, but if you guys are going to be practicing, do you want me hanging out or to get lost? Either way is fine."

Devon gave me that killer blue-eyed gaze of his and I had to catch myself before I reached up and checked my pulse.

Marcus looked at him and then at me with a raised eyebrow. "We absolutely want you there," he said. "That's the point of you being with us."

I nodded and figured I should give the full disclosure to him about my little habit. "I told Devon, but I should let the rest of you guys know that I sketch. A lot. I'll try not to be intrusive but I usually have a pencil and sketchbook with me all the time. Is that going to be too weird?"

I should have known he would be fine with it. He kind of puffed up his chest a bit and gave me his best sultry-model face. "Sketch away, dahlin."

Devon gave him a shove and said, "C'mon, Fabio. Let's get to work."

I bit back a laugh, Marcus looked perturbed, and Devon just gave his half smile. I sighed. This was definitely going to be an interesting couple of weeks.

FIVE

I went to my room to grab my sketchbook and pencils and checked my phone. Mackenzie had already left me five text messages. I sent her a quick *"I'm fine, I'm working, you should be too!"* answer and dropped the phone on the bed. I didn't want it distracting me so I wasn't going to keep it with me.

As I headed down the stairs, I could hear the guys starting to warm up their instruments. I was actually looking forward to watching their creative process. Live music was thrilling to me in any form. Being here while they created what would hopefully be another successful album would be a once-in-a-lifetime experience.

Star's drum set was on the little stage. It was a stripped-down set, probably not what he'd use live. The other guys were in a half circle around the front of the stage. Jade and Mage stood next to each other, tuning their guitar and bass, respectively. Devon was off to the other side with a collection of acoustic and electric guitars. He was warming up with a Les Paul, but I could also see a Fender Stratocaster, a Flying V and an Epiphone acoustic. My eyes couldn't help but be drawn to his long fingers flying over the fretboard. He hadn't plugged in yet so I couldn't hear what he was playing.

Plugged in... This might get loud.

I looked around and at that moment, Mage walked over and handed me a box of earplugs. "Here. You might need these."

I thanked him. But if I was going to need earplugs, wasn't everyone outside going to hear? Then I noticed that egg-crate foam was put up all along the windows in the front. Aha. That was how they hoped to keep folks from hearing what was going on.

There were a couple of huge beanbags thrown over by the bar, so I figured that would be a comfy place to watch. I could see them all fairly well from that vantage point. Marcus was lining up sheets of paper at the foot of the stage. Star ran through some beats, and Jade and Mage had plugged in and were tuning.

They started by playing a few instrumentals, perhaps some songs they were working on? The first one started out with a fast, pounding rhythm, followed by Jade and Devon playing a harmony that was reminiscent of an Iron Maiden or Judas Priest song. I could dig this for sure. There were a lot of changes and then they just kind of stopped. Ah. Not quite finished yet.

Marcus bobbed his head along, writing occasionally. The second piece was a slow groove that had Devon playing a very soulful intro. It reminded me of something Slash would have played on later Guns tracks. Marcus was watching, not bobbing his head this time. Instead he was studying Devon with a frown on his face.

Jade and Mage were following along, eyes closed a bit. Star was playing a soft, almost jazz-like rhythm, not overpowering the melody.

Marcus appeared to grow increasingly impatient, finally motioning for Devon to stop. "Okay, okay. I'm just not sure what you want me to do with that one, D."

Devon just shrugged and walked over to a stool to get a drink of water. "It is what it is, Marcus. You want us to work on stuff. This is what I came up with. It's just where my head's at right now."

Whoa. If that's where his head was, it was a bluesy and beautiful place. I figured I shouldn't play the cheerleader right now, but if I were, I'd say Go Team Devon.

Marcus walked back over to his papers and then grabbed one of the guitars by Devon. "I was thinking something more like this." He played a riff that sounded squealy and full of feedback to me, but that was my uneducated ear.

He repeated it and looked over at the other guys, who were kind of scratching their heads. They fell into a supporting groove with him. His playing was in the realm of earsplitting but he had some talent. It just didn't seem as natural for him as it was for Devon. Or was I choosing sides?

Bad, bad. I couldn't do that. I was supposed to be observing.

But what I was seeing was some major tension coming off two men who were in totally different places musically, for sure. Maybe those differences could be seen in other ways, too.

I picked up my sketchbook and started to draw. I was listening to them start to argue and found myself drawing a heart split in two. One side had jagged edges. The other just seemed to melt toward the bottom of the page. Then I was doodling and each side of the page became distinctive. One side was filled with anxiety and frustration, the other with sadness and despair.

After a while, I started hearing some familiar tunes. It seemed Devon was trying to teach the guys to play a blues riff. I didn't know whose it was originally but I liked it. Jade and Mage joined in, with Star supplying the rhythm.

Eventually Marcus started to play, although he still seemed frustrated. He wore his guitar slung low and his movements were kind of jerky. Devon played effortlessly. His arms were loose, his limbs hanging low. I didn't know what had come between them, or why the rift, but I was sure it wasn't going to be pleasant for anyone to discuss.

The guys played for another couple of hours, with a few breaks in between for smokes out back. Through it all, I just sketched each of them playing their instruments and tried to capture what their essence brought to the group. Devon's and Marcus's sketches were probably the most detailed, though, because it was obvious that the root of the band's problem was something between them.

Star came over during one of the breaks and flopped down into the beanbag next to mine. He was trying to look over my shoulder with subtlety. He had zero. Marcus and Devon had gone outside together, and the other two were grabbing drinks from behind the bar, stretching out their hands and arms.

I handed my sketchbook to Star with a sly smile and said, "If you want to see my drawings, Star, you just have to ask. They're all going to belong to you anyway."

He blushed and said, "That obvious? I'm sorry. I've just always wished I could draw. I was never any good at it." He started to flip through the pages and blew a breath out in a whistle. "Damn. Jaylene, these are amazing. You totally got us all. Where did you learn to draw like this?"

I shrugged. "I don't know. Around, I guess. I had a few classes but I never did well in them because I wanted to do my own thing, you know? I probably had lower grades in my art classes than anything else because the teachers were always like 'You have so much potential, Jaylene, blah blah blah, if you'd just do it like this.'"

He nodded in agreement. "Totally. You should have seen us in music class. Our band teacher hated us, huh, Jade?" Jade wandered over to us and asked if he could look at my book, too.

"Of course. I told Marcus and Devon it's a habit of mine. I draw all the time. Sometimes they turn into something, sometimes it's just a way for me to process what's going on around me."

He was looking thoughtfully at one drawing in particular. "That's so weird. That's how you see us? That's so cool though. Isn't this cool? Mage! Dude, come check this out. You look fuckin' crazy, dude, look at this one."

Mage came over with a cup of coffee in his hand and peered over Jade's shoulder. In the drawing of Mage, for some reason I'd added swirls around him, like a cyclone of energy, and above them there was a face with hollow eyes. It was kind of freaky, but like I always say—I draws 'em like I sees 'em.

"No shit, really?" He looked from the book to me, and back again. "Jaylene, these are really deep. You can really *see* us." His eyes met mine, searching. "You sure you don't have any of the Gift in you, eh?"

I frowned. "I don't know what you mean."

"It doesn't always have to be about that freaky shit, Mage. You're going to scare her off." Jade was looking worried so I shook my head.

"Jade, it's fine. His beliefs are his beliefs and that's cool. It doesn't bother me. I've heard a lot of people's views on things, and it's like... whatever rings true for them. We all have to find our way, right?"

Mage was looking at me like he'd just had an epiphany. "Yesssss. See? That's *exactly* what I've been trying to tell you assholes since seventh grade, but you just gotta see everything like skeptics. Haven't you ever seen something or been through something that you just couldn't explain? Like it had to be something else, man?"

Star and Jade just groaned.

"He's right, I think. There's a lot that goes on that there are no good explanations for, true, Mage. And hey, the way I look at it is, if people believe in something, it gives it power, so I try to suspend disbelief. It is what it is."

Their looks weren't as disgusted when they gazed back at Mage this time. Maybe they were seeing things through his eyes.

Then Mage hurriedly turned and ran over to pick up his bass. "Hey, Jade, come check this out."

The two of them put their heads together and started in on that demented musician speak Devon had warned me about. I just watched the magic happen. Star wandered around them slowly and climbed back up to his drum set. The beginnings of a riff were coming together when Marcus and Devon came back in.

Marcus looked pissed, Devon just looked sad.

The three continued to play and the music began to get faster and faster. Star pummelled the drums. But instead of the shrill sound I'd heard when Marcus had started them off, this was powerful. The kind of stuff you could feel in your gut. I couldn't help but bob my head a little.

Devon wordlessly picked up his guitar and caught up to them. In a few eight counts, he started playing notes all over the place, complementing what Mage and Jade were laying down.

Marcus's face went from angry to engrossed. He just stood there, seemingly engaged at a pretty deep level.

So that's how it happened. That was how a metal band wrote a song. Or at least, I was seeing the beginnings of how a song comes together. They started it over, Mage said a few things to Devon, who just nodded, and they played it out for a solid seven or eight minutes, until Marcus waved them off.

"Now that's what I'm talking about. I sure fucking hope someone remembered to turn on the recorder."

Star raised a hand and they all thanked him. Mage was writing things down quickly, the chords, I guess. I had no idea. This was all foreign to me.

"Mage, I'm going to listen to that and see what I can come up with for lyrics. Nice work." Mage seemed very pleased with the compliment. My guess was that those didn't come often from Marcus...or at least not lately.

Marcus walked over to me then and said, "Now *that* is what we're trying to accomplish. This is how it's supposed to work. It just hasn't for a bit. Maybe you're our good luck charm." He glanced down at my sketchbook that had been forgotten in the creative burst. The drawing of Mage was still on top.

Marcus bent down and picked it up, looking at it closely. "Can I borrow this?"

I nodded, "Sure. It's all yours. Just take it out."

He carefully ripped out the page, looked at the drawing of Star—on which I'd added silly devil horns—and he laughed. "Yeah, I guess you really do see us. Star, she's already got you figured out."

Star blushed and played a silly drum roll. The tension dissipated and the camaraderie of earlier was back.

I stood up and stretched, stiff from being hunched over my sketchbook for the better part of two hours. But I felt good. I felt like I could illustrate what was going on and they could see it from an outside perspective. No words, no judgments. Just pictures.

I giggled, thinking about those "artist's renderings" from court sessions, and hoped there wouldn't be any drawings of angry conversations. I'm not much good with confrontations; I tend to be a bit passive. I already didn't like it when the guys were mad at each other. If I could get it out through my drawings then I could process it better, and maybe so could they.

The guys went back upstairs to watch TV and play video games. I decided to do some exploring. I knew there was a back patio and I wanted to get a breath of fresh air. I thought that would be appropriate, considering the afternoon we'd just had.

I walked back between the bar and the stage into a narrow hallway. I could hear kitchen sounds, so I thought I'd take a peek. Devon was in the kitchen with an older woman, who was peeling potatoes and singing to herself. Devon was washing dishes, and for some reason it didn't seem out of character for him to be doing that. It seemed almost natural. Could it be he knew his way around the kitchen?

"Hey," I said to announce my intrusion. "Is there anything I can do to help?"

Devon turned around and looked from the woman to me. He walked over to the door, wiping his hands off on the back of his black jeans. "Jaylene Charles, this is my mother, Marie Doucette Boudreaux."

The woman turned around and gave me an all-business handshake.

I tried not to react. Boudreaux? That was Devon's last name? Did that mean Margaret was his wife? It would make sense why he was so full of sorrow.

That thought hit me like a punch in the gut. I tried to shake it off and make nice.

His mother was thin and taller than me, probably 5'10", with black hair streaked gray in a messy bun on top of her head. She was wearing a black t-shirt with the name "Houma City Bar and Grill" on the front, and a pair of khaki Bermuda shorts.

"Pleased to meet you, Mrs. Boudreaux."

She smiled at me and said, "You as well, Miss Charles. I've heard a lot about you from that rascal brother of mine, Daryl. He speaks highly of you and your work." She glanced at my arms and hid any displeasure she might have had at my tattoos. That was a welcome reaction.

"Thank you. Daryl has been very kind to me since I arrived here. I couldn't have opened my shop without him." She smiled and nodded.

"He does a lot for the people he cares about. He took care of us after my husband passed. Helped me keep the business open, he did." She smiled, but there was that sadness I'd grown used to with Devon in her eyes. If he'd lost his father, that could explain some of the sadness...but it seemed deeper than that.

"I was actually just trying to shoo Devon out of the kitchen. Maybe you could encourage him to let me be?"

Devon looked at his mother with his half smile. "I guess I know when I'm not wanted. I was just trying to help, Mama." His drawl was a bit more pronounced in here with her. It was sweet to see him with his mother. He obviously cared deeply for her.

She snapped a towel at him and said, "You aren't here to work in the kitchen, son. You're here to make music with dem boys. You run along with Miss Charles."

He walked over and kissed her on the top of her head. "Don't work too hard, Mama. I'll be back in a bit to check on you and help you feed those monsters."

She laughed and waved us off. "Ain't nothing I can't handle, son. You go on, now, I've got this under control."

She was friendly but reserved, and I could see a lot of her in Devon. She was a beautiful woman, probably in her early fifties, but you could tell she'd worked hard in life by the slight bend in her back and the tired lines on her face. Her beautiful blue eyes shone just as brightly as his, and were just as intense. I hoped I'd have more of a chance to talk to her. Maybe she could help me understand just what they'd all been through.

"It was very nice to meet you, Mrs. Boudreaux, and please, let me know if I can help. I'm not a great cook but I can bake a little."

She waved me off and said, "Nonsense, you young'uns go enjoy yourselves. Dinner will be in about an hour."

"Thanks, Mama." Devon motioned for me to leave the kitchen before he did, always the gentleman, and I thanked him.

He leaned back in the door to say something to his mother and I heard her say, "You a good boy, son. Go have some fun." He shook his head and then we were in the hallway, facing each other.

"I was just, um, exploring a little. I didn't mean to interrupt."

He looked at me questioningly, looked back at the kitchen. "Oh, no, you weren't interrupting. I was just trying, rather unsuccessfully, to help my mother in the kitchen. You might have noticed she didn't want my help. She's like that I guess, always trying to do for everyone."

I smiled at him. "I guess that's where you must get it from? Or does it just run in your family? Because I know Daryl is the same. Well...he doesn't cook too well, from what I've experienced."

He laughed. "No, he can handle a grill some but he's banned from our kitchen, and probably Katie keeps him away there, too." He shook his head and then we were just standing there.

"Listen, if you..."

"Hey, do you want..."

We both spoke at the same time and laughed nervously. I said, "I'm sorry, I was just going to say if you have things to do, don't mind me. Just tell me where's off-limits and I can certainly entertain myself."

"No place is off-limits, but I'm sure you don't want to walk into bathrooms or bedrooms without knocking first, or you might get an unpleasant surprise."

I laughed out loud at that. "No doubt. I'll take that under advisement. I do tend to forget about that after living alone for so long."

He nodded. "I forgot, no brothers and sisters. That must have been weird. My sister learned early on to not barge in on us. The guys were over a lot when we were younger and she caught us in many embarrassing situations." There was that sadness again. "I was just going to go out back, want to join me?"

"Sure," I said, and then I tried to lighten up the conversation. "What kind of embarrassing? Like barn-animals embarrassing? Hormonal-teenage-boy kind of embarrassing?" It worked. I got him to crack a smile.

"There was the time she caught us watching porn in the garage. She screamed at us about how awful it was, how we shouldn't be doing it. But she was most angry that we were watching *crappy* porn that had horrible actors. Like we were actually paying attention to the acting. When Marcus told her that, she smacked him upside the head and threatened to tell on us. She was eighteen at the time and I guess I was fifteen, and the other guys were fourteen. Man, that was horrible."

"Well, did you learn anything from that experience?"

He shrugged. "To watch better porn? Not to do it when my sister was around? We were teenage boys, what were we supposed to do?"

I couldn't tell if he was being serious; he spent so *much* of his time being serious. "I don't know. You could have gone out and found girl-friends instead of sitting around in a garage watching bad porn."

He burst out laughing at that, and the sound was music to my ears. "No girls would have even come close to letting us touch them back then. We were total nerds. We couldn't even talk to girls. Well, except Marcus. He had the confidence, even if he didn't have anything to back it up." There was a twinge of bitterness in his tone. "Anyway, we just took all that pent-up angst and poured it into our music, I guess."

I spoke as nonchalantly as I could. "It seems to have paid off for you."

He scoffed. "Yeah, well, I wouldn't exactly say that."

Was he really going to play that one off?

We stepped out the back door into a quaint courtyard with a fountain and benches all around. The high wall in back blocked the view from neighbors, so we were safe. I sat down on a bench in the corner near the fountain and continued my line of questioning. "Really? No girls hanging out backstage? Groupies in your tour bus?"

He snorted. He chose the bench next to mine and took a seat. "Maybe, but those weren't exactly the kind of girls I'd have picked. Some of the other guys might have been a little less choosy. I'm not naming names." His lips twitched a bit, like he was trying not to laugh.

Pity. He was even more beautiful when he laughed. But I needed to stop thinking like that right now. If he'd just lost a wife, there's no telling what shape he was in emotionally, and having a woman flirt with him would probably make him extremely uncomfortable.

He lit up a cigarette and took in a long drag. He looked at me apologetically. "Is this going to bother you?"

I shook my head. "No, it's fine."

He took another long drag and closed his eyes. "I quit for a long time. Maggie hated it. But after everything that happened, well...I guess we all fall back on our comforts."

I didn't know what was safe to ask him about her. I was assuming that was a pet name for Margaret? I decided a little disclosure of my own might make him feel better.

"I smoked on and off when I was younger. I quit when I learned I had asthma, at around twenty years old. After my father died a year and a half ago, I took it back up for a while. Until I moved here, I guess. Fresh start and everything." I gave him a sad smile.

"I'm sorry about your father, Jaylene. It's rough. Mine died so long ago, but I still remember how awful I felt after."

"Thanks. It's still weird, but being here has made it much easier to get perspective on it. How old were you when your father died?"

He took one last drag on the cigarette and put it out in a large urn. He took out a pack of mint gum from his pocket and offered a piece to me, which I gladly took. He unwrapped one and popped it in his mouth.

"I was sixteen when he died. He used to fish in the gulf so we'd have fresh-caught options at our restaurant. He was out when a storm came in and didn't make it back. My mom ran the restaurant while he was away fishing and they had a couple of other employees, but after he died, I went to work there in my spare time. My sister was moved out by then, so it was just me and Mama until I went to college."

"Where did you study?" I was learning more about him in this conversation than at any time previously, and I wanted him to continue unraveling his mysteries.

"I had a music scholarship to Tulane, but I left after three semesters. Mama was sick a lot and needed me, although she was pissed that I gave up school. Guess she's always been trying to get rid of me and thought that was her best chance." He snickered but it sounded like he really felt that way.

"Devon, I can't believe your mother was trying to get rid of you. Is it possible she just wanted bigger things for you?"

He shrugged and looked down at his feet. "Yeah, I know that's it. I hated disappointing her. Besides, she didn't really have much choice but for me to come back. And that's how things happened with the boys, anyway. If I wouldn't have come home, I guess there'd be no Maggie's Bones." Somehow he didn't sound pleased about that.

"So you came back home and started up with the boys then? I thought y'all were from New Orleans?"

He shook his head. "Nah, we grew up in Houma. We spent as much time bumming around Uncle Daryl's as he'd let us. He snuck us into bars when we were younger, and then after we put the band together, he got us a few gigs. Then Marcus decided we needed to go to L.A. Daryl promised me he'd help Mama out with the restaurant, so we left. The rest is fucked-up history, I guess." He stood up and started pacing a little.

"But Devon, you guys have truly made the world a better place. Without Maggie's Bones, you'd have no masterpiece like 'Mystikal Stick'," I deadpanned. "I'm not sure what the world would do without such an ode-to-my-magic-cock kind of song."

He gave me a sly smile, which I would have to categorize as my favorite smile so far. It was evil and sexy and it gave me a shiver. "So you *have* been listening. Is that one of your personal favorites, or do you prefer something like 'Sin on My Face'?"

I clapped both hands over my mouth to keep from laughing hysterically. He laughed too, thankfully. "Hmmm, I'm afraid I'm not familiar with that one. Is that one of your early tunes?"

"Those would be off our debut, yes. I'd like to think we've grown since then, so to speak. Now we just play songs about dysfunctional relationships and sexual predators." That pissed-off look was back. I liked playful Devon so much more.

"You don't seem happy about that. Are you missing the early Bones material?"

He shook his head. "I'm not really missing any of it, to be honest. I'm kind of done playing this shit. I mean, I'm proud of what we've accomplished, even if we had to sing songs about magic cocks, but we're a little old for that now. Or at least *I* am." He paused and rubbed the back of his neck. "I'm ready to do something a little more serious with my music, I guess."

This was quite an admission. It explained a lot about what was going on between him and Marcus. "I take it Marcus doesn't feel the same?"

He looked over to me and nodded. "Yeah. He wants more of the same. He's always just wanted the big time." He lit another cigarette, obviously getting more upset. It was good for him to be talking but I hated to see him upset like this.

"And you want more? I gotta say, I really liked what you were playing earlier. I worried whether I should say anything, like maybe I should stay impartial, but... Well, I can't. There was a lot of soul to what you played."

He froze, and I thought I caught a sparkle in his eye. When he spoke again, it was in such a quiet voice, I barely heard him. "You liked that?"

I nodded and he smiled. He started pacing again, slower this time, keeping his eyes on me.

"It was really powerful, it had feeling. I'm no music critic or expert or anything. I just know what I like and what I don't." I was afraid I was overstepping my bounds, but I wanted to be honest with him, since he'd been so open with me.

"But you liked it, really?"

Why was he unsure? "Yes, Devon. It was really, *really* good. But the important question is—did *you* like it?"

He paused in his pacing. "Yeah, I did. It felt good."

I smiled at him.

He walked over and stopped in front of me. I had to crane my neck to look up at him, which he noticed, so he crouched down. "Look, Jaylene. I'm glad you're here. I *want* to work things out with these guys. I love them like brothers. But I just don't know if there's anything here for me anymore."

I had the suspicion he might feel that way, just based on the little I'd observed so far. "What about the album and the label?"

He shrugged and looked down at his hands. "I'll meet my obligations. After that, I don't know." He looked up at me, his eyes imploring. "I haven't told them what I'm feeling yet, so if you don't mind..."

I touched his shoulder. "I understand. It's not my place to say anything to them. You'll tell them when you're ready." I tried to give him an encouraging smile. His eyes were so blue they were almost glowing in the fading afternoon light.

I took my hand back and he grabbed for it, holding it in his for a minute before letting it go. He stood up and smiled down at me. "I'm *really* glad you're here. I'll see you at dinner?"

I nodded to him and waved, watched him retreat through the door, slightly ducking his head. My hand tingled where he'd touched me.

I smiled to myself. I was really glad I was here, too.

. . .

Dinner was spaghetti, meatballs, garlic bread and salad, and was served buffet style on the back counter in the hall. We all took seats in front of the bar. It was a nice, antique-looking, solid wood bar that had aged well. The rest of the building varied between work-in-progress and work-not-even-started. I assumed the owners were in the process of restoring it.

The guys had saved me a seat in the middle of the bar between Mage and Marcus. Devon sat at the end, eyeing them with a smirk.

"So why is this building empty? What is this place?"

Mage wiped his mouth daintily with a napkin and said, "The current owners rented it to us with an option to buy. It seems after Katrina, he was unable to continue with his renovations and plans to open a burlesque club."

"We were thinking of opening one up ourselves after our next tour. What do you think, Jaylene?" Marcus was looking at me intently, waiting for a reaction.

"It's a beautiful old building. I guess burlesque could be cool, if it's done in good taste and the club is nice." I gave him a challenging look, waiting to see if he was going to push it further. But Mage came to my rescue.

"There are stories of paranormal activity in the building. Ghosts and spirits, that kind of thing. I still think Club Haunt has a nice ring to it."

I heard the other guys giggle. Jade elbowed Mage in the side.

"Dude, you are obsessed. I'm telling you, the only thing going bump in the night around here is Star sleepwalking to the bathroom."

Jade snickered and Star said indignantly, "I do not sleepwalk! It was only once and we'd just watched a scary movie."

"What happened?" I asked.

Star groaned and put his head down on the bar.

Jade took over the narrative. "We'd just watched *The Grudge* for the hundredth time, and Mage got up to take a leak in the wee hours of the morn. He found this dumbass curled up in the tub in his boxers. Said he didn't know how he got there."

I laughed. "That's okay, Star. Often people sleepwalk after a traumatic experience. It has to do with the body's subconscious and how it tries to help us deal with trauma."

Mage shuddered. "Shit, the real trauma would have been if I'd found him in there naked."

They all laughed and I tried to console Star. "Like you guys have never been caught with your pants down."

I looked over at Devon—who promptly spit out his milk and grabbed frantically for a napkin.

The guys looked between Devon and I. Marcus asked, "What did you tell her, D?"

Devon took another bite of his spaghetti and ignored Marcus.

"Did you break the Bro Code? Damn, dude. How could you? After all we've been through?" He started mock sobbing. The other guys were shaking their heads.

Devon recovered and shot back, "What? It's not like I told her about the time you and Bernadette got caught on my daddy's boat because you forgot to check that you were tied up and drifted out into the Gulf."

"Yeah—and you guys left your clothes on the dock," added Jade, and the guys all started laughing.

"Okay, funny guy." Marcus turned on Jade. "What about the time I caught you in Mama's underwear drawer?"

Jade blushed and said, "That was for Mardi Gras and you know it, asshole." He threw a bread crust at Marcus that just barely missed me. Marcus grabbed an ice cube out of his tea glass and chucked it back.

Star leaned into Jade and said, "Dude, what about the time Marcus sang that Michael Bolton song at the talent show in middle school."

Okay, that one got me laughing—and prompted another ice cube thrown by Marcus.

"I won, didn't I? Y'all were just jealous you didn't have the balls to get up there."

Mage and Devon kept shaking their heads, trying to stay out of the path of Marcus's ice cubes.

"What song did you sing, Marcus?" I asked.

He lifted his chin and smoothed back his hair. "I covered his version of 'How Am I Supposed to Live Without You'. It was a huge success."

The other guys were laughing hard.

"He even had the long mullet to go with it." Jade was holding his sides and gasping for breath.

"My hair was awesome. I didn't hear any of the girls complaining." He was trying awfully hard to remain untouched by their razzing.

"Yeah, I'm sure it kept Bernadette warm out there on Uncle David's boat."

At that, Marcus kicked back his stool and Jade took off running. They chased each other while the other guys continued to roar with laughter. Jade flew up the stairs and continued to taunt him from the gangway, warbling out lines to the Bolton tune.

I couldn't stop laughing either. It was fun, watching them acting like boys and giving each other a hard time. I'd never had that kind of relationship with anyone until I'd met Mackenzie and I was still new to it. It had taken me a long time to not get upset when she teased me. It was different in the tattoo shops I'd worked in. There was hazing and pranking and that kind of thing, but this was true brotherly love I was witnessing here, and it was strong, despite their current dilemma.

"So what's on the agenda for tonight?" I asked Mage and Devon.

They shrugged. "I think there's an *Evil Dead* marathon on tonight. You game?"

I beamed at Mage for the suggestion. "I *love* those movies. Although, you can really do without the first one. *Evil Dead II* is the best."

Mage was looking at me in wonder. "You actually like horror movies?" He put his arm around my shoulders and said, "Guys, can we keep her? I mean, she likes *Evil Dead.* That's like perfection."

He dropped his arm and I patted him on the shoulder. "You have to give me up in sixteen more days, I'm afraid, or Mackenzie will make Ash's girlfriends look harmless."

They all laughed at that, except Star. "What's her story, Jaylene? She got a beau?"

I knew he'd taken a liking to her. I raised an eyebrow at him. "I don't think I can answer that unless I know your intentions, young man."

He smiled sheepishly. "She's awful pretty. I like all that pink hair she's got going on and those legs... I, ah, I mean, she's pretty talented with a needle. Shit. I mean shoot." It was so charming how they tried not to cuss around me.

"She does not have a boyfriend, Star, but she *does* have a line of guys who would like to take her out. She doesn't just go off with any guy with a cute smile. So while you *do* have a cute smile, you have to have more going for you than that. Are you gainfully employed?"

The other guys laughed at that. "Depends on your definition of gainful," said Marcus, who was dragging a red-faced Jade through the room in a headlock.

"You know—like in a respectable profession." I crossed my arms and tapped my foot at Star.

"Would you call a professional musician respectable?"

I narrowed my eyes. "A musician? A person who travels around, wooing women in every city, using his music to lower unsuspecting women's inhibitions? I think not! What other skills do you have?"

He was seriously trying to come up with something. "Uh, I'm good with my hands? Ah, that didn't sound right. I mean I can fix cars and shit—I mean *stuff*. I restored a nineteen sixty-five Camaro with my uncles when I was a teenager, and not hanging around with these knuckleheads."

"Hmmm, classic cars are certainly a weakness of Miss McGowan's. Would you be respectful with her? Take her on proper dates to respectable locations?"

He frowned for a minute. "Would a bar on Bourbon Street count?"

"Seriously? That's where you'd take a woman on a date?"

He shrugged. "Why not? If they've got good music and drinks. Isn't that what women want?"

"I suppose some women might like to do that, but that's not really a date. That's more like hanging out, hoping to hook up, isn't it?"

He looked confused. "Marcus, what's she talking about?"

Oh Lord. Dating advice from Marcus. This was about to get ugly.

"Star, my fine young friend, I believe what Miss Charles is trying to say is that respectable women want to be taken out and treated to the finer things in life...before they give it up."

The guys started chuckling—until they saw my face.

"Is that right, Marcus? And just how many *respectable* women have you actually dated?"

He gave me that creepy smile of his that reeked of his imagined sexual prowess. "Probably none. But if I ever tried, I'm sure I wouldn't have to go out of my way to wine and dine them before they gave me what I wanted."

I rolled my eyes. Did guys really think that shit worked?

Unfortunately, in his case, with those bedroom hazel eyes and that arrogant swagger, he was probably right. They did absolutely nothing for me. I needed to put him in his place.

"You know, Marcus, I'm sure there are plenty of women out there who are immune to your idea of charm, and who prefer men who respect them and at least *pretend* to care about other things than getting laid. You might try it sometime. You might find your pool of potential mates to be a little higher on the intelligence scale that way." I smiled sweetly at him, took a long drag on my ice water, and put my glass on the bar firmly.

The other guys sat there, eagerly waiting to see how he'd react.

He eyed me coolly and said, "You might be right, Miss Charles. But I intend to continue having my fun with the vast number of women who are easily seduced by my charms. It's not as much of a challenge, true, but it sure beats celibacy." He winked at the other guys and headed off to go upstairs.

The guy sure knew how to make an exit.

"Well, fellas, that was enlightening. Anyone else care to tell me my logic is flawed?" None of the other guys dared to speak up and Devon just stared at me with what seemed like appreciation. I wasn't trying to take sides but Marcus sure pushed my buttons. I'd have to get past that if I was going to work on him. It was never a good idea to tattoo someone you had negative feelings about. It could really affect your work.

"I'm going to check my messages and take a quick shower. Mage, what time does the movie start?"

He started grabbing plates off the bar. "Eight o'clock, I believe. I'll knock on your door when it's on."

I started to help grab plates but he and Devon shooed me away. "We've got this, dinner's our meal. Marcus and Jade have lunch, and

Star has breakfast. You're our guest, you don't need to help," Mage finished.

I shook my head. "No, I'm going to do my share to help, too. Star, I'll help you with breakfast from now on, okay?"

He smiled appreciatively. "Great, thanks, Jaylene." He bounded off up the stairs. "Hey, Marcus, care to try to beat me at pool? Notice I said *try*?"

Marcus shouted back but I wasn't listening. Devon was taking my plate from me and smiling his half smile.

I took a chance. "Are you joining us for the movie?"

He shrugged. "I might. I've got some things I want to work on but I'll come up."

I nodded and walked up the stairs closest to my room. I didn't want to seem like I was coming on strong with him. I was so not good with these situations. And this wasn't exactly the right time to try to start something with an obviously wounded man who may or may not be a grieving widower.

It had been an eventful day and I'd learned a lot, but I still knew very little about Margaret—other than she was likely Devon's wife. Other than looking at their website, I hadn't researched anything about them, and since Sherry told me they wanted to tell me about Margaret, I was trying to be compliant with the contract. One thing was abundantly clear: these guys had a long road ahead of them if they were going to meet their label's demands.

Six

I got up to the room and found three voice mails. The first was from Sherry:

"Hey, Jaylene. I hope your first day went okay. I just thought I'd call and check in with you. I spoke to Marcus earlier and he said you were all settled in. He also said you weren't taking any of his crap. Good girl. That I love to hear. Call me if you need me. I'll actually be coming out there next week to see what kind of progress they're making with the material for the new album. Talk to you soon."

Ugh. They weren't making much progress at all. I hoped they had more than what they'd played today.

The next message was from Mackenzie.

"I'm dying for an update! CALL ME!"

Nice. I'd call her.

"Hi, sweetheart. I wanted to tell you how much we enjoyed our time with you. We're back and tucked in here at home. I also wanted to tell you how proud I am of what you're doing. I wish I'd had the guts to live my dreams at your age. Never mind what Shannon says, your father would be very happy for you. He loved you very much, even if you weren't the daughter he imagined he would have. So you just keep doing what you're doing and have fun. I love you. Goodbye."

My heart hurt so much, I crumbled. Too many emotions flooded me at once, and I was floored. Their visit had threatened to unlock the vise grip I had on my feelings about my father's death. A few words from my beloved grandma and I was done.

I don't know how long I sat there before my phone started buzzing in my hand.

"Why the hell haven't you called me yet, girl? I'm sitting on pins and needles at Pins and Needles—ha ha ha. Get it? Hello, Jay? Jay! What's wrong?"

I sniffled a little and tried to talk but she was fired up.

"What did they do? I'm coming over there right now. I'm—"

"Kenz, I'm fine. I just got a voicemail from my grandma, is all." She was quiet, which let me catch my breath for a minute. "How's the shop?"

She didn't answer right away, and when she did, her voice was low and full of concern. "Today went well. Troy had a couple of walk-ins and Grant came in to get his piece done. He liked your drawing and was cool with Troy doing the work, so it was okay."

"Thanks, I feel better knowing things went smooth there." I walked into the bathroom and grabbed some tissue.

The door opened on the other side and Devon's eyes were wide with surprise—and then concern.

I waved at him that it was okay and held up a finger to tell him I'd be off soon. "Mackenzie, I gotta go. Thanks for calling and I promise I'll call you tomorrow, okay?"

She protested but then said good night. I could tell she was worried but I wasn't going to get into it.

I hung up and turned towards Devon, praying my face wasn't a total disaster but knowing it probably was. "Sorry, that was Mackenzie. I'll get out of here so you can have your privacy."

I turned to leave and Devon grabbed for my shoulder. He turned me gently to him and said, "You don't look okay. Did something happen here?"

I shook my head and reached for another tissue when it felt like the waterworks were going to start up again. "No. No, it wasn't anything. It was just…my grandma called." I suddenly didn't know what to do with my hands and just stood there feeling lost.

He must have sensed it, because the pressure from his hand grew stronger until he pulled me into him.

Then I was up against his amazing chest and his strong arms were around me. All I could do was tremble. My hands curled up between us and I tried to get control of my breathing. He stroked his hand over my hair, which I'd taken down from the ponytail as soon as I came upstairs. I took a few deep breaths before moving to step back.

I didn't get far, though, because his hold didn't budge. He reached down with one hand under my chin and tipped my face up to look at him. "What is it, Jaylene?"

I laughed nervously. "Where do I start? It's just a grandmother thing?" I sniffled again and he handed me a fresh tissue. Strangely, I didn't feel embarrassed. "I promise I'll be fine. She was sending me some encouragement. It meant a lot to me." How much to say? "I didn't get much encouragement growing up, so it's nice to hear her say I'm doing the right thing."

He pulled me into him again…and my sadness was quickly replaced with something much more overwhelming. He was so close, and so tall, and this moment was getting so heavy.

He rested his chin on the top of my head and I just couldn't take it anymore. "Devon?"

"Hmmm," he replied, and I felt the vibration in his chest. Oh boy.

"Just how tall are you? Because this feels strangely like I'm hugging a tree." *D'oh*. What a weird thing to say.

His laugh melted away the rest of my sadness. I don't know what it was about him that his laugh meant so much. Maybe because I knew it was rare.

"Last time I checked, I was around six-six, I think. This is probably the first time I was compared to a tree. I'm not *that* tall."

I looked up at him and he laughed again. "Maybe you're just shorter than you thought."

And then realization hit that we were standing in the bathroom in an embrace, and while it didn't seem like either of us wanted to let go, at any minute someone could—

"Hey, D, are you coming to wa—" Star came around the corner from Devon's room and stopped in the doorway, a shocked look on his face.

My cheeks immediately burned and Devon turned around and pulled me behind him so I could collect myself. Always the gentleman.

"Yeah, I'll be there in a minute."

Star left and I felt Devon take a deep breath, as I was now pressed against his equally amazing back. He was built lean but was more muscular than I had originally thought. I could see lettering across his shoulders, through his thin white t-shirt. It looked like Boudreaux.

I swallowed hard and stepped back from him.

He turned around, the concern still etched on his face. "Are you better?"

I smiled weakly and nodded. "Yes, I am. Thank you. Although I'm afraid I may have just made a mess of things."

He frowned. "You mean Star? Whatever. You were upset."

I shrugged. "I just don't want to cause any problems for you. I'm supposed to be here... You know, I'm not even sure *what* I'm supposed to be doing here. But I'm sure the intention wasn't for me to be holed up in the bathroom, crying on your shoulder."

I stepped over to the sink, splashed my face with cold water, and then dried it off. When I looked up, I could see he was leaning against the wall with his arms crossed, looking bemused.

"It was my chest you were crying on, and I'm certainly not complaining." I looked over my shoulder at him and he gave me my favorite smile. He pushed off from the wall and said, "Movie is starting soon. You going to join us?"

"I should probably go to bed. I'm not sure I'd be good company right now."

He frowned again and I was already missing his smile. "That's exactly why you need to come out and join us. The guys made popcorn and will probably cry if you don't. They're already total saps when it comes to you. And it's just your first day." He seemed mildly perturbed at that, and I wondered why.

"Total saps? Those guys need to get out more. Fine. Let me just take a quick shower and I'll be out there. Tell them to start without me."

He nodded. "I'll lock the door this time. I wouldn't want anyone else coming in here."

The tone of his voice warmed me to my toes, which I should not have allowed. He was quickly getting under my skin and I couldn't muster up any desire to have him not be there.

"Thanks. I'll just be a few minutes." I made sure the other door was locked and I took off my clothes.

The shower looked a little scary but it was clean. It took me a minute to figure out how to turn on the showerhead and when I did, I was practically blasted out of the tub with the force of the water. I shampooed, conditioned, shaved and exfoliated, until my skin was nice and rosy in between the designs inked on it. There was a small cabinet against the wall with lots of big, fluffy towels that felt wonderful against my skin.

This place might not be a luxury hotel but I was already feeling pampered. No cooking? Little cleaning? A nice shower? If the bed was comfy, I might not ever leave.

I slathered on some lotion and twisted my wet hair up into a bun. Out of curiosity, and against my better judgment, I peeked in the cabinet on the left side of the sink—Devon's side.

Nothing too exciting, some pomade, a razor, deodorant and aftershave. I took a little whiff of the latter and found myself feeling his arms around me again. He smelled really good that close. And most guys would freak if they walked in and found a girl crying. They'd make a lame excuse and run out the door. But he didn't run. He didn't even hesitate. It was obvious he had some inkling of how to treat a woman. Either his mom had taught him well, or his sister, or his wife.

Crap. There went that good feeling.

I sighed, closed up the little bottle and left the bathroom as I'd found it.

Back in my room, I put on a sports bra and plain white cotton panties, grabbed an old Led Zeppelin tie-dyed shirt that was roomy and lived-in, and threw on a pair of boxers. No sense in being uncomfortable. I took a minute to text Mackenzie and tell her *"I'm really OK, vmail just turned on the waterworks. I had a chest to cry on. Spill more tomorrow. Nite nite, luv ya."*

I knew that would drive her crazy. I was probably a little mean to leave it unexplained, but hey, I was doing what she wanted, right?

I grabbed my sketchbook, as I was feeling a little restless and thought it might relax me to draw a bit. I stepped out into the hall and could hear the very beginning of the movie. I hesitated for a minute.

Was I really up for this? And what if Star had told the others what he'd walked in on?

I shook it off. I could worry about it or I could just get on with my purpose for being here. Helping these guys come up with ideas for memorial tattoos.

I walked around to the rumpus room and found the guys sprawled on the couches and beanbags. They were eating popcorn, drinking sodas, and calling out the lines to the movie.

Star jumped up when he noticed me. "Hey, I saved you a spot." He'd been sitting where the two parts of the sectionals met in the middle and Devon was at the other end. He looked up and smiled as I stepped around him, and Star waited until I was sitting to be my waiter. "You want some popcorn? Something to drink?" He smiled eagerly and walked over to the mini fridge.

"Um, water's fine, Star, thanks."

He came back and handed me the bottle. When he sat down, he leaned over and whispered in my ear, "You doin' okay, chère?"

I smiled and nodded. "It was a Grandma thing."

He nodded and patted my knee before going back to the movie. It was a very sweet gesture.

I looked over to Devon and he was giving me a small smile, but this one was different. Maybe I detected a hint of satisfaction in it? Whatever it was, it made me feel a little giddy.

I stretched out my legs on the ottoman in front of me—grateful for the hasty pedicure I'd given myself—and alternated between watching the movie and sketching. I had a goofy drawing going of Ash's girl-friend's headless dance. That was one of my favorite parts of the movie. That, and when he loses it in the house and everything starts laughing at him.

Jade walked by on his way back to the bar and stopped to look over my shoulder. "Oh, that's awesome. That's it. I gotta have that. Will you tattoo that on me? Like right now?"

I looked back at him in surprise. "Really? *This?* I was just messing around."

But he was dead serious. He pulled up his sweatpants and showed me the back of his calf, which was bare. He had a tower of skulls on his shin with a dagger through them. "How about here? Will that work?"

Once I got over the shock, I looked at the picture again and then at his leg. I held the sketch to his leg and it was a perfect fit. "I could make this work here. But let me redraw it. You want black and gray?"

He nodded. "Yeah, and can you put in the words 'Swallow Your Soul' underneath? That would be badass."

Devon leaned over, concern in his voice. "Jaylene, it's almost nine-thirty. Are you sure you want to start this tonight? He can wait until tomorrow; he's not a little kid."

I laughed at that and looked at Jade, who had a very disappointed-kid-like look on his face.

"Aw, but it's so cool, Dad! Can't I just have it tonight, puleeeeezzz?"

Devon chuckled and I couldn't resist razzing him a little too. "Yeah, Dad, can't he get a tattoo tonight? All the cool kids are doing it."

He gently elbowed me in the side. "You're as bad as he is. Very well, but remember you've got homework to do."

"You're such a buzzkill." Jade was hopping from foot to foot. "I can't help it, that's how it's been with all of my other tattoos. I see something, I want it, I have to have it *now*, so I go get it done." He had such a boyish quality about him. His bright hazel eyes lit up and dimples showed in both cheeks when he smiled. He was taller than Marcus but had a slighter build. His face was very expressive. I bet he sucked at poker.

Marcus looked up from his spot, half on and half off a beanbag on the floor. "Yeah, remember when he made us drive him to a shop three hours away at seven in the freakin' morning? All because he woke up from a dream about a mermaid and he had to have her tattooed right then so he'd never forget."

"That's kind of romantic, Jade. Do you think she represented anyone you knew?"

He blushed. "Naw, I just remembered reading about them as a kid and how they supposedly lured sailors to their death with their beauty. After that dream, it just seemed like a good idea. Maybe then I'd be immune to them and could just look at them all day but not succumb to their charms."

"Or maybe you're just a psycho who needs to quit getting tattooed." Marcus threw that last comment over his shoulder and then proceeded to stuff his mouth full of popcorn.

"If you've got room, why not get more, is what I always say." I winked at Jade and showed him the revised sketch.

"*Yes!* Can we do it? Can we do it?"

I chuckled. "Sure, just give me a bit to get set up. I'll be right back."

"You need any help getting your stuff?" Star jumped up to help me.

"I think I'm fine. I'll just go grab my table and my bag."

He got up to follow me anyway.

"Hey, Jaylene, you really *don't* have to do this now. Aren't you tired?" Devon still looked worried, and while it made me gooey inside that he would be so concerned, I really was fine, and I told him so.

"The shop stays open until eleven on weekends anyway. I'd probably still be tattooing if I were at work. Besides, you guys are paying me to work, right? So I'm getting to work."

"Yeah, but..." He was frowning now.

Oh, that was just making me feel even gooey-er.

"No yeah-buts. I want to. It's not every day that I get to tattoo scenes from one of my favorite movies. There aren't as many horror junkies in New Orleans as you might think. This is good; this way, if you guys think it's crap, you can send me packing." I smiled sweetly at him over my shoulder and heard him groan and slide back down the couch.

"If you show me where your table is, Jaylene, I'll carry it over. What else do you need?" Star was so eager to help it made me smile. I was looking forward to sharing my craft with the guys after watching them practice today.

"I'll need my lamp, a chair, and something to set my inks on. Then I need to sterilize the workspace. I have all I need in my bag."

I had packed everything in my travel case so it made things easy. Star carried my table out and I set it up while he nervously watched to make sure I didn't hurt myself. I couldn't imagine what it would be like to grow up as a little girl surrounded by men like these. In my family, girls were expected to be seen and not heard and to act appropriately for every occasion. Other than that, they were mostly ignored.

It seemed as though with *these* guys, at least from what I'd seen so far, girls were to be treated like they were fragile and it was important to make sure they were taken care of. It was precious.

"There. Now, Jade, since I don't have my copy machine here, I'm just going to freehand this on your leg and then tattoo you. Sound good?"

He frowned. "Freehand? You mean not use a stencil? Can you do that?" He was totally serious, so I couldn't help but mess with him.

I shrugged. "I don't see why not. It can't be that hard." His eyes got wide and you could have heard a pin drop in the room, even over the screams from the movie.

"I'm kidding, Jade. I do this all the time. C'mon, let's get that leg shaved." He looked only slightly less nervous. The other guys were laughing hysterically.

"Dude, you should have seen your face." Mage was shaking Jade by the shoulders. Jade hadn't completely recovered and still looked worried.

"Oh, relax. I already told you, I've only almost messed up once. I've got a pretty good track record." I grabbed his hand and walked him down the hall, taking him into my bathroom.

He looked back over his shoulder at his brother. "Marcus? Uh, if I don't make it back, tell Mama I love her." More laughs followed us from the other room. I had him prop his leg on the edge of the tub.

"What are you going to use?" Jade asked as Star followed us into the bathroom. I guess he wanted to see the entire process.

"I've got a rusty straight edge I thought I'd use. What do you *think* I'm going to use? Haven't you done this before, Jade?"

"Well yeah, but usually in a tattoo shop and, well...by a guy."

I stood up and narrowed my eyes. "Are you seriously weirded out because I have boobs? I thought we were past this as a society." I turned on the water and grabbed a pink Bic and my soap spray bottle.

"I don't know, I'm pretty sure some of the guys who tattooed me had boobs." He shook himself. "But that's not what I meant. I meant I just haven't been tattooed by a woman before and I haven't gotten shaved in a bathroom before by a woman, and I certainly haven't been drawn on before by anyone."

I paused with the razor on his Achilles tendon. "You need to live a little." I smiled, he sucked in a breath, and I slowly dragged the razor up the back of his leg, careful not to nick him. He relaxed a little. I looked over at Star in the doorway and gave him a wink. Star jumped right on it.

"You mean you've never let a chick shave you? It's kind of hot, Jade. You should try it."

I snickered and Jade wobbled a little. "Be still if you want to keep your flesh intact."

"Sorry, Jaylene, it tickles." That made me snicker even more. "And no, I've never let a chick shave me. Although one time, this girl let me take my trimmer to her, and we..."

Star cleared his throat loudly. "You sure you want to continue that story in mixed company?"

I rolled my eyes but at my angle, I guessed they didn't see. "You guys really don't have to hold back around me. I'm used to working with guys, remember? I'd be more grossed out if you were talking about soap operas or makeup."

They both laughed and all Jade's anxiety seemed to be gone.

When I was done, I cleaned up his leg with a washcloth. "See, all done and no blood...yet."

Some of the color washed out of his face, but he was hanging in there. We got back to the rumpus room and the guys were all waiting for us. I covered the bottom half of the table with plastic wrap and had Jade lie down on his stomach and relax while I finished setting up.

Someone had brought over a card table, so I covered that with wrap too. I put out my ink caps and a dab of petroleum jelly to keep things moving smoothly. I'd serviced my machines before I left. They were in good working condition and this one was already wrapped in plastic. I snapped on some rubber gloves, and then reached for the roll of paper towels and spray so I could clean his leg again.

I used a marker to transfer the outline from my drawing onto his calf. When I thought it was centered and looked good, I had him go look in the mirror.

"Damn. That looks awesome. How did you do that?"

I shrugged. "I just draws 'em like I sees 'em."

Jade got comfortable and the other guys gathered around to watch. I was feeling more in my element. I flipped on my machine and got to work. I did a quick line to see how he handled the pressure. "How was that, Jade?"

"Is that it? I barely even felt it. You have such a light touch." He put his head down on his arms and closed his eyes. "Shit, I could totally sleep through this. Wake me when she's done, D."

I just shook my head and kept on with the outline. They watched for a bit in silence, a few murmurs of appreciation coming out every once in a while.

I figured it would take about two hours tops to finish. *Evil Dead II* finished and then came *Army of Darkness*. I laughed and shouted out my favorite Ash lines, and Marcus and Mage went back over to the couches to watch the film.

Devon was still on the edge of the couch next to where I'd set up the table and he was watching me closely. His eyes on me felt comforting. I didn't need to look over at him to know that he was giving me a ghost smile.

Star dragged a barstool over to watch me work. He seemed really interested, and asked me, "How long you been doing this?"

"I started working in a shop when I was eighteen, but I didn't start my apprenticeship until I was almost nineteen. It was kind of by accident. My boss found my sketchbook and threatened to fire me if I didn't start learning how to tattoo. The apprenticeship lasted a year and a half, and then I continued to work there for four more years while I finished college and grad school."

"Grad school? You tattooed and went to college? Are you some kind of overachiever?"

I laughed. "No, just couldn't choose. And tattooing paid the bills so I didn't have to take out student loans."

"What was your degree in?" Star asked.

"Counseling Psychology. My undergrad degree was in Psychology and Sociology. I had a hard time choosing, so I did both. I earned my Masters almost three years ago."

Devon spoke up after a minute. "You opened up your shop here a year ago, right? What did you do in between?"

I sat back in my chair and took off my gloves. Jade had nearly fallen asleep and I needed to stretch. "After grad school, I landed an internship with a prominent Berkeley psychotherapist. One of my professors knew someone and had it arranged." I took a swig of water and rolled my head around on my shoulders.

"That sounds promising. So what happened?" Star was looking over the work I'd done so far. He shook his head and murmured appreciative noises.

"It wasn't my cup of tea. The clients were mostly wealthy, middle-aged women who were unhappy in their marriages and with their children. They really just wanted some good drugs rather than to examine themselves. I didn't have a whole lot of patience with them, and the therapist I worked under didn't have much patience with *me*. Then my father died and I quit. I landed here in New Orleans and you know the rest."

I took one final drink of water and put new gloves on. I spread some petroleum jelly over the work and that woke Jade up a little.

"Are we done?"

I patted his good leg. "About halfway there, dear. Go back to sleep."

He nodded and closed his eyes. He was really sitting well for this. I hoped they all were this good.

"Do you miss it? Counseling, I mean?" Devon was looking at me intently and I thought about what he asked.

"Not really. A lot of my work as a tattoo artist involves some sort of counseling. Everyone's got a story to tell, and I like to listen and try to turn it into art."

They both nodded their heads and smiled. Star said, "That is so cool, Jaylene. I bet your clients come away from your shop in good spirits, they do."

"I hope so. I'd hate to take their money if they didn't." I put the last bit of shading on Jade's headless lady and started on the wording. That was a bit trickier to get on straight. I made the letters look like they were made of bones. Lettering was a challenge for me, and I really liked to make it stand out, so I took extra time.

Jade was starting to get a little twitchy toward the end. I was working on the area right above his Achilles and that can get tender. I finished the last L and wiped him down with soapy water.

"Ta Da! Mr. Lambert, would you like to see your new lady friend?"

His eyes bright, he hopped down from the table and walked gingerly over to a mirrored wall behind the bar. "Holy Mother. Jaylene, that is fucking cool! You nailed it. Thank you so much, chère." He hugged me from behind and kissed me on the cheek. The guys all complimented me on a job well done.

"See?" Mage said. "I told you she was meant to be here. Who else would we have taken this numbskull to at this time of night to get a naked dead lady tattoo?"

They all laughed.

"You're welcome. I think. Now, Jade, come over here so I can wrap you up." I had him stand on a chair so I could carefully wrap him in pads and plastic wrap. "Keep this on until the morning. Only wash it with this anti-bacterial soap and use this bacitracin for the first forty-eight hours, then switch to Aquaphor."

"No A&D?" Jade asked.

I shook my head. "This will heal it better. I'll take a look at it to make sure you aren't having any problems but seeing how well your others healed, either you take good care of them or are a good healer."

"Aw, man, Maggie would have loved this one, huh, Devon?"

All eyes went to Devon and he looked at me, that horribly sad look back in his eyes. "Yeah, Jade. She sure would have." He stood and walked toward the hallway. "Good night, everyone," he called over his shoulder, then he went into his room and shut the door quietly.

Everyone looked at each other. Jade's chin trembled when he spoke. "I'm sorry. I just miss her, and she would have liked it, right? I mean, she loved that movie."

Marcus gave him a tight hug and ruffled his hair. "It's okay, little brother. She would have really liked it. He just needs more time." Then Marcus gave me a determined look.

"How much longer until we can say her name without him taking off? I mean, fuck, we *all* lost her. Grief is a process, man. You have to work through it. He's not even trying," said Mage. He was glaring at Devon's door.

Marcus got in his face and pointed a finger in his chest. "You fucking know why he's not able to talk about her. Jesus Christ, Mage! He lost more than the rest of us, so don't go bitching about D. He's our brother, and we will fucking be there for him as long as it fucking takes, do you hear me?"

Mage lowered his eyes and nodded. "Yeah, I'm sorry, Marcus. It's just...it's death, right? It's not the end for her. But it's sure as hell going to be the end for *us* if we don't get our shit together." He walked off in a huff towards his room and slammed the door.

"Star, will you help Jaylene clean up? I'm going to put Jade to bed."

He nodded. "Sure, if she'll let me." He tried a smile and I gave him one back to reassure him.

"You can help me. You can put on some gloves and take off all that plastic wrap and throw it in one of those blue garbage bags from my case. I'll take all that stuff back to the shop with me when I go; we've got a special container for that and the sharps."

He nodded and followed my directions. He then folded up my table and carried it back to my room.

Marcus had come back and was standing there like he had something to say.

"Did you need something?" I finally asked him, because it was getting a little awkward.

"Yeah," he said. "I need you to get through to him. We don't have much more time."

I put down my case and put my hands on my hips. "You can't really put a time limit on this kind of thing, Marcus. Grief doesn't work that way. I'm going to do what I can for all of you, but if he's not ready, he's not ready. And if you push him, you might not get him back."

He stepped closer to me, almost as if he thought using his size might intimidate me. I wasn't easily intimidated—certainly not by him.

"Listen. It's your first day. I don't expect miracles from you yet, although you've gotten him to smile more than anyone since she died. But I'm telling you, I've got three other guys, not to mention our whole support staff, who have a lot riding on this next album. He's got to get it together. Talk to him, tattoo him, whatever the fuck you need to do. Just get his head in the game so we can get this album done."

I looked at him closely. He was angry, for sure, but under that he was afraid. I wasn't ready to call him on it.

"I can appreciate your situation, but I told you all from the beginning that I am not a miracle worker. If you want miracles, you'd better start praying. I'm going to bed...unless there's anything else?"

He looked surprised. I was sure most women didn't talk back to him. I was not going to be like most women, where he was concerned.

"No. That's it."

I nodded and continued packing up.

He started walking down the stairs but stopped three from the top. "Hey, Jaylene?" I looked over at him. "That was a great tattoo you gave my brother. Thank you. He loves it."

I nodded and closed up my case. I was finishing my water bottle when I heard the piano playing downstairs. Apparently that was how Marcus was going to work off his frustration.

As I walked toward my room, Star stepped out of Devon's. "He's going to sleep. He said to tell you good night."

"Thanks, Star. For your help tonight, too. Hey, if this rock 'n' roll gig doesn't work out, you can come be my shop boy."

He smiled sadly. "Yeah, I might need that. Listen. I heard what Marcus said to you. We just want to play music together, you know? And we just want Devon to smile again. He blames himself for what happened to Maggie, no matter what we say, or what anyone else says to him."

I touched his shoulder. "Hey, nothing anyone says or does is going to help him until he's ready to be helped. But being there for him *until* he's ready is the best thing you can do. He loves you guys. That much is very clear. Let's just all get some sleep and we'll talk more tomorrow, okay?"

He seemed like he needed a hug, so I opened my arms and he stepped into them. "It's been a long day. I'll see you for breakfast duty. What time?"

He stepped back. "How about eight? No one should be up before that."

I nodded. "Eight it is. Good night."

"Good night, Jaylene."

He turned and walked toward his room with his head down. The piano played on downstairs, and I thought if Marcus and Devon could make such beautiful music together, they had to be able to work things out. I paused in front of Devon's door, wanting to comfort him but knowing that it was too soon for that. I brushed my teeth and crawled in bed.

Sometime in the night, I woke up and heard the soft strumming of the guitar playing next door. It was a melancholy sound. A tear slid down my cheek before I forced myself to turn over and go back to sleep.

SEVEN

I woke up early, around 6:30, and rolled out of bed to do some yoga. Stretching helped keep my back in decent shape. I'd seen too many tattoo artists have to give up their work prematurely because of back and neck problems. I know I had my degree to fall back on, but I wanted to have the option to keep tattooing as long as I desired.

I knocked on the door to the bathroom softly to be sure Devon wasn't in there. When I heard no response, I crept in quietly. I reached over to close his door and I...well, I had a compulsion to peek. In the pale morning light, I could see him lying across his bed. The sheet rode low across his torso. He was shirtless and in sleep, he looked so peaceful. If I could have been stealthier I would have loved to sketch him in this pose. Truly breathtaking.

I didn't want to disturb him so I silently closed the door, wincing when I heard a squeak. I kept the light off, brushed my hair, used the loo and brushed my teeth quickly. I opened his door just a crack and then closed my door on the other side. This bathroom sure made these living arrangements interesting.

I tiptoed down the stairs into the kitchen and turned on lights. Mrs. Boudreaux and the dinner crew had left things spotless. I walked over to the pantry and took out a box of pancake mix and the syrup. I found the necessary cooking utensils without making too much noise and commenced making pancakes and bacon. I'd scramble up eggs at the very end. In the cold storage, I found some fruit, so I placed it carefully on a tray and was backing out of the door when Star walked in.

"Hey. Why are you up so early," he asked me through a yawn. He was wearing a rumpled tee with his boxers and his hair was sticking up all over.

Star was lean all over, probably from the high metabolism that had him almost constantly in motion. He was the kind of guy who put you at ease, like he didn't want anything from you other than to be near you. He had an enthusiasm for things that made him seem younger than he was. But the morning showed a few lines on his face I hadn't noticed before. At just twenty-five, he'd already been around the block. I wondered if the block hadn't been too kind.

"Just woke up, and once I'm up, I'm up." I smiled cheerfully. I had a pretty good stack of pancakes going and the bacon was sizzling on the grill.

He looked around and a hand involuntarily came up to his stomach.

"You hungry," I asked him. "Help yourself. The early bird gets the worm."

He laughed and rubbed his stomach. "It smells awesome, thanks. Is there anything I can help with?"

I shook my head. "You can eat before any of your drool falls on the bacon."

He kissed my cheek and said, "You're a peach, Jaylene. This looks fantastic." He loaded up a plate and was making groaning noises when the door cracked open and three more shirtless guys in boxers came stumbling in.

"What smells so good? Jaylene, did you do all this?" Jade came in last, yawning and rubbing his eyes.

"Hey guys, help yourselves. I'm about to scramble a bunch of eggs and then I'll bring them out if you want to go take a seat." They each walked by and mumbled some sort of thanks and kissed me on the cheek as they passed by to get their plates.

"Oh, Star. I forgot to make coffee. Does anyone need some?" A chorus of grunts followed and Star shoveled one last bite into his mouth before he started making a pot of coffee.

"Sorry, guys. I don't drink it so I always forget. There's fruit, too, so make sure you get some."

More male morning noises followed as they served themselves. I tried to ignore the various scratching going on and was glad they'd at least thrown on shorts. All this skin was a little overwhelming, though, and with the grunting, at any time I thought they could come to blows over the food or try to drag me off by my hair.

After making the eggs, I put a plate together and carried it out of the kitchen. One of the boys was missing and I wanted to make sure he ate breakfast. I wasn't sure what shape he'd be in after he'd played his guitar for most of the night, but I was going to try.

I pushed his door open and set the plate on a small table near his bed. He was still sprawled as I'd seen him earlier. His hair was disheveled and I hadn't realized that the top was so long. Pieces of it touched his chin. He usually had it pomaded back. It looked just like black silk; so smooth, I wished I could put my hands in it. I sat on the edge of the bed and touched his arm gently.

He stirred, rolling towards me, and the sheet slid down farther. Revealing a fine covering of black hairs over pale skin that gathered in a thin line before disappearing under the sheet.

He grabbed my hand and pulled it to his chest.

My breath caught and I froze. He looked so incredibly sensual. I wanted to reach out and stroke his hair, his face... I looked away and cleared my throat.

He pulled my arm in closer, almost pulling me onto his chest. I stopped myself from falling with my right arm and I giggled, I couldn't help it. He opened one eye and I giggled some more.

His eyes went wide and he loosened his grip on my arm, but only slightly. I pulled it back and felt my cheeks flush.

"Hey. It's you." He smiled a sleepy smile, closing his eyes for a minute and stretching. When he opened his eyes again, he spied the food. "Is that for me?" He was smiling even more, and I so wanted to touch the crinkles next to his eyes.

"I cooked. I wanted to make sure you got some before the cavemen downstairs ate it all." That wasn't an exaggeration. I was glad I'd been nibbling at it as I cooked, because there were slim pickings after they came through.

"That was real sweet, thank you. You cooked all this?" I nodded as he sat up, rubbing his face.

My cheeks were on fire. I could barely act normal while sitting there with him. He was absolute perfection. He could have stepped off Mt. Olympus and into this room. His skin was like alabaster, making his tattoos that much more severe and stunning. His eyes and lips were a little puffy, making me wonder if he'd shed some tears during his solo jam session last night. But he seemed happy, in a much better place than when he'd gone to bed.

I watched him take a few bites and he downed half the glass of OJ I'd brought. "This is really good. Thought you said you didn't cook much?"

"I'll tell you a secret...it's hard to screw up breakfast. And besides fried chicken, which I *can't* make, it's my favorite meal. Any time of the day."

He chuckled at that. "Breakfast food is the best. Thank you. Thanks for breakfast and..." He paused and really hit me with that soulful gaze of his. My skin rippled with goose bumps. "Just thanks for being here. I'm sorry I bailed last night." He took another drink of his juice and looked down.

I touched his hand. "Hey, I understand. It was a heavy moment and you needed a break. I think I get it."

He looked up at me. "You do?"

I nodded and smiled. "I do. And you don't have to tell me what it was about unless you want to. I know there's a lot of pressure on you and I don't want to be the cause of any more. I just want you to know that I'm here if and when you do want to talk about her."

His blue eyes were dark and he looked so pained, I wanted to take him in my arms and fix it all for him.

"I want to. I want to talk about her, I do. I just don't know where to start, I guess. I can't find the words." He put his plate aside. He'd barely eaten anything. He pulled his knees up and rested his head on his forearms.

"Maybe you could start by telling me something about her? If you want, that's a place to start. It's obvious that you all loved her very much. She must have been amazing."

His head lifted and his chin now rested on his forearms. "Maggie was everything. A best friend, a cheerleader, a mother. She took our sorry asses and whipped us into a successful career, never letting us slack off or forget what we were supposed to be doing. She was there for us when we needed a shoulder to cry on, when we needed a kick in the pants, when we needed a drinking buddy."

He cringed at that and looked away, toward the window.

"A person like that would be difficult to be without. And it takes a special person to be all those things." I wanted to keep him talking but I didn't want to push.

"She *was* special. To all of us. For me, it was like she was the only one who got me. She knew I loved the music and hated all the popularity shit. She'd listen to me complain and then remind me how much I loved to play and loved the guys. Without her, it just feels like...what's the point anymore? Why keep playing?"

I was glad that he'd clarified that. I didn't think he was suicidal, what I got from him was just a deep, deep sorrow.

"What do you think she'd want you to do now?"

He looked at me confused, then his chin quivered and he looked toward the window again. He took in a shaky breath before he answered.

"She sure as hell wouldn't have wanted me pining away in a room somewhere, running away from my problems. I just have this weight on my chest, squeezing me. When I play our stuff, I feel like I can't breathe. It hurts." Another shaky breath. He rubbed at his chest with the heel of his hand as he spoke.

"I'm so sorry, Devon. This is going to sound kind of shrink-y, but bear with me, okay?" He nodded and looked down at the sheets. I thought about how to put this gently. "Devon, that pain in your chest is grief, and it's weighing on you. The worst thing about grief is that it can manifest in physical symptoms, like a panic attack does to people who experience extreme anxiety."

He looked at me, engaged but wary. "I know about that. My mama had those after my daddy died. That's why I came home from school. They were getting worse."

This was progress. "And what did she do to help, do you know? Did she ever talk about it?"

He shook his head. "I'm not sure. I know she saw doctors about it. It seemed to get better after a while. I was just so grateful that she wasn't having a heart attack like she'd thought."

"It's hard to tell the difference for some people. It feels very similar. Doctors treat it with medicine. Sometimes people try talk or behavior therapy. Others find the root of whatever is causing the anxiety and try to deal with that."

He shook his head, seeming a little irritated. "I won't take drugs. I won't do that. And a head doctor? I don't know if I could do that either."

"I understand. Lots of people don't want to see a therapist. It's uncomfortable, they feel like they're crazy or people will *think* they're crazy. I'm not suggesting you need to do any of that." I took a deep breath and went for it. "Sometimes it helps to just face the things that frighten us head on. If we can determine exactly what it is that's holding you back, or for lack of a better word, what's got you afraid to move forward, we can start to chip away at that weight on your chest, give you some breathing room to start making some decisions."

He blinked. "You sure you shouldn't have done *this* for a career?"

I frowned. I wasn't sure what he was saying.

"I mean, you're great at tattooing, for sure. But you seem to know what you're talking about with this stuff." He gave me his small smile and I breathed a sigh of relief.

"I just want to help, however you need me to. I'll tattoo you guys from head to toe and listen to whatever crazy music you guys want to play for me. Hell, I'll cook breakfast for you every day if I can just see that smile of yours a little more often." He blushed.

He pulled me by my hand, pulling me forward, and he took my face in his hands. "If you'll just be here, I'll smile. A little. And if your breakfast cooking is this good, they'll all be begging you for it every day." He sat up and kissed me on my forehead. "Thank you, chère. This was a great way to wake up." His lips were still against my forehead as he spoke.

It was so very wrong of me to be this attracted to him, to be thinking inappropriate thoughts. I desperately wished I had the guts to look up and kiss him. Instead I pulled back and said, "Well, now that you're awake, want to tell me what that was you were playing last night?"

He cocked his head to the side, curious, and then closed his eyes. "I woke you. I'm sorry. When I can't sleep, I play. It helps to get it out."

I stood up and nodded at his plate. "That's probably cold by now. Why don't you come downstairs and I'll heat it up for you?"

"I'd be glad to, but I think you might want to leave first."

It was my turn to cock my head to the side. "Okay?"

He laughed at my expression. "Uh, I think I promised you we'd be dressed around here, and I'm not exactly, ah, presentable."

Gods, my cheeks were on fire. Could he tell that I'd been ogling him in his morning glory? I was pretty transparent and my poker face was nonexistent. "Right. I'll just take this and you can finish it downstairs. When you're dressed. Okay. I'll see you, after, you know...yeah."

I made a beeline for the door, desperate to get out of there without further embarrassing myself. Beautiful, naked men were completely outside my scope of expertise. Partially naked in my tattoo shop was one thing. Trussed up in bed looking like Adonis, not so much.

I hurried down the steps and almost slammed into Star.

"He didn't eat?" He sounded worried.

"No. I mean, he did, but he needed to get dressed and it was getting cold."

He pressed his lips together to keep from smiling.

"Oh, you know what I mean. He's coming down to finish."

"Oh he is, is he? He's going to *finish* down here?"

He was so in trouble. "Really, Star? It's like that? I thought we were kitchen buddies and now you're going to mess with me?" I made like I was going to dump Devon's plate on him and he cowered away.

"I don't think I'll be messing with you at all if *he* has anything to say about it." He ran away from me laughing.

I yelled to him that I'd get him back. I couldn't be really upset, though. I felt a little giddy after my conversation with Devon.

But then my heart dropped. Why was I getting excited about this? He was off limits on a couple of pretty major levels. He was probably a widower, he was grieving a woman he obviously loved, and I had no business being as attracted to him as I was.

I was here for sixteen more days to do a job. That did not involve getting intimate with the most troubled member of the band. No matter what Marcus said last night, I would be there for him to talk to, I'd tattoo him if he wanted, but anything other than that would be highly inappropriate on my part.

New rules had to go into effect: No more breakfast in bed, no more *anything* to do with his bed or looking at him in bed. Too tempting. No more goose bumps. My libido needed to get a hold of itself. I could melt about him after the job was done and I was back snug as a bug in my shop.

These were the new rules and I needed to stick to them.

I made it into the kitchen, still mentally going over this list, and saw that Star had cleaned up the entire mess. I may have been good with the cooking, but he far bested me with cleaning abilities. I put Devon's dish in the microwave for him so he could heat it up when he came down and I stepped back out into the bar area. I heard the shower running upstairs and behind the stage, I heard a loud humming.

I went back into the hallway and looked inside the doorway opposite the kitchen. Marcus was running on a treadmill and Mage was lifting free weights. They both had headphones on, so I waved and they waved back. I thought I'd better check on Jade, so I went around the rumpus room and knocked on the door I'd seen Marcus take him into last night.

"Jade? I just wanted to check your leg."

He opened the door in just a towel. "Hey. It looks good. I took the bandage off and washed it in the shower, gently, with that soap you gave me. It's a little red but it looks *so* good. Thanks again." He was beaming...and dripping water down his chest. There was way too much male skin around here this morning.

"Great. I'm glad you like it. I'm just going to go change."

He nodded and stepped back into his room. That meant Star was in the shower I'd heard. I went back to my room and found the bathroom door closed and that shower running as well.

I flopped down on my bed with my sketchbook and scanned over the sketches I'd drawn yesterday, minus the one of Mage I'd left with Marcus. I opened to a fresh page and was just doodling when my phone started buzzing incessantly.

"Good morning Mackenzie—"

She cut off my greeting by yelling, "How *dare* you leave me a message like that last night and then LEAVE ME HANGING!?"

I had to hold the phone out from my ear. I got her to calm down and explained what had happened. She was quiet until I finished.

"And that's it? He hugged you and that was it? Oh, my darling little needle pusher. Have I not taught you anything about men?"

"Mackenzie, I am here to *work*. I've created a list of rules to live by that don't involve being anywhere around him in his bed, the bathroom, when he's mostly naked..."

"*You saw him naked?* Oh, why couldn't they have wanted to hire a piercing artist instead of a tattoo chick who might as well be from the convent? What I could do with a needle and all that yummy flesh."

I groaned loudly. "Kenz, you are not making this any easier. He's beautiful and sweet but this is horrible timing. Okay? He's probably a widower, for goodness sake."

Mackenzie was quiet for a second. "Margaret was his *wife?* Oh my gods. Oh honey, you're right. That is not something you want to mess with. You're sure about this?"

I told her about meeting his mom and realizing they had the same last name. "See what I mean? He's not in any position to be getting involved with me. Not in any way I'd want to be involved with someone."

"Hmm," she said. "What about a ring? Is he wearing a ring?"

I frowned. "I don't remember seeing one. But that doesn't mean anything."

She sighed. "You're right. What about any of the other guys?"

I groaned again. "Kenz! Snap out of it. I will talk with them, I will draw them, and I will tattoo them. I will come home. Life will return to as normal as it can be with you as my shop mate. The end. That's how this story is going to go. Speaking of which, I gotta go. I think they're going to have practice today so I should be there for that."

We said our goodbyes and she made me promise to call her again this evening.

After hanging up, I was lying on my bed, doodling in my book when I heard a knock at the door. "Yeah?"

Devon opened the door. "Hey. We're going to be practicing for a while so I brought you your earplugs." He left them on the desk.

"Thanks. I'll probably need them."

He gave me the ghost smile and started to leave, then stopped. "I'm going to play for them what I wrote last night. If you want to...you know, come down. You can hear it." He looked so sheepish. He was killing me.

"I do. I'll be right down. I'm just going to change." He nodded and shut the door behind him.

Okay, wardrobe. What should I put on today? I decided on a sundress, as it was fairly warm in the building. I stayed shoeless. It was kind of nice to go barefoot all day. I braided my hair really quick and brought my sketchbook. They were already playing as I came down the stairs.

Marcus waved at them to stop and addressed the group. "So I have a plan. Since we've got to have material ready to record by next week, I thought we'd start today by going through what we've come up with so far. It looks like we've got the three I came up with, and D, we can try that one you played for us yesterday but I'm not sure about the lyrics yet." Marcus was handing out notes to the other guys.

"I actually wrote some. They're rough still. And I've got a new piece I messed around with last night."

Marcus looked at him for a moment and gave him a grateful smile. Devon just looked down and started tuning his guitar. Marcus made eye contact with me and mouthed "Thank You."

I just shook my head at him.

"Okay, let's start with track one." Star counted them off and they launched into a gritty, down-tuned number with a slower beat. Marcus had some lyrics he would sing over what I guessed would be the chorus:

· · ·

I am the leather, you are the lace
  I hold you close and caress your face
  You are the leather, I am the lace
  I'm bound to you tightly, I crave your embrace

Not bad, not as slutty. I liked the beat. It was kind of sexy. When that one finished, they all gave notes and fell into communicating in their secret language of sounds.

Today, I focused on sketching Jade, as I hadn't drawn him yet. When he played he was frantic. I could tell he was somewhat contained in this practice but I could imagine his frenetic energy on the stage would really be something to see. His long hair flicked off his shoulders with every beat and he swung it around to free his face.

They started track two, which was the piece they'd played yesterday that had a lot of changes. They stopped abruptly and then Jade said, "Could we add the..." And then I lost him again. It was impressive how cohesive they were, how they could communicate through the music and make changes through eye contact. They tried one last change then repeated an earlier part and then ended together on a beat. Marcus seemed pleased.

"Yeah! That sounds good, guys. Let's do it again and then let's hear what D has for us." They launched into it again and it was cleaner, more together. It sounded really cool and I found myself trying not to start rocking out.

They played it through three more times and then took a break. I walked behind the bar and got a bottle of water. I watched Marcus and Devon out of the corner of my eye. Devon was showing him something he'd written.

Marcus was chewing on a fingernail and reading it, nodding. "This is deep, D. Really good, man. Want to sing it?"

Devon shrugged and plugged in his acoustic. The other guys sat and listened intently. My heart pumped wildly when I heard the first notes of his singing. His voice was rich and husky. It was so sensitive, as if you could discern every emotion he was carrying in one line of a song. He didn't seem super confident with the vocals but did his best to get through the very emotional lyrics.

Heavy is the weight on my chest
　　Heavy are the burdens I carry
　　Heavy is my heart
　　Heavy is my soul
　　Heavy is the only thing that keeps me

Here, I'm flattened by this pain
　　It rips at my heart
　　It tears at my soul
　　Heavy is the only thing that keeps me

Living alone
　　Living without you
　　It's crushing me inside
　　Why can't I move?
　　Why can't I move on
　　From this heaviness inside?

Heavy are the memories
　　Heavy is the love I felt for you
　　Heavy is my heart
　　Heavy is my soul
　　Heavy is the only thing that keeps you

Here, you left me behind
　　I'm buried in my guilt
　　I'm buried in my pain

Heavy is the weight that drowns me

Living alone
  Living without you
  It's crushing me inside
  Why can't I move
  Why can't I move on
  From this heaviness inside?

He played a few more chords and then stopped. The room was completely silent.

Marcus stood up first. "That was beautiful, D. Just beautiful."

Devon gave a ghost of a smile and put down his guitar. His blue eyes looked wet as he took a deep breath. "I'm going to go get some air." He went out the back door and closed it behind him.

I looked around at the guys—and they were staring at me. Jade and Star both had tears in their eyes, Mage gave me a suspicious look.

"What?"

Mage walked over to me and took my hand, kissing the back of it tenderly. He spoke quietly. "You might not believe you have a gift, but no one else could have moved him to write that song. *Merci*, chère."

I looked at the others and they were all nodding at me.

"Whatever you're doing, please continue." Marcus took a long drink of water and followed his friend outside.

I frowned. Why were they looking at me like that? I hadn't done anything.

"I'll be right back." I ran up the stairs and into the bathroom. I made sure both doors were locked and looked at myself hard in the mirror.

Gods, that song was achingly beautiful. Was this what he wrote last night? Maybe the music...but this morning, we talked about those things. Maybe somehow that had helped him put into words what he was feeling.

Devon was in such pain, I could barely breathe while listening. He was pouring his heart out, telling us all exactly where his head was. Maggie must have been his soul mate for him to be feeling this much.

I leaned forward on the counter and realized my knees were shaking. I can't even fathom what it would be like to be loved by someone so deeply. Even worse, how could you carry on after they left?

But there was something more. He'd talked about guilt.

What the hell happened for him to be feeling guilty?

I had to find out what happened to her. This was getting ridiculous. I'd never been much for solving mysteries. It was time I got some answers.

When I went downstairs, only Star and Jade were there. "Hey guys, are you still practicing?"

They shook their heads. "Nah, they left to go pick up lunch," Jade answered. "We might try to learn that song this afternoon. If Devon can play it again." They looked at each other and then looked down.

This was an opening—and I was going to take it. "Guys, I think I need to know what happened to Maggie. I was going to wait until you were all together but that seems to not be the best way to go about this. Will you tell me what happened?"

They looked at each other again and Jade shrugged. "I guess we can tell you. It's not like it's a secret."

Star nodded. "It was bad, Jaylene. Real bad. We were all kind of in a bad place when it happened, too, and that's what made it so horrible."

I sat down on the edge of the stage near them and waited for them to continue.

Star took a drink of water and heaved a big sigh. "When *Burns Like Ice* was about to drop last December, we were all insane. We'd been touring nonstop for two years, partying too hard, never in one place longer than a week. We were wrecked physically but pumped for the release.

"The label planned a big party for us at the Whisky in Hollywood. All of our friends, people who worked with us, industry people, radio people, shit like that. We played a few songs from the album and then shit got crazy. We were all drunk and high on whatever was there. Devon got in a huge fight with our producer, Richard. I'd never seen him so pissed. He even pushed him, and D never puts his hands on anyone.

Anyway, Maggie got pissed at him, told him to quit acting like an ass, and that she was leaving. He told her to fuck off. Again, not something he ever did. Then she left with Thomas."

I wasn't surprised to hear about the excess, although that seemed a long way from where they were now. I also wondered who Thomas was, but didn't want to interrupt. I waited for him to continue.

"A half hour or so later, Thomas came back all bloody and his clothes were all fucked up. He said they wrecked on Sunset in his fucking Porsche and that Maggie was gone."

My mouth had gone dry. It was more awful than I could have imagined.

"He hit a pole and she was ejected from the car. He left the accident to come and tell us what happened. One of the execs drove him back there and he was arrested. They pronounced her dead on the scene. We brought her home to Houma and had her service. Devon was a mess. We had ten weeks of shows scheduled to promote the new album. He didn't speak to us the whole time we were doing the shows and when we were done, he came home and that was it. He said he wasn't going back to L.A."

Jade wiped at his eyes. "So here we are. Marcus figured if he wouldn't come to us, we'd come to him."

Star got up from where he was sitting on the stage a few feet away from me. He cracked his knuckles and the bones in his neck. He hopped down from the stage and stood next to Jade.

"Did any of you ever talk to anyone about what happened that night?"

Jade shook his head. "Marcus said we just needed to keep moving, that Maggie would have wanted it that way. So we did the shows. Star talked about it some. He spent some time in rehab when we were through."

I looked over at him, figuring my guess had been correct about him and the block. "Did it help?" I asked him.

"Yeah, it did. I was drunk or high all the time, just to stay numb. While I was there, I talked about it a little with my counselor but really just focused on quitting the drugs and drinking. It sucked. I needed to get away for a bit."

I reached out and touched his shoulder. "I'm glad you got some help. Was drinking always an issue for you?"

"I guess. My dad was an alcoholic and I was always around him and my uncles. My parents fought all the time. I had plenty of reasons to drink before. It was never this bad though. I was a functioning alcoholic for years, since I was about fifteen. I've been clean and sober for two months now and I feel pretty good. Just gotta stay busy."

"I'm proud of you, Star. I know how difficult it is to find a healthy way to cope with your stuff."

He smiled and blushed. He was so like a young man still. I loved the innocence about him. I was glad I was getting the opportunity to know him.

"Thanks for telling me, guys. I know this isn't easy on any of you. You have your own grief to deal with. I understand you were all close to her."

They nodded. "She was a natural mom type, a nurturer. She was the Sharon to our Ozzy," Jade said with a humorless laugh. "She believed in us and pushed us to keep coming up with better stuff, to become better musicians."

Star nodded. "She was just like the sun, man. You felt warm in her presence. She would laugh at us being stupid, liked to play pranks on us, dress us up. She tried to knock the small-town mindset outta all of us."

Jade laughed. "She did. She showed us all around L.A., and whenever we went anywhere, she always took us around to museums, historical places, shit like that. And she knew the business. She may have been young, but she was so damned smart. Marcus really tried to learn from her; he lives for that stuff. He's basically taken over the business side of the band since she's been gone and Devon won't step up. Sherry might be our manager now, but he's kept us moving forward, kept us together. He's a pain in the ass, but if it weren't for him, we'd be in deep shit right now."

"Who's a pain in the ass?" cried out Marcus as they came in the back door. Mage was right behind him, carrying bags from Frenchmen Deli. Devon brought up the rear, his aviator shades back on.

"You are, my brother. What'd ya get for chow?"

They all hovered around the bags and it took Marcus slapping hands away to get them to snap out of their hunger-induced frenzy. "Go wash your hands, you heathens. No one eats until you've washed your hands."

So Marcus was a lothario *and* a mother hen? A man of contradictions.

I went upstairs and washed up, leaving my sketchbook upstairs. I had a lot to process and really wanted some time alone, but I was afraid I'd offend them if I didn't have lunch with them. When I went back down, however, they'd all grabbed lunches and were going over the new songs, discussing the parts.

I quietly grabbed a small container with salad and a roll and tried to slip upstairs unnoticed.

"Jay? You okay?" It was Star at the bottom of the stairs.

"I'm fine, I'm just going to eat a quick bite and then work on some drawings. I'll be down a little later."

He nodded, looking unsure but letting me be.

I plopped down on my floor, turned some music on my iPod and put in my earbuds. I ate a few bites of my salad while the sounds of Tab Benoit helped me relax. Blues seemed appropriate for my mood at the moment. So many thoughts were running through my head, it was kind of exhausting.

I didn't know how I was going to make it for two more weeks. Not only was their grief so heavy, their problems so massive, but their energy was exhausting. One minute they were playing around and acting like the teenage boys I suspected they still were at heart. The next they were brooding, arguing, and on the verge of sobbing. They could get so angry at each other. It was like an emotional roller coaster that I had just exited, and I couldn't get my legs to work again.

I picked at the salad but couldn't make myself eat much. After I'd stared at my sketchbook and then back at the salad for about an hour, I got up and threw the box in the trash. I sat on the bed, looking for inspiration to draw some more.

EIGHT

The next thing I knew, I was being gently shaken and my face was smashed against the paper.

"Jaylene, wake up chère! You alright?"

I looked up and could barely make out anything in the dark room. I squinted and realized it was Daryl.

"What are you doing here? What time is it?"

He looked at his watch. "It's four, dahlin'. You been sleeping for hours now. Dem boys was afraid to come wake ya. You feelin' alright?"

I tried to sit up and wiped the drool off my chin. Attractive. "I don't know what happened. I was going to draw and I guess I just crashed. But you still didn't answer my question. What are you doing here?"

He chuckled. "I'll tell you after you go clean up. We got more company downstairs, so hurry your pretty little self." He stood from his crouch and headed for the door. "And wear something nice, you."

I threw a shoe at him that hit the door as he was closing it. "Smartass!"

I kind of felt hung over. I never did well when I napped in the afternoon. Especially when I got half a night's sleep. I stumbled into the bathroom and noticed the door on the other side was closed. I could hear muffled voices from downstairs and wondered who the hell could be here.

I took a moderately long shower. I needed to clear my head, and it was a great shower after you got over the initial blast. When I turned the water off, I heard music being played downstairs. It wasn't rock. It was some sort of bluesy zydeco mix that sounded fun. I'd taken a liking to zydeco since coming to New Orleans. There were some great bands that played around the Quarter. I tried to catch a show occasionally when I wasn't working.

I dried my hair, left it down, and went back to my room to search my wardrobe. Did I dare wear the halter?

Yes, I did. It was black and I had some white capris with black skulls on them that I loved to save for special occasions. A pair of black sandals rounded out the outfit, and a dash of eyeliner and gloss made me feel like a new person.

When I opened the door, I was assaulted by a savory scent...

Someone had fried chicken down there.

I slowly descended the staircase and recognized the band playing on the stage as Dwayne Dopsie and the Zydeco Hellraisers. They were one of my favorites. But what the hell were they doing here?

"Jay!"

I turned to see Mackenzie racing across the floor to me in a polka dot pencil skirt and cami with stilettos on. "Whoa, Kenz, slow down before you hurt yourself."

She pulled me into a rib-crushing hug before kissing me on the cheek. "You look fucking hot, baby girl," she whispered in my ear.

I stared up at her. "What are you doing here?"

"Surprise! Daryl and Katie came and picked me up from the shop this afternoon and said we get to come visit. How exciting." She was bouncing on the balls of her feet and looking around in wonder. I knew she'd love this old building as much as I did. It had character. I felt like if I could stand still and be quiet, I could almost hear the voices of those who'd been here before.

Daryl and Katie came over and both hugged me. I elbowed him for not giving me some warning about the event. "For some guys who are trying to have a covert operation going on, they sure have a hard time staying hidden."

Katie rolled her eyes and Daryl laughed. "Since when do boys have any idea how to be subtle? These guys have been trying to be slick since they were teenagers and they still haven't learned a thing."

Katie had me cracking up. I'd forgotten she'd said she was friends with one of the guys' sisters. Maybe I could get some more info from her about what they were all like growing up. For some reason, I really wanted to know what Devon was like as a teenager.

Was he the cool cat he acts like now? Was he goofy like the other guys? It was apparent to me that this Devon I was getting to know was a small part of the overall Devon package.

Hmmmm... And a package he was. Sigh. Too bad he was so unavailable.

When I came back from my mental wonderland, Daryl was arguing with Katie about his ninja-level skills and I couldn't help but snort.

"Ain't you never heard that hiding in plain sight is sometimes the best option?"

I raised my eyebrow at him. "Maybe in some bad spoof on spy movies. Seriously, what is all this?"

"This," said that deep voice that curled my toes, "is a birthday party for a special lady." I spun around and there was Devon, smiling down at me, dressed in jeans and a white button-down shirt with his hair brushed back. He pulled me into him and gave me a hug, kissing me on the cheek. He whispered in my ear, "You look beautiful, chère."

I was dumbfounded. "But..."

He looked at me and dropped his hand to my back. A sharp intake of his breath let me know he appreciated my wardrobe choice. Score one for the formerly fashion challenged.

"This is us needing to blow off some steam, Cajun-style, and us wanting to celebrate you."

I still couldn't understand why they would care about my birthday. Who was I to warrant such a celebration? I told him as much and he looked stunned.

"Birthdays are sacred around here, Jaylene. We *have* to celebrate them. It's in our blood. Now come dance with me."

I looked at Mackenzie in a panic and she just gave me an evil grin while biting one long, hot-pink nail.

"But Devon, I don't know how to dance like this."

He took me by the hand and pulled me onto the dance floor, where Marcus was already dancing with a woman I hadn't met and Jade was dancing with Mrs. Boudreaux. Daryl and Katie came out, too, followed by Star with Mackenzie in tow.

Devon leaned down to whisper in my ear, "You'll be fine. Just follow my lead."

He slid his right hand around my lower back, his fingers skimming my skin where there was a gap between the top of my pants and the bottom of my top. I shivered and he pulled me closer. He took my right hand in his left and started to rock us back and forth gently to the beat.

I must have still looked petrified because he threw his head back and laughed. "Jaylene, relax. I'm not going to let you fall. Trust me?"

I nodded at him, wide-eyed, and I prayed silently to the gods of grace that I not make a fool of myself.

He kept his blue eyes trained on me the whole time as we moved together. The beat was a slower one but when that song finished and a faster one started, he sped us up, never breaking eye contact. Then he was grasping my hands, pushing me out and pulling me back in to him. He lifted me up and spun me around like I was nothing but a waif.

I was in shock. All I could do was go along with it. Pretty soon, I found myself laughing, too.

For a tall guy, he was a helluva dancer. I wasn't surprised he had good rhythm, but the fact that he was very coordinated as well? Amazing. I was the one trying not to step on his feet. I could move alright by myself. I just didn't have much experience partner dancing. I kept my eyes on him and held on tight.

Devon was very moved by the music. He closed his eyes sometimes and a small smile would play on his lips. The rest of the time his gaze shone down on me with happiness.

He was truly happy. It was the first time I'd seen him so relaxed.

One song ended and another started up, this one just as fast. Dwayne Dopsie, the leader of this band, was wailing away on his accordion and singing his heart out. The man on the washboards was hopping around the room, letting some of the other folks play his spoons.

Mage cut in and had his fun spinning me around. Then Jade stepped up, and even Marcus took a turn spinning me around the floor. I was dizzy and laughing so hard my stomach hurt.

I ended up back in Devon's arms just in time for a slow number. He held me so close, I was forced to rest my head on his chest. He stroked my back with his thumbs while we swayed along to the music. I closed my eyes and just let it all in. It felt so good to be in his arms, with his cheek resting against my head. I could feel his breath on my neck and goose bumps started to rise on my moist skin.

So much for my rules.

"Thank you for agreeing to come here, Jaylene. After our talk this morning, I feel like I can almost breathe again."

I looked up at him, startled. His lids were low on his eyes and he was smiling that half smile. "I'm glad we talked, too. That song you wrote was beautiful, Devon. It really moved me."

He closed his eyes and pulled me in tighter against him. I felt him sigh and I couldn't help but snuggle in closer.

Daryl cut in then and Devon took up dancing with Katie, giving me a devastating smile as he moved her away. Daryl watched them go, shaking his head. "I don't know what you done to that boy but there's new life in him. I tol' you you'd be good for them."

I groaned. "I've been here less than thirty-six hours. All I've done is draw some pictures, do one tattoo on the fly last night, and watch them play. It's got nothing to do with me."

Daryl gave me a stern look that meant I was in for it. I couldn't help cowering a little. I knew he'd never hurt me but he was an intimidating man.

"Now you listen to me, Jaylene Renee Charles. Devon has been inconsolable since Maggie died. He and my Marcus haven't been able to be in the same room without bickering and arguing. All dese boys had long faces since the accident—and today? They're laughing, dancing. They say they even got a couple of songs going. Dat's *something*, chère. Dat's some magic whether you want to believe it or not."

I blew my bangs out of my face and tried to look away. I hated all this pressure. I just knew I was going to disappoint someone. I spoke in a quiet voice. "Daryl, I'm just a tattoo artist. Maybe they're just ready to open up to each other. It's got nothing to do with me being here."

"Jaylene, I known you for a year and a half now, and I ain't seen nothing but beauty come outta your hands. You've softened up some of the meanest motherfuckers I ever knew. What you done for Ted and Bobby, tattooing them when they came back from Iraq... Dey was in bad shape. I thought we was going to have to put Bobby in rehab. But after he talked to you and got that tattoo, he's talking through shit, and he stopped drinking. He swears it was just being able to talk about their fellow soldiers with you that helped them. And most importantly, Katie and the girls adore you. You know we all love you, but if you keep talking like this, I'm going to put you over my knee, little girl."

I started giggling at that. "Bet you'd like that wouldn't you, you dirty old man."

That got him to smile. "I'm serious, Jaylene. You doubt yourself too much, girl. Just do me one favor, you."

I raised my eyebrow at him, waiting for him to continue.

"Just whatever happens, if he ain't for you, you let him down easy, you hear? Dat boy ain't never acted around no woman like I see him with you."

I was so confused. "What's that supposed to mean?"

He sighed and rolled his eyes at me. "Are you so dense, woman? Ain't you seen the way he looks at you? Devon never paid no attention to girls. Hell, he had to fight most of 'em off growing up and he *still* couldn't care less about 'em."

"What about Maggie?" I asked, exasperated.

He frowned at me like I'd grown a third eye. "What do you mean, what about Maggie? Her death rocked us all. I still can't believe she's gone. But dat girl was headstrong and she was gonna do what she was gonna do."

This was getting more confusing the more he went on, but then the music was over and everyone was heading over to get food. Katie grabbed Daryl and pulled him away to get cuddly in a corner.

I noticed Mackenzie and Star sitting at the bar eating, so I wandered over to them. "I thought I smelled fried chicken, you can't hide it from me." I took a piece of crunchy skin off Mackenzie's plate and she fake-slapped at my hand.

"I can't believe I'm supposed to be your best friend and I didn't even know it was your birthday. How is that possible?"

I shrugged and grabbed some more chicken skin off her plate. This time she *did* slap me, and I pulled my hand back, shaking it off. "It's just a birthday. I've had twenty-five of them already, what's one more? I want a bite of your chicken, Kenz."

"Go get some yourself, silly. Mrs. Boudreaux made it for *you*."

The smile fell from my face. This was just too weird. "I'm just going to go get something to drink."

I heard Mackenzie call after me but I kept going. I walked around the end of the bar and down the hall to the patio. When I got outside, I took a deep breath. My head was buzzing. I hadn't eaten much and I definitely hadn't had enough water. I sat down on my bench from yesterday and put my head in my hands.

What the hell was happening? I'm here a day and they throw me a birthday party? Who does that? I felt so unsure of myself that I was starting to shake.

I'd always been a loner. It was easier that way. Don't disappoint anyone, don't get disappointed. I loved my life here in New Orleans but I was still an outsider. I didn't understand the way they were all so close with each other. I definitely didn't understand what Daryl was saying about Devon. Could it be that he really liked me? But he'd just lost his wife four months ago.

Worrying about this was exhausting and against my rules, so I decided to just go back inside and try to have fun with my friends.

As I reached for the back door, it opened from inside.

"Hey, I was just looking for you. What are you doing out here all by yourself?" Devon was so handsome tonight. It was hard to look at him.

"I just needed some air. And now I need some food. Is it in the kitchen?" I moved to pass by him and he grabbed my wrist.

"Is everything alright? You seem awful quiet."

How did I tell him what I was feeling?

Simple. I needed to quit acting like an idiot and start practicing what I preach. "I'm just feeling overwhelmed. I appreciate that you wanted to throw a party, I'm just not used to anyone doing anything for my birthday. It's a lot. I mean, it *means* a lot. I just don't know how to be...you know?"

"Why would no one do anything for your birthday? You grew up with your father and stepmom, right? Where was your mama?"

I shrugged. "She left shortly after I was born. My father already knew Shannon, so they ended up together almost immediately. She did a good job with me, the best she could, but neither of them was the warm-fuzzy type, you know? So this whole thing you guys got going on, it's just different than what I'm used to."

He nodded. "I'm sorry you grew up without your mama. That had to be hard."

"It is what it is. She and my father didn't get along. It was best for everyone that she just went her own way. I used to wonder about her, but I realized that she wasn't meant to be a part of my life and I moved on. Here, everyone has been so friendly and warm with me. I just don't want to let anyone down."

"The only way you'd let anyone down around here is if you would have said no. We've all been having so much more fun with you around. And..." He stepped outside and let the door close behind him. With his hands in his back pockets and a nervous smile, he said, "I just like you being here."

I crossed my arms and frowned at him. "Why? You just met me."

His grin moved into dangerous territory. "You need me to spell it out, huh?" He stepped toward me.

I stepped back. "I..."

He took another step and then my legs were already backed up against the bench. We were just two feet apart. I felt like I couldn't breathe.

"What's not to get, chère? I like you being here. I like to look at you." His voice was so low and it sent shivers through me. "I liked seeing your face first thing when I woke up this morning." His eyes were searching mine. "And I like talking with you, it's so easy. That's why."

He reached out for my hand and I looked at it for a moment before putting my hand in his. "Devon, I like being here with you, too. But I feel like I'm not being fair to you."

He frowned at me and squeezed my hand. "How are you not being fair to me?"

I let go of his hand and stepped away. He was just too close for me to think straight. "Devon, I'm supposed to be here to help you guys through a rough time and to design tattoos. I like being here, but I don't want to make anyone uncomfortable. I certainly don't want to make things difficult for you."

"I don't understand, Jaylene. How would you be making things difficult for me? I feel better today than I have in months. Today was a good day, thanks to you." He smiled and walked toward me, sliding his arms around my waist. I had to tilt my head way back to look up at him. "I just want to say thank you. Is that okay? So thank you..."

He leaned down and my heart jumped out of my chest as I realized that he was going to kiss me.

His lips gently brushed mine and my body jolted from the shock of it. He was searching my face for a reaction—and I just froze.

"Devon, I—"

He put a finger against my lips. "Jaylene, I'm not asking anything from you other than to stay with us. Spend some time with me. It just feels good to be around you and I need that right now. Is that too much for you?"

I shook my head. "I can do that. But what about the other guys?"

He shrugged and smiled. "What about them? They want you here, too."

I still wasn't sure if he understood my hesitation so I had to ask the tough question. "Devon...what about Maggie?"

His face fell a little. He looked confused.

"What about your feelings for her? If you're thinking about getting involved with someone, have you really dealt with your feelings for *her*?"

He looked even *more* confused. "What do you mean? Jaylene, Maggie was—"

The door opened and Mrs. Boudreaux came through. We were still standing in an embrace. Great.

"There you are. Devon, can I see you in the kitchen, son?" She was smiling sweetly at him.

He looked down at me and moved his hands to grasp mine. "We'll continue this conversation."

He looked worried so I smiled to reassure him. "Sure. I'll see you inside." I stepped away from him and walked to the door. Mrs. Boudreaux held it open for me.

"Did you get some chicken, Jaylene?"

"I'm afraid not. Is there any left?"

She looked upset. "Well there better be. I made it for *you*. If those boys ate it all, I will whip them to within an inch of their lives. I've done it before and I don't care how big they get, I'd do it again."

"No-no, no whippings necessary. I'm sure I can find some. Thank you so much for everything you've done tonight. I hate that you've gone to so much trouble for me."

She pulled me into a hug. "Nonsense, sugar. You've been good to my boys. Now go find you some chicken."

I smiled and thanked her again, heading for the kitchen. Devon met her at the doorway and she smiled just as brightly at him. He looked so adoringly at her, it melted my heart. This man was too much. Beautiful, smart, talented, generous and loving.

This was going to hurt.

I found a few pieces of chicken at the far end of the bar and I took one around to the other side of the stage. It was delectable. I hadn't had homemade fried chicken since before my grandma had moved in with Shannon and my father.

About a year before he died, she moved in with them because it was just getting too hard for her to keep up a household by herself. Before that, most of our family gatherings were at her house. She was a fantastic cook. She made to-die-for fried chicken.

But *this* chicken, with its touch of Louisiana flavor, was just a smidge better. I felt like a princess eating this chicken. Even if I was hiding in the shadows and shoving it in my face like a wild animal.

"There you are. I wondered where you'd gotten off to—or who you'd gotten off with." Mackenzie was so naughty. I loved that about her, but in this situation, where I was already so nervous about everything, it just made me that much more uneasy.

"I had to find me a piece of chicken before it was all gone. Are you having fun?"

She nodded, licking her lips. "Absolutely. That Star is one fine-looking young man. What do you think of him?"

I was glad it wasn't Marcus who'd caught her eye. I couldn't give him a ringing endorsement in the eligible man department. In the friend department, that remained to be seen. "Star is a good guy. He's been very sweet to me and he's completely devoted to his boys. He seems like he's had a rough time of it, but he's got great energy. I think you've chosen well."

Her femme fatale facade slipped a little, showing me the vulnerable woman I knew her to be. She might act the part of vixen, but really she put that on for show. She was sensitive and a bit like me, in that her appearance gave people the wrong idea about her from time to time. She'd been really hurt a few times by douchebag ex-boyfriends. I felt very protective of her. If I had any inkling that Star wouldn't be good to her, I'd tell her.

"Really, Jay? We've been talking all night and he's just so..."

"Yeah, I get it. Just be careful, Kenz. I love you, girl, and I don't want to have to kick his ass for not being good to you, because I kinda like him."

She smiled a totally girly smile at me and kissed me on the cheek. "You are my best friend, Jay, and I love you. Now tell me what the *hell* is going on with Devon? I looked up some stuff on line after we talked and—"

"Jaylene, can you come over to the bar?" Mage was suddenly standing next to us with a mischievous grin on his face.

I looked questioningly at Mackenzie and she gave me a guilty smile. I squinted my eyes at her before I followed Mage.

I saw a glow from behind the bar, which was surrounded by even more people than had been here earlier.

"Happy birthday to you, happy birthday to you, happy birthday dear Jaylene, happy birthday to *youuuuuuuuuuu!*" Devon was standing in the middle of everyone, holding a birthday cake covered with candles. The light from the flames played across his face. It illuminated his gorgeous smile and painfully perfect blue eyes.

I stepped up to him, feeling hands patting me on the back.

"Make a wish, chère," he whispered, and I wished with all my might before blowing the candles out in one breath.

Everyone cheered then Mrs. Boudreaux took the cake out of Devon's hands. Daryl grabbed me and gave me a hug, followed by Katie, Mackenzie and the rest of the guys. Then Devon and the Bones grabbed their instruments and jumped onstage.

Marcus stepped up to the mic and said, "Ladies and gentlemen. Thank you for joining us here tonight. The guys and I want to thank you for coming out to help us blow off some steam. We needed our families tonight to help us celebrate our newest family member's birthday—Jaylene Charles!" Applause from the audience had me blushing and I waved my thanks.

"She's been a good sport, coming to hang out with us, and we thank her. I also want to thank Mrs. Boudreaux for the feast." Everyone clapped for her and she blew him a kiss. "And I want to say thanks to Dwayne and the boys, to the Lambert and Doucette families, Mage's mom and Star's uncles for coming out. I know it's a hike from Houma, but we missed you guys and wanted you here tonight.

"We've put together a few songs for the new album. They're still rough, so bear with us while we try them out on *you*, our most treasured audience."

Everyone clapped and hooted and whistled. I was nervous for them, especially Devon, but they all seemed so happy and easygoing with each other tonight.

Mackenzie came to my side and grabbed my hand, bouncing excitedly. I felt the curious gazes of some of the other guests on me but when Devon struck his first chord, my eyes couldn't leave him.

He'd unbuttoned his shirt halfway, rolled up the sleeves, and he slung the strap of a red and white Les Paul over his head and shoulder. He and Marcus stood shoulder-to-shoulder as they played, looking down and feeling the music. Marcus was gathering up momentum with his vocals. Growls, screams, and husky choruses had everyone jumping around and dancing along. Mage and Jade were playing face-to-face and grinning at each other. Star was in his own whirlwind of drumming heaven. He was all over the place and completely in control of the rhythm he and Mage were laying down.

Here, I was seeing the professionals; they were confident and seemed much larger than life than the silly boys I'd been hanging out with. It was probably good that I'd seen them in that context first. They weren't intimidating to me now. If I'd have met the band first in their performer personas, I don't think I would have been so willing to work with them. They seemed like, together, they could take on the world.

I wanted that for them. So no matter what my feelings for Devon were becoming, I was going to stay so that what I was seeing right now would continue.

Mrs. Boudreaux handed out plates with cake to everyone and Mackenzie and I clicked our forks together before we dug in. The cake was smothered in chocolate buttercream frosting with a rich fudge filling. I thought I would pass out from the sheer joy it brought me. This woman had uncanny skills in the delicious food department. All of her cooking so far had been to die for.

The look on Mackenzie's face told me she completely agreed. She reached over to wipe a smear of chocolate from my chin and I wiped some off her chest with a napkin. We both giggled around mouths full of the stuff and tried to bounce along to the music without dropping a morsel.

Devon looked my way a few times and gave me the devastating smile, leaving me breathless. After the first two songs, he took off his shirt and it was all I could do to keep to my feet.

Mackenzie was having a blast, too, and when Star took off *his* shirt, she was done for. We were like two teenage girls together at a show, drooling over the rock stars and wishing they could be ours.

In this case, could we dare hope that was possible?

Devon was a different kind of irresistible tonight. This morning, he was god-like perfection. Tonight he was a sexy bad boy dream come true. It was overwhelming to say the least.

I felt even more strongly that there was no way I was anywhere near his league. Not even the outskirts of the suburbs of his league. I'd enjoy my time here with him and try not to let my feelings get hurt when it was time to go back to reality.

I thought about the spark I felt when his lips brushed mine in the courtyard, the thrill I felt watching him play, watching those unbelievable fingers run up and down the fret board, his well-sculpted muscles glistening in the lights from above the stage. That smile, the sparkle in his eyes... He might think he's not up for staying in the limelight, but from what I was witnessing, he was made for this.

Soon they were taking a break and everyone was cheering loudly. Devon pulled up a stool to the microphone and grabbed his acoustic. He looked questioningly at Marcus, who nodded at him in encouragement.

My hand went to my chest. He was going to play his song. I looked over at Mackenzie, worried about how he was going to be after singing it. She took one of my hands and turned to watch him.

I wasn't standing very close to the stage. There were several people in front of me. But his eyes found mine—and they showed fear. I smiled reassuringly at him, nodding my head.

He looked down at his guitar and started to play the song. He didn't look around. He either had his eyes closed or was looking down.

He very well could be the one singing in this band. He was that talented. However, I imagined that didn't go along with his dislike of the spotlight. His voice was so pure, so full of pain. I noticed several people wiping their eyes and hugging each other. I was glad that he felt comfortable enough to share with his friends and family how he was feeling.

When it was over there was a very appreciative applause. Daryl and Mrs. Boudreaux stepped up on the stage and hugged him. His smile was gone and I thought I saw him wipe at his eyes once. Daryl was offering him encouragement and he was listening intently.

Mackenzie put her arm around me and I hugged her tightly. "That was about her, huh?" I nodded. "Wow, he really loved her." She didn't say it but I could see worry for me in her eyes.

I gave her a reassuring smile. "This is good for him. I'm so glad he did that." She raised an eyebrow in a look that told me she didn't quite believe me but she'd let it go for now.

By this time it was getting late, but they showed no sign of wanting to slow down. The guys from the Hellraisers got up onstage and the whole group of them played a bunch of crazy Cajun music. Mackenzie and I danced together with abandon.

Dwayne and Marcus traded off vocals and harmonized together well. Marcus had more range than I thought he did. He slipped into a bluesy vocal like second skin. I was starting to let go of some of my apprehension about him. Didn't mean he didn't still push my buttons.

Daryl and Katie came by to say good night, claiming they needed to take Mrs. Boudreaux back to her place and pick up the girls from their gran's. He promised he'd be back soon, and made *me* promise to call if the boys got out of line.

I kissed his cheek and whispered in his ear, "Thank you for making me do this. You're the best." His return glance was surprised but pleased.

"You take care now, dahlin'. Take care of my boys."

I winked at him and waved to Katie and Mrs. Boudreaux. Mrs. Boudreaux dabbed at her eyes with a handkerchief while smiling at something Daryl said to her.

After another hour or so, I was pooped. I grabbed two waters and told Mackenzie I needed to rest. She agreed it was time to call it a night. She and I headed upstairs to the rumpus room and flopped down on the couches. We laid up there and listened to the music, talking about everything and nothing like we always did. Before long, I drifted off to sleep.

The next thing I knew, I was moving and smelling something really good. I opened one eye and realized I was being carried. I sighed and tried to move.

"Shhh, I'm just putting you to bed. Go back to sleep." His voice rumbling in my ear was so comforting.

My arms snaked up around his neck and I felt him hoist me up higher. I heard my bedroom door close and after a few steps more, he lay me gently on the bed. I couldn't make out his features in the dark. My eyelids were so heavy I couldn't keep them open. I felt him take my sandals off and pull the covers over me. A dip on the mattress had me registering that he was sitting on the bed. I felt his hand stroke my hair, and I sighed as I snuggled into my oh-so-comfortable bed. "Devon..."

I felt his lips on my forehead and heard that exquisite voice whisper, "Sweet dreams, beautiful."

And then I was deep asleep, dreaming about the divine way his lips pursed together when he played his guitar.

NINE

When I woke the next morning, still in my clothes, I had conflicted feelings.

Last night was magical and scary. Exciting and confusing. I thought about the many conversations I'd had...with Daryl, Mackenzie, Mrs. Boudreaux and Devon. I felt like I was still missing a piece of the puzzle. I couldn't bring myself to worry about it as I floated to the bathroom.

Once again, Devon's door was open and I couldn't resist a peek. Seeing him sprawled across his bed with a smile on his face had my cheeks flushing and other parts of me warming. The idea of crawling in bed with him and curling up next to that piece of heaven was tempting. It was the same way a jewel thief might crave the crown jewels. Frustratingly close yet utterly unattainable.

I shut the door quietly and turned on the light. A note was taped to the mirror in a masculine scrawl.

Good morning, beautiful. Don't worry about breakfast. Mama is bringing us beignets around 10. If you wake before then, please just rest your pretty self. We've got a long day planned and we need your help. I hope you slept well. I know I will. ~D

I couldn't contain the huge smile that broke out on my face. I stripped and got in the shower, taking my time to shave and exfoliate. I hoped the shower didn't wake him but it felt really good. I braided my hair and wrapped it up on my head. I went back into my room and put on a bra and panties and did some yoga stretches. I decided on a black tank with Motley Crüe written in red and black shorts for the day, not knowing what was in store.

I snuck out of my room—and then panicked.

What had happened to Mackenzie last night? I couldn't believe I hadn't made sure she had a place to sleep.

I heard snoring from the couches and tiptoed over there, finding the cutest sight ever.

Mackenzie was curled up on the couch with a blanket thrown over her, her head directed at the center of the two couches. Star's head was inches away. He'd slept on the other couch, and he was the source of the snoring.

I giggled and came around the front, kneeling next to Mackenzie's sleeping form. "Hey gorgeous. You awake?"

She opened an eye when she heard me whisper and then sat up quickly, knocking foreheads with me.

"Ow! Shit, Jay what are you doing?" We both burst out laughing and Star rolled over against the back of the couch, snoring louder. That had us giggling even more. I took her by the hand and led her back to my room.

"I'm so sorry I left you, Kenz. I was so out of it. Devon must have carried me to my room and tucked me in. I didn't wake up enough—"

She shushed me. "I was fine, honey. Star came upstairs with Devon and I woke up then. Devon said he was putting you to bed, assured me it would be *your* bed, and Star offered to walk me home or stay with me on the couch if I was too tired to walk. Then we just started talking and... Oh Jay, he's just too precious. I hope I get to see him again." She looked much younger without her makeup and with a little sleepiness hanging on.

I hugged her and showed her the note.

"So what do you think?" I asked her.

She shrugged. "Um, besides the fact that he's completely smitten with you? What else is there to tell?"

I growled at her, frustrated. "But how? How could that even be possible?"

She gave me her most patronizing smile, patted my leg and said, "Let me explain this in the simplest terms. You are a gorgeous, talented, though sometimes dim-witted blonde bombshell, and he is rock 'n' roll perfection who thinks you're the cat's meow. Now, you can either remain clueless and make him work for it, which isn't a bad option, or you can just give in to your feelings and let things progress as nature intended. He is a boy, you are a girl... Do you need me to remind you how this stuff works?"

I smacked her thigh and she giggled.

"C'mon Jay, relax. Just go with it. Let him woo you and if it feels right, let him in. I know it's scary for you, I do. You don't let people in. I know *I've* had to work hard at it." She looked a little sad.

I took her hand in mine. "Kenz, I'm sorry. I know I'm a pain. It was just always easier to be alone before and now, I get overwhelmed sometimes. Not by you. You keep me grounded, dollface."

She hugged me and squeezed tight. "Well, now that that's settled, I gotta get back to the shop. I have to open at ten for a couple of clients and then I think I'll go to bed until we open up again on Tuesday."

We laughed together. I gave her a hoodie, a pair of sweats and my Vans to change into, as she was in no shape to hobble the few blocks to our shop in her stilettos.

I grabbed my sketchbook and walked her downstairs to the back patio. I let her out the back gate, kissed her on the cheek, and told her I'd call her later. She waved, put her hood on and walked stealthily down the street. No one was out and about so I was sure she was safe.

I went back inside and started cleaning up the kitchen. Most of the dishes had been washed but I wiped down the counters and then went out to the bar to wipe it down as well.

Star came down in a few and grumbled something about making coffee. I waved him on and walked around picking up plastic cups and napkins from the room. Once things looked neat and orderly, I went back into the kitchen and found Star resting his head on the counter next to the coffee machine. I tried to send him back up to bed but he pointed to the machine, grunted, and laid his head back down.

I shook my head and went into the cold storage to put together another fruit platter.

Suddenly the door closed—and arms embraced me from behind.

I jolted but quickly relaxed as I took in a familiar, tantalizing scent.

"Good morning," Devon breathed onto my neck. I put my hands on his arms and tilted my head, giving him better access. His lips brushed the side of my neck, his teeth grazed my shoulder and a small moan escaped me.

His hands wrapped around my upper arms and he turned me to face him. His head bent to my throat and his thumbs grazed my jaw. His breath was hot and minty and my pulse sped up in anticipation.

"I thought I told you to rest this morning. This isn't resting." He spoke against my neck, giving me chills and causing me to arch my back, pressing my body closer to his. I held onto his biceps for dear life. It was his turn to groan, his hands now gripping my hips.

"I rested," I said in a tight voice that didn't even sound like me. I cleared my throat and whispered, "I had to see Mackenzie out since I was such a bad friend. I left her out on the couch all night."

He laughed. "Star was there to keep her company." The rumble from his chest made my skin break out in goose bumps.

I scoffed. "Hmm, I bet. It's a good thing he's a gentleman or I'd be groveling for forgiveness with her right now." I could barely form a coherent thought with his hands on me. His lips grazed my throat once more and I thought I would probably have oxygen deprivation soon, since I couldn't breathe.

I pulled back and looked up at him. His lips mere millimeters away and I sucked in a shallow breath, ready to finally taste his—

"Star, do we have any more O— Shit. Good morning." Marcus was grinning from ear to ear as he caught us in a most compromising position. "You know, there are more cozy places to make out in this building. Although, cold storage certainly has its *perks*."

He laughed at his own joke and I looked down and saw just what he thought was so amusing. "Ah, cold. Yes." I tried to cover up the girls, but judging by the wideness of Devon's eyes and his attempt to rearrange something else that had come up, I had failed.

"I'm so sor— No. I'm not. I'm not sorry. That felt too good to be sorry for. It's a shame we'll have to continue this later." He kissed me firmly once on the lips, grabbed a jug of orange juice and headed for the door, leaving me gaping at the sight of his retreating back and low-slung jeans.

He'd neglected to put on a shirt this morning. I was right about the name on his back. It was enough of a cold shower for me.

Fruit platter in hand, I emerged into the bright light of the kitchen to find the guys all huddled around the coffeepot, silently urging it to give up the goods. I hoped I wasn't too red-faced and guilty looking as I hurried by and stepped out to the bar.

Mrs. Boudreaux was just setting out the beignets with small plates and a can of whipped cream. She smiled cheerfully at me as I came in.

"Well good morning, Jaylene. You look bright and shiny. I trust you rested well?"

Gods, she could probably see right through me. For all I know my neck was still red from Devon's stubble. Had he left any teeth marks? "I slept just fine, thank you. How 'bout you?"

She nodded. "I sure did. It was a crazy night last night."

"You sure looked great dancing with that brother of yours."

It was *her* turn to blush.

"Mama used to be quite the dancer back in her day, didn't you?" Devon carried two cups of coffee into the room and handed one to his mother, whom he kissed sweetly on the cheek. He walked around behind her and winked at me over her head. I turned and tried to hide my flushed smile.

"Oh, you! That was eons ago. I gave all that up for the love of a fisherman and a thriving business. Then along came two crazy kids and there went my dancing days." She was teasing but there was certainly a hint of sadness to her voice.

"Well, you were wonderful last night, Mrs. Boudreaux. You haven't lost your touch." She thanked me and drank the rest of her coffee in silence.

I frowned at the beignets. I had chosen all black to wear today...with powdered sugar. Not the smartest plan. Perhaps that was why Devon was still shirtless and the rest of the guys were again just in their boxers.

Once they had some food in them, they started talking about the songs they'd played last night, which ones felt good, which ones still needed work. I listened intently and doodled in my sketchbook.

"So let's run through them again this morning after we get Jaylene started."

I looked up as Marcus said my name. "Get me started on what, exactly?" The guys grew a little more serious and Devon's smile was gone.

When Marcus spoke again, it was with a somber voice. "We asked Mrs. Boudreaux to bring her photo albums for you to see. She's got ones of us as kids, ones of us getting started...and pictures of Maggie. We thought maybe you could go through them and, since they're all annotated with dates and places, you might be able to see a pictorial history of us."

It was a great idea but none of them looked very enthused. Marcus pointed to a large table that had been set up last night and to the boxes on the floor next to it. "Those are the important ones. There were others but these cover the most pertinent stuff. The wedding album has the best ones of Maggie, I think." He cleared his throat.

Any euphoria I had been experiencing was replaced with dread.

I didn't want anything to do with those pictures. I didn't want to see wedding photos of Devon and Maggie. Especially after this morning. I looked at Devon and he was standing with his back to me, his arms crossed, talking to Jade. He hugged himself like that, I'd noticed, whenever he was feeling his grief.

Devon glanced over and those damn blue eyes of his were back to their deeply sorrowed state. His look was enough to break through my dread and make my gut freeze up. It also told me that I needed to do this, that this was an important step in getting to the mystery of why Maggie's life, and death, had affected them so.

"Okay. You guys go on with whatever you're going to do and I'll just get started."

They congregated around the stage and started warming up. I ran upstairs to get my sketchbook and to take a few deep breaths so I didn't have a total freak out. Why couldn't I be spending this time with Devon under different conditions? It just wasn't fair. However, a temper tantrum wasn't going to help me right now.

A quick look at my texts had me giggling. Mackenzie had sent me a pic of her standing over Troy, pouting. The text said, *"Wish you were here xoxo."*

I loved that girl. I texted back, *"With what I'm about to do, I wish I was too. Muah."*

I dropped the phone on the bed and went downstairs. The guys were just getting started practicing their new songs. They were taking them piece by piece and adding notes and changes as they went. It would grow a little tedious after a couple hours of hearing the same parts over and over again, but I figured that was part of the program.

I picked up a book that was labeled "Middle School Graduation – 1998." Inside were pictures of boys in their dress clothes next to girls in dresses. I stifled a laugh when I finally found Devon with the guys around him. He was already towering over them at fourteen. Then there was him with his mother...and I was guessing his sister? I still didn't know much about his family. She looked vaguely familiar, though. She was obviously older, wearing a "Class of 1998" tee in a few pictures taken after the ceremony. She resembled him but there was no seriousness to her. She smiled widely in the pictures, compared to Devon's smirks and half smiles.

The next album showed the guys with long hair and instruments, playing in someone's garage. They were such babies. One had Devon with a cigarette hanging from his lips while he played, his hair pulled back in a ponytail. Not a bad look for him, but I preferred his current hairstyle.

And there was the famous Marcus Lambert Mullet. I figured these pictures were probably worth a lot of money to their fans.

Devon's sister was back in some of these as well, but she looked way more sophisticated. She had an edgy haircut and she was dressed like a businesswoman with style.

I definitely remembered her now. I'd tattooed her several months back. Daryl had asked me if I would tattoo someone at his house. I showed up and she was there waiting for me, but Daryl and Katie were out. I thought I remembered her name was something Stone. Weird.

Small world. I guess I *had* met Devon's sister. I wondered why she wasn't there last night.

I closed up the second book and saw that the wedding album was next. I felt a little sick to my stomach so I opted to go for a drink instead.

I'd avoided the beignets earlier so I grabbed a plate, put two on it and went into the kitchen to give them a quick whirl in the microwave and find a Diet Coke. Nice breakfast, I know.

I was just finishing the first beignet when Devon walked past the kitchen and out onto the patio. The morning had been intense for the guys. They were working hard so he probably needed a smoke break. Poor guy. He'd said he didn't want to smoke, but I understood that now was probably not the time for him to be trying to quit. I wanted to check on him but I needed to get through these pictures before I faced him again.

I finished my snack and made sure I washed my hands well so I wouldn't get sticky stuff all over the albums. Miraculously, I'd made it through with zero powdered sugar contamination. Thank goodness.

Back in the bar, the guys were flipping through the other photo albums and laughing about some of the pictures.

"Dude, that mullet was grotesque." Mage was laughing hard, holding the book I'd just looked at.

Marcus shot back, "It beats your first forays into facial hair. Remember the moustache he grew for Jr. Prom?" The guys laughed hysterically at that and Mage told them to shut up.

"Chicks dig mustaches, don't they Jaylene?"

I thought briefly of how I could torture him on this, but the look on his face said I should be honest.

"It completely depends on the mustache, Mage. For example: Sam Elliot? Perfection. Jack White's Fu Manchu? Strange. Justin Timberlake's? Ridiculous." They all laughed.

Marcus brought the album around and showed me a picture I had missed of Mage and Devon together, both sporting scraggly excuses for mustaches. "And how would you classify these, Miss Charles?"

Again, I didn't want to hurt his feelings so I went easy on him. "I'd say these had potential. They hinted at sophistication to come." I winked at him and walked around to my seat.

"Aha! Spoken by a true genius. Thank you, chère." He leaned over and kissed me on the cheek, sticking his tongue out at Marcus after.

"Real mature, Mage. So, Jaylene, do you have any questions about the pictures so far?" He walked around to peek over my shoulder.

"Not really. Well, maybe. Who told you guys that polyester was a good fabric for your formal dance wear?"

He rolled his eyes at me and Jade spoke up. "It was a seventies-themed dance party and we were by far the best dressed. We had the moves and everything. John Travolta would have been begging us to take him out cruising."

Star nodded. "Yeah, man. We even had the killer ride. Devon had a souped-up nineteen seventy-two Challenger convertible that we cruised around in. We were the hottest dudes at the disco."

Jade started singing the Bee Gees and demonstrated some hip rolls and arm waves.

"I can see that. You would have been impossible to resist." They all laughed and I reached for the wedding album. Time to quit stalling and get it over with.

"You know, I met Devon's sister once. I tattooed her out at Daryl's place back in December." I had my head down so I didn't see their reactions.

Marcus spoke very quietly. "You must be mistaken, she didn't have any tattoos."

I looked up at him, and then back down at the page I'd opened up. The picture was of her in a wedding dress surrounded by four of the guys trying to look tough. "That's her, right?" He nodded.

Strange. I had assumed this was Devon and Maggie's wedding album, but it was still nice to see the guys all cleaned up and in formal dress.

"Yeah. She asked Daryl to set it up when she was in town for a visit. She moved away, right? Anyway, I tattooed a small fleur-de-lis on her hip with angel wings. She said she wanted a memento of home."

I looked up—and they'd all gone white. They were looking back and forth at each other.

I frowned. "Funny, though. I thought she said her last name was Stone."

Marcus looked at me gravely. "It was." He turned the page. On it was a picture of her with a blond guy with a Ken doll haircut and equally plastic smile. Their wedding photo.

Marcus cleared his throat. "After she left home, she started going by Meg. Then when she married Thomas, she was Meg Stone. But to us, she was always Maggie."

My head snapped up. I was stunned. I stared at him, unable to speak —or breathe, for that matter.

This was Maggie? Meg Stone was Margaret Boudreaux?

My voice came out sounding very weak. "Maggie was Devon's sister?"

They all frowned and looked at each other again. Jade spoke first. "Who did you *think* Maggie was?"

I had been so wrong. But then, no one would tell me much. "All I knew was that she was your manager. When I learned Devon's last name was Boudreaux, I just assumed they were, uh...married. I thought Maggie was his *wife*."

None of them spoke...but they were trying not to smile.

I looked at them, feeling like a total idiot but also feeling a wave of relief. He hadn't been married. That changed things for sure.

Finally Jade said, "Uh, that's kind of gross. Why would he be married to his sister? They don't even allow that anymore." The other guys started laughing.

"You dumbass," yelled Star, and they were all razzing him and laughing about Devon being married.

"Who's married?"

Devon came in and I wished to the heavens above to please come and swallow me up. I was mortified. How could I have been so wrong? I blew my bangs up out of my face in frustration and Devon's eyes shot straight to me, the intense look on his face hitting me like a blast of heat. How the hell was I going to get out of this one?

"You, apparently." Marcus was snickering. My face was so hot I thought for sure I'd break out in blisters.

Devon looked confused. "When did I get married?"

Mage pointed at the album and said, "Jaylene thought Margaret Boudreaux was your wife."

"Wife? *Wife!* Oh, no. Jaylene?" He was looking at me with that damn bemused expression of his.

I jumped up from my chair, already tired of being the butt of this joke. "It's not my fault. None of you thought it wise to tell me *anything* about her. Anyone could have made that mistake."

That just made them laugh harder. I was fuming and Devon was just staring at me incredulously.

"No, really. No one could make that mistake who knows this dude. He could never even *talk* to girls. He would totally freeze up. He could barely even get laid, much less get a girl to marry him." Devon socked Marcus in the arm for that one, which only made Marcus laugh harder.

"I guess I just don't know him then, do I? Excuse me."

I grabbed my sketchbook and ran up the stairs to my room and shut the door. I rested my back against it and felt hot tears of humiliation threatening to run free. How could I have been so stupid...and why were they laughing at me? What happened to "you're one of the family, Jaylene?"

Chapter Ten (check this)

Devon pounded on the door. "Jaylene, open up, please? I'm sorry. I should have told you. Please."

I couldn't hide in here forever but I was so embarrassed. I unlocked the door and trudged over to my bed, sitting with my back to him as he burst in.

"What do you want, Devon? Want to laugh some more?" I was too upset to speak over a whisper. I heard his footsteps coming closer and then he was kneeling in front of me.

"God, no. Jaylene. I wasn't laughing. I would never laugh at you. I'm so sorry. I just assumed you knew Maggie was my sister. With all the big-mouthed jackasses around, I thought you knew. God, please just look at me."

I couldn't do it. His eyes were always too intense. I told myself I should never have let him get close to me. I was such a fool.

"Hey, chère. I'm sorry. Please? Say something."

I bit my lower lip to keep from crying. I took in a breath. I couldn't look at him right now. "Look. I don't do this well, this...whatever it is we're doing. I didn't even *want* to get involved with you because I thought you were a widower. That's what I was trying to tell you last night. I don't play games and I certainly don't like being the butt of someone's jokes. So please, just leave me alone so I can process this little humiliation of mine in private?"

He sat back on his heels. "I'm sorry if we screwed up, Jaylene, but please don't do this. I was going to talk to you about her today. That's why I had my mama bring the pictures. I thought it would be easier to explain her that way. If you're upset, be upset with *me*. Everyone's gotten so used to not talking about her in front of me. I guess they didn't know what to tell you. I'm such an idiot. Please, Jaylene. I never meant for you to get hurt." He put his hand out and rested it on the bed next to me.

I could hear the pain in his voice and I couldn't bear to be the cause of it. Slowly I turned toward him and he looked up at me with worry. I gave him a weak smile. "At least no one made this into a blonde joke. Then I really *would* have had to kick someone's ass."

The relief sagged through him and he leaned forward, putting his head in my lap and grabbing hold of the sides of my thighs. "I'm so sorry, Jaylene. Please forgive me. That was a terrible thing for me to let happen."

I gave in to my urge to touch his hair. It was exactly as silky as I'd imagined. "You didn't do anything, Devon. I'm the one who jumped to conclusions. I just thought she had to be someone intimately close to you, and...I don't know, I guess not ever having a sister, I just didn't even imagine that you could love a sibling that deeply. And then when I heard your song, it was obvious how much you loved her. I felt so guilty, thinking about how attracted to you I was when I was supposed to be helping you grieve for your deceased wife. *I'm* the one who made the mistake, not you."

He sat up and grinned like he'd just won a prize. In this position, we were almost at eye level with each other. His powerful shoulders and long arms swallowed me. "You're attracted to me?"

I groaned and he pulled me closer, so my legs had to part for his chest.

"Really? That's what you took away from what I just said?" He was so on the money, though. I was incredibly attracted to him. With him this close, I was on fire.

He leaned in and kissed the bottom of my throat and then my chest. "So...you're *not* attracted to me?"

I groaned even more dramatically and grabbed his face, forcing him to look at me. The sexy grin he had on his face froze me in place.

"Devon, you know damn well I'm attracted to you. I've been a mess since you first came to my shop and stood there with your sad eyes and your many smiles."

His eyes lit up even further. "You were? But you were so professional. And then when you came here, you were so close to me, but *not* —you know what I mean? You asked questions but gave nothing away and I couldn't tell if I was being out of line or not. But I couldn't stop wanting to be close to *you*."

I was growing dizzy with him so near. I thought about the way I'd felt when he'd just given me a quick kiss and wondered if I'd be able to handle more without spontaneously combusting.

I cleared my throat nervously and said, "Well, now you know. What do you have to say?"

I was shaking, I was so nervous.

He pulled me tighter to him, so our chests were touching and my thighs were spread wide to accommodate him. "I think what I have to say is that I'm dying to kiss you and I'm hoping you'll let me."

I licked my lips—and that was all the invitation he needed.

He was on me immediately. His full lips kissed me softly but with just enough pressure to let me know he was barely containing his passion. His arms locked around me and my hands tangled in his hair.

"Jesus, Jaylene, you taste so good. I've wanted this so much." We were both shaking and breathing heavy. His eyes searched mine for any sign I wasn't totally okay with this.

I brushed his hair back from where it had come loose. I'd never been this affected by a guy before. "I was afraid to want this."

He grabbed my face in both of his hands. "Why?"

I didn't know what to say to make him understand. "Devon, you don't know me. The only guys who have ever shown interest before just thought I was someone I'm not. And I would never think someone like you would even want someone like me."

He hit me with those eyes again. They penetrated me.

"Jaylene, you amaze me. You are so beautiful...who you are, what you create. Whenever I'm around you, that's the only place I want to be, like the world could just fall away and that's alright. Don't you feel it too?"

I nodded. "I feel like I'm drowning. It scares me."

A pained look crossed his face. "No, chère. Don't be afraid of me, of this. Just be here, with me. Please?" He kissed me again. This time he started slow and then moved us back onto my bed. I was on my back with Devon holding himself above me. He slid his leg between mine and I ran my hands timidly along his back, under his t-shirt. His skin was so soft, completely at odds with the hardness underneath it.

And his lips were intoxicating. They were so full and feather-soft. He smelled so damn good. He was invading all of my senses, taking over, and I felt helpless to stop it.

He started to lower himself on top of me—and I started to panic. He was just so much, and while I wanted to be in this moment with him, it scared me.

"Devon, please. Just give me a minute."

His eyes grew wide and he lifted himself off me. "Of course, chère. Are you okay? Is this okay?"

I nodded and he moved over to lie beside me. I curled up next to him and his arms pulled me close. This was truly the best feeling.

He unwound my hair that was starting to come out of the wrap I'd done this morning. He slowly unbraided it and ran his fingers through the mass, sending delicious shivers through me. We lay there in silence for a while and I felt peaceful.

"Talk to me, chère. Don't keep me out." He held me tight to his body. It was just as heavenly as I imagined it would be when I'd thought about curling up with him yesterday.

"I don't mean to. I'm sorry. This feels really good." He nuzzled my neck and kissed my shoulder. I guess that meant he agreed with me.

"This feels incredibly good. I could stay here forever." I giggled at that.

"That would certainly get me in trouble with the guys downstairs. They're expecting me to get you back with the program, not change the channel." He chuckled.

"Whatever. They know I'm going to do what I said I'd would do. Doesn't mean I'm not going to do what I *want* to do, too."

I was smiling so wide my face hurt. "You are very loyal to them."

He rolled over on his back and sighed. I turned and placed my head on his chest. He brought his arms around me and caressed my shoulder and my back, tracing lines with his fingers. "I guess it's loyalty. I just do what I say I'm going to do. I wouldn't bail on them. I just couldn't come up with any new material and they started to panic. I didn't feel it. What was I supposed to do? I know Marcus would just keep regurgitating the same shit, but I want us to grow."

"You guys definitely have a distinctive style. But then you play stuff like you did last night, and that sounds terrific, too. Why does it have to be all the same? I think your fans will love you no matter what you play."

He rolled over on his side to face me and rested his head on his hand. "Do you really think so?"

I nodded. "Of course! I know it's hard to mix it up when you're trying to establish your fan base but once you do, I think fans *like* to hear a little bit of mixing it up. I mean, think about Guns n Roses. *Use Your Illusion* was very different from *Appetite for Destruction*. And of course, Metallica. Their range has blown the doors off of what was expected of them."

His face showed he was taking in what I'd said. He seemed to be working something around in his head. Then he narrowed his eyes at me. "You're pretty incredible, you know that?" I rolled my eyes at him and he frowned, hard. "Why do you do that, Jaylene? I'm serious. I love how you always say what you think and don't let anyone intimidate you. Even if it might not be the popular thing to say."

I snickered. "Maybe that's why I was never popular. I couldn't stand the posturing. I liked what I liked. I still do." I shrugged. "I never got people who said what they thought others wanted to hear. Not until I went through my grad program. Now I understand but it doesn't mean I could ever do it."

He kissed my forehead and continued to play with my hair. It was so relaxing. It helped to ease my anxiety. When he spoke, his deep voice rumbled against my ear and tickled me, giving me chills. "That's why being with you is so refreshing. So many people who've been around us had their own agenda with our music or they were just hoping we'd give them a boost. They'd say anything sounded good, even if it sounded like shit. I mean, there was a time when I thought songs like 'Mystical Stick' were the height of sophistication..."

I giggled. I couldn't hold it in whenever he talked about their more ridiculous songs.

"Oh, you think that's funny? Better not tell Marcus. He'll explain the whole concept to you, and why it's highbrow entertainment. He'll give you a thorough demonstration," he said, as he made vulgar faces and gestures. I was really laughing now, and he started to tickle me. "Your laugh is the best medicine, I swear. I could listen to it all day."

I stopped, suddenly self-conscious. I pushed myself up onto my elbows and looked into his eyes. "Who are you, Devon Boudreaux? Who are you and why are you in here with me?" I looked at him in wonder. I could see so much more than his pain, with him this close to me. He was a completely different person alone. One whom I liked so very much.

"I'm in here with you, Miss Charles, because it nearly killed me to see you so upset. I promise I won't let that ever happen again. I don't want to ever be the cause of that again. I just want you smiling and laughing and frowning at me. Even rolling your eyes at me. That part is kind of sexy."

I gently slapped at his arm and he snaked his hand up my exposed skin and let his fingers drift along my side.

"And I want to see you blowing your bangs out of your face when you get frustrated. And I want to see your face relax when you sleep. And I want to see your eyes light up when I kiss you."

He leaned in closer to me with his eyes open and staring into mine. He kissed me tenderly, his tongue gently urging me to let him in. I moaned and our tongues met and danced together, reminding me of how good it felt to dance with him last night. Everything about Devon made my body feel more alive. But he still scared me.

I pushed the fear to the back of my mind, where I vowed I would keep it until my time with him was up. I thought about what Mackenzie said and knew that being with Devon made me happy. And I wanted happy. I wanted *him*. I'd been alone for too long.

He rolled me on top of him and my hair fell all around us, like a fort we could hide in and play. He pushed it back off my face and our eyes held each other. My legs straddled his hips and his hands slid up the outside of my shorts.

I sat up and put my hands on top of his. "While I'm certainly not in favor of ending our current activity, we kind of left things a mess downstairs. I meant what I said about not wanting to make things more difficult for you. You have the guys waiting for you down there and I should go finish my task." I searched his face to get a read on his reaction. His smile was gone but I didn't see the pain in his eyes.

With a gigantic sigh, he sat up, pulling my hips dangerously closer to his. We groaned at the incredibly good feeling that movement brought us both.

"Oh wow," I breathed, and he grinned back at me.

"Yeah, I second that."

We were now face-to-face, our chests touching, and his hands gripped me tightly. I was afraid if I moved at all, we'd both fall apart. He started kissing my neck and it grew increasingly difficult to think straight.

"So what are we going to do about this...mmmmm...situation we seem to have found ourselves in?" He spoke this against my throat, finishing by running his tongue up the side. I breathed hard, my legs liquid.

"Well, it's certainly a predicament. What do you suggest?"

He laughed softly. "If I have to go downstairs, a cold shower might be in order."

I giggled and kissed my way along his chin to his earlobe, bringing his thick silver hoops between my lips and pulling gently. I felt him push against my core and we both moaned.

"God, I don't think even a cold shower will help this." We both looked down at the evidence of our dilemma.

Oh. Impressive. Even through his jeans.

My cheeks reddened, and so did his.

"Serious talk, Devon. Just what *is* our situation? What do you want?"

He did his best to answer my question without letting his hands roam anymore but I was extremely aware of the pressure against my hips. His hands were so large they covered me from hipbone to tailbone, his fingers touching in the back. And I was not skinny by any means.

"Serious talk? I think my situation is that I'm emphatically attracted to you. I want to be with you however you'll have me. I also have work to do." He smiled sadly. "Which means that this can't continue at the present time."

He gently lifted my hips off of his and I immediately felt the absence of his warmth. We sat on the bed facing each other and he tucked a piece of hair behind my ear. "Jaylene, what do *you* want?"

I smiled at him and looked down at my hands for a moment to regain my composure. "Well, Devon, I want to get to know you. I like Smiling Devon, and I really want to soothe Sad Devon. I also want to further explore possibilities with Sexy Devon. But I don't want to take you away from your duties. So we have to have ground rules." I hoped he agreed with me.

"Agreed," he said with a business-like sternness that was still very sexy. "I have to practice, you have to draw. I have to agree to share you with those knuckleheads down there during business hours. You have some tattoos to do. I have to keep my hands to myself when we're not alone. When we *are* alone, though..." He started to lean towards me for another kiss and this time I put my finger against his lips, which he promptly kissed.

"When we *are* alone, Mr. Boudreaux, we need to have rules, too. I'm your employee, for all intents and purposes. You may not think that's serious, but I do. As much as I want you to *not* keep your hands to yourself, we need to think about that. I. Do. Not. Want. To. Cause. Problems. For. You." I tapped my finger against his lips with each word.

He sighed and ran his fingers through his hair, which was coming down around his face in his current relaxed state. When he looked up at me, his eyes were full of worry. And hurt?

"So does that mean this isn't going to happen between us? Because I'm not okay with that."

I reached up and cupped his face in my hand, running my thumb across his lips. Gods, I loved those lips. "I'm not okay with that either. I want this, but like I told you, I have a hard enough time just trying to date someone, much less navigating the world of employer/employee relations." I smirked at him and he at least gave me a sad smile. "And I should also tell you that I haven't been physically involved with anyone since, well...ever."

His eyes snapped up at me in disbelief. "How is that even possible?"

I frowned at him. "Well, maybe you're used to having women throw themselves at you, but the world I live in? Yeah, it's only been populated by guys who either thought I would be an easy score or who wanted a BFF. So you'll forgive me if I'm a little inexperienced because neither of those were particularly pleasant options." There was a hint of defensiveness in my tone.

He grabbed for my hands and when he spoke, the concern in his voice touched me. "I only meant that how is it possible the men you've been around couldn't see how special you are? It just makes me even more sure that I want to do right by you. Whatever it takes."

His words took my breath away. "You just need to be honest with me, always. Even if it's to say that you're moving on. Okay? I'm not fooling myself here. I know what kind of lifestyle you have. I'm not asking you for any commitment other than to tell me the truth, always."

I could tell he was bothered by what I said but it *needed* to be said. He pulled me into a tight embrace, his face buried in my hair. "I will always tell you the truth, Jaylene. I know you don't know me well enough yet to believe me, but I always keep my word. And I plan to show you."

"Thank you," I whispered into his shoulder.

He reluctantly let go and started to get off the bed. He stopped to look at me over his shoulder. "You don't need to thank me. I promise I'll do my best but it is going to be damn hard to behave like nothing's going on. I want you so bad it's downright painful."

I couldn't help but giggle at that.

He raised an eyebrow at me. "You find that amusing, chère?" There was humor in his voice.

"Nope. I'm just glad I won't be the only one suffering. I may be inexperienced, Devon, but how you make me feel is driving me crazy. I can only imagine how much better it could get from here."

His eyes lit up and that damn sexy smile of his was back. "How about how much better it *will* get? There are how many days left on your contract?"

I started Friday and today was Sunday... "Fourteen," I answered him.

He licked his lips and rubbed his hands together. "So two weeks for me to show you that you can trust me. Two weeks. I can do two weeks. In the meantime, I'll still get to look at you, watch you work, and dream about you in the bed right next door... Okay, that's probably not a good idea. I'll dream about all the things we can do when the two weeks are up."

I smiled back at him. "A lot can happen in two weeks. You might just realize there's a reason Mackenzie always tells me I'm a pain in the ass."

Devon stood up from the bed, shaking his head at me. He walked around the foot of the bed to my side and stood with his hands on his hips. "Oh, you're a pain, alright. But it's an exquisite pain. One I will revel in for the time being, until I can be with you again."

With that tasty morsel, he left the room and left me to try to pull myself together. I could still smell him on me and it made it difficult to stop smiling. I tamed my hair in the bathroom, and I splashed some cold water on my face to hopefully calm the redness and swollen lips.

I looked at myself for a long time in the mirror. Before all this insanity, when I'd looked, I'd see an average-looking woman. Gobs of blonde and whatever-color-I-was-in-the-mood-for hair, dark brown eyes and pale skin. My tattoos were the only things I thought made me anything more than ordinary. I was medium height, medium build. I was pretty much nondescript, other than the ink.

But today I saw a sparkle in my eyes, a glow to my skin, and surprisingly, a few curves. My skin was flushed from recent activity and the color made my features stand out. I smiled at my reflection, almost like a long-lost friend I was seeing again after a lengthy separation.

I silently thanked Devon for waking these feelings in me. I could still feel the warmth from his skin against mine, and a pleasant ache in all the right places from his attentions.

So this was what all the fuss was about? Oh, I'd been kissed before, absolutely. But kissing to me brought memories of beer breath, slobber, and overeager lips trying to devour my face. I pictured hands trying to maul me and get my clothes off.

Devon had done none of those things. He was gentle yet persistent. He was full of passion, but restrained enough to respect my limits.

That led me to a tantalizing thought: How would it feel if he lost some of that restraint? The small amount of his passion I'd felt so far was consuming. What would it be like to touch all of him?

A knock on my bedroom door had me shaking off my fantasies for the moment. "Yeah?"

The door opened and I heard Star. "Jaylene? Hey, we're sending out for lunch. What do you like on your pizza?"

Lunch? I checked the clock to see that it was one. Devon and I had been up here for almost two hours.

"Oh, uh...pepperoni and mushroom? Is that okay?" I peeked out of the bathroom and he had just stuck his head in the door.

"That's great. And Jaylene? We're all really sorry. I can't believe we were such idiots. Can you forgive us?"

I smiled and walked over to the door, opening it all the way. "There's nothing to forgive, Star. It was my mistake, and frankly, I can see why you guys would think it was humorous. Let's just promise not to keep anything that major from Jaylene in the future, sound good?"

He blushed. "Yeah. I'm so sorry."

"Not to worry. I'm fine. Devon and I talked."

Star's face split into a huge, relieved grin. "He was so worried. I'm glad you talked. We were all afraid that you would leave."

This seemed to be a common thread. I tried to answer him with a mild voice filled with conviction. "Star, I'm not going to leave. I'm going to probably ask y'all more questions from now on, but I'm not going anywhere. Okay? So just forget about that."

"That's good. I'm glad. And I'm happy for Devon. He hasn't been this happy since..." Star scratched his head. "You know? I don't think I've *ever* seen him like this before. He's always been fun to be around, kinda quiet and reserved, like you've seen him. But he hasn't smiled, really, in a long time. Even before we lost Maggie."

I wasn't surprised to hear that. It sounded like things were out of hand for a while before then.

"Well, I'm glad he's smiling more. But we have more work to do, right?"

He gave me a sad smile and nodded. "Yeah. We do. So pizza should be here in about forty-five minutes. After that, we've got more to practice today. Sherry's flying in tomorrow and we need to have something ready for her so she can tell the label we're making progress. We may even start recording week after next, if they like what we've got so far. Shit, we've got a lot to do though. I hate this part. The pressure really sucks." He was running his hands through his hair, making it stand on end.

"It seems counterproductive to put time limits on art, doesn't it?"

He looked at me quizzically. "Yeah, you're right. It's not like I'm writing a research report, I'm writing to express myself. But they pay us, I guess, so we're kind of on their dime."

"No doubt. When I'm in the same situation with a client, I just draw word for word exactly what they ask for with minimal interpretation. Usually they'll look at it and say, 'Hmmm, that's sort of it, but can we add a little of this or a little of that', so I end up getting more time to work."

He chuckled. "Ah, so you're sneaky too, eh? Maybe we should try that, like perform some country shit or even some pop rock and have them say, 'Weeeelll, we like where you're going with that, but maybe something a little more...oh, say...heavy?"

We both laughed at that and headed down the stairs together. Star just really had a way about him that eased peoples' discomfort.

"I got a question for you. About last night."

Uh-oh. Devon and I hadn't talked about what we would say to the others. "Okay, what did you want to know?" *Please don't let it be about Devon, please don't let it be about Devon.*

"It's about Mackenzie. She left so quick this morning. I didn't get to even say goodbye and find out if she enjoyed herself at all." Poor guy was seriously bummed out. I had to give him a little help here.

"Hey, buck up little camper. It just so happens, she told me she had a great time with you, really enjoyed your talk. She also said she hopes to see you again."

His eyes lit up like the fourth of July and he hugged me tight. "Oh, awesome, thanks, Jaylene. So should I call her? Like, should I ask to see her again?" He was so eager.

"I tell you what. I'll text her later and ask if I can give her number to you. Then it's up to you kids." I winked at him and his grin spread.

I knew Mackenzie wanted to see him but I had no idea how she would play this one. My best friend had game when it came to dating. I had tried to convince her to be straightforward with the men she dated, but she complained that they were never honest. She felt she had to seem aloof, uninterested, or even a little hostile to keep their interest.

Hence the reason I'd never done much dating. I didn't like constantly trying to figure out how the other person felt or what they were thinking. Being by myself had always been simpler.

But I'd change all that in a heartbeat for Devon. And as much as I believed all the stuff I said to him about maintaining a professional relationship while I was here, I had fantasies about sleeping in his bed and curling up in those arms every night.

TEN

Downstairs, the guys were all standing around their equipment talking about what they were going to play for Sherry. Marcus was making notes and speaking to the group.

"I definitely think we should play your track for her, D. What do you think about adding in the electric and beefing up the sound a little?"

Devon shrugged. "I think it's cool acoustic. We haven't done that before. Let's leave it for now."

Marcus nodded. "Okay then. We've got 'Leather and Lace' worked out pretty good. What do you guys think?" They all nodded and murmured that it was a good one.

Jade strummed his guitar a couple of times. "How about that one we were playing around with last week?" He started playing a riff that sounded promising. It was really fast, almost a punk-like vibe. Star gave him a backbeat and Mage started following along on the bass. Marcus was frowning.

Devon was nodding, looking amused. "Sure, Marcus. You add some of your manwhore lyrics to that one and it will suit us just fine."

He rolled his eyes at Devon and smirked. "Manwhore. Nice. Okay, let's think about that one. Anyone else got any ideas?"

They all kind of shrugged and looked at their feet. Marcus seemed very frustrated.

"Well, Sherry's not going to have much to take back the label then, is she? We better see what else we can come up with."

For the next three hours after lunch, the guys played riffs, played some of their favorite songs, but still they came up with nothing new. Anything the guys suggested, Marcus thought didn't sound like them. They seriously needed a break.

Mrs. Boudreaux came over to me while they were arguing. "It doesn't sound like they're making much progress, does it?" she whispered.

I shook my head sadly at her. "It started off okay, but they just don't seem to have enough material for their visit with Sherry tomorrow."

She patted my shoulder. "They will. They're already doing better, just by talking to each other." We listened to them for a bit longer and then she asked me if I would help her in the kitchen. I agreed and we walked back together. When I passed Devon, who was playing along with the guys to Pantera's 'Walk,' he smiled at me knowingly and I felt his eyes follow us to the kitchen.

"Boy, I love hearing them play but it gets so loud. How have you been holding up, hearing it all day, dear?"

I laughed. "I work in a tattoo shop and we usually have the music up incredibly loud. It helps cover the noise from the needle, keeps the clients calmer in a way."

She smiled at me and started unloading some bags of groceries. "Do you mind peeling potatoes?"

I shook my head. "Whatever you need me to do."

I washed about ten pounds of potatoes and got to work peeling them over a garbage can. Mrs. Boudreaux was seasoning pork loin chops and cutting up some fresh vegetables to steam.

"We'll be boiling those potatoes to mash so you can put them in that pot over there."

I pulled the pot closer to me and kept at it. I wanted to talk to Mrs. Boudreaux. I thought I'd try to get to know her a little since she had been very nice to me so far.

"So Devon told me you ran a restaurant back home, in Houma?"

She nodded. "Well, I did. We sold it to some cousins about three years ago. It was getting too difficult to run it by myself, and with the boys and Maggie all in California, I was getting too run down. We still have the house there, but Devon bought me a place here in the Quarter so I could be closer to Daryl and Katie." She sounded so tired.

"How do you like living here?"

She shrugged. "There's a lot going on, that's for sure. I have a couple of girlfriends from high school who live in the Garden District that I see, but I haven't found much to keep me occupied. I was glad to come cook for the boys."

"But...if you could be doing anything right now with your time, what would you choose?"

She got a dreamy look on her face. "I don't know for sure. I hadn't thought about it 'til now. But you're right. I can do what I want, can't I?"

I laughed. "You sure can. I bet it's a tough adjustment after running your own business and being a parent. Are there any skills you wanted to learn to do when you were younger? Art? Crafts? Music? I know you were a dancer."

She sighed and shook her head. "I always wished I could have stayed a dancer. I liked working in the restaurant, working with food, but there was so much more than that involved. With my husband gone out fishing a lot of the time, I was there all day. Thankfully Maggie was around to take care of Devon. They were four years apart but she was a little mama from the beginning." Her smile disappeared and she was quiet for a bit.

"You miss her a lot, don't you?"

She looked at me, surprised. Then she nodded and her eyes watered. "I'm sorry. I'm just not used to talking about her. It makes Devon so upset."

I saw a box of tissues on the shelf above me so I took one over to her. "It does make him upset, but I think I've got him convinced that it will do him some good."

She looked at me and damn if she didn't have those same blue eyes that held her pain in them.

"It was hard when I lost his father. I cried a lot and felt like I couldn't keep going. But losing Maggie has been like losing a part of me. She was such a joy. It just doesn't seem fair."

I nodded and reached for her hand. "Mrs. Boudreaux, will you tell me about her? Maybe just a little? If I have just a bit more information, I'll know better what questions to ask them to get them to open up a bit."

"Of course, anything to help them. I couldn't do much to help Devon when he lost his father. I have to help him through this. He's too young to spend his life devastated like he is."

I put the potatoes on to boil and she put the pork loin in the oven to bake. That gave us some time to chat. "Can I bring you anything to drink?" I asked her as I headed for the door.

"Thank you, sugar. I'd love some iced tea. Do they still have those bottles out there?"

"Sure do. I'll be right back."

I passed Devon in the hall. "I was just coming to check on you two. Is that dinner I'm smelling?"

I nodded. "I'm helping your mom. We're having some girl time."

He smiled at me, and he seemed somewhat astonished and grateful at the same time. "Thank you, chère. She could really use that. I'm afraid I haven't been much fun to be around."

I raised an eyebrow at him. "Well, duh. You're a guy. Can't have girl time with your son."

He rolled his eyes at me and I skipped past him to get drinks for his mama and me. I might have heard a groan before he turned away. I might have been hoping for one. A girl can enjoy herself, can't she?

When I came back, he was in the kitchen hugging Mrs. Boudreaux.

"Mama, are you okay?"

She nodded. "I'm fine, son. Your friend and I were just talking about your sister."

He grimaced at that. "I'm sorry, Mama. Please don't cry. You don't have to talk about her if it makes you sad." His voice had gone scratchy and he was trying to keep himself together.

"Of course it makes me sad. But *you* being sad is worse. I don't want you to hurt anymore, son. I'm afraid I haven't been a very good example."

He held her tight to him and she cried quietly. I waited just inside the doorway because I wanted to give them space. He noticed me at that moment and the look on his face had me concerned. Would he be angry with me for upsetting his mother?

I couldn't worry about that. I had to assure myself that this was what they needed. "Mrs. Boudreaux, I brought your tea. You probably want sugar for it though, right?"

She looked up and laughed. "Of course. I forget you're not from these parts, are you?"

I shook my head. "No, ma'am, and where I grew up, we drank our iced tea black and strong."

She made a sour face and laughed some more. It helped to make Devon relax a bit. "That just sounds awful, you poor thing. Isn't that terrible, Devon? They don't even know how to drink tea in California."

He gave his half smile. "I'm sure they drink tea just fine, Mama." He kissed her on the top of her head. "I'm going to go out and bang my head against an amp for a while, maybe that will make the music miraculously happen." He was joking but the tension was rolling off his shoulders. I wanted to check on him so I told his mom I'd be right back again.

"Hey, headbanger," I called out to him. He turned around and smiled a very sad smile. I put out my arms and he came to me for a big hug, picking me up off my feet. "I'm sorry I upset your mom, Devon. But I think she really needs to talk. Are you okay with that?"

His eyes bled sadness but he was trying so hard to keep it together. "Whatever you think is best, chère. But please, be careful with her. She's tough but breakable, you know?"

I nodded grimly. "I know. Dinner should be ready soon."

He kissed me on my cheek and put me down. "She's all I've got, Jaylene."

I shook my head and he raised an eyebrow at me.

"No, she's not." I winked at him and turned to go back to the kitchen, hearing him chuckle behind me.

Then Marcus yelled, "Hey, quit fraternizing and get your ass back in here, D."

Devon answered him with a creative suggestion of what he could do with his own ass.

Back in the kitchen Mrs. Boudreaux was tossing a salad and smiling to herself.

"Sorry about that. Did you need help with anything else?" She pointed over at the loaf of French bread. "You could slice that. There's a bowl and a towel to wrap it in over there."

I got to work and waited for her to talk if she was ready.

"You know," she said after a few minutes. "My son is very protective of me. Too much, probably. He really took on the man-of-the-house role when his father died, and Lord forgive me, but I let him." She sniffled a little, cleared her throat and then kept talking.

"Maggie left home as soon as she turned eighteen; she wasn't due to start college for a couple of months but she wasn't waiting around. She didn't want life or its vast possibilities to pass her by, she'd tell me. So she rented an apartment in Hollywood and knocked on every door in the music industry until someone would give her a chance. She interned while in college and loved every minute of it. After she finished, she was hired on with the boys' label. Then she met Thomas."

This was more than anyone had spoken about her to this point. I itched to have my sketchbook but it would be difficult to sketch and help her around the kitchen at the same time.

"Thomas was her supervisor and she fell madly in love with the man. He was older than her, experienced. She was naïve, and there was nothing I could say to change her mind when she decided to marry him. At least they were married here."

I thought about the wedding album. Their wedding happened in a beautiful place. It looked like one of the nearby plantations.

"She and I weren't real close during that time. I had a hard time keeping my mouth shut about Thomas. He was aloof around me, didn't say much and didn't want her coming home often. Devon wasn't happy about it either. After he and the boys had formed the band, they sent her some recordings and she flew them all out there. Devon was sorry to leave me, but we both thought it would be good for him to be near her, make sure she was okay. He couldn't stay home and take care of me forever, now could he?"

She turned to me and smiled that sad smile. She was trying so hard to do the best she could by her son despite her sadness. I admired her for that.

"So they all went out to California and made it big?"

She snickered. "Yes, I suppose. Although at first Maggie was just a gopher for Thomas. She went behind his back to play the demo she'd had the boys record for one of the executives. They went wild and gave her a big promotion. Thomas was furious when he found out. Even though he tried to keep his thumb on her, my Maggie was destined for greatness." There was pride in her voice, and maybe even a little envy that her daughter was willing to fight for her own career when Mrs. Boudreaux had not.

"The boys put out their first album about eight months after they left here, and they've toured nonstop for most of the last four years. I hardly saw any of them. Devon sent me money every time they were paid. He probably sent me *all* of his money.

"I worried about him. I knew he was having fun, sowing his oats in a way. But they were all drinking a lot, and from what I understand, there were drugs going around. Maggie assured me she had it under control, that she was looking out for them."

I had been watching her closely and as she said this last part, she gripped the counter hard, her knuckles turning white. Very quietly she said, "I guess no one was looking out for her."

I walked over to her and handed her another tissue. I stood next to her, trying to will her some strength. "It must have been so hard to be away from them and know something wasn't right. Who did you have for support?"

She frowned. "Why would *I* have needed support?"

Okay, maybe I was going about this the wrong way.

"I guess I meant...did you talk to anyone about your concerns? Did Daryl know what was going on?"

She nodded, understanding now where I was coming from. "He knew. He went out there a couple of times and tried talking to all of them, but they was surrounded by people who only cared about how much money they was making off of my kids." She grew tense.

"Daryl told Maggie she needed to get things under control or he was going to bring the boys back to New Orleans to clean them up. She begged him not to and said she'd get them to clean up their act. Things were better for a while, until a few months before the accident. There was so much pressure on them with their new album coming out. They were promoting it around the clock. Every time I talked to Devon, he was exhausted and irritable. He wasn't my little boy anymore. I knew that. But the man he'd become was not the warm and loving young man I'd raised. That part of him is back, now that he's away from all that insanity out there, but his sadness and guilt are weighing him down."

I nodded and looked toward the door, where I could hear raised voices that didn't sound playful. "He's in a lot of pain. And it's going to get worse before it gets better, I'm afraid. But if I can get him to talk about what happened, maybe it will help."

When I looked back at Mrs. Boudreaux, she had turned those blues on me like a spotlight. "I think he'll listen to you, Jaylene. He's very taken with you." She studied me for a minute, and then smiled warmly. "And I can see why. I think we're *all* taken with you." She squeezed my arm gently. "Thanks for listening to an old woman prattle on."

"You are far from being an old woman, Mrs. Boudreaux. And thank you. I've been treated like a queen since I met Daryl, and now these guys. I've been more spoiled this past year than ever."

She laughed. "Well, you deserve every bit of it. And while I'm not too sure about tattoos, I have to admit what you do is incredibly beautiful. You've got a lot of talent, sugar." I blushed and thanked her. "And if I'm not an old woman, then you better start calling me Marie or I'm going to continue with that delusion."

I laughed and agreed.

The oven timer dinged, saving me from further embarrassment, and I hurried to help Marie get things set up for the deluge of the cavemen. I told her about breakfast that first morning and how I was afraid for my life if I got between them and the food, and she cracked up.

"Oh, you should have seen what they were like when they were growing up. All five of them boys kept my pantry empty. I was cooking all day at the restaurant and then cooking when I got home and it was never enough. Especially when Devon hit his growth spurt? Lord! He went from being five-six to six-six in just over two years. I couldn't keep him in clothes and shoes, much less food!"

She had a flair for storytelling once she loosened up. It tickled me to see her smiling and laughing. We got the food set up buffet style and I went out to tell the boys.

The scene I entered was not a good one. Marcus and Devon were facing off, Marcus yelling in his face. Jade yelled at Marcus to back off, which didn't help diffuse the situation. Star and Mage sat with their heads down, trying to ignore the tension.

"Why can't you just hear him out, Marcus? It's okay for us to throw in some different sounds, man. Isn't that what we're doing this for?" Jade was red in the face, but Marcus was redder.

"Jade, if I want your opinion, I'll fucking ask for it. Pipe down."

Devon stepped closer to him and lowered his voice. "Marcus, you're being an ass. Be mad at me, I don't give a fuck. But don't talk to your brother that way. We'll work this out, alright?"

He put his guitar back on the stand and walked past me to the back door, his cigarettes already in hand.

I watched him walk past and then turned to Marcus. "Hey, Marcus, can I talk to you for a minute?" He looked irritated but followed me upstairs to the rumpus room and plopped down on the couches. I got us each a water bottle from the fridge and heard Marie come out and tell the other guys to come eat.

Marcus threw his head back against the couch and let out a huge sigh. "I know, I know. I'm an asshole. Go ahead and say it."

I sat down across from him on the ottoman and handed him a bottle. He uncapped it and took a huge drink.

"I wasn't going to say that."

He frowned at me and rolled his eyes. "Then what? I can't carry this. They don't want to listen to me. The label is expecting Maggie's Bones, not Maggie's Shell of a Band. And Devon's head isn't in the game. He's so miserable he can only play miserable shit, and that's not us. We do angry. We do slutty. We don't do heartbroken."

"I hear you. So what do we do to get them in a better frame of mind?"

He looked at me shrewdly, like maybe I was an ally instead of just one more person to bite his head off. "You got ideas, I'm all ears. I thought bringing them home might help, but fuck, I don't know. You being here at least got D out of his catatonic state. He can't keep wallowing. It's not helping anyone."

I took a breath and calmed myself. It was infuriating sitting here listening to him piss and moan about how this was everyone else's fault, but I needed to get him focused on solutions. "Okay. So he's not catatonic. The other guys are starting to talk a little. How about you? Are you ready to talk? Because I don't see how pretending like you can all just move on is going to fix things." I hoped he didn't take that as an attack.

He looked away and closed his eyes, leaning forward to put his head in his hands. "I know. You're right. I just felt like she died and I was left trying to keep us all from drowning. No one else was in any shape to lead and the label was like, 'Wow, we're sorry for your loss. Now get back to work and make us some money.'"

He finished the rest of his water in one gulp. He looked ready to get down to business. "Alright, Tattoo Girl. What do you suggest?"

I was so hoping he would ask me that.

"For one, I think last night was a good idea. Trying to blow off some steam seems to have helped at least get people waking up, am I right?" He nodded. "So even though it seems counterproductive, I think more fun might help get things moving again."

I had a crazy idea that I thought just might get them out of their mindset and back to their boyish ways. Marcus's eyes lit up and he belly-laughed when I told him.

"I love the way you think, girl. I'll make the call right now."

I really hoped this worked. I went downstairs and fixed a plate of food for each of us and brought them back upstairs.

"So you'll get it all here? How soon? Okay. The sooner the better. Thanks, Uncle Daryl." He hung up and grinned wickedly at me. "Baby girl, we gonna start us a war."

I clapped my hands together. I couldn't wait to get started.

We talked strategy over our meal and then Marcus and I went downstairs to tell Marie we'd clean up later and that she'd probably want to get out of there as soon as possible. She looked confused, but I assured her I had a plan.

She kissed me on the cheek before she picked up her purse and headed out. "Good luck, sugar."

I waved to her from the back door and spotted Devon in the corner smoking. He said goodbye to his mama and then we were alone.

"You guys seem to have had a nice talk." He only sort of seemed happy about that. I walked over and sat next to him, kicking his foot with mine.

"We had a great talk, and no, I won't tell you what we talked about." I grinned at him and he just shook his head, taking a long drag on his cigarette. I could tell this was not his first. "Did you get some dinner?" I asked.

He shook his head, so I urged him to go make a plate. He looked over at me with those sad eyes and I hoped again that my plan worked.

"I'll go eat. Then we'll probably practice some more." He groaned. "I'm sick of this already. I hate fighting with him."

I leaned over and kissed him on the cheek. "You guys will find a way. I'm going back inside, gotta go check my messages. See you in a while." I bounded off, leaving him with a look of complete bewilderment.

I ran upstairs, happy to see the other guys were busy eating and arguing by the bar. Maybe they wouldn't see what we were about to do.

I found Marcus and Daryl out on the balcony. "This is the best I could come up with, chère. Think this will work?"

I nodded, excited. "It's perfect. Now if you can just get the fog machine and strobe lights set up and then hit the lights, we'll take it from there."

Daryl appeared to be having a hard time containing his amusement. He and Marcus stared at me like I'd sprouted a second head.

"Trust me, guys. This will get them working together and hopefully get them to get out of their heads a little."

They both shook *their* heads. "You're either a true genius or out of your pretty little mind. Alright, dahlin'. I'll do my part, you two go get ready."

I grabbed Marcus's hand and we inched along the gangway to his room, trying to be as quiet as possible. We quickly put on the black coveralls over our clothes and night-vision goggles. We checked our equipment and made sure we had enough ammo. Then we crept silently to the rumpus room, where Marcus queued up the music and waited for the signal that Daryl was ready.

As soon as he hit the lights, I heard shouts from downstairs.

"What the fuck?"

"What happened to the lights?"

"Shit, I can't see anything down here!"

We heard them banging into stuff and yelling out names.

Marcus and I signaled to each other to split up. With our night-vision goggles, we could see the guys flailing around.

I took aim with my gun and hit Mage in the thigh.

"Holy shit! Someone's shooting at us. Ow, what the..."

The strobe lights started and Mage was wiping at his leg, finding fluorescent paint.

"What the hell is going on in here?" I heard Devon coming in the back door and I couldn't resist. I let one fly, hitting the wall next to him. "What the fuck?"

Just then, Marcus's maniacal laugh came over a bullhorn. "Alright, you weenies! Find your gear. It's hidden in plain sight. Last one standing wins a prize to be named later."

Then Slipknot's "Spit it Out" started screaming from the stereo. A spotlight came on, illuminating a pile of coveralls and guns and goggles.

"Marcus, you son of a bitch! I'm going to nail your ass." Devon was the first one to the pile, followed by Star, and they scurried out of the light to get dressed. Marcus and I took random shots to keep them moving.

Mage was still yelling about his leg. "That hurt, motherfucker! I'm going to get you, Lambert!"

More maniacal laughing.

That's good, Marcus. Keep them coming after you so I can sneak up on them.

I crept quietly around the gangway, looking for my next victim. Jade was dressed and started yelling, "Where are you, Marcus? Dammit, I can't see anything." By this time, the fog machine had filled the downstairs and the strobe lights made it tough to see anything in front of your face. I had the urge to cough but knew they might hear me.

Suddenly, Devon broke out and ran across the floor. I took two shots but missed. I could hear him laughing as he ducked behind the bar and then shot back. He missed me by several feet but I kept my chuckle to myself.

Jade stood helplessly in the middle of the floor looking around. I couldn't resist nailing him in the ass when he turned around.

"Ow! Man! That's not fair, I can't see anything! *Marcus!*"

Hearing his whiny voice and watching him rub his poor little tushy was too much. I couldn't help the giggle that burst out.

"Is that you, Jaylene? Are you a part of this too?" Mage was yelling at me.

I giggled some more and then ran for cover. Shots were fired in my direction but they all missed. I dove behind the couch and waited, trying to smother my laughter. This was working perfectly. I could hear Star and Mage strategizing and I heard footsteps pounding on both sets of stairs.

I ran into their room and hid behind the door. When Star came in and his back was to me, I couldn't resist but to pop him one in the calf, where I hoped it wouldn't hurt too much. These coveralls were padded but the paintballs didn't feel good. As he spun around, trying to find his attacker, I snuck into the bathroom and out the door into the adjoining bedroom. I heard his voice go out into the hall so I waited for a few minutes before I attempted to sneak out.

I heard shouts and laughter from all over the building. I was elated that they were working together, even if it *was* to find Marcus and "destroy him."

I was just about to the door when arms closed around me from behind and a hand covered my mouth. I froze and felt lips at my ear.

"Well, well. Look who I've found here with her guard down." Devon turned me in his arms and flipped up his goggles, and then mine, before disarming me. Then he laid a victorious kiss on me that left me gasping.

I couldn't see him in the dark but his hands were all over me. He turned us around and backed me into the wall, picked me up, and wrapped my legs around his waist.

"Devon, oh...mmmmmmm...," I panted, my whole body alert.

He murmured softly against my skin while he nipped and sucked at my exposed neck. His hand came around the front and cupped my breast through the coveralls, thrilling me to my toes. My hands grabbed frantically at his biceps, which were fully flexed as he pressed me into the wall. He rocked ever so slightly against me and I could feel him becoming incredibly aroused.

My breathing started to get out of control. I tapped him on the arm and he dropped his head to my shoulder. We both tried to catch our breath, not letting go, not moving from this sensual position. I couldn't believe he'd hoisted me up with little to no effort. His muscles didn't even feel like they were straining.

"I think I caught you, chère. What's my prize?" he whispered, rubbing his lips gently against mine.

I smiled wide. "You haven't nailed me yet."

I could faintly see his eyes in the dark. They were practically glowing with excitement. "That's true, chère. And I would so love to."

I giggled and wiggled to get him to let me down. When he did, I reached up and kissed him softly. "Fourteen more days, remember?"

He pouted and I nibbled at his lower lip. He groaned in frustration. His hands grabbed my ass and he pulled me against him firmly. I tried to stifle a moan but it escaped anyway. I was in danger of falling for his seduction if I didn't get away from him.

I had to distract him. "I know of one way to make this sweeter."

He pulled back from kissing my neck, which I thoroughly enjoyed, and whispered, "Going to my room and locking the door? Unzipping those damn coveralls with my teeth?"

I was panting again. I had to take control of the situation before I let him do just that. I grabbed his face to still him. "While that sounds delectable, let's focus on the task at hand. Let's. Get. Marcus."

He smiled wide and that evil glint in his eye had me even more turned on. "If I can't have my prize, that's a perfectly acceptable consolation." He handed me back my gun and swapped me for the night vision. "Follow me, chère. I know just where he is."

We crept out the door and heard Mage yell, "You can't hide forever, Lambert."

Just then I saw Devon's head swing to the left and I followed his line of sight. Marcus was over by my doorway, directly across from us.

Devon crept up to the railing and knelt down soundlessly. He took aim and let three paintballs fly.

All three hit Marcus in the chest.

"Damn you, Boudreaux. You were always a better shot than me. Very well, I surrender."

With that, the lights came back on and we could hear Daryl laughing. The other three guys were staring up at us in awe. Marcus pulled off his night vision and laughed, looking down at his shots.

Jade looked up at me with a completely befuddled expression. "Jaylene? You were in on this?"

I smiled. "Hey, you guys needed some fun. What better way to blow off some steam than a little paintball action?" I tried for an innocent look but they started grumbling.

"How come no one hit *her*? Girls don't get special treatment in this game!" Mage had his hands on his hips.

Star laughed. "That's why she hit you first." Everyone fell into peals of laughter until we were all groaning and in pain.

I raised my hands in surrender. "Hey, Devon caught and disarmed me. Technically that makes him the winner."

They all smiled knowingly. "Oh, I bet he disarmed you," snickered Star to the guys downstairs.

Marcus and I shared a wink across the room and he mouthed, "Thank you." I nodded back to him.

Devon leaned down and whispered in my ear, "Don't think you're off the hook, chère. I still get to claim my prize." He swatted my behind as he walked by me and I was sure my cheeks turned five shades of crimson.

The guys took off their coveralls and dumped them in a big pile. Daryl opened the windows upstairs to air out the smoke and Jade opened the back door. We dropped our equipment on top of the pile and the guys were still looking at me in disbelief.

"Wherever did you learn how to shoot like that, Jaylene?" Mage seemed irked to have been bested by a girl.

"My old shop mates back home and I used to go paintballing at least once a month. It was serious business. I was the only girl so if I wanted to keep up, I had to learn to be better than them. Story of my life." I shrugged and looked innocent. They weren't buying it.

"Just you wait 'til we take you back to Houma to our old stomping grounds. There's no way you can beat us there." Jade hi-fived Mage and they started plotting in whispered voices.

Star came over and fist-bumped me. "Nicely played, Tattoo Girl." I winked at him and he went upstairs to wash off the paint that had splattered him in the face. I was glad no one had gotten hit in an uncomfortable place.

"So what now?" Marcus asked the guys when Star returned. They looked around at each other. He was trying to give them an option, as hard as it was for him to give up control. He was making an effort.

Devon jumped on it. "Let's try something. Hey, Mage? Remember that bass line you used on 'Feeling Your Pain?' Hit that for me, would ya?"

Mage hurried over and plugged in his bass. The other guys followed and picked up their instruments.

Marcus came up behind me and held up a hand for a sly hi-five. I nonchalantly hit him up and he leaned in, whispering, "I like the way your mind works, girl. Let's see what happens now." I nodded.

Mage had a strong rhythm going and Devon played a riff that was completely hot. It was one of those songs that just grabbed you by your spleen and yanked you in. Star began drumming a simple beat and then added in some complex rhythms. Jade managed to harmonize with what Devon was laying down. Marcus's face lit up and he gazed at them like a proud papa.

They played on for what seemed like an hour, changing it up, adding parts, and it grew and grew into a monster of a jam. Marcus furiously scribbled notes on his pad.

When they stopped and huddled, I grabbed for my sketchbook and did my own form of creation. None of my drawings made any sense tonight. They were just random images. I felt like the band's energy was feeding me.

They worked for another hour on the song. Marcus even added some pretty crazy lyrics, obviously inspired by tonight's fun.

There is no light, there's only sound
The noises screaming, boots they pound
I hear your breath
I feel your panic
This time I'll win, you'll hit the ground

You are the Hunted
There will be no tomorrow
You are the Hunted
No days to follow
You are the Hunted
All your pride you swallow
You are the Hunted

And when tomorrow comes
You will surrender
You will be mine
Mine alone forever...

"Those are rough, guys, but I think this whole thing sounds pretty badass. Jaylene, what do you think?"

I was absorbed in my drawing and didn't hear the question.

The bullhorn, unfortunately, had been left behind when Daryl packed up.

"JAYLENE CHARLES, YOU HAVE BEEN QUESTIONED. HOW DO YOU ANSWER?"

Mage's voice scared the shit out of me and I dropped my sketchbook on the floor, nearly falling on my ass out of the chair I had reclined onto two legs with my feet on the table.

"Thanks for that. Um, what do I think? I agree. Badass territory. But I'll just have it be known that a girl bested nearly all of you. Maybe *you* should be the 'Hunted.'"

I laughed at my own joke and the other guys chuckled. Except Devon, he shared a particularly sinful smile with me that turned my cheeks hot.

"I could turn it around, sure. Let me think about that. Not a bad idea to let the ladies have control from time to time, don't you guys agree?"

I rolled my eyes. Lothario Lambert was back. "Seriously, Marcus? Does that shit work in real life with women who have no idea you're a rock star? I'd love to think it doesn't." I was still scribbling when he walked over.

"I certainly haven't had any complaints." The guys all pulled up chairs and decided to take a break. Devon passed out water bottles and Jade brought out some cheese and cracker platters Marie must have put together and left in cold storage.

Hmmm, I kind of liked that cold storage.

"Do you give them any time to complain?" I really didn't want to have this conversation with him. I was enjoying Marcus on a Mission earlier tonight. I'd say mission accomplished.

Thankfully, Star changed the subject. "So what time is Sherry coming in tomorrow?"

Marcus frowned. "You know, I don't remember what she said. I'll have to check my texts. But we've got at least three or four solid tunes to play for her, you think?" They all nodded and murmured their agreement. "We've made progress. It might tide them over, but it means we've got to really get on it this week. What do you guys think?"

Mage spoke up. "I'm all for the hard work. I think we can do it. My question is, are we going for a focus on this album? Or are we just throwing together random songs that sound okay? Because I feel like we have the beginnings of a really solid concept coming. I mean, so far the songs are kind of about us, right? D's song, this one tonight is about our journey. Well, that and Jaylene kicking our asses."

There were some grumbles of reluctant appreciation. Who were they kidding? They'd had a blast. But Mage was on a tangent.

"The other two, well, they reflect Marcus's insatiable side." This prompted giggles. "But if we want to make this about us, what if we really get into it, man? What if we all spill here, get our shit out there? About Maggie? About the shit we were doing in L.A. before things got bad? About where we want to be? I think we can really make this meaningful if we do."

There was some shuffling of feet and some clearing of throats. What he was proposing was going to be painful for all of them.

"What do you think, guys? We've been through some shit, for real. Let's just fucking get it out and put it out there."

The others remained quiet but pensive. I could feel their minds churning.

"If we do that, we need to be willing to take it if the critics and fans hate it. If we're getting that personal, can we take it if they slam us?" Marcus brought up a valid point.

"I'm so beyond that right now." Star was doing that thing with his hair, making it stand up all over. "So what if they criticize us? It's not like they've never experienced pain and loss. Hell, a bunch of our fans have either been through rehab or need to go. I for one think if my story would help one person *not* have to feel like this, it would be worth it. Who gives a shit about the charts or the label?"

I meant to stay quiet during this conversation. But... "Star, that's really brave." I said it just above a whisper and his grateful smile told me he needed to hear it. "You guys have all been haunted by what happened, as well as other things. Putting it out there will be tough... but might feel extremely rewarding."

Five sets of eyes bored into me. I felt myself shrinking back into my chair. Did I just blow it? I only wanted to encourage them.

"Anyone else just completely in love with this woman right now?" Jade's emotions came through in his soft tone. Star was sitting next to me and leaned over to give me a hug and kiss me on the cheek.

"Absofuckinglutely. Haunted. That's brilliant." Mage looked at me knowingly and mouthed, "Told you."

Devon's deep blues were on me, but this time sadness wasn't

pouring out. It felt more like determination. I smiled at him and he sent a hopeful smile right back, wordlessly letting me know that loving me was pretty on the mark for him.

The realization hit me like a gentle wave, working its way through me. I'm sure I was blushing again.

Marcus remained quiet and slowly the focus moved from me to him. He appeared to be contemplating in a business-like manner whether this would be a good idea.

Devon kicked his chair. "You're awful quiet over there, Marcus. What do you think?"

Marcus's eyes didn't waver from me. "The question, Jaylene, is what do *you* think? Are you willing to go there with us?"

My heart felt heavy in my chest. Was he testing me? Did he think I wasn't up to the task?

"I'm willing to go wherever you guys need to go. I want to listen to your stories. All of them. I'll hold your hand. I'll let you cry on my shoulder. I'll even let you yell and scream at me. But I can't fix anything. Only you guys can fix things. And there's no guarantees you'll get an album out of it, although it seems to me like you've all got something really beautiful to say." My voice sounded calm but I was panicking inside.

Could I really do this and not let them down? Gods, give me the strength, because I wanted them to do this.

"I trust you, chère."

Devon's words shattered me. Spoken in such a husky voice, his feelings were right there on the surface.

Star grabbed my hand and said, "Me too, Jaylene. I trust you. You've been so good to us." Star was fast becoming one of my favorite people. His belief in me did a lot to make me feel competent to do this with them.

Jade swallowed hard. "Count me in, too. Maybe if we do this, then we can quit being so mad at each other all the time." It struck me how childlike Jade sounded when he was stressed. So vulnerable.

Marcus looked at Mage, who was standing with his arms crossed. "No-brainer for me, man. I already told y'all she's got some of the Gift in her. I don't ever question that." I wish I knew what the hell he could see that I couldn't.

"Well, then it's settled" Marcus said with a shrug. "Who's going first?"

They all looked at each other, wide-eyed.

When no one spoke, I offered a solution.

"It might not work for you guys to just jump in and start talking. I do have another idea. How about you guys each take a photo album and pick out your favorite picture of Maggie? Pull it out; here, you can use these sticky notes to mark the spot." I handed each of them a small pack of stickies I'd found in the back office, along with a pen.

"When you find one, think about what was happening in the picture or your favorite memory of her. I'll hang up some poster board on the wall, and you guys put the picture up on the board, with a few notes beneath it with the memory. That will give you guys a place to start and it will give *me* some more information about her. Because see—you've shared a few pieces with me, so has Marie. But I don't *see* her yet. I want to see her. I may have tattooed her once, but I didn't at all get to know her like you did."

The guys all grabbed albums, chatting and laughing with each other. Except Devon. "Jaylene, would you come outside with me, please?" He held up his cigarettes.

Aha. I nodded, grabbed my water, and followed him down the hall. Star looked up, concerned when he saw the pace Devon had set. I waved at him and he went back to his photo album.

Devon pushed open the door hard and the dark night sky greeted us. It dawned on me that I hadn't been outside much the past few days. I was kind of missing the sun. I made a mental note to find a way to spend time outside every day, no matter what was going on. Vitamin D —kind of important.

When Devon turned to look at me, his face was a mask of anger and hurt. "What did you mean when you said you tattooed her? What are you talking about?" He was really agitated. His hands shook when he lit his smoke. He took a long drag and then blew it out with his eyes closed. When he turned those intense blues on me this time, I felt like I was at the cop shop being interrogated. I fidgeted where I stood.

"I forgot you weren't in the room when I realized that yesterday. Back in December, Daryl asked me to come to his place to tattoo someone for him. He wasn't there, just her. And she told me her name was Meg Stone."

The memory was coming back to me more vividly, now that I'd seen her picture. Another reason I had no idea she could be Devon's sister was that they looked nothing alike. Her hair was a dark golden blonde, and curly. It was nothing like Devon's straight black hair. Marie and Devon looked so much alike. I guessed Maggie favored their father.

Devon paced, growing more agitated as he sucked down half a cigarette in one drag. This likely wouldn't be the last one he smoked while we were out here. "So what happened?" he asked, his voice cracking. "What did she say to you?"

I couldn't tell what had him so upset. I wanted to tell him the rest of the story and then maybe I could help him figure it out.

"I got there and she was alone. Daryl and Katie were out with the girls. She told me what she wanted, a fleur-de-lis with angel wings, something to remind her of home. She told me she'd grown up here but was now living in California. We talked a little about California, places we liked. We talked about college. She never said what she did for work. She mentioned she'd sort of had to run away to make the trip, that her husband wasn't pleased she'd left, since he didn't see anything good about Louisiana."

Devon grunted. "Thomas came out for the wedding and bitched about it the whole time. They left immediately after the reception and never came back. At least, I didn't *know* she'd come back." His eyes were wet but he was still pacing angrily. "They got married three years ago and she barely saw Mama after that. He never wanted her to go anywhere without him."

There was venom in his voice when he talked about her husband. He fell silent, his gaze urging me to tell him the rest.

"The tattoo was on her right hip. She didn't want it to show, she wanted it to be just for her. She said her husband was going to throw a fit but she didn't care. She missed home and wanted a piece of it to carry with her."

Devon stopped pacing and stared down at me where I sat on the bench. He growled and cursed under his breath. "Why didn't she ever tell me she came home? I would have come with her. He had her so fucking tied up in knots all the time. She had to sneak around to do what she wanted to do. *Goddamn him!* I swear, I never want to see that fucker again as long as I live!" His anger was so fierce. It was tangible in the air.

"What happened to him? After the accident?"

He turned on me, his eyes full of hate. "What the fuck do you *think* happened to a rich white dude? He got fucking probation, some community-service bullshit. Not even enough of a fine to be a pretend slap on the wrist." He wiped at his eyes and ran his forearm under his nose. "His goddamn lawyer got the blood test thrown out in court and without that, it was just an accident. He fucking *killed her* and he's out there living his life!"

He stopped and shook his head, rested his hands on his hips for a minute. Then he took out his pack and smacked it hard against his hand.

I'd known this anger had to be inside him, but I was surprised at the vehemence in his voice. It was gone almost as soon as it surfaced, though, and his next words were sorrowful.

"The funny part is...I'm the one who should have paid. I'm the one who sent her off with him that night." His voice broke and he threw the pack against the wall. He collapsed onto a bench and dropped his head into his hands, which then pulled viciously at his hair. "If only I wasn't such a dick that night."

His body was trembling wildly. I hurried to his side and put my hand on his back, gently rubbing circles between his shoulder blades.

This was pain. Pure, guilt-laden suffering poured out of him. I wished I could take it all away. "If you could change anything about that night, Devon, what would you have done differently?"

His breathing slowed down a little as he tried to get himself back under control. "I sure as hell wouldn't have been so drunk. I wouldn't have tried to talk to Richard about why he was remixing guitar parts at the last minute at that party. And when Maggie intervened, I never would have yelled at her like I did." He looked up at me, his eyes blood-shot in the patio lights. "I killed my sister, Jaylene. As sure as I told her off, I sent her to her death."

I held his face in my hands and he closed his eyes, trying to pull away. He wasn't successful. "Devon, did Maggie listen to you? You know, when she was making decisions about her own life?"

He looked at me, puzzled. "No. I was her little brother. She could boss me around all she wanted but she'd blow me off anytime I tried to talk to her about anything to do with her life." His eyes searched mine for a clue as to where I was going with this.

"So if she never took advice from her little brother, what makes you think she would have listened to you that night? Especially if she thought you were being unreasonable?"

He cocked his head to the side. "Yeah, but...if I wasn't so out of control, I would've made sure she didn't get into the car with him when he was high. That guy snorted so much coke, his brain should be completely gone by now. But she was going to do what she was going to do." He seemed so heartbroken.

"You just said it, Devon. She was going to do what she was going to do. Had you voiced your concerns to her about him? Had anyone?"

He nodded. "All the time. We were okay with him when they were just dating but as soon as they moved in together, he became a total control freak. She didn't make a move without his permission, especially not after she went behind his back and got us signed. That's when things got *really* bad. She tried desperately to get him to forgive her for that."

"Devon, women who are in relationships like that rarely take the advice of the people who love them, especially if their partners convince them that their families are out to keep them apart. She had to want out herself. It doesn't sound like she was ready to get out. Especially when I met her. She was still head over heels in love with him and wanted desperately to please him. Sadly, I don't think you or anyone else could have gotten through to her until she was ready."

His pain was so heavy. He took a shuddering breath and dropped his head from my hands to my shoulder. I smoothed back his hair, just trying to ease him however I could.

"I feel like I failed her. If I could have just talked to her, made her listen to me... Maybe she would have started taking better care of herself. Maybe she wouldn't have gotten in the car with him that night."

His voice was so weak it was breaking my heart. I took in a shallow breath and said what I knew he had to hear.

"Maybe. Or maybe she would have told you off, and cut you out of her life because she felt like you didn't understand, didn't support her. I've seen it happen, Devon. I don't know that anything you did could have changed things at that point."

He looked up at me again, resignation starting to show in his eyes. I opened my arms to him and he leaned into me, letting me hug him and stroke his shoulder. Devon being so much taller made it a little awkward but I held him to me and willed some solace into him.

"I miss her," he whispered, his voice gone.

"I know, baby. I'm so sorry you lost her."

He squeezed his eyes shut and heaved a huge sigh. We sat like that for a while, until he seemed to be breathing normally again.

"I'm glad I got to meet her. I do recall she had an infectious energy about her."

He took one last deep breath and the shuddering stopped. "She would have loved you. She would have tried to convince you to move to L.A., change your style and possibly your name, and convince you the stars belonged to you, because you were that good." He chuckled sadly. "In your case, she'd be right." He wiped his eyes with the bottom of his shirt and took one more deep breath. When he turned to me, his smile was terribly sad but hopeful. "Thanks, chère. I know I needed that, but it fucking hurts."

I gave him a squeeze. "I know. It's like when annoying people always say 'the things in life that are painful are more worth it' or some shit like that. Whatever."

He chuckled again and turned in my arms to put his forehead against mine. "You're amazing, Jaylene. I feel like I can talk to you and I'm not going to die. It still hurts, but I can breathe when I'm with you. I don't know what I would have done if I hadn't met you." He reached up and grazed my cheek with his thumb.

I leaned forward and kissed his lower lip gently. "You are a brave man. I'm so glad I can be here for you. I just want you to feel better."

He breathed out hard. "How much better?"

This time I bit his lower lip. "You and this lip of yours are going to be in trouble if you don't behave."

He groaned. "But you make it so hard to be good." He stuck his lip out farther into a ridiculously sexy pout.

"Ugh, really? That was a Marcus Moment if I ever saw one."

He grabbed me and pulled me onto his lap, laughing. "He would be proud of that one." He kissed me on the nose and then I stood up.

"Alright, Mr. Boudreaux. Time to get back to work. You haven't picked out a picture yet." I might have swung my hips a little excessively as I walked to the door. This time I was *sure* he groaned.

"You're killing me, Miss Charles. If I don't behave, will I get detention?"

I turned on him, one eyebrow raised pointedly. "No preferential treatment for you. Get inside, mister, or no more private tutoring."

He jumped up and hurried inside. "Yes, ma'am. I'll be a good boy from now on." He winked as he scooted past me and I couldn't resist kicking him in his perfect ass.

"Ow! I didn't think corporal punishment was allowed in school anymore." He ran into the room rubbing his backside, laughing. The other guys were huddled over a bunch of pictures. They barely looked up as we came in.

"Remember this one? Wasn't this when Uncle Daryl caught her and Katie driving around in Aunt Marie's car without a license?" Jade was showing Marcus a picture and they were all laughing. "He was so pissed at them both. Maggie just kissed him on his cheek and said 'Sorry Uncle Daryl, we were just having fun.' He totally forgave her, too. Not like when *we* got caught doing the same thing."

Marcus was holding the picture and shaking his head. "But remember, Jade, they were like sixteen when they did it—we were thirteen and fourteen. And it was his *Cadillac*. Kind of a difference from Aunt Marie's Ford Taurus." There were more snickers.

Mage held up one for the others to look at. "I remember this one. This was when we were going to Homecoming our freshman year and

Maggie was a senior. Remember? She got her group of friends to take us. Man, I was sporting wood most of that night. Marcus was the only one who even got close to scoring." Mage said that last with disgust.

The picture was of the four boys dressed in slacks and dress shirts with ties on. Four older girls, including Maggie, were wearing very mature dresses. The boys all looked adorable, fairly clean cut, with the exception of Marcus's remaining mullet. Maggie was posed with Star and he looked like he was flying. Jade was standing with Katie, and the other two girls I didn't recognize.

I frowned, confused. "So you four were all in the same grade?"

They nodded. "Yeah. Marcus's birthday is in January so he's the oldest, and mine followed in November, just making the cut-off, so we were in the same classes." Jade seemed much younger but birth order had a lot to do with that.

I turned and looked at Devon. "Where were you that night?"

He shrugged. "Probably taking the pictures, I don't know."

Marcus snorted. "Yeah, I told you, Devon had no interest in girls in high school. He was a year ahead of us and we rarely got him to go out to dances. He was eating, sleeping, and breathing music and his car."

I looked back and smiled. "I've heard about this car. Do you still have it?"

He gave me a half smile but I saw the excitement in his eyes. "I do. She's back in Houma. I couldn't bring myself to get rid of her."

I secretly hoped I'd get to see it before this was all over.

That thought left me with a sick feeling. When this was all over.

No matter what Devon said, when my contract was up, they'd all go back to business as usual. I'd be here, doing my thing without them. I felt unbelievably sad all of a sudden. I looked around for a clock. "What time is it, anyway?"

Mage had a watch on. "It's three already. Shit. No wonder this has felt like the longest day ever. I need sleep. Can we finish this in the morning?"

I nodded and also turned to go upstairs, calling "good night, guys," over my shoulder. They called back and I heard chairs scraping as they got up to follow.

I went straight to my room and dropped off my sketchbook before going into the bathroom.

"Oops." Devon said as we both entered at the same time. "You first."

He shut his door and I locked it, did my nighttime routine, and then opened his door. "All yours, Devon." He stepped to the door in just his jeans, shirt off.

I sighed and turned to leave. It was a shame to have to walk away from that.

"Thanks. And thanks for earlier...I'm sorry I dumped all that on you."

I turned to look at him from the doorway. "You don't ever have to apologize for confiding in me, Devon. I want you to be able to talk to me."

He gave me a small smile, his hands resting on his hips. Another sigh.

"Good night."

"You too. Sleep well, chère." It was obvious neither of us wanted to go our separate ways but I closed the door and a moment later, I heard the lock click.

I fell asleep as soon as my head hit the pillow. I was exhausted from these past couple of days. My feelings for Devon had also left me drained. There were only so many ups and downs my emotions could take on so little sleep.

But I was not meant for sleep that night.

About an hour later, I heard Devon scream next door. I ran in to find him on his hands and knees on the floor next to the bed. "God, No. Not, Maggie! Please, please..."

I crouched down next to him and touched his shoulder, unsure if he was awake from his dream. He instantly collapsed and curled up with his head in my lap, his arms crushing me to him.

"Please...please no...!" He kept repeating it over and over.

Star opened the door and helped me get Devon back onto the bed.

"I'll stay with him. Thank you, Star."

I let Devon wrap himself around me and I held him, stroking his back and trying to calm him. He still hadn't fully awakened. He was crying and shaking. It took another few minutes until his breathing leveled out and he was back to sleep. Obviously our discussion had hit him hard and his subconscious wasn't done dealing with it.

The room eventually started to grow lighter with the rising sun. I looked at Devon to find him finally at peace. I smiled and kissed his forehead.

He snuggled closer—and then opened one eye in surprise.

"Jaylene? Hmmmm, Jaylene. I thought I was dreaming. Am I dreaming?"

I smiled at him. "No, it's me. You were having a bad dream. Are you okay now?"

He nodded. "No bad dreams. Not with you here."

I smiled. He was so adorable. His hair spilled over his cheeks and his lips curled into a smile as he pulled me closer. In minutes he was back asleep, snoring softly.

Lying with him like this was bittersweet. He was still painfully beautiful to look at, but even more so now, because I knew that as much fun as we were having and as much as he thought he was going to be with me when this was over, I couldn't feel confident in that.

Before the moment was totally ruined for me, he shifted again, rolling onto his back and pulling me across his chest. I waited until he was snoring again before trying to extricate myself.

Once out of his death grip, I crept downstairs, needing to be moving around. My back was stiff from lying at a weird angle and my head was spinning with all kinds of nonproductive thinking.

I ended up in the kitchen and used what I could find to put together a breakfast casserole. I put it in the oven to cook, poured myself an OJ and went out back to enjoy the rest of the sunrise. The morning was chilly but the promise of a warm spring day was in the air. Birds circled the tall ferns in the corner and others dipped into the fountain's water for a quick bath. The sky was all pinks and purples like a watercolor painting. I wished I had my sketchbook. Instead, I made myself just sit and enjoy the quiet. It did a lot to calm me.

I went back inside in time to check on the casserole and leave it in the warmer for the guys. I still had some restless energy in me so I went into their makeshift weight room, spied an iPod and headphones someone had left behind, and hit the treadmill. The music selection was decent. I chose some Queen, and was jogging at a good pace when Jade came in, dragging his feet.

"Good morning, Jaylene," he said quietly before putting his own headphones in and starting on some free weights. I waved to him and was glad I could take a few minutes longer to put my thoughts in order for the day. First, I would go upstairs and take a shower. Second, I would call Mackenzie to check in and ask her to bring a few of my sketchbooks so I could find the drawings I had done for Maggie's tattoo. I wanted to show them to the guys. Third, get these guys to finish with the pictures.

Then take my sketchbook outside and work in the sun. I wanted some time alone today and I hoped I could manage it.

I heard voices in the kitchen as I passed by. Star spotted me. "Jaylene, thith ith delishuth," he said with an obviously full mouth.

He, Mage, and Marcus were all gathered around the casserole dish, eating my creation with sighs and grunts. And no silverware. *Ew.*

"Thanks, glad you guys like it. I'm going to take a shower. Anything planned for the day besides practice?"

Mage said with an equally full mouth, "Shewy ith coming tonighth."

I nodded. "Great, I'm looking forward to meeting her. See you guys later." They waved and I was glad to see they were at least taking breaths between shoveling more food in their mouths.

I went straight to my room and promptly ran out of steam. Instead of the shower, I fell on the bed and crashed.

Sometime later, I woke up to the sound of nervous throat clearing. I opened one eye and found Mage, Jade and Star all sitting around the edge of my bed.

"Kinda creepy to be watched while you're sleeping. What time is it?"

They looked at each other and Jade cleared his voice again. "It's three-thirty. We wouldn't have woken you up, but Devon was worried when you were still sleeping and he had to go." He looked to my nightstand and nodded. "Those are from him. He wanted to give them to you himself, but he and Marcus went to pick up Sherry and take her to dinner."

On my nightstand was a gigantic bouquet of the most lovely coral and pink roses. Coral fell under the category of passion and desire, the pink for gratitude. I was curious if he knew just what message he was sending with them, then figured he probably did, since it was an unusual combination. They were unbelievably lovely.

I looked back at the guys, the stupid smile still on my face. "I'm sorry I slept so long. The last thing I remember was sitting down for a minute before I was going to take a shower."

They chuckled. "Yeah," Star said. "I guess that's what happens when you hang around with us. We don't keep a real consistent schedule. You were up the whole night, after all. I'm not surprised you needed the sleep."

I sat up and smoothed my hair back, thinking that these guys have sure seen me at my worst, and they still hadn't run for cover. "So why did just Marcus and Devon go to meet with Sherry?"

Mage answered. "They thought it would be better if they just went alone. We're not where we're supposed to be with the album and she's not going to be happy. So yeah, they're going to take the brunt of it, explain our plans."

Uh-oh. That didn't sound good. "Is she really going to be mad?" I was still confused by this whole deadline thing. "I mean, it's not like you've all been hanging out in the Bahamas, drinking fruity beverages. She can't rush genius."

They all smiled at me and I just raised my eyebrow.

"Why are you looking at me like that?"

Star blushed, his cheeks mottled with color. "You sounded a little like Maggie right then. She always stood up for us."

I crossed my arms. "Well it's true. And you have a plan, right? Right. So. Is she coming back tonight?" They nodded. "Okay, so let's finish the pictures and see what we can come up with. Then after she's gone, we can all talk some more. I have an idea but I need Mackenzie to bring me some of my books. Is that okay?"

"Sure. Of course, Mackenzie can totally come over tonight." Star bounced with excitement. I winked at him and he beamed back at me.

"Now I *really* need that shower. I'll meet you guys downstairs." They got up and left in a hurry and a minute later, I heard the three of them practicing.

I took a shower and got myself cleaned up, putting on one of my dresses. I thought I should dress up before meeting this woman. She seemed so nice when we spoke on the phone but now that I'd met the boys, I felt protective over them. They were vulnerable and sweet under their heavy-metal glamour. And they were in pain. I hoped she realized that, if she continued to push them, they would be worse off than they were now. I tried to keep myself from getting angry; I didn't know the whole story and I was just a hired hand.

After my shower, I called Mackenzie and told her what I needed.

"I'll be there. No need to ask me twice! What time?"

I told her I'd call her with a time to come over and we hung up with a giggle. I knew Star was excited to see her. I smiled at the memory of them curled up on the couches, their heads next to each other. It was a rare moment of innocence, and it made me hopeful.

Hopeful that these guys could all beat their demons and find happiness.

Before I left my room, I lightly touched the petals of the bouquet and inhaled the sweet fragrance of the roses. That man was too perfect. He was beautiful, he was thoughtful and sensitive, and if I wasn't mistaken, he was trying to charm the pants off me.

All of his actions didn't compute with the shy, awkward guy the others tried to make him out to be. He seemed to really know what he was doing. I'd always heard you needed to beware of the quiet ones. Now I knew what that meant. I was falling hard for him. I had to admit it. And this was going to hurt, a lot. But right now, it wasn't about me or my feelings. It was about getting Devon and the others on their feet so they could do what they needed to do.

Marie was in the kitchen when I went downstairs, so I asked her if I could help finish dinner. When she saw me, she grabbed me into a tight hug.

"Bless you, dear. I heard what you did for my boy last night."

I pulled back and shrugged. "He was having some sort of nightmare. Has he had these before?"

She nodded grimly. "After he came home, it seemed like every night I heard him screaming in his sleep. I would run in and find him curled up on the floor. I tried to help him but all I could do was cover him up and hope he got back to sleep. He was a wreck, tired all the time. He stopped eating. Being back here with the guys, at least that's brought his appetite back." She laughed and gave me a mischievous grin. "You *have* heard where their name came from by now, haven't you?"

I shook my head, anxious to hear. "I assumed it had something to do with Maggie."

She giggled. "They had a studio at my place, in the garage. They were trying to come up with a name for their new band. They had all these tough names like Love Blade and Universal Foe, and when they called Maggie and asked her, she snickered and told them, 'Boys, you're just bags of bones, not some tough guys. That should be your name, Bag of Bones.'

"They decided on Maggie's Bones after they got to L.A. They were a scrawny bunch back then. They would eat and eat and try to compare their sad excuses for muscle. I had such a hard time not laughing. But Maggie never held back. She told them just how much work they needed, had them seeing trainers and eating right, working out. Well, they've just turned out to be the best bunch of young men. I'm so proud of them."

"As well you should be, Marie. It's refreshing to be around guys my age and a little younger who actually respect women and can hold a conversation."

She chuckled. "That's another thing you can thank Maggie for. She practically beat it into them from the time they were small. Devon's father was also on them about being respectful." She frowned for a moment. "I'm not sure it sunk in with Marcus. That boy, he worries me."

"All it's going to take is one woman to put him in his place, and that will cure him of his lothario ways." She agreed with me, and we discussed how that scenario might play out.

When dinner was ready, the five of us ate together, waiting for the others to return. The guys were quiet. I think they were worried about what Sherry would say.

Around seven-thirty, we heard the back door open—and the roar of screams and laughter filtered in.

The door slammed shut and Marcus came forward with Sherry behind him, Devon bringing up the rear.

"Well, my friends. Our little hideaway has been discovered. We got recognized at Antoine's and unfortunately, they followed us back. There are probably about twenty screaming women out there right now." Marcus only seemed slightly bothered by this pronouncement.

Devon, on the other hand, was visibly frustrated, but when his eyes found mine, his face relaxed in a hesitant grin. I smiled back and mouthed, "Thank you," to him. He nodded and winked, prompting me to blush profusely just in time for Sherry to march up and stick out her hand.

"And you must be Tattoo Girl. So glad to meet you in the flesh."

She was a stunning woman. Her corkscrew curls bounced playfully and her features and shape were super-model material. She had the most gorgeous caramel coloring, and huge green eyes shaped like a cat's. She was dressed in black slacks with a lime-green sleeveless blouse. Her hand-shake was firm and enthusiastic.

"Nice to meet you, too. How was dinner?"

She looked at Marcus and back to me. "I'm in New Orleans. It was fantastic! I have to say, I've been secretly excited that they came here, so I'd have an excuse to visit and eat my way through town."

I looked down at her perfect shape and thought she was probably exaggerating. "That *is* one of the more dangerous aspects of this fair city."

She smiled at me before turning to the others. "So I'm ready to hear what you guys have been working on. I understand it's not where you want to be."

The guys got ready to play. A few nervous glances were exchanged. Sherry and I sat on chairs a ways back from the stage. She grabbed a pair of earplugs out of her handbag and I found mine. We made small talk while they warmed up, but when they started playing it was too loud to hear each other.

They played the four heavy songs that they'd worked out and they all sounded great. Some of the lyrics were unfinished but Marcus had explained to Sherry that the songs were still rough. She alternated between smiling appreciatively and listening with her business side. I could only imagine that she was thinking about which songs would sell.

Then Devon grabbed his acoustic and sat down to play "Heavy" for her. This time, however, Marcus sang it. I guess I missed him learning it today. While I much preferred Devon's voice, (I know, so bad of me), Marcus was doing a nice job of adding some vulnerability to the words.

Sherry frowned a little when the song started—but by the end, she was tearing up as well.

When they finished, it was quiet like it was the first time, but they were all looking at Sherry. She pulled a tissue out of her handbag and just stared back. "Wow. That was beautiful. Different, but beautiful. It's for her, isn't it?"

Devon nodded and looked at me. Sherry looked at me out of the corner of her eye, picking up on whatever was traveling the ether between us.

"So that's what you have? It's a start. How do you guys feel?"

The guys shrugged. Mage spoke up. "It's okay. 'Heavy; is a for sure, I think. But we've also talked about changing the focus a little, writing more about us and about Maggie. 'Heavy' fits in perfect for that. Jaylene has been talking to us and we want to make this a really personal album." He looked to Marcus to make sure he wasn't speaking out of turn. Marcus smiled and nodded.

"That would certainly be a departure," she answered pensively. We all waited for her to speak. Devon bent forward, his elbows resting on his knees, eyes on the floor. He was motionless except for his right heel, which bounced at a rapid pace. I wanted to do something...Hold his hand, touch his shoulder... Something. He seemed so alone in his pain.

Marcus could see that Devon wasn't able to talk, so he spoke up. "Devon and I spoke to Sherry a little about this at dinner."

She nodded. "Yes, and while I have some reservations, it's really up to you guys. Your fans will want to know everything, though, and legally, with Thomas's case tied up in all this, I'm just..."

Devon's eyes narrowed and he blurted out, "Excuse me, Sherry... But *fuck Thomas*. This isn't about him, it's about *Maggie*."

She raised her eyebrows high, probably not used to being spoken to that way by Devon. I was actually a little surprised to hear him speak that way too, but I agreed with the sentiment.

"I understand how you feel, Devon, but with Thomas being a former employee of the label, not to mention Maggie, and the fact that she died on her way home from a label-sponsored event...I just don't want there to be any repercussions for you guys."

Marcus spoke up this time. "Repercussions? Sherry, we lost our best friend and manager. We've basically lost the past four months of our lives. We want to move forward and we are taking steps to do that—no thanks to the label. If the label can't see its way to being supportive of what we want to do, then perhaps it's time we start speaking with some of the other labels who've been courting us."

She looked completely shocked. "Marcus! I don't think you need to do anything so rash as that—"

"And furthermore, Sherry, if you can't stand behind our decisions, then perhaps we need to hire a new manager."

She clamped her lips together so tightly they lost some of their color. She started to speak a couple of times and then closed her mouth, a muscle twitching in her cheek.

Finally, she said, "I don't know where this hostility is coming from. I flew out here to try to help you guys. I'm not trying to tell you what to do. As your *manager*, it's my job to look at the bigger picture that can affect your art. I have worked my ass off to advocate for you! If you friggin' want to do an album of polkas, then that's what I'm friggin' going to sell to the label. So before you decide to fire me, I just want you to know that I completely support what you want to do. Maggie was a friend of mine, too, as some of you seem to forget, and I would love to see her memorialized." A tear rolled down her cheek as she crossed her arms over her chest and glared at Marcus. I was struck again by just how much Maggie meant to so many people.

"Sherry, I'm sorry. I didn't mean to be rude. I know Maggie was your friend. I just really don't want Thomas's name being mentioned anymore. If you don't mind." Devon's voice trembled as he spoke and Marcus stood closer to him in support.

"I'm sorry too, Devon. You're right. Now, I can go back and tell them that you have a plan and need more time. They might not like it, but I will remind them that they are partly responsible for all of you *being* in this position." She had a sly smile at that statement. I loved that she was willing to fight dirty to get them what they needed.

"That would be great, Sherry. Thank you. We've made a lot of progress in the past couple of days and I think that trend will continue." Marcus eyed Devon and a look passed between the two of them that spoke volumes about their relationship with each other.

When it came down to it, they were in this together. They were committed to the band and their friends and family, and committed to ensuring Maggie's legacy was respected.

Sherry looked around at all of them, and the determination showing in their faces. "Well then. It's settled. I'll tell them to back off and you guys do what you need to do."

They nodded and Marcus gave her a hug. He spoke low to her, letting her know he was just doing what he had to do to keep things together. It was obvious they had a close relationship. She seemed mostly immune to his charms. I hoped he didn't try any of his slick lines on her. I liked her too much for that, especially now that it seemed as if she was going to fight for them.

The guys went back to working on their songs and I waved Sherry into the kitchen. She looked completely relieved.

"Whoa. I don't know what the hell has been going on in this building, but that is an entirely different group of guys than I was working with in L.A. How much can you tell me?"

I thought about it and figured since she was technically one of my employers, I would give her the basics.

"I won't give you specifics but I can tell you a few things. First of all, *Evil Dead II* makes a great icebreaker. Second, they really loosen up after some good zydeco. Third, and most important, they really suck at paintball." I tried to keep a straight face but her look of confusion had me cracking up.

"You have completely lost me. What is an *Evil Dead*?"

I figured I'd better start over from the beginning. I gave her a brief synopsis of what we'd been up to, leaving out the part about me thinking Maggie was Devon's wife. "But the catalyst, I think, is that for whatever reason, Devon is finally talking, and that has given them hope.

It was apparent from the beginning that without all of their parts functioning together, they weren't going anywhere."

She nodded and looked at me quizzically. "Somehow I don't think these things just happened without intervention. Marcus told me that Devon really likes you."

It was my turn to blush.

"I don't know if it's that, or he just feels like he can talk to me. Maybe it's because I'm an outsider? I don't know."

She gave me a knowing glance. "Yeah, pull this leg and it plays 'Jingle Bells.' Girl, I don't care what you say. I've known these guys for the past couple of years and I've *never* seen Devon talking to a woman before, at least not more than polite conversation. He barely speaks to *me*. So if he wants to talk to you until he's blue in the face, please let him."

We both laughed at that. I didn't really want to discuss anything more personal with her, but I just found it so odd that everyone was convinced Devon was so awkward in the girl department. I told her what I was thinking and she raised an eyebrow.

"Put it to you this way, Tattoo Girl, I've known several women who have tried to get intimate with him. He's always been polite, but never shown more than a gentlemanly interest in them. Between you, me and the fence post, I even knew an executive at the label who went to his hotel room clad in only a trench coat and heels and was turned away—politely, of course—and left in a state of complete sexual frustration."

I must have looked shocked because she laughed at my reaction. "You can't be serious?"

She nodded, a laughing fit taking over her ability to speak. "God's honest truth. And this woman wasn't used to being dismissed. She'd been a Playmate and had lots of men chasing after her, so the fact that he wouldn't hit that surprised those of us she told." She was looking at me speculatively. "But none of those women have what you have, Jaylene. You have natural beauty and you don't come across as pretentious." She shrugged. "Maybe that's what he wants. There isn't a lot of that in L.A., for sure."

I really needed to direct this away from me. "So what happens now? Will the label really back off of them and let them work? Because I think with a little more time they'll put it all out there, and if what they've written so far is any indication, you're going to get some beautiful music."

"Then that's what is going to happen. I know they don't fully trust me yet, but I'm damn sure not going to lose them as my client because the stupid execs can't see what they've got. These guys are brilliant. They could be the next kings of metal and hard rock. They just need the right album."

"Let's just see if we can get them to make it."

We shook hands and I let her in on a few of my plans. I told her about the pictures and then I was thinking more blowing-off-steam needed to happen. "I think one of the saddest things about what has happened is that they forgot how much they care about each other and about the music. They're so goofy and have so much fun when they forget about being pissed at each other. You should have seen them dancing to Big Time Rush."

She rolled her eyes and groaned loudly. "Do you know they made me listen to their last album for three hours once while stuck in traffic? I don't know what it is about them and their dance music fascination. Maybe they should just make a dance album and get it over with. Hey, that's not a bad idea..."

"NO! Please!"

We were both laughing when the guys came in to get some snacks. Marcus eyed us suspiciously. "What are you two laughing about in here?"

Devon came around behind me and put his hand on my back. I looked up at him and smiled and he took out his pack, gesturing for me to come outside with him.

I nodded and said, "We were just hoping you guys aren't going to end up putting out a dance album."

Jade perked up. "Ooooh. Maybe we could get Skrillex and do some dubstep metal."

Mage shook his head. "Nah, Korn already did that. We'd have to, like, add some beatboxing or something, take it back to the old school days."

They all started rapping to "Paul Revere" by the Beastie Boys and

Sherry covered her ears, pleading, "Make it stop! Make it stop," as Devon and I walked out of the kitchen together.

I was giggling as we walked out the back door. "That would really be too much, you guys opening for Justin Bieber on his next tour."

Devon rolled his eyes. "While I don't mind dancing to some zydeco with a pretty lady, I highly doubt they could get me up on stage in some boy band nonsense. I think they're forgetting we're a little old for that. It would be kind of pedophile territory for us to get into that market."

"Ew."

I slapped at his arm and he just shrugged, his unlit cigarette pursed between his lips. "I told you it wouldn't be pretty."

I laughed and he took my hand, gently pulling me towards our benches. Funny how I'd claimed them for us. Then again we'd done a lot of talking out here.

"I haven't really been able to talk to you today and I just wanted to make sure you were okay and that you liked the flowers."

I could feel the color creeping up into my cheeks. I spoke quietly. "The roses are beautiful, Devon. I want to draw them when I go back to my room tonight. They're perfect."

He blushed this time. "I'm glad you liked them. It was just... You just..." He rubbed at his soul patch and ran his hands back over his head, obviously agitated.

"Devon, it's okay. Whatever it is." I knew he was trying to get something out and I wished I could make it easier on him. He looked at me for a long time, took a couple of deep breaths.

"I talked to Star and he, uh...he told me what you walked in on last night. I just...I'm sorry, that you had to, ah, see that."

I took his hand in mine. "You were still processing what we talked about yesterday. I'm sorry you had to go *through* it. I didn't do much, just held on to you."

He took his hand back and stood, needing to pace. I watched him quietly, hating to see him so upset.

"The thing is...when I woke up with you this morning? It wasn't there. That pressure in my chest. And part of me felt guilty for that, like it wasn't okay for me to feel that good because Maggie—" He stopped and lit another cigarette with shaky hands.

"Because Maggie's not here?" He nodded. I blew my bangs out of my eyes. He watched me out of the corner of his eye and smirked. "That's survivor's guilt, Devon. You're feeling bad when things are going good for you because the one who passed had that taken away from them. It kind of goes with the territory."

He nodded and started pacing again. "Right. That's how it felt. But I didn't want to let go of you, Jaylene. I *don't* want to. Is that wrong?"

We were quickly leaving territory I was knowledgeable about. "I can't answer that for you. I don't think it's wrong to want to be happy, especially because you know in your heart that Maggie would want that for you."

He watched me so intently. I found myself squirming under his scrutiny.

I swallowed around the gigantic lump that was forming in my throat. "I guess it all depends on why you want to hold on to me. Is it because it's me? Or is it because you just need someone to hold on to?"

He frowned, and it was apparent that the question made him more agitated.

"I'm only suggesting that you think about that. You don't have to answer me. I'm going to be here for you regardless of whether you need *me* or just need *someone*."

He stopped and his hands rested on his hips, his frequently used frustrated pose. "Of course it's because it's you. Damn, woman! Is this why you told me Mackenzie says you're a pain?"

It was my turn to frown. My voice was low when I answered him. "I don't understand."

He took one last drag on his cigarette and tossed it in the urn. "What I'm trying to say is that I wanted to hold *you*; I want to hold *you*, not someone else. But I want to know if that's *okay* with you!"

I blew my bangs out of my face again and that only made him more frustrated. "God, when you do that I just want to carry you up those stairs over my shoulder and kiss you senseless. I feel like a goddamned cave man."

I felt my face flush. "I'm sorry, Devon. I'm not trying to be difficult." I drew my knees up to my chest and wrapped my arms around them.

His whole demeanor changed at that. He got down on his knee in front of me, taking my hand. "No, *I'm* sorry. I don't know how to say what I want to say and I keep fucking it up. I just want you, Jaylene. I want to be close to you. I'm not trying to sound like a stalker here or anything, I just feel better when I'm with you. Even if you're sitting on the other end of the bar, talking to someone else. I can't explain it."

I blinked at him a couple of times and smiled. "You're doing a good job."

He exhaled in a laugh. "No, I'm not. You're not the only one who has trouble with this. I've never felt like this before and I don't want to scare you. I don't want you to go. I'm trying to get better..."

I dropped my knees and put my other hand on his shoulder. "Devon, I should be the least of your worries right now. I'm not going anywhere, okay? You have me for another couple of weeks here, and after that, I'll still be around."

"That's not what I mean, though. I'm not just talking about this gig. I could give a shit about the contract you're under. I mean, I do because I'm trying to respect your rules. But I just have this fear that when it's over you're going to walk away from me—and I don't want that."

"How can you know what you're going to want? You don't even know me, Devon."

"Then let me, chère. Let me know you. I know you think you're only supposed to be here for *us*, but I want to know *you*."

I didn't want to upset him, but I was so afraid he just needed a crutch. And I would be that for him. I was afraid to want more than that because once he was able to live *without* the crutch, *he* would leave. To want him to still need me was selfish on my part.

"Getting into a relationship—or whatever you're thinking about—with me or anyone else is not really a good idea when you're grieving for someone. So whatever I want or think is irrelevant. Let me be here for you, to help you grieve for your sister and try to save your career. When that's all said and done, if you still feel like this, then we can talk about what *I* want."

He sat back, stunned. Myriad emotions crossed his face—hurt, anger, and resignation among them. "So nothing I say right now is going to change your mind?"

I smiled sadly at him. "It can't. I'm sorry."

He cursed and stood up. He turned his back to me and took in a shuddering breath. "I'm going to get through this because I have to," he said over his shoulder. "You've helped me see that I don't want to feel like this anymore. But you've also showed me that I can want more. And no matter what you say, I *do* want more, and I *will* want more. I'm going to consider this conversation to be continued."

He stalked back inside and dragged my heart along the concrete behind him, slamming it in the door.

ELEVEN

When I went back inside some time later, Star caught me in the hallway as he was coming out of the dark kitchen.

"Hey, you okay? What happened?"

I sniffled a little and smiled. "I'm fine. I— Oh! *Shit.* I was supposed to have Mackenzie come by with my books. *Shit!* What time is it?"

He pulled out a cell phone from his back pocket. "It's nine-thirty. What do you need me to do?"

"I need that book. Care to break the rules a little?"

His face crinkled into an adorably sneaky smile. "Let's do it. Let's be rebels. We're supposed to be fucking rock 'n' rollers, right?"

We bumped fists. I was so glad I'd run into him.

I had him run upstairs and get us some hoodies so we could sneak out the back. He brought them downstairs and I slid one on. It was so giant on me, I was swimming in it.

We peeked out the back gate and there were still a few people around the front of the building. We decided we needed a better escape route. Star boosted me up to the top of the back wall, which was interesting in my dress. The ledge was just wide enough for us to walk along. We followed it around to the next property and then cut through their courtyard out to the street.

There, we blended in with folks who had spilled over from Bourbon Street. We caught up to a haunted tour and followed them down Ursulines, then cut over until we hit Frenchmen.

The night was very pleasant and the walk felt great. Star was good company. He kept humming the theme from *Mission: Impossible* and a demented James Bond mashup that sounded more like Austin Powers. He had me giggling and it did wonders to dispel the ache in my chest.

God, was I being an idiot? Devon laid his feelings out for me and I held them away like a stinky diaper. I wanted to just grab them up and hold them close to me, hold *him* close and not let go. But if I did and anything went wrong, I would forever blame myself for taking advantage of a grieving man. Plus, would I ever know if he loved me for *me*, and not just for the support I was giving him?

I must have stopped giggling because Star put out a hand and stopped me. We were a few blocks from my shop when he pulled me over to someone's front steps. We sat down and I took a deep breath.

"Jaylene, please tell me what has you so sad tonight?"

I blew up my bangs and tried to decide what to tell him. "Tell me what you would do in this situation. Say you have this friend, an acquaintance really, but let's just call him a friend. And this friend lost his best friend; they got into a fight or whatever, and all of a sudden he was hanging out with *you* all the time. You did everything together and you thought, 'Hey. This is cool, I'm happy to have this friend.' But then you start wondering, 'Would we be hanging out like this if he hadn't lost his best friend? Would he still like me if he still had his other friend?' How would you know? How could you be sure?"

He regarded me with deep understanding. "You mean can Devon really love you if he's grieving over his sister."

I put my head down on my arms, crossed over my knees. "Okay, maybe that was a little obvious." I felt his hand on my back, trying to take care of me, and I shook myself. "I'm sorry, Star. I shouldn't even be bothering you with this."

He shook his head. "Jaylene, of course you should. Look. I know we asked a lot of you. 'Come on over and help us save our band.' But truthfully, you're just the catalyst for us. That's not to say you aren't amazing, because you are. Your art is brilliant and you are so easy to talk to. But we didn't ask for a therapist; that's *not* why you're there. I know from my time in rehab about boundaries and shit like that, but this is a different situation."

"Yeah, but how unprofessional of me to even consider the possibility of getting involved with someone I'm working with. Or working for. Jesus, I fucked up. Why I ever let Daryl talk me into this—"

"Whoa, whoa, Jay. What are you talking about? You haven't fucked *anything* up. Unless there's something you're not telling me?" He gave me a look of exaggerated shock. "Have you sold our secrets to TMZ? Are you really a tabloid spy?"

I rolled my eyes and he hugged me to him. "Your goofy secrets are safe with me, for sure. No, I fucked up by getting too..."

"You're falling for Devon."

I looked up at him, wide-eyed. His reassuring smile did little to ease me this time.

"It's perfectly understandable. Hell, if I swung that way, I probably would, too." I elbowed him in the side and he grunted. "I'm serious. He's been a good friend to me, to all of us. He's one of those people who doesn't have time for the bullshit. It's probably why he hated L.A. and all the shit we were doing out there. He's passionate about his craft, a perfectionist at what he does, but he's completely selfless. He's never wanted anything for himself. He's always helping everyone else through their stuff.

"He was the one who drove me to rehab. He set the whole thing up, drove me there, didn't hardly talk the whole six-hour drive. When we pulled up he said, 'Get better, Star. Do what you have to do and don't worry about anything else. It will all be here when you're ready. You deserve to be happy.'" Star teared up at that. "The thing is, of all of us? *He's* the one who deserves it the most. And he's the happiest I've ever seen him around you. How can that be wrong?"

"It's not wrong. I want him to feel better. I'm glad he feels like he can talk to me. But that's just it. What if he's confusing the two, you know? And I can't help but worry that if I let my feelings get too mixed up, he's going to realize he only needed me to get through his grief. He'll realize that he really isn't into me the way he thinks he is."

Star tsked at me. "My darlink, zat sounds like a leetle beet of projection." His Freudian accent had me giggling again. "See? I know my psychobabble. Seriously, what if I turned that around on you? Are you only into *him* because you're helping him?"

"Gods, no. He's such a good person, Star. In just the short time I've known him, he's given me so many reasons to think he's the bee's knees. I'm just afraid..."

He nodded and I felt like his arm around me was the only thing keeping me grounded at the moment. "You just said it. You're afraid. But why?"

I shrugged. "You're the Junior Freud, you tell me." He tickled me and I tried not to yelp too loudly. He started back up in his accent and I could barely contain my giggling fit.

"Vell, to tell you ze trooth, I zink you are afraid of puttink your feelinkz out zere and havink someone not reciprocate. Or is eet zat you zink you vill let him down?"

"Yikes, guess I'm pretty easy to read."

He shook his head. "Nah, it just takes one to know one. Look, all I'm saying is, you should give yourself a break. If you were going to take a chance on a dude, Devon's a pretty good bet. Just think about it."

I nodded and kissed him on the cheek. We started to walk again. He kept his arm around me to steady me. "You're pretty awesome, Star. Maybe *you* should have done the Master's degree."

He laughed and shook his head. "No way, ADHD, remember? School and I weren't friendly like that. But I have thought about maybe helping out with some support groups. I try to go to AA when I can find a meeting. Maybe someday I can be someone's sponsor. That would be cool."

"Yes it would," I answered him, and I meant it. He was such a wonderful young man. I found myself praying that Mackenzie wouldn't eat him alive as we stepped up to the back door of the shop. "Hey, Star? Where'd your name come from? It's not very Cajun."

He sighed. "No, it's not. My mama used to call me her 'Shining Star.' She had a pretty shitty life. I was sorta her bright spot. Anyway, the name stuck. What can I say? The guys were the only ones who didn't give me shit about it growing up."

I smiled at him and ruffled his messy hair. "I agree that it suits you.

Definitely." I turned to the back door. "We have to go in quick and shut the door so I can turn off the alarm, okay?"

He nodded, the secret agent once again. He was even whisper-humming the silly music again. I got the door open and then I shut us in, working on the alarm code. The beeping always made me nervous. I screwed up once before I got it in correctly.

All of a sudden the light came on at the top of the stairs and there was Mackenzie, in her micro-mini baby doll nightie, wielding a frying pan.

"Who the fuck is breaking into my shop?" She flipped on the light at the bottom of the stairs. Her eyes went wide and she dropped the frying pan with a loud clang when she saw us. "Oh my god, Jaylene. You are so lucky I haven't bought a shotgun or you'd have some more holes in you."

Star and I giggled but he was staring at her in awe.

"Good evening, Miss McGowan. It's nice to see you again."

She blushed and then looked down and tried to cover up a bit. "It's nice to see you, too, but what the hell are you two doing sneaking around?"

"Sorry, Kenz. I never got a chance to call you back and this evening kind of went to hell, so Star and I snuck out to come get my book."

"Yeah, I was waiting for you to call and I decided to just go to bed. Someone kept me up late the other night." She smiled wickedly at Star. His blush was adorable as he kept staring at her.

"Okay, well, I'm going to pop into my flat and see if I can find it. Star, why don't you wait with Mackenzie? I'll just be a few minutes."

His phone started buzzing insistently. "Oh shit. It's Devon. I didn't tell him we left."

My heart dropped. "Please tell him we just ran a covert operation and that we'll be right back. I don't want him to think...you know, after the talk we just had."

"Roger that, partner. I'll settle down the chief."

I laughed and ran up the stairs to my flat. Mackenzie invited Star in for a drink. I thought it would be nice to give those two a few minutes to catch up so I wasn't worried.

As I passed my dinette, I saw the drawing I did of Devon the day they came into the shop. I smiled when I thought of how much my impressions of him had changed from when he was just this aloof, mysterious guy in my shop with aviator shades on. Then I thought of him on his knee tonight.

Was Star right? Could I trust him when he told me it was really *me* he wanted? Could I have enough confidence in myself to trust him?

I sat down and drew him again, this time from the memories of the afternoon in my room, when I discovered he wasn't a widower, that he was in fact very unattached and attracted to me. I poured all of my feelings for him into that drawing, him looking up at me with eyes so full of emotion.

Maybe if I gave these drawings to him, how I saw him in the beginning, how I saw him yesterday, how I see him today, maybe he would know what I was feeling. I wasn't skilled with words like he was. But maybe through my drawings, he could see how I felt about him.

When I was finished drawing, I walked over to my bookshelf and pulled down the December book. I flipped through it until I found the drawing and the picture of Maggie's/Meg's finished tattoo. I thought they should see it. Maybe they would want to incorporate it into what I did for them. I still needed more ideas for their tattoos but I was feeling her more. I thought about a portrait of her or a symbolic representation of all the things she meant to them.

Star came in a few minutes later, a huge smile on his face. "Now that lady right there is going to be the death of me. Jaylene, there's no doubting I am in a bad way over her." He looked so sweet, and after our earlier talk, I had no qualms about him pursuing my best friend.

"She's a lucky woman then. You are quite a catch."

He gave me a hug and took my hand. "C'mon. We need to get back before Devon completely blows up my phone. He wants to be sure you're okay, and *he* won't be until he knows you're back."

I sighed. "Man, I really botched things up."

"No you didn't, Jay. But if any of us needs to get out of their heads, it's you right about now."

I groaned and we went out the back after resetting the alarm. The walk only took about twenty minutes but by then it was late. The party had moved away from the building so we could easily walk in the back door. It was dark inside, the only lights coming from the rumpus room upstairs.

We snuck up the stairs and he ran interference for me as I went into my room. I closed the door and went into the bathroom to get ready for bed. These weird hours had me a mess. I knew I should sleep, but I wasn't tired after sleeping through the afternoon. I peeked my head into Devon's room to let him know I was back—

But instead of seeing him, I caught a view of Sherry sliding a very lacy negligee over her head.

"Oh, sorry, Sherry! I was just closing the door here..."

"No problem. Yeah, this bathroom situation reminds me of the *Brady Bunch*. Did you ever watch that show? The kids had that weird bathroom between their rooms?" I nodded and we laughed about that.

"Hey listen, I'm glad we talked earlier. And I'm really glad you're here. Marcus told me how much of a help you've been, getting them on track, so I just really want to thank you."

I waved her off. "It's been great. Doesn't feel like work at all. Maybe more like babysitting a set of quadruplets and a conniving older sibling, but it's been good, no problem."

She laughed at me. "I hear you. Listen, I'm here one more day and then I have to go back to L.A. Maybe you and I can chat some more tomorrow, while they're practicing?"

I nodded and said, "Sure. Good night, Sherry."

"Good night, Jaylene. See you in the morning."

With that, I closed her door and proceeded to do my nighttime routine. I was feeling disappointed that Devon wasn't there to say good night to. I figured he must have gone to one of the other guys' rooms.

I changed into sleep clothes and tried to lie down, but I was still wired and I felt like I needed to at least see Devon, so he'd know I hadn't run away. It seemed really important.

I poked my head out my door and all was quiet upstairs. There was a light on downstairs and I could hear a guitar being lightly strummed. I peered over the railing and saw Devon sitting in one of the huge bean-bags, strumming his acoustic with his eyes closed. He was bathed in golden light, just in his jeans, and his hair was falling all in his face. I watched him for a minute before I slowly crept down the stairs.

He kept playing as I approached. He'd opened his eyes and was staring at me warily. I sank down on the floor next to his beanbag. His eyes never left me. I didn't speak and neither did he; he just kept playing for a few minutes. The music coming from him sounded like a sensual lullaby.

I leaned into the beanbag next to his, resting my head on my arm, just letting the music wash over me. It was so relaxing, except for his eyes on me.

He eventually put the guitar to the side and just sat there looking at me. I wanted to touch him so badly, but I hesitated after how we left things. I broke the silence.

"You gave up your room for Sherry."

He nodded.

"Where are you sleeping?"

He shrugged and ran a hand through his hair. When he was shirtless, that movement was so sexy it should have been illegal. "I was going to bunk with Star but as you know, he snores. I'm not really sleepy anyway." His gaze was still on me and I didn't know what he was thinking.

"In that case, can I show you something? I brought some things from my place. I'm sorry we took off without telling you. It was kind of a spur-of-the-moment excursion. Actually, it was an oh-shit-I-forgot-to-call-Mackenzie-back kind of trip."

He smirked and moved to stand up. I stood quickly and ended up face-to-face with him. Well, nose to chest. He watched me closely and it made me anxious.

I turned and went up the stairs with him right behind me. We went to my room, hearing feminine giggles and a sigh coming from Sherry's room. I turned to him and raised an eyebrow. He put a finger to his lips and motioned for me to keep going.

Once inside, we closed the door. He wordlessly closed the bathroom door and locked it from our side, locking the hall door as well. I walked over to my dresser while he sat on the edge of the bed. I pulled out my drawings of him and laid them side-by-side on the bed next to him.

I whispered when I spoke. "I seem to screw things up when I talk so I thought I would show you."

He studied the pictures intensely. I moved around the other side of the bed and lay on top of the covers to watch him. His expressions changed from picture to picture. He took a long time looking them over before raising his eyes to me. There were questions on his face.

I wanted to say something but when I tried to speak, he just shook his head. He turned around, his back facing me. I wanted to trace the name across his shoulders.

He sat that way for a moment, collecting himself. Then he slowly stood, gathered up my drawings, and carefully placed them on the dresser. He leaned over and turned off the light next to the bed, covering us with darkness. He pulled back the duvet and crawled into my bed.

I did the same and still, neither of us spoke. When I settled down, I noticed a crack of light from the window illuminated his face and mine. He was still staring at me.

I don't know how long we lay there looking into each other's eyes but I felt like we were having an entire conversation.

When he finally closed his, a small smile appeared on his face and he settled into my pillow to sleep. I tentatively reached over to smooth his hair back. I couldn't resist. It felt so nice and he looked so handsome lying there.

He brought his hand up to cover mine gently, and then turned his face to press a single kiss into my palm. He turned to his back and slipped into sleep.

I smiled at him and followed him there.

TWELVE

ometime in the night, he reached for me and took my hand. When I woke the next morning, he had my hand tucked into his chest, cradling it. I watched him for a long time. He stirred in his sleep, rolling to his side and enabling me to slip my hand from his. He frowned but kept sleeping.

I reached for my sketchbook and finally drew him how I'd wanted to. In his sleep, he was so peaceful. The strong line of his jaw, those full lips, the long lashes. I couldn't have imagined a more perfect man.

The sheet had slipped down almost to his waist and his arm was lying across his stomach. The morning light was coming through the same crack from the night before, shining on his chest and perfect abs. I drew all of that perfection and was doing the final shading when one of his eyes popped open.

"I wondered what all that scratching was about." His voice was so deep and husky in the morning. It gave me shivers.

"I didn't mean to wake you. You presented an irresistible opportunity, so I took it." He smiled with his eyes closed and rolled over onto his back to stretch. The sheet slid down to reveal the waistband of his jeans. The top button was undone.

"Did you sleep okay?" I asked nervously.

He nodded and opened an eye again. "I did. How about you?"

I nodded and smiled at him. Suddenly, I realized I hadn't brushed my teeth, my hair was probably a mess, and I hadn't put on a sports bra last night under my thin white t-shirt. I scrambled back off the bed.

Devon sat up quickly, looking worried. "What's wrong?"

I covered my chest. "Uh, I need a minute."

His eyes got big and then he smiled and sat back. I hurried into the bathroom.

"No fair, I haven't brushed either," he called out as I closed the door.

The door to the adjoining room was closed but I heard voices coming from inside. Just what had Sherry been up to last night?

I had just pulled on a sports bra and was pulling my t-shirt over my head when Devon walked in. He smiled slyly at me and walked over to his cabinet. He pulled out his toothbrush and toothpaste and then motioned me over to the sink.

I held out my toothbrush to him and he pasted it for me. We stood side by side, brushing and watching each other in the mirror. He spit first, leaning down to catch a mouthful of water from the faucet. He stood, gargled, then spit it back out. He smirked before grabbing for a towel.

There was no dignified way to do this, so I went for the spit and rinse and then snagged his towel from him. I wiped my face and went to climb back in bed.

Devon followed me, crawling under the covers. We continued to stare at each other like we did last night.

"I should probably go help Star get breakfast ready." I so didn't want to get up, but the shoulds were getting to me. I should get out of this bed before I—

"Don't get up." He gave me a small smile. "Stay." He snuggled down farther under the covers. I did the same. Then he pulled the covers over our heads.

"How long are we going to hide under here?" I asked with a giggle.

He smiled back, but his eyes were wary. "As long as it takes," he said in that husky voice.

I looked at him questioningly. "For what?"

He smiled that devastating smile. "As long as it takes for you to talk to me."

I raised my eyebrow. "About what?"

His smile never faltered. "Everything. About you. About your drawings. About us."

"Where do you want me to start?"

He reached out and pulled me to him. I instantly curved into his body. We fit really well together. The last thing I wanted to do was talk with him this close, but I was the one who set the rules, and I couldn't expect him to respect them if I didn't.

"How about you start with you? Tell me about you. If I needed to know one thing about you, what would it be?"

"Wow, start with the heavy ones, geesh."

He squeezed me tighter and kissed my hair. "Not heavy, it can be anything you want." I blew my bangs out of my face and he groaned. "You're killing me. Do you have any idea how adorable that is?"

I blushed. "I can't help it, you get me flustered. And who are *you* to talk? When you get frustrated, you put your hands on your hips and it, um, accentuates stuff. That does things to me, too." I couldn't believe I'd said that out loud, but since we were making confessions...

"What kinds of things?" He narrowed his eyes and that damn bottom lip of his poked out.

I rolled my eyes at him. "Do I have to spell it out?"

He rubbed at his soul patch, something else that drove me nuts.

"That doesn't help either."

"What?"

His innocence was too much. "What do you mean, 'what'? You! *All* of you. Don't play innocent with me. I've heard the stories, I know you've had women chasing you your whole life. I can see why they would."

He seemed surprised by that. "I don't know what you've heard. I never had girls after me. I was really nerdy in high school, I wasn't a jock, I didn't go out much. I was either working at the restaurant, working on my car, or playing music with these guys."

"What about in college?"

He frowned. "I went out, but never more than a couple of dates. Then I came home."

"So no girlfriends? Just a few dates? That had to be lonely."

He shrugged. "I don't know. I wasn't lonely. I never really got lonely until I went to L.A. There, I was always surrounded by people but they were all so empty."

"That sounds unpleasant. How were you able to write music in that environment?"

He pulled at his soul patch again and I bit my lip to keep from groaning. Thankfully he was thinking and didn't see my struggle.

"I had a lot of time to write; it was my only outlet. The only people I talked with much were Maggie and Marcus, maybe the other guys. I was lonely and that came out in my music. I was also angry about how things were going. I never bought into the scene there. I started drinking, I guess, to kind of turn it off when I was with others. If I wasn't drinking, they would bug me until I did. If I drank, I didn't have to talk to anyone, and most of the time they would leave me alone."

Sadness seeped into our little sheet fort and I wanted to chase it away. He apparently did, too, because he turned the tables on me then.

"You succeeded in changing the subject, Miss Charles, but I'm not letting you off that easy. Not until you tell me about you. What were you like in high school?"

I frowned. "*Very* nerdy. I'm sure my nerdiness was nerdier than yours. I hung out with the art kids and the emo kids. When I say 'hung out,' I mean I had friends at school but I didn't *go* out. I went to the movies but that was by myself. I loved to go hide out in the theater and get lost. I probably went at least once every weekend. Sometimes I'd sneak from picture to picture just so I wouldn't have to go home."

He chuckled. "I did that once, I saw three movies in one day before they caught me and kicked me out."

I looked up at him and grinned. I felt a new kind of bond growing between us. It wasn't just about his grief anymore. We were relating to each other on a different level. I curled against his chest so I could hear his heartbeat. I needed to know this was real.

"Anyway, I made sure I had dates to the major dances. My art friends were capable of dressing up every once in a while. They made a pact to go to all the high school stuff so they could sit back and laugh at how the other kids took it so seriously. Me, I just wanted to make sure I didn't miss out on anything. I kind of looked at it through the lens of my future counselor self. I loved watching how others interacted. I did a lot of people watching back then. And drawing."

He rubbed his chin on the top of my head, every once in a while kissing my hair. "So then how did you end up here? It's a long way from home for you."

I sighed and snuggled closer. "I came here once in college during spring break with some guys from the shop. They were doing a convention and I thought I would tag along. I hadn't done much travelling. I was immediately sucked in. New Orleans had it all for me. The architecture, the people to watch, the music... Oh, the music moved me. I ate and ate and ate. We stayed at the Maison Dupuy and I would sit on the balcony every morning and evening and the drawings were coming out of me like crazy. I always knew I wanted to come back. After my father died, I took the opportunity. I wanted a fresh start and I got it. Best move I ever made."

"I would have to agree. Best move you've made."

Devon kissed my forehead. I closed my eyes and breathed him in. His scent was enough to make my mouth water. I swallowed and tucked my head down so those lips wouldn't be tempting me anymore.

"So what now? You've found the place you are meant to be. What now?"

I looked back up at him, confused. "What do you mean, what now?"

He shrugged. "I don't know. Are you going to stay here? Is there someplace else you've wanted to check out? I'm just trying to see the future for you. Guess I'm not as good at it as Mage."

I giggled. "Does he think he can see the future, really?"

He shook his head. "No, but if anyone could, it would be him. He's really in tune with people and he reads them well."

"If you must know the future, then this is it. I opened my shop and I love what I do. I have no plans to do anything else. Well, I didn't before coming over here. This was totally out of my norm. The whole situation has been an adventure. Not one I would have seen myself doing, but I'm glad I did."

This time he didn't let me hide. His hands turned my face up to his. "I'm glad too, chère. I'm so glad our paths crossed." He kissed me softly and I couldn't hold back a sigh. He smiled against my mouth and then deepened the kiss, his hands moving over my back and hips. He moved his knee between my thighs and I squeezed. This felt too good.

"Devon, I'm sorry I was so difficult yesterday. Please know it was never because I didn't want you. I just couldn't see that you'd want me, too."

He pressed his forehead against mine. "I hoped it wasn't that. I'm glad it wasn't that," he said with a chuckle. He pushed my hair back from my face and ran a fingertip along my jaw. "I really didn't mean to push so hard. It's just that when you finally find someone you want to be with, it sucks to sit back and wait."

I looked up at him and took in a shaky breath. "I want that, too. But how do you know? Have you ever been in love, Devon?"

He smiled. "I was in love once before. She never knew it. It was in college, she worked as a receptionist in our dorm. Every day she'd say hello when I came in and goodbye when I left. That was the most I'd ever say to her. I tried for a long time to work up the courage to talk to her and when I finally did, it was the night her boyfriend proposed to her while she was at work." He laughed at himself. "I watched the whole thing, how bright her eyes were, how happy she looked. I wasn't even jealous. I was just happy *she* was happy. I was such a sap."

I ran my finger along his jaw and over his lips. "Sap or no, she missed out."

He smiled down at me and kissed me again before pulling back. "Have you ever been in love, Jaylene?"

"I thought I was. There was this guy I worked with, Toby. He was a great artist, very in demand. Our stations were next to each other. For a year we sat next to each other, talked all day, even brought each other lunch. One night he asked me out to dinner and I was so excited. I thought, 'This is it.' Maybe I'd finally have a real date. It turned out that he'd asked me out so he could pick my brain about our shop girl, Kristen."

Devon grunted. "Sounds like he was too much of an idiot to see what he was missing."

I rolled my eyes and shook my head. "Seems he'd been pining for her and didn't know what to say. I helped him out and the two of them got together shortly after. She ended up getting pregnant. They got married and moved away. I figured I did the right thing, even though I was pretty bummed out for a while. He was just another one in the long line of guys who wanted me for a BFF, not a girlfriend."

Devon looked at me while his hand crept down my side, and then he pulled my hips into him. "I hate to say it, but I'm really glad. I already have a best friend, Jaylene. I damn sure don't want you for that. But I could definitely use a hot girlfriend."

I snickered—until he slipped his hand below the waistband of my shorts and caressed my skin. I took in a shaky breath. "Oh, well then. I'm sure you'll find one if you really work at it."

I shivered as his hands skimmed over my bare skin, over the curve of my ass and down my thigh. He pulled my leg over his hip and pressed me closer. I could feel his length hardening against me and I imagined just what we could get up to if we had a bit less clothing on.

But then he pulled back. "God, Jaylene. I'm sorry. I'm trying to follow your rules, but I really just want to get your clothes off and feel all of you."

Well if that didn't just make things hotter. "I was thinking the same thing."

His gaze was so heated and his bottom lip was swollen from kissing me, and maybe because I'd sucked on it a little. "Jaylene, I want you. But I want it to be right. Not here, not with those guys right outside, and not with a time limit. I want to make love to you like you deserve."

"Devon, you're pretty perfect, you know that?"

He smiled shyly. "Nah, I'm not perfect. But I want *this* to be perfect. You make me want to make *everything* perfect."

I smiled and kissed his beckoning lips again. "And that's why you're perfect to me. And it *will* be perfect because it will be with you."

He kissed me harder and we were starting to get senseless again... when we heard *things* get going next door.

"Devon, shhh. Did you hear that?"

He was kissing my neck and lifting the bottom of my shirt. "Hmmm, I didn't hear anything other than you."

"Oh...oh, gods Devon. That's...mmmm..."

And then we heard something crash, and we heard a male and female moan together.

Devon sat up and looked at the wall. I covered my mouth to hold back a laugh. "What is going on in your bed, Devon?"

He snickered and pulled the covers back over us. "I guess we aren't the only ones up to no good." The moaning got louder and we both giggled.

"Who's she with in there, do you think?"

He rubbed at his stubble. "If I had to guess? I'd say probably Marcus."

I rolled my eyes. "Really? I wanted better for her. He can be such a dog."

Devon laughed. "All that is just for show. Sure, he's had his share of women, but he's had a thing for Sherry since before she became our manager. I think it was the whole unattainable thing because she didn't fall for his crap."

"It sounds like she may have fallen for it." Then I squinted at him. "No good, huh? I think we were up to something *very* good."

He smiled at me and licked his lips. "Come here, very good thing."

He pulled me in for another kiss and I felt like I was melting. A very delicious ache settled in my pelvis and his kisses and touches pulled that ache tighter and tighter.

His hands skimmed under my shirt and along the bottom of my sports bra. I arched my back, pushing into his touch. His large hand cupped my breast and I had to bite his shoulder to keep from crying out. That got a groan out of him. Then his thumb slid over my nipple—and he jolted.

"Oh, chère." His voice was tight, his face pulled even tighter. "What do we have here?"

Oh shit. The dare. "Ummm, you know how I work with Mackenzie and she does piercings?"

He nodded. The devastating smile was back, and his eyes were full of liquid fire.

"Let's just say I can't ever turn down a dare."

His eyes rolled back in his head and he fell away from me. "Jesus, woman. You are seriously going to destroy me. You say these things and all I can think about is…"

"I know. That's all I can think about, too." We both breathed hard, our chests heaving.

He was staring at me, playing with the ends of my hair. "So where do we draw the line here? I'll do or not do whatever you want."

I sat up to look down at him and tucked my hair back over my ear. I smiled, feeling brave all of a sudden. "I guess it couldn't hurt to let you see them…if you want. Unless you think we should wait."

He sat up as well, pulling at his soul patch again. He rubbed his hands together and I couldn't help giggling. "I don't know if I could just look, chère. I might have to do more than that if you show me."

And right on cue, there was a knock on the door.

We both looked at each other and pouted. I whispered, "Later?"

He nodded and fell back, groaning, adjusting himself in his now too-tight jeans. It took every ounce of willpower I had to look away from him and walk to the door.

"Hey, Star. Sorry I wasn't down to help with breakfast."

He smiled knowingly. "No problem. It was just me and Mage anyway. Jade wasn't hungry and, well. Yeah. So, can you ask Devon when we're going to start practice? Just trying to figure out if I have enough time to get in a workout and a shower."

I looked over at Devon and he covered his face with a pillow. "He'll be down in a couple of minutes. He might need a workout, too."

Star turned red and stifled a laugh. "Alright, tell him to meet me in the weight room. I've got some ideas I want to talk with him about."

"Sure, see you in a few."

He turned around and jogged down the steps. I closed the door and turned back to Devon. He sat on the edge of the bed with his head in his hands.

"It's probably for the best. One look at what you've got going on and I would have been done for."

I giggled and stepped into his arms. "Yeah. We should probably save the 'you show me yours and I'll show you mine' game for another time."

That pained look was back on his face. "You weren't kidding about me needing a workout. That and a cold shower. Come here."

He kissed me deeply and I felt my knees start to buckle. Regrettably, I said, "Shower time, you evil man. You run downstairs and get all hot and sweaty without me."

He groaned again and pulled back, eyes level with my chest. He groaned louder and pushed me away from him. "I'm going to be thinking about those all day. Man, this is going to be rough. Tell me, chère. Are both of them...?"

"You'll have to wait and see." I blew him a kiss and stepped into the bathroom, locking the door.

"You're cruel," he whined before I heard the door close.

Cruel was the fact that I so wanted to stay locked in there with him, and now I was headed to the shower alone.

Thirteen

The shower was lonely. As the water and soap ran down my body, I imagined it was his hands again. They were so warm and big. He was definitely a tactile kind of guy. I could appreciate that a hell of a lot. I shaved and took my time with my hair, using a deep conditioner. I wanted to feel good for him if and when we had a chance to be close again.

Hmmm, if Sherry was staying another night, perhaps we could have another sleepover.

I got out of the shower and took my time putting on lotion, gathering up my hair and adding a little makeup. It was warm so I opted for my second halter and a long swishy skirt. Devon had left me feeling pretty and wearing the skirt contributed to that feeling. Thank you, Mackenzie, for forcing that shopping trip on me.

When I came out of the room, I heard voices and a radio playing downstairs. Sherry was sitting at the bar with a cup of coffee and a bagel. My stomach grumbled so I figured I should eat too.

"Good morning, Sherry. Let me grab some food and I'll join you."

She smiled and winked at me over the rim of her cup. I guess we both had reason to feel good this morning. I just hoped what Devon said was true, that Marcus was mostly all talk when it came to his manwhore ways.

As I passed the weight room, I could hear the treadmill running and weights clanging. I had to pinch myself to resist the urge to peek inside. I did not need to see Devon working out. I could even hear singing—I could hear *Devon* singing. He must have been singing along to an iPod, although I couldn't make out the words. I heaved a huge sigh and slipped into the kitchen.

With a glass of orange juice and a chocolate muffin in hand, I floated back out to the bar. Jade and Mage were working on their guitars and Star was writing something down on the table by the pictures. That was what we really needed to do today. Time to get on task. A shower was running upstairs, which had to be Marcus.

Sherry was casually dressed in a pair of yoga pants and cami. She had no makeup on. She didn't need any with her amazing features.

"I trust you slept well," she said.

I raised an eyebrow at her. "About as good as you, I'd suspect."

She shook her head. "I tell you what, girl, they know how to make their men down here in Louisiana, for sure."

I giggled. "You'll hear no complaints from me." I didn't know how comfortable I could get with her but I was about to find out. "So, Marcus? Really?"

She took another sip of her coffee and rolled her eyes in a sinful way. "He may act like he's all that around other people, but he definitely puts the 'toy' in boy toy. We have an understanding. He entertains me and we have fun together. The minute I'm not entertained, I'm done."

"I can admire that stance, I suppose. He just really lays it on sometimes and I hate to think that it works for him."

She scoffed. "You think I'd let him get away with that? Please. He knows better. He also knows I'm not interested in anything other than fun, so he doesn't have to pretend to be anything he's not. In our business, it's hard to find people you can trust. When you do, it's nice to keep them around, for business *and* pleasure. It's mutually beneficial, since we're looking for the same things."

That statement didn't sit well with me when I thought about Devon. She must have sensed that.

"That's probably why Devon has never been happy with the business side of the business. He's a true artist, that's rare. And the rare ones are worth investing in."

I smiled guiltily at her. "He's definitely worth it. And thanks for taking his bed."

She laughed out loud. "It paid off for both of us." We clinked glasses and laughed until we realized the guys were listening to us.

"I think it's dangerous to let those two sit together, Mage. Look at how much damage Jaylene did with a paintball gun. Imagine if there were two of them."

Sherry let out a maniacal laugh that had me a little afraid of her. "Better watch out, Jade. You have to sleep sometime."

His eyes got big and he glanced nervously at Mage and Star, who were quite amused.

Sherry turned to me and whispered conspiratorially, "He's so easy to get, isn't he?"

I nodded. "But he's so sweet, I've been trying to take it easy on him ever since I freaked him out before tattooing him."

"Oh, you already tattooed him? Jade, let me see." He walked over to her and showed her the back of his calf. It was healing nicely. There was just a little bit of flaking from the ink.

"That's cool but what is it?"

I forgot she didn't know what *Evil Dead* was all about. "That, Miss Jordan, is from *Evil Dead II*. Jade, how is it that your manager hasn't seen the masterpiece?"

He narrowed his eyes at her and put his hands on his hips. He was so freaking cute I could barely stand it. "Yeah, Sherry, how come you've never seen it?" He shook his head and continued. "Anyway, this lovely lady is Linda, Ash's now departed girlfriend, dancing headless for him. You like?"

She was frowning, obviously not sure what to make of it. "The tattoo looks very well done. Wait, does that say 'Swallow Your Soul'? Really?"

We all giggled. I shrugged at her and threw up my hands.

She smacked herself in the forehead. "You guys are strange."

The door to the weight room opened and my eyes involuntarily looked to see Devon emerging, dressed only in a pair of basketball shorts, dripping with sweat. He draped a towel around his neck and paused as his eyes found mine. Damn him and that devastating smile.

"Dude, hurry and hit the showers, we got work to do," shouted Mage.

Devon lifted his chin at him then walked straight for me. He pinned me against the bar and reached around for my orange juice. He took a big drink, slammed the glass down and, with his other hand, picked up my muffin and took a bite. He winked and then ran up the steps to his room. A minute later, we heard the shower come on and him singing loudly.

Every person in the building, including Marcus, who had just joined Sherry, had their eyes trained on me.

Ignoring the fact that I was probably ten shades of crimson, I picked up my glass, gave them a small smile and raised it before taking a drink and turning back to the bar.

"Alrighty then...that's new," said Mage. He shook his head and went back to tuning his bass.

Jade looked completely bewildered, and then it was like a light bulb went on and he said, "Ohhh." Then he smiled approvingly at me and continued playing his guitar.

Gods, this was embarrassing. I couldn't wipe the stupid smile off my face.

Until Marcus spoke.

"See? I knew she'd be a good investment."

I turned on him, pissed that he was about to ruin my good mood. "Marcus, you're much more fun when you aren't being an ass. Why do you have to make everything sound so vulgar?"

His smile fell. "Hey, I didn't mean anything by— Ow!" Sherry knocked him back off his barstool and he barely caught himself before falling on his ass.

"I know you didn't just call this lovely lady an 'investment.' Boy, do you have any idea how completely disrespectful that was?"

He looked genuinely confused. "What? I just meant I knew having her here would be good for us. Him especially. That's all I was saying." He rubbed his ass like maybe his fall wasn't without trauma.

"Well next time, don't insinuate a woman has monetary value when it comes to something like this. You kiss your mama with that mouth?"

He looked shocked but then his smartass smile was back and he whispered loudly in her ear, "I kissed *your* mouth—and I'm pretty sure you liked it."

She smacked him in the chest but she was smiling.

Still annoyed, I went back to finishing my breakfast. One of these days, he and I were going to have it out, and it wasn't going to be pretty.

A few minutes later Devon was back to various shouts along the lines of "It's about time, pretty boy," from the other guys. Then they were playing with an energy I had yet to hear from them. They spent the rest of the day playing and fine-tuning the songs they had. Jade and Mage played them something new that they jumped all over. Sherry had some work to do on her laptop, so I just worked on some sketches and listened.

Sherry and I pulled out sandwich fixings a couple hours later. They came over as a herd, devoured what was there, and went right back to playing.

Around six, Daryl showed up with some barbeque so they decided to call it quits for the day. He motioned me over and gave me a hug.

"How's things going?"

My stupid smile must have given something away, because when I said, "Good. They're getting a lot accomplished I think," he just smiled knowingly.

"Uh-huh, dat all dat's getting done around here?"

I smacked his arm. "Don't be rude. No wonder Marcus has such a potty mouth."

At this, he frowned and put on the scary face that most people ran from. "What dat dumbass do? Do I need to have a talk with him?"

I shook my head and placed a calming hand on his chest. "No, Daryl. He hasn't done anything. He just has an uncouth way of putting things sometimes. Don't worry. Sherry already knocked him on his ass today."

He smirked but didn't seem appeased. "Nevertheless, dat boy needs a good ass kicking like you heard about. I don't give a shit if he grew up without a father, he knows better than to talk to a lady like dat."

I frowned. "What happened to his father?"

His eyes darkened. "My sister picked a pansy-ass motherfucker with no qualms about leaving her high and dry with two young boys when he found something a little less domestic. Marcus was probably about eight or nine, I suppose, Jade less than a year younger. I did what I could to teach 'em to be good men, but I was having my own troubles around dat time. I might not have been the best influence. Dey was close to David, Devon's daddy. When he died, dey was on dey own. Marcus is a little too much like his daddy for my liking."

I forgot sometimes just how much life Daryl had lived, and that it wasn't always warm and fuzzy like it was now with his beautiful family.

"I understand your frustration, Daryl. But there comes a time when everyone has to answer for their own behavior. I just hope that when his reckoning comes, it's not in the form of a two-by-four upside the head. Or worse."

Daryl smiled at me appreciatively. "Jaylene, you ain't bigger dan a minute but you a spitfire. I love dat about you. And I ain't the only one."

At that moment, Devon joined us, shaking hands and doing the bro hug with his uncle. Then he turned to me and kissed me on the cheek tenderly. I smiled at him, and his eyes were full of such happiness, it made me want to cry.

Daryl cleared his throat. "You two enjoy the food and I'll see you later. Oh, and Jaylene? I checked in on Kenzie Kitten today and other than being a little lonely without you, things was good. She told me on the QT dat Troy was doing good work and already talking about his next gig, so you ain't got to worry about him moving in for the long term."

I couldn't help but breathe a sigh of relief. "Thanks, Daryl. That makes me feel better. But I'm sad for Mackenzie. I don't want her to be lonely."

Devon pulled me into him and said, "Why don't we invite her over tonight? We can play games or something, give her a chance to, ah... mingle." He looked over at Star who was scribbling something down again. I was curious as to what he was writing.

"I think that would make someone very happy."

He winked at me and said, "Why don't you go call her, chère."

I hugged Daryl goodbye, taking a moment to look up at the two of them. "You know, I never felt like a small person, but around the two of you, I feel downright petite."

Daryl laughed and said, "That's cuz you are, sugar. You're perfect. Now get up there and call Kenzie and tell her to get her pretty little self over here before she gets teary and ruins dat makeup of hers."

I rolled my eyes and reached up on tiptoe to kiss him on the cheek. "Thanks Daryl. I'll be right back."

The two of them watched me walk up the stairs. I glanced down and saw Daryl put his arm around Devon and talk seriously with him. Devon smiled and his joy lit up his entire face. My heart raced in my chest and not from exertion.

When I got up to my room, I sat down on the edge of the bed for a minute to catch my breath. It was a week ago today that the guys came into my shop.

Only eight days and already my life felt so different. I'd been so preoccupied with the band and their needs and my feelings for Devon that it felt like it had been more like a month. I still had a week and a half to go, and I wondered what else I was going to learn about them... And myself.

I sighed and looked back at the mess of sheets and blankets Devon and I had made this morning. I felt my face get hot, along with other things, and I really hoped that he'd be back with me tonight. And if I wasn't kidding myself, I hoped for every night after that as well. The fact that we fell asleep staring into each other's eyes the night before was so precious to me. It made me feel that much more for him.

I shook myself and grabbed for my phone.

Mackenzie picked up on the third ring. "You've reached the winter of my discontent, care to leave a message?"

"Kenz, it's me. Your long-lost gal pal. Why so down in the dumps, dollface?"

She sighed. "Oh, because I miss you, and it's no fun working with a boy. Well, at least not the boy I'm working with. He took over the stereo and keeps playing that death metal stuff that I hate so much. I miss *your* metal, even, that's how much I hate his stuff." Her little whiny voice was music to my ears.

"Well, cheer up and get your fine little behind over here. The guys' manager Sherry is here, Daryl just brought barbeque, and we're thinking of playing some games tonight."

"Really? I can come play? Oh that sounds like fun. What should I wear? Wait a minute, why am I asking *you* that question? Wait. What are you wearing?"

I sighed, kind of pleased she asked. "I've got on that black flowy halter I got at Sabrina's and a brownish long skirt."

"Hmmm, I'm impressed. How did you do your hair?" I told her I'd piled it up. Then she asked about my makeup, and I assured her I had on the bare minimum. She sounded pleased. "Sounds like someone found some motivation. Tell me, Jay, have you let that boy touch your feminine side."

I could only giggle, and that was enough of an admission for her.

"You *did*? You go, girl! Was it great? Is he a good kisser? Oh, is he good with his hands?" She knew I wasn't going to give her details, but *I* knew she couldn't help herself.

"It was wonderful, Kenzie, and frighteningly enough, I seem to have fallen for him. Like completely, crashed and burned with no hope of recovery."

She was quiet for a minute. "He better be good to you, that's all I have to say. That, and it's about time. I'm so happy for you."

I thanked her, feeling better that I could admit it to my BFF. She said she had to finish up at the shop and that she'd be over around eight-thirty.

I went back downstairs and looked over at the pictures the guys had put up. They'd written little stories to go with each one.

Star chose the picture of him with Maggie for the dance. Underneath he wrote, "Thanks for the date, Maggie, and the lessons on being a good man."

Wow. I wondered just what happened with those two.

Mage chose a picture of Maggie and him holding up a human skull between them. They were looking at each other with intense facial expressions, like two boxers getting ready to face off. Mage had a wand with feathers and chicken bones and beads hanging off it in his other hand. Maggie was wearing a sparkly, low-cut robe and glittery makeup. Under the picture, Mage wrote, "The best All Hallows Eve ever. Maggie came with me to a gathering at the Lafayette #1 and we got to see some of the masters at work. Thank you, Maggie, for always listening to my crazy talk."

So Maggie had a wild side. It seemed like there was nothing she wouldn't do for them—or *with* them, for that matter. I was glad someone had listened to Mage's talk and taken him seriously.

Jade's picture was of him and Marcus looking pretty roughed up, sitting on a couch with ice packs on their heads. They were clearly pissed. His note said, "Maggie always covered for us, no matter what stupid shit Marcus got us into. In this case, we beat the crap out of each other after Marcus asked out my best girl, stealing her from me. When mom found us all bloody and scraped up, Maggie told her we'd fought off some guys that were giving her a bad time. She bought it and left us alone."

Why did that story not surprise me? Man, they looked awful. They must have really beaten each other good. I couldn't imagine brothers doing that much damage to each other.

Marcus posted a picture of he and the band with Maggie holding up their gold record, shaking hands with some executives from the label, I assumed. The guys were all decked out in what were probably the clothes they would perform in. Marcus was even wearing eyeliner, which made him look more dramatic for sure. Devon had on his shades and was wearing a simple tight black t-shirt, black jeans, and a belt with a huge skull buckle. Great look for him.

Marcus wrote, "Maggie was our biggest supporter. Without her we would still be a bunch of fuck-ups from Houma. God bless her and keep her safe."

Devon still hadn't posted one. In all fairness, he hadn't had much time to peruse the pictures, and he *had* written his song.

More pieces of the Maggie puzzle: a sister who was the glue that held them all together, a devoted cousin who ran interference and brought out the artists in them, a trusted friend who would go to the ends of the

Earth for you, and a woman who taught a boy to become a man. Now how to bring this all together in one drawing?

I stood there looking at the pictures for a long time. She was very beautiful; in every picture she was gorgeous, no matter what look she was sporting at that time. She had a blinding smile that changed her whole face. I could see so clearly why they were lost without her.

They needed to learn from each other how to make things work. They had to depend on each other and learn to trust people like Sherry, who had their best interests at heart, even if they weren't family.

I found a chair and sat with my sketchbook doodling for a while, losing track of time. Eventually I became aware that the others were gathered around me, looking at the pictures on the wall.

Mage pointed at the one of the brothers bloody. "I remember that. Man, you guys beat the shit out of each other that day. What was that girl's name, anyway?"

"Janice," they replied in unison. Jade gave Marcus a dirty look and Marcus just smiled innocently. "What? You should be glad I took her off your hands. She was a terrible kisser. No doubt any other activity with her would have been lacking."

"Fuck you, Marcus, that wasn't the point. You broke the code and ruined my plans for the summer."

Marcus looked a tad bit guilty. "Sorry, Jade. If I had known how much you liked the girl, I would have left her alone. But if she was so quick to run off with *me*, she would've hurt you anyway. Either way it sucks, but at least I ruined things before she had a chance to break your heart."

Jade just shook his head and bit on a fingernail. It must have been rough to be Marcus's brother. Jade clearly loved and respected him, but struggled with his feelings.

Sherry looked at Marcus with disdain and said, "I hope he kicked your ass, Marcus. You deserved it for being a dick to him and to that little girl."

He narrowed his eyes at her...and then acceptance was clear in his expression. "He gave me this scar on my cheek and broke my nose, so yeah, I guess he won."

She nodded, an eyebrow raised. "Good."

He looked really uncomfortable. I liked the effect Sherry was having on him. If he had any desire to continue this...whatever it was they were having, then he'd better learn to have a different attitude.

Sherry looked at the board and frowned. "How come you haven't put up a picture, Devon?"

I looked around and found him standing behind me to the left. He shrugged and put his hands in his pockets. "I don't know if I can pick just one. If I did, it would probably be one of us as kids. That was when I knew she was fearless and would always take care of things." He was quiet for a moment, still looking at the pictures.

"There was this one morning when we were home alone together. I think I was around seven, so she would have been eleven. Mama was at the restaurant and Daddy was out on the boat. Anyway, I tried to cook breakfast for her because she had been sick and was still in bed. I was trying to fry bacon in the skillet and it started popping all over and burning. I started screaming and crying because I couldn't get close enough to turn it off. I just wanted it to be perfect for her and it was ruined.

"The smoke detector went off and she came running out to the kitchen. She was so brave. She grabbed the lid to the skillet and covered it, burning her hand in the process. She didn't yell, she just hugged me and held me until I stopped crying. When the smoking stopped and she could lift up the lid, the bacon was burnt to a crisp. She picked up a piece, nibbled it, and said, 'Mmm, thank you, Devon. Thank you for cooking me breakfast. Now go on and get washed up and get your clothes on and we'll go to the restaurant for some hot chocolate.' I smiled at her, feeling so proud of myself, and I took off for my room. She cleaned up the mess and probably chucked the bacon in the trash. But she handled it. She handled all of the messes in our life with style."

I looked over my shoulder and smiled at him. His eyes looked sad but he smiled back at me. He was really doing great with all of this. I wanted to tell him how proud I was of him.

"Would you guys mind if I chose a picture?" Sherry was asking them all but looking at Devon.

"Of course," I said. "Take a look." She started to flip through the albums and found the one after Maggie had left for L.A.

"I met Maggie at a work function. We were both interning at the label and I really admired her because she just seemed so competent. I'd heard how all the execs loved her. I went up to her and asked her, 'Hey, Meg? What's your secret? You have them all eating out of your hand around here.' She just rolled her eyes and waved me in for the secret. 'I'll tell you but it ain't pretty.' I was so surprised, I leaned in closer and she said with a total straight face, 'Blow jobs. Just blow as many of them as you can and they'll let you get away with murder.'

"I remember my heart dropped into my stomach because I thought, 'Oh Lord. My mama warned me about this and how am I going to tell her?' But then I looked back at Meg and she was just laughing her ass off. 'Got you.' she said. I was so embarrassed. She apologized and said, 'Honestly, I just tell 'em like it is and for some reason, they listen. I don't know. I just hope I get a job here because otherwise I'm going to have to go home to Louisiana with my tail between my legs.'"

The guys were listening intently and I noticed Devon had come closer to me. His hand dangled beside me so I took it in mine. He looked down and squeezed *my* hand. He still had that sorrow in his eyes but he seemed to be laughing at what Sherry said.

"She told me that, too, when she called home. I threatened her I was going to tell Mama that's what she was doing and she threatened me back with even more severe blackmail. That was her way. She'd have my back no matter what but if I tried to cross her, she'd point out all the good dirt she had. You could never win with her."

They all laughed at that. I noticed Marcus looking at us holding hands and then looking at Devon—and I'll be damned if he didn't look a little envious.

Good. Maybe he'd keep his mouth shut and I wouldn't have to smack him.

"Here's one," Sherry pulled out a photo and made sure to mark the spot before holding it up. It was a picture of Maggie in L.A. with some of her friends at a bar, wearing a very slinky party dresses. They had on Happy New Year's tiaras and had glasses of champagne in their hands.

And in the middle of them all stood none other than the Working Class Dog himself.

"Oh my goodness, is that who I think it is?" I walked over to look at the picture up close. "Holy shit, that's Rick Springfield! Did she know him?"

Sherry laughed. "Honey, Meg got to know everyone she could. I remember her telling me about that night. She said she'd had a huge crush on him as a girl and had too much to drink that night, which resulted in her spilling her guts to him and almost puking on his shoes. She classified that as a major no-no, and after that, I made sure to not drink at functions where I knew I might meet an idol. It came in handy when I met Tony Bennett." We all laughed.

"She had posters of that guy all over her room. She was old school like that. We used to tease her all the time." Devon was even laughing about it.

Sherry taped the picture up on the wall with the others.

I figured this was a good time to show them the drawings and her tattoo. "Guys, can you give me a minute? I want to show you what I found last night." I jogged up the stairs real quick and brought down my book. I motioned for them to join me around the table, making sure Devon was closest to me so he could see it first. I flipped to the correct page and laid it out.

"I wanted to show you the drawing I did for her and the picture of her finished tattoo. It looks pretty raw. I hate to say it, but she didn't sit very well for it. Her skin was pretty sensitive so I don't have a good picture."

They all crowded around looking at it, murmuring their appreciation for the design and wincing from the redness of her skin in the picture.

Devon found my hand and squeezed it. "She never did handle pain very well. She always said she'd never get a tattoo, was too chicken." He pulled me away from the table a little and into his chest for a hug. His breath tickled my neck as he whispered, "I'm glad you were the one who tattooed her, Jaylene. Thank you for showing us." His voice trembled and cracked with emotion.

I whispered, "I'm just glad I had the chance to meet her." He pulled back and looked into my eyes for a moment before he kissed me sweetly on the lips.

Now *I* was trembling, and had completely forgotten about the others, who were openly staring.

Mage broke the silence. "It's about fucking time, man. Good for you."

Devon looked over at Mage, who slapped him on the back. Devon blushed and shook his hand. I bit my lip to stifle a nervous laugh. Devon was still holding me to him. "Thank you, I think. It *is* time." He turned back to me with that devastating smile.

"As long as you don't start writing sappy love songs, it's cool with me." Marcus walked over and pulled him into a hug.

Devon looked surprised and hugged him back. "I might do that, asshole, just for you. How could I *not* want to write sappy love songs? She's pretty amazing."

I was thoroughly red and completely mortified. "Okay, enough gooey stuff. He's still yours, guys." They all laughed and hugged both of us. I didn't understand what all of this meant but I gathered it was about acceptance, relief that they were finally talking about Maggie without fighting, and letting each other know they still loved each other.

Star gave me an extra-long hug. "Glad you got out of your head, chère."

I smiled brightly at him. This felt way too good to be true. I was still waiting for the bottom to drop but right now, in this room, I just wanted to hold on to the good feelings as long as I could.

"Hey, am I late for the love-in?" Mackenzie came strolling in from the back towards us. "You guys really should lock that gate back there. Anyone could just come in."

I ran to her and hugged her hard then stepped back, confused.

She actually looked kinda earthy and almost normal looking. The pink hair was gone. Her natural black was back and flowing around her shoulders. She wore a pale-pink gauzy sundress with wedge sandals on. Her makeup looked flawlessly applied but was more subtle than usual. She smiled brightly at me and I almost teared up again at the sight of her.

"You look stunning, Kenz."

She winked at me and batted my hands away. "Just got bored, that's all." Her gaze shifted to someone behind me. I turned to see Star looking as though he was about to faint.

"Star? You okay, buddy?"

He nodded and slowly moved toward Mackenzie. Her blue eyes grew wide and she bit down on her glossed lips. Star stopped in front of her and bent to kiss her hand. I'd never seen Mackenzie blush before. It was very becoming on her.

"*Vous etes belle, mademoiselle*," he said in a low voice.

Her eyelashes fluttered in surprise. "You speak French?"

He smiled at her and I was tickled to see just how much she affected him. He grasped her hand and led her over to our little group. I took that opportunity to introduce her to Sherry.

"Sherry, this is Mackenzie McGowan, my shop mate and best friend."

She and Sherry shook hands. "I'm the manager of this ragtag group of hooligans."

They both laughed and Mackenzie looked around. "Do I offer condolences or congratulations?" The guys all groaned and she winked at Sherry and me.

"Hey, how about we take this party upstairs? I set up Trivial Pursuit. We can play teams!" Jade was so excited and we all agreed. Sherry and Marcus went to the kitchen to grab some snacks and the rest of us headed up the stairs, Mackenzie and Star taking up the rear, still looking at each other that way that people do when they are completely undone over the other person. I kinda knew how that felt now.

Devon led me over to a corner of the couch and pulled me down onto his lap, wrapping his arms around me and resting his head on my shoulder.

I turned and asked him quietly, "I'm not too heavy for you?"

He balked at that. "Chère, you really don't have any idea how tiny you are, do you? 'Cause you weigh nothing and you fit here just perfect. So quit worrying. It makes you frown." He touched my forehead right between my eyes and I blew up my bangs at him in frustration. That got a groan out of him and he shifted a little underneath me.

"Good. Now behave."

He slid his finger up under the strap of my halter. "Do I have to?" he whispered.

"Yes you do...for now. If you're good, maybe I'll let you take this off later."

His face flushed and he squeezed my hip tight. Between clenched teeth he said, "You really can't say things like that to me right now—and don't even think about getting up."

I bit my lip to keep from bursting out laughing.

"Okay, obviously Jaylene and Devon are on a team together, and me and Mage will be on a team. Who else is on the two teams?" Jade hopped back and forth between two feet, he was so excited. Little did he know that he didn't have a chance. Nerds like me spend a lot of time racking up useless trivia for just these opportunities.

Mackenzie and Star joined us, and Marcus and Sherry joined Jade and Mage. Jade pulled out a beat-up '80s version that looked well used. We played for a couple of hours and I was delighted that, while Jade's team did respectably well, we kind of crushed them. I was able to answer all of the history and science questions. The music questions were a draw because both teams knew them all. The film questions, Sherry and Mackenzie really battled over. It was so much fun.

"I still say it's not fair because Jaylene has a freakin' Master's degree and Devon went to college some." Jade tried unsuccessfully not to pout.

"You could go to college, too, you know," I pointed out to him.

He looked at me, surprised. "I never thought about that. It's always just been the band. I'll admit when Devon went, I was kind of jealous but I never really cared much about homework and stuff in high school. I barely graduated."

"A lot of people who wait to go until they're older do better in school because they appreciate it. It's just a thought, Jade. I only mentioned it because you seem to have a lot of knowledge already, and I think college classes just might be something you'd enjoy."

He smiled and had a thoughtful expression on his face. "I *will* think about it, thanks. But for now, my loser ass is going to bed. G'nite."

We all wished him sweet dreams and Mage followed close behind. That left the six of us. It was late, we had all been laughing a lot during the game, and now it was just chitchat.

Marcus whispered something to Sherry and she nodded. "Guys, I'm going to turn in. I've got a long flight tomorrow and I still have some reports to work on in the morning. Thanks for a fun night."

We all said our good nights, assuming Marcus would be going with, which he did.

Mackenzie and Star talked quietly together. Her legs were drawn up beneath her, and Star was sat next to her on the couch with his arm along the back, behind her.

"Kenz, do you want us to call you a cab or are you staying?" She looked to me and then at Star, who waited anxiously for her answer.

"I can't stay. I've got appointments in the morning. Star, would you walk me home?"

He nodded enthusiastically. "Sure, let me just grab us a couple of sweatshirts and I'll be right back." He ran to his room and Kenzie watched him go, her eyes flaring.

"Mm mm mmm... Thank you guys for inviting me." I knew she was thinking of what she could do to my poor friend when she got him to her place. I raised an eyebrow at her, and she said, "Don't wait up for him."

Devon snickered behind me. Then Star was back and he held out his hand to help her up from the couch.

"I'll see you guys in a few," he said excitedly. Kenz bent down and kissed me on the cheek.

"Thanks, Star," I said. "Just text Devon when you're on your way back so we don't worry."

He nodded and they were off.

I turned to look at Devon and he was studying my sleeve, tracing my tattoos with his fingers. Goose bumps appeared instantly and I shivered, which had nothing to do with the temperature.

"It seems my bed is still occupied." He was looking down at my arm, still tracing, and his bottom lip was pursed out.

"It does seem that way. I can't say I'm disappointed." His gaze flickered up to mine for a second before resuming his perusal of my arm. He lifted it out to the side so he could see the designs underneath. In a low voice, I said, "I was kind of hoping for another sleepover."

His hands gripped me tighter at that and I saw his eyes flare again.

"I love your tattoos, chère. I love the way the colors look on your skin." He held up my hand and looked at the Celtic knot I had tattooed on my index finger of my left hand. "What does this mean?"

"It's a wisdom knot. I figured I could use all the wisdom I could get."

He held my hand up to his lips, closed his eyes, and pressed them against my finger. A sigh escaped me and he turned his blue gaze on me. "I would love to share your bed tonight. But before we go, I just want us to set some limits." He was so serious.

"I can appreciate that," I said softly.

He still had my left hand in his and he turned it over, gently kissing my palm. "If we don't decide here, when I get you in your room I'm afraid I won't be able to hold back. And I meant what I said before. I want it to be special when we make love the first time."

I reached across with my free hand and smoothed his hair back from his forehead. He closed his eyes and his head fell back. "How specific do we need to be about those limits?"

He smirked and opened his eyes. "Specific. Mmmmm, this could be fun. Tell me, chère, what did you like about this morning?"

I felt my face flush. I couldn't believe we were going to talk about this. "Um, well. Besides waking up next to you? I loved feeling your hands on me. I loved being close to you." I felt shy. I didn't know what to say to him. His gaze on me felt so intimate. I was still sitting on his lap but my shoulder was pressed against the back of the couch so we were face-to-face, our chests only inches apart.

"I loved that, too. I want to touch more of you. Would you let me, Jaylene?"

I nodded, biting on my lower lip, feeling my chest tighten with excitement. I pressed my thighs together and moved just a little.

Devon's eyelids fluttered and when they opened again, they were heavy. "That's good. Will you let me take your clothes off to touch you?"

My breathing was labored and I nodded again. He groaned quietly.

With his left hand, he touched my chest and ran his fingers down my breastbone, over my stomach and then gently grazed the tender spot between my thighs. I sucked in a breath and felt things getting way hot.

His breath was very husky when he spoke again. "Is there any place you *don't* want me to touch you?"

I was starting to tremble and feel that tightness low in my belly again. I shook my head, licking my lips. This elicited another groan and he let his hand continue down my thigh and over my knee, down my calf and to the instep on my foot. "Good...that's good Jaylene. Because I really want to touch you."

I placed my hand against his chest and he covered it with his own. I could feel his heart pounding and felt better knowing he was just as aroused as me. "Only if I get to touch you, too."

His eyes rolled back in his head and he gripped my hip tightly. "God, you can touch me to a point, chère, but I don't know how much I can take."

I cupped his face in my hands and made him look at me. "Thank you, Devon. For being so patient with me."

His eyes softened and he smiled at me, pulling me in for a gentle kiss. "It's got nothing to do with patience. It's just about making sure you're totally with me, because it'll only be good if you are totally with me."

I kissed him again and pulled back with a devious grin. "I'm *so* with you. Can we go now?"

He nodded quickly and slid his arm under my knees and around my back. "Hang on, beautiful."

He stood, picking me up and carrying me effortlessly to my door. I reached down and turned the knob, he pushed the door open, and then I reached back to close it and lock the knob. He smiled, took me over to the bathroom door to do the same and then placed me gently on the bed, where I reached over and turned on the lamp next to the bed. He leaned close, with his fists resting on the bed on either side of my hips. Then he knelt down in front of me.

We looked into each other's eyes for what felt like forever. I think he was just making sure I was okay, and it made me that much hotter and that much more ready to explore him.

He kissed me for a long time before gently removing my sandals, one at a time. He even massaged my feet. There was so much love in the way he touched me. He ran his hands up my calves. Thank goodness I'd shaved. He stopped on the outside of my thighs for a moment before sitting back on his heels to look up at me. "Stand up, chère."

I placed my hands on his shoulders and did what he asked. Our eyes locked as I rose above him. He smiled reverently at me before closing his eyes and rubbing his face gently against my stomach. When he looked up again, I felt lost in the blue of his gaze. My heart was bursting for this man kneeling before me.

"Hey, you okay?"

The concern in his voice made it crack and I was quick to reassure him. "Just feeling so much right now. Devon, I..."

He squeezed my waist with his hands. "I know, beautiful. Me too."

I ran my fingers through his hair then placed my hands on his. I moved his thumbs to hook over the top of my skirt and started to move his hands down. His eyes widened, as if to make sure I was okay. I smiled down at him and nodded.

I saw him swallow and then his eyes followed his hands as he pulled my skirt down to the floor. I stepped out of it and he laid it carefully to the side.

He smiled at the tattoos on my thighs, caressing and kissing them both. "I'm going to want to know about these later."

I giggled and he looked up at me and smiled. But then his eyes got serious and his gaze lowered to my plain black cotton panties. He toyed with the elastic on my hips and around my thigh before placing a kiss right below the waistband.

"Oh," I whispered and felt my knees start to buckle, but he was there to catch me. I watched him through hooded eyes and his gaze drifted up to check on me. He continued placing gentle kisses over the top of my panties. It was intense. I felt the heat throbbing just below where his lips were travelling.

When he looked up again and saw that I was so moved by his touch, he took pity on me and gently pushed me back to sit on the bed. He stood and placed his hands on my shoulders. "Is this the part where we, uh, you know..."

I smiled and got exactly where he was going. "I show you mine and you show me yours?"

He rubbed at his soul patch, which sent jolts down to my lower belly and below. Things were getting critical and he still had all his clothes on.

"I think so, but since I've already lost my skirt. I think it's your turn."

He smirked at me. "Is that right? So what should I lose first?"

My eyes immediately went to his waist. I'd seen him with no shirt on and I knew how erotic that sight was. I wanted to see more of him but I wanted to feel his skin against mine. "I can't decide. I want it all gone."

He laughed and tilted my head up to look at him. "Give and take here. How 'bout my jeans join your skirt first?"

I nodded, reaching for his button fly.

His hands stopped mine. "Careful, chère. I'm trying to stay in control, but this is torture. Just, be careful." His voice was so tight when he spoke I could feel the tension.

I smiled and undid the first button.

His eyes closed and his hands fisted at his sides. The second and third buttons went quickly and revealed the waistband of black boxer briefs and a further hint of where that light covering of hair on his abs disappeared to.

I looked up to find him breathing fast and looking a little pained. I hoped it was good pain. I watched his face as I undid the last two buttons and placed my hands on his hips. He sucked in a harsh breath and a small sound escaped him. I ran my hands down his hips, slowly lowering his jeans past them, and then they slid the rest of the way down themselves.

His erection was massive and pressing firmly against his boxer briefs. My eyes must have gone wide when I got a look at what he'd been working on, because he chuckled low. "Yeah, told you so."

I blushed and grinned up at him. He raised me to my feet and switched places with me on the bed, turning my back to face him. He murmured his praise of the tattoos running up the backs of my thighs and traced his fingers lightly over them before cupping my ass and kneading it gently.

"Damn, Jaylene. It just keeps getting better and better. You are so damn beautiful." I giggled—and he squeezed harder. "Why are you laughing? I'm serious. I can't believe how good you feel right now."

I sighed and peeked at him over my shoulder. His expression was like that of a kid in a candy store, trying to decide which confection to put to his lips first. He looked up at me and the excitement in his eyes had me giggling again.

"You are too much, Devon. But please, continue."

He muttered under his breath, "Hell yeah I'm going to continue. Woman, you're deadly."

I couldn't help the giggle that escaped that time.

"I'm glad you're enjoying this," he chuckled. Then his face got serious. "But now for the reveal." His fingers deftly untied the knot at the nape of my neck and the straps of my halter slipped down my front. I turned to him, clutching them to my breasts. He gazed at me in wonder with an excited smile on his face.

"So did you decide? One or both?"

He cocked his head to the side and then his eyes bugged as he remembered. He groaned again and reached down to adjust himself. "I don't think I can take much more of this."

I decided to draw this out a little. "You're the first person to see these besides Mackenzie and me. I'm curious as to what your reaction will be."

"Are you kidding me right now? Chère, I don't have to see them to know that you blow my mind. Do you have any idea how much fun I'm going to have with them?"

I laughed and let one strap side slide down, and then the other. I watched him closely for his reaction. It was priceless.

"Oh, god bless you, Jaylene, for not being able to resist a dare. Those are the sexiest things I've ever seen in my life." He just sat there staring forever and I was beginning to get a little self-conscious. I started to cover back up and he reached up to still my hands. "Oh no, please. They are so beautiful. I just want to look for a minute." He stared at them while he finished removing my top.

"Devon, they're just boobs."

He looked at me in shock and grabbed me around the waist, bringing me in closer to him. "No, they're not. They're much more than that. They're *yours*." He placed gentle kisses on the swell of my breasts, all the while watching my reaction. I was breathless, those lips felt magical on my skin.

He stopped for a moment, smiling at me. "Are there any added benefits for you?"

I shrugged. "Don't know, told you you're the first to see them."

He sighed happily and brushed his soul patch across a nipple. I shuddered—and then I was lost as his tongue snaked out and he flicked one of the tiny barbells.

The sensation was unbelievable. This time my knees *did* buckle, and only his arms braced around my hips kept me from sliding to the floor in a puddle.

"Oh, dear gods, that is intense," were the last words I got out before I lost the ability to speak.

It seemed that Devon was beyond that faculty as well, as his mouth went to work worshipping one nipple and then the other. His tongue and his teeth licked and tugged until the ache between my thighs became unbearable and I was reduced to whimpering.

"Is that good, chère?"

I couldn't speak, could only nod, and then my hands grasped the sides of his face. I kissed him hard and I swear he growled, his tongue plunging into my mouth.

Thankfully he took the time to turn me around and lay me back on the bed, as my legs were no longer functioning. All I could do was rub my thighs together to try to ease the growing sensation there.

Devon stretched out next to me and ran his hands down my hips as he continued to kiss me deeply. My hands tangled in his hair and I worried the frenzy that was building would be heard outside our room. I could barely breathe and I couldn't get close enough to him. In a frustrated bid for something more, I pushed Devon over on his back and crawled up his chest. But damn, his shirt was in the way.

"Off. Please, off. I need to feel you."

He grunted and moved out from under me to tug his shirt roughly over his head and throw it on the floor, immediately grabbing for me and pulling me back on top of him. I straddled his hips and when my core touched the hardest part of him, we both groaned.

"Remember what I said, chère. Just be careful. I can't hold back much longer."

I smiled down at him. And kissed him. And rocked against him.

"Oh god, Jaylene," he moaned, and I kept it up, moving slowly above him, hitting both of us in a crucial spot.

He kissed me roughly on my neck, and then his lips tugged on my piercings. I cried out in sheer pleasure. The pressure built and built where our bodies met and then his hands were on my ass, pushing me harder against him.

"Devon...Devon, I'm..." My legs shook as my body experienced passion like I'd never thought possible. The pressure was giving way to something way more intense.

"I'm with you, baby," he said in a tight voice.

One more pull on my nipple and that intensity heightened until I felt like something came apart inside of me and I broke into blissful little pieces.

"Oh...*Devon!*" And then he gave one last thrust and groaned as new warmth spread between us.

He gripped me to him, his body shuddering. We both panted hard. His eyes closed, his face completely relaxed. I tried to slide off him, afraid I was squishing him, but his arms clamped around me and he whispered, "No, please. Just stay with me a little longer. Jaylene, that was so...oh my god."

"Mmmmm...so that's what all the fuss is about," I sighed against his neck and he chuckled.

"What? That was your first...?"

"Mmm-hmmm. My first orgasm. Thank you, Mr. Boudreaux."

At this, he rolled me over and buried his face in my hair. "Oh, chère. I'm so glad I could make you feel even a little of what you make me feel."

It was my turn to laugh. "Uh, Devon? There's nothing *little* about you. Nothing little about that whatsoever."

He slapped a hand to his forehead and laughed deep from his belly. "You're too kind, chère." We continued to chuckle together and I thought that nothing could have made the night more perfect.

"Give me a minute?" He moved to get up and I reluctantly let him go.

He went to the bathroom and closed the door. I heard the faucet turn on and when he came back a minute later, he had a towel wrapped low around his hips and another one in his hand. He handed the other towel to me. "I'm sorry, I'm afraid I made a bit of a mess. I did warn you."

I laughed. "You did. Did it appear that I was concerned about that?"

He walked around the other side of the bed and slipped under the covers. I slipped my now-soaked panties off and crawled under the blankets with him. We both lay on our sides a foot away, just looking at each other like we did the night before. This time there was less curiosity and more satisfaction.

He cleared his throat before he started to speak and it appeared he was trying to hold back a smile. "So about your rules. I'm afraid we just trampled all over them."

I grinned. "Rules schmules. As long as my boss isn't angry, then I guess it's okay."

He smirked. "I don't hear any complaints from anyone, especially not me. But I don't like being called your boss." His smile slipped a little at that and I raised an eyebrow.

"No? What should I call you?"

His blue eyes got that vulnerable look about them like they did when he was unsure. "If it doesn't sound too strange, I'd rather be called your boyfriend."

I shook my head quickly, not wanting to see that vulnerability any longer. "Not too strange. I like it. It's sort of old fashioned, but I like it."

His relief was sweet. "I'm glad. Because I *am* old fashioned. I believe in one guy, one girl and all that stuff. I might live...what did you call it before? An unconventional lifestyle? That's not by choice. I like conventions like this."

I giggled and reached across to take his hand. He held it between his two much larger ones. "I like this, too. A lot. Devon, you made me feel so good...like cherished, I guess."

He smiled sweetly through his blissful gaze. "I do cherish you. I'm grateful you trusted me enough to be intimate with. I want all that and more. I've got it bad for you."

My heart leapt into my throat. "Devon, I'm falling for you so hard it scares the shit out of me. But I don't want to stop."

His voice was impassioned when he said, "Then don't. Don't stop. And don't be afraid, chère. I'll be so careful with you. I promise."

Those words broke down the last of my defenses and I crawled across the open space between us and pressed an emotion-filled kiss to his beautiful lips.

"Please be careful," I whispered so quietly, I didn't know if he heard me.

His eyes searched mine for the right words to say. Instead, I closed them and turned over, tucking my body into his. His arms tightened around me and he kissed my neck gently.

A buzzing sounded jolted me in his arms. He got up quickly and walked around the floor, looking for his jeans. He pulled his cell phone out of the pocket, glanced at it, and his lips curled up into a smirk. "It seems as though we don't have to worry about Star tonight. He's staying at Mackenzie's."

I sat up, clutching the sheet to me. "Are you serious? Wow, that's...I don't know. Cute?"

He turned out the light and then came around the bed and got back in. "It's very cute. Now get back over here, I'm not done with you." He was holding the sheet up and waiting for me.

I guess it was a little late to be shy but he hadn't seen all of me yet. I tried to stay covered as I scooted into him. He wrapped me in his arms and kissed my hair.

I didn't want to fall asleep but my body had other ideas. I stretched up to kiss him one more time and when our lips met, it was like heaven. "Good night, Devon."

He sighed and pulled me in tighter, our legs wrapped around each other. "Sweet dreams, beautiful."

FOURTEEN

I woke to the most heavenly sensation the next morning. I was on my stomach. Fingers trailed lightly along my back, followed by feather-light kisses. I sighed and turned to face him. "How long have you been awake?"

He was leaning on his elbow, head in his hand, and grinning like he'd won a prize. "A while. I just couldn't believe you were here next to me, that I could be so lucky. I tried not to wake you, but your skin is just too lovely not to touch." I wiggled into the mattress a little more. "Besides, I couldn't sleep. Too much running around in my head."

I looked at him closer and could see dark circles under his eyes.

I rolled over quickly to sit up and realized I was still naked. I grabbed for the sheet too late, and then my breasts were on display for him.

His eyes flared and any hint of tiredness was gone. "That's exactly what I meant. So lovely." There was a dangerous glint in his eyes as he leaned down to kiss me, his hand gently brushing over my breasts. I clenched his biceps before I remembered—

"Mm-mm!" I covered my mouth with my hand. "I haven't brushed my teeth."

He gently pulled my hand away and laid a deep one on me, obviously not bothered by my morning breath. Sighing, I molded my body to his and realized as I came up against him that his towel was gone, and I was feeling every inch of him.

"Wow, you feel incredible." I rubbed my feet along his calves and our legs tangled together. I could feel his growing length against my hip, nestled in his soft hair.

"Jaylene, I want to see you—can I look at you? I fought the urge all morning. I just need to see all of you."

I could only nod. His expression was so intense. His hair was perfectly mussed from sleep and his eyes and lips were puffy. Devon in the morning was probably at his most beautiful. But at any time of the day, he took my breath away.

He pulled the sheet down slowly, uncovering me inch by inch. He sucked in a breath as it passed my hips and uncovered my legs.

I had tattoos covering both arms and legs, but my torso was only marked by the dragon that ran from the left side of my ribcage down to my thigh. I hadn't had my chest or back tattooed yet and wasn't sure I would, unless something really jumped out at me. My right thigh had mermaids swimming together and both shins and calves were covered by smaller pieces. Skulls, butterflies, antique keys and locks... Some I'd even done myself after running out of friends to practice on during my apprenticeship.

Devon took his time appraising every inch.

"There's so much to appreciate here, I could take forever getting lost in your body."

"I don't know about forever, but I do have a lot of ink." I was looking forward to doing the same to him. The way the sunlight made his skin practically glow had me itching to touch him but he only shook his head when I tried.

"It's my turn to look."

I blew my bangs out of my face and his eyes immediately locked on mine.

"I told you that was dangerous, Jaylene. Do I have to show you what I mean?" His chest was level with my thighs, his head right at my hip.

"Dangerous how?" I whispered.

His eyes were on me, looking extremely wicked. Without looking away, he pressed a kiss right in the middle of my nest of curls.

"*That* kind of dangerous. Do I need to show you more?"

I'd never had a man be this intimate with me before and I was scared and excited at the same time. I started to tremble. "I'm not sure."

He splayed a hand on my belly and kissed me again, still looking into my eyes. Having him so close was unbearable. I didn't know if I wanted more or if I truly couldn't *take* any more.

He must have seen the indecision on my face. "I won't, not if you aren't sure. It's something that will make us both feel amazing. But I'll wait 'til you're ready." He was smiling, and I was feeling really hot all of a sudden.

"It's not that I don't want to or am afraid. I've just never, um...no one's ever done that before." I felt like an idiot trying to explain to him. "Pretty much anything that's ever happened before has been with most of my clothes on; greedy fingers and sloppy, slobbery kisses." He snickered and I felt more relaxed. "Everything *you've* done so far just makes me laugh even more about those experiences."

"Aw, chère. I'm sure I was just as bad my first time. I still don't know everything—but I know what I want to do with *you*." He was blushing a bit and I reached out to tousle his hair. I was suddenly curious to know just how much experience he had.

"When was your first time?" I asked him.

He put his head down and when he came back up, he looked sheepish. "Are you sure you want to have this conversation? I want to be honest with you, and will answer anything you ask me. I just hope you aren't too disappointed."

I smiled down at him and said, "I'm sure. I want to know. It won't change my opinion of you; you don't have to worry about that."

He snorted. "Oh, I *do* worry. I've always been careful, but I've done my share of experimenting, I'm afraid."

Strangely, I was turned on by this confession. "I want to know, Devon. I'm actually really curious. Being a virgin at my age hasn't necessarily been by choice. It's not been because I'm not curious or interested in experimenting. Just hadn't found someone I wanted to share it with until now."

He closed his eyes and kissed my thigh, rubbing his soul patch over my skin. "That was a pretty powerful thing to say, chère. I'm so grateful you want to share this with me."

I giggled. "I do, but I really, really want to hear more about you."

He looked up and frowned. "Really? It doesn't bother you?"

I shook my head, and he shrugged and got comfortable with his head on my stomach. All the better for me to run my fingers through his amazing hair.

"Okay then. I was a gawky sixteen-year-old the first time a girl let me touch her. She was two years older than me and she worked at the restaurant for my parents. Over the summer, before she left for college, we fooled around. At the end of the summer, we had sex in my car. It wasn't pretty, but she was fun, she taught me a lot. Her name was Sarah."

It sounded cute, something I wished I would have had the guts to do at that age. "Older women, huh? Sounds fun. Now I'm even *more* eager to see this car of yours." He laughed shyly. "Okay, so then what?"

He cleared his throat and looked up at the ceiling. "I already told you I had a few dates in college, some of them involved sex, and that's really all they wanted. I didn't mind. I still didn't know what *I* wanted, and figured I'd better see what was on the menu."

I poked him at that and he grabbed for my finger and kissed it. This was actually fun. I loved talking with him in bed like this.

"So then you became a big rock star. I've heard stories about what happens backstage." I was daring him a little, and I could see from his face he wasn't sure what he wanted to tell me. "Devon, it's okay. If you don't want to tell me because you'd like to keep it private, that's fine. If you're afraid I'll be upset, I won't. I know other women have had the privilege of your company, but you're with me now, and that's what matters."

His gaze was intense when he looked back at me and I felt my stomach clench. "It's not that. I don't care about it being private. I just don't like who I was in L.A. I let it go to my head and I did a lot of things I wasn't proud of, things I have no interest in repeating now that I've left. No one forced me. It wasn't the drugs or alcohol, although they were often involved. It was about me trying to fill a void in my life, you know? Music had always been a part of my soul and it got twisted out there. It wasn't enough to fill me...so I looked elsewhere."

He was frowning and I reached out and ran my finger over his eyebrows. "I'm sorry you felt like that. I can relate to having that void. When I quit tattooing and was doing my internship, I felt that way. I was smoking a lot. I couldn't even draw; it was like I was being smothered by my clients' dramas and filth. It was awful. And then when my father had his heart attack, that was it.

"But I think whatever happened with him, whether he lived or not, I was already going to quit interning and go back to tattooing. I missed the atmosphere and the creative energy. I think being in a place that isn't nurturing your energy as an artist isn't healthy."

"That's exactly why I don't want to go back to L.A. I hope I don't have to."

This was good stuff but I wanted to remind him where we were headed. "So tell me about the craziest thing you ever did with someone else. Ever been with more than one person? Another guy? I'm very curious."

His eyes got wide and he smiled. "Really? You want to know the dirty details."

I wiggled my eyebrows at him. "Are there dirty details? Yes, yes I do. You forget, I've worked with all men for years. They were horny, slutty, pervy guys who didn't know the meaning of TMI. There's not much you could say that would shock me. Just because I haven't done it doesn't mean I haven't heard about it, so spill."

I wanted to dispel this notion he might have of me being innocent. I wasn't innocent, just inexperienced.

"The craziest thing? Hmmm..." He stared up at the ceiling again but this time he was grinning instead of frowning. "See, I'm not sure I can tell you the craziest thing because I shouldn't tarnish your image of anyone here." He looked over to gauge my reaction.

"Ooooh, you mean there's tarnishing involved? Wow. All right, tell me, just leave out identifiers. It's not like I'm going to say anything."

"Alright, I'll confess. There was one time we were on tour in

Europe, it was our first time being there for an extended period, and I saw firsthand that sexual attitudes are much different there. Every night there were basically orgies going on back at the hotels. One night after a show in Amsterdam, we had gone for a walk through the red light district, and you know there, the drugs and sex run freely. Anyway, the guy I was with got recognized and soon we had a crowd of girls around us asking us to go back to their flat. There were probably eight of them and two of us."

I tried not to squirm but his story was getting to me. "So eight exotic women take you and another guy back to their flat. That sounds hot. Then what happened?"

He chuckled and sucked in a breath. "Honestly, a lot of it was just watching *them* go at it. They had all kinds of toys and stuff and liked us watching. We did eventually get invited into the activity. There wasn't much for us to do; they were pretty much in control." His face had turned a little red.

"Did you like that, Devon? Having a woman in control like that?"

He looked at me, trying to discern how I felt. "I liked watching them with each other. They certainly knew what they were doing. It was actually hot watching them with the other guy as well. I don't know why. I guess I'm more visual than I thought." His voice was lower, softer now.

"How many times did you come that night?"

His eyes jerked to mine, that fiery intensity back in them. "I came four times that night. It was very erotic—and exhausting." He grinned and then let out a shaky breath. "I've never told anyone about that experience before."

"I'm glad you told me. Four times, eh?" I blew up my bangs, this time to help release a different kind of frustration.

His eyes flared. "Four times. Yeah. I have pretty good stamina."

I was breathing heavy again, every intake pulling the sexual energy throughout my body. "I bet. I practice yoga most mornings. I'm pretty flexible."

His eyes rolled back and he groaned. "Now why you gotta torture me like that, chère?" He sat up and the sheet fell dangerously low on his hips. "You make me burn, Jaylene. Just talking to you, just looking at you...I can't get enough." He leaned forward and took my face in his hands, kissing me passionately.

I met his passion equally in the kiss and soon he had me under him, my thighs spread eagerly for him. He stopped with a shudder and a groan. "Not like this, not like this. I won't..."He buried his face in my neck, panting.

I ran my hands down his powerful back. "Then touch me, Devon. Show me how good it will feel."

He groaned again and kissed me harder. His hands masterfully stroked my breasts and then he followed that with his equally skilled lips and tongue. He slid one hand down my stomach and brushed my mound first with his knuckles, then with his fingers.

"I need to touch you."

I let my legs fall open farther and he rewarded me with long strokes against my folds. I cried out, clenching my fists against his shoulders to keep from scratching him.

"This feels like heaven right here, chère. You feel perfect. Can I touch you more?"

I nodded. "More please. I need more, baby."

He sighed. "I think I love it when you call me 'baby'. Tell me if it hurts, okay?"

I looked into his eyes and nodded again. He held my gaze as he inserted one very long finger.

"*Ohhhh*." we both said together in wonder.

"You're so tight," he murmured. "I'm not hurting you, am I?"

I shook my head, smiling sinfully at him. "Only if you stop."

He chuckled and kissed me lightly. "I'm not going to stop until I make you feel good, that alright?"

"That sounds great— Oh!" The pressure felt invasive. It sent shock waves of pleasure through me. He moved his fingers slowly in and out, and my hips matched his movements. When he grazed my clitoris with his thumb I bowed up, clutching him to me tighter.

"Feel good?"

I could only moan in response and he moved to kissing my neck and jaw, his morning stubble scratching me deliciously. He kept up with those amazing fingers of his, and in a few tantalizing minutes more, I came hard against his hand, once again biting his shoulder to keep from screaming.

"I think I love it when you bite me, too," he whispered, kissing me softly.

"Well if you keep doing that, I'm going to end up drawing blood. Gods...I mean I knew you had talented fingers and all, but that was ridiculous."

"You're too kind, chère. I could do that all day, every day. You look so amazing when you come. Your face relaxes and you have a glow about you. It's awesome."

I cringed and hid my face against his shoulder. "No fair. I want to see you, too."

He shivered. "You will; no hurry. We have all the time in the world to explore each other, and believe me, I intend to thoroughly explore you."

We kissed some more until my stomach started growling.

"We better take care of that," he said, leaning down to kiss my belly. "Plus, if Star isn't back, there'll be no one else to get breakfast for my fellow cavemen, and I think by now they've forgotten how to pour cereal. Let me get dressed and I'll help you."

I pouted at him. "What about taking care of *you*? This is two mornings in a row I've left you in an uncomfortable position."

He smiled that devastating smile at me. "I feel perfectly fine. A little tension just makes it a sweeter release." He winked, crawled off me, and slayed me with his naked walk to the bathroom.

"Goddess of creation, that is the most perfect ass on the planet." I blew up my bangs, thankful he didn't see, but he must have heard me because I heard *him* chuckling in the bathroom.

Voices through the wall let me know he had gone next door to grab some clothes. I hoped he grabbed a towel because that ass was sure to set Sherry ablaze. How could it not?

And he wanted *me*. That thought and the delicious pulses still moving through my womb had me feeling more complete than ever.

When he returned, he found me stretching languorously on the bed. He stopped with a hand on his hip and smiled, pulling at his soul patch. "Enough of that, beautiful. Time to get up. Why don't you meet me downstairs? I'll help you get breakfast going and then I'm going to work out." He had another pair of basketball shorts on and was still shirtless.

"You go on ahead and work out. It won't take me but a few minutes to get breakfast going. Besides, I don't think I could concentrate with you in the kitchen." I winked at him and he smiled back before heading out the door.

FIFTEEN

After a quick wash, I threw on sweats and a matching short tank. I piled my hair up and jogged downstairs. Breakfast was going to consist of some hastily thrown-together omelets. There were diced tomatoes and onions already in the cold storage, so I put all the fixings out and as the guys came in, I made them omelets to order one at a time. Mage started the coffee for me and Jade poured juice for everyone.

"Hey, where's Star?"

"He walked Mackenzie home last night. Guess he must have gotten lost."

He walked in at that moment. "Very funny, Jaylene." He came over and kissed me on the cheek. He and I probably had the same goofy smiles on our faces. It was a good thing the others were still sleepy or we would have been in for a world of shit.

"Thanks for getting breakfast ready. Mind if I go clean up?"

I shook my head. "No worries, I got this. You go on upstairs."

He looked relieved. "Thanks, Jay."

Marcus came in next, shirtless, and as he passed me to get to the coffee machine, I noticed scratch marks all down his back. I didn't breathe a word but I was worried that Devon wasn't wearing a shirt this morning. I hoped no one would get an eyeful of *my* vampiric tendencies.

"Practice in a half hour guys?" The others grunted. "We've got a lot to do. I've got some new stuff and so does Devon, so we'll be at it most of the day." Then he turned to me. "Jaylene, maybe we can talk some more tonight and finalize ideas for the tattoos? I don't know about the rest of you but I'm itching to get this thing done, get some new ink."

I grinned. "And I better get started tattooing you guys or I might get rusty. Wouldn't want me making any mistakes, right Jade?"

"Huh? Oh, right. She's really scary with the razor too." He winked at me and I couldn't help but reach over and give him a big kiss on the cheek, which made him blush.

"Yeah, you need to get started tattooing so we can finish up here and get back to L.A. Now that we've got some material, we need to get into the studio and start moving," Marcus continued.

My heart dropped a notch at that statement. L.A.? Did Devon know or was Marcus just making decisions for them all? "Sure. And remember I have to go back to my shop Saturday. I have out-of-town clients coming in. Sherry said you guys were good with it."

He nodded. "Of course. Take the day off. Maybe the rest of us can do the same if we get enough done. Hell, maybe we'll be able to take the weekend off." He smiled at me and left the kitchen as a sweaty Devon came in.

"Hey, you, how do you like your omelet?"

He kissed the top of my head and grabbed a bottle of water from the fridge. The rest of the guys left the kitchen on their way to work out or get showered. "However you'd like. Oh, hold the onions though." He downed the contents of the water bottle and was leaning into the fridge, looking for the orange juice.

Damn. His ass looked just as nice covered up in shorts. Okay, not quite. But it had the same effect. I cleared my throat and fanned myself.

"Coming right up." I got to work on his omelet and minutes later, flipped it onto a plate for him.

He took it with a smile and kissed me on the cheek. "Thank you, chère."

I gathered he didn't just mean for the omelet. "No, thank *you*." I teased and started putting things away. "It's my turn for some yoga and then I need to get cleaned up for the day. I want to have some drawings for you guys to look at tonight."

His eyes travelled my body. He took another drink of his juice. "Yoga?" His voice was barely more than a squeak.

I nodded and bounced away. "See you later."

I heard him groan as I left the kitchen.

Back in my room, I put on some slow music and tried to relax. I'd been so off my routine this past week that my body was starting to feel off as well. A little yoga would get me back on track. And there were some new muscles I had discovered recently that needed some attention —after the attention they had *already* received. Sigh.

After I was thoroughly stretched out, I showered and dressed in a tank and shorts. I braided my wet hair and let it hang. I could hear the guys downstairs playing their hearts out but I was enjoying the peace of my room. It was very sunny outside, so I sat at the drawing table and utilized the natural light to draw out some ideas for their tattoos.

I used the basis of Maggie's tattoo and added some details. Some of the feathers were falling from the wings. There was a skull at the base of the fleur-de-lis. I also did another drawing, this one of a traditional weeping angel. Nah, that wasn't right for them. I put that one aside.

I did my own take on the sculpture. Instead of an angel, it was a beautiful woman with black wings, leaning over the tomb, and she was looking up with a tear falling from her eye. Skulls lined the bottom of the tomb.

None of these seemed right for Maggie though. Cool, but not Maggie. I needed some ideas from the guys.

I texted Mackenzie to see if she was okay.

"More than OK, baby doll. Had a great night. Hope you did too. Can't wait to have you back Saturday, even if only for a day. Karen called and confirmed and so did Jonathan. They'll be here. TTFN. Gotta go pierce some guy's dick."

She frequently ended texts on a shocking note. That was my Kenz. I debated whether I should tell her that my "dare" paid off. Then figured it would make her day.

"Thanks, Kenz. BTW, the girls made their debut appearance to rave reviews."

It only took a few seconds for her to hit back:

"YES! Bout fucking time! Enjoy them. I do!"

Oh, I did enjoy them. I was starting to quiver just thinking about him touching me again. Which got me thinking...

I made another call, this one to my doctor. With things progressing as they were, it made sense to take precautions. She agreed to call in a prescription to the pharmacy across the street and I'd pick it up Saturday, before heading to the shop. She explained it would take a cycle before I was protected, so I wanted to get started as soon as possible.

Of course, if Devon was leaving soon to go back to L.A....

Nope, not going to think about it. If he did, I hoped he'd come back. I had to believe him when he said he wanted to be with me. Although no time frame had been mentioned.

Whatever. Not thinking about it.

I decided to get some air and check on things downstairs. As I descended the steps, they were playing a slower song and the lyrics Marcus was singing...well, *breathing* into the mic, were pretty intense.

One kiss from you and I'm no longer a boy
*   You taught this boy just how to be a man*
*   And this man wants to show you just how good*
*   A man you've helped him to become*

But it wasn't Marcus. It was Star.

He was singing in a breathy voice, one higher than Marcus's, way higher than Devon's. I sat on the steps and listened to him sing, smiling wide.

I wallowed so long in a world of pain
*   I fought the bottle but it was all in vain*

I never thought I'd be worth anything
Then you taught me what love could bring

You made me see there was a light
Just one kiss and all the strife
Was gone and now I'm ready to fight
You showed me there was more to life

So this was what he must have been scribbling down the past couple of days.

They finished the song and the guys all congratulated him. Devon hugged him. "I knew it would be beautiful, man; that was great."

"So you're not mad I kissed your sister?"

Devon socked him in the arm. "Nah, as long as you kept your filthy paws to yourself, dick." They threw a couple more fake punches at each other and then Mage and Jade were hugging him.

"I like it, Star" Marcus said thoughtfully. "I think I can make that work. How 'bout we add in a little more crunch to the guitars on that one part and speed it up a notch?"

Star shrugged then nodded. "Whatever you think, man. I'm just glad I got it off my chest."

"Me, too," I said, walking towards him. His eyes were glassy as he reached for me and I hugged him tight. When he didn't let go for a minute, I pulled back. "You want to take a walk?"

He nodded and I led him out back, calling over my shoulder, "We'll be right back."

I heard Devon yell, "Take your time, chère."

I kept my hand on his back until we got out the door and led him over to my bench. I sat next to him and he pulled me to him, sobbing quietly. I held him and rubbed his back for several long minutes until he was able to breathe normal again.

"Better?" I asked him.

He nodded. He wiped his face with the inside of his shirt. "Much, thanks. I started writing the other day when I found that picture. Man, that night was so great. It was just the first of many times that Maggie was there for me. Did I tell you she bailed me out of jail a few times?"

I shook my head and he laughed.

"Yeah. Once for fighting at a bar, once for a DUI... Once after I beat the shit out of my dad for beating the shit out of my mom. She saw me at my worst, no doubt. But that night at the dance, man. She and I danced. We talked and laughed. Then afterwards when we had all gone out to her mom's restaurant after it closed, she asked me if I'd ever kissed a girl. I told her not really, not a real kiss. She turned to face me—she was as tall as me with her heels on—and she said, 'Star, I'm going to make sure you do it right.' And she planted one on me. I was in shock. She showed me how to kiss like girls *like* to be kissed...and she told me I better not ever treat a girl bad. She even told me that if I learned to be a good kisser and a good lover, I would find the perfect woman for me and get away from all the drama that was my parents. She talked to me about not being jealous and possessive..."

He frowned and looked teary again. "It's too bad she didn't take her own advice about that."

"Did she ever talk to you about her husband?"

He shook his head. "No. I confronted her once and she just kissed my cheek and said, 'Babe, I got this. Don't I always got this?' But she didn't. One night at a bar, I saw them but she didn't see *me*. They were arguing because she'd gone out with some girls from work and they'd run into one of the bands she'd signed. The guys were buying her shots when Thomas showed up. He got pissed. He dragged her outside by her arm and I followed to make sure she was okay. He yelled at her, she took it, and then he started crying and she hugged him. Then they went home. That was it. I told Devon I was worried, and he was, too, but she wouldn't listen to us. She wouldn't even listen to Mr. Daryl."

His breathing was shaky and I took his hand in mine. He smiled down at our hands.

"I miss her, but talking to you helps a lot. You're different than her, though. There's a peace around you that she never had. Her energy was wild and crazy. Yours is more comfort and peace." He smiled at me. His eyes were red from crying and his cheeks were blotchy. "I can't thank you enough, Jaylene. For me, for Devon, for all of us."

I hugged him again and he kissed me on the cheek.

"You're welcome, Star. I'm just glad I can be here. I'm glad I got to hear you sing your song, too. It was beautiful. Maggie would have been honored that you felt that way about her."

He smiled a little too wickedly. "She was a helluva teacher. Devon was so pissed when he found out. I thought he was going to beat me up, and like I told you before, Devon didn't fight. He wasn't like that. But that night he was beyond pissed." He laughed and stood up.

I stood with him and squeezed his hand. "So I'm guessing last night went okay?"

He turned to me and sighed. "I feel like a total kid with a crush. I fucking love her, Jaylene. I mean it. I love being with her and talking to her. I told her everything, you know...about rehab and shit, and she didn't freak out. She's great." He literally had stars in his eyes.

"I'm glad, but be careful. I love her too, but she's finicky. It takes patience and tolerance to be a part of her life. Just be careful with your heart, okay? I don't want to see either of you get hurt."

He looked at me seriously and nodded. "Okay, sure. Thanks. And I'm so fucking happy for you and Devon."

It was my turn to blush. "Me too."

We went back inside and he stopped behind the bar to grab a sweet tea. Devon looked up from his guitar and smiled at me, giving me a nod to say thanks. I nodded back and felt butterflies in my tummy. He had a serious effect just by hitting me with that blue-eyed gaze of his.

The guys took a break to have lunch and we sat around and talked some more. I told them I'd been working on some drawings for them to look at and they were excited. They planned to practice for a few more hours and then Mrs. Boudreaux was coming to fix dinner.

The rest of the day passed quickly. Practice went well. They now had Star's song, Devon's song, and three Marcus had written; they had two more rough songs that Jade had come up with, and Mage was working on lyrics for another. The way they were collaborating was amazing. Even though Marcus wore the pants in the family, they all had things to contribute and they were all gifted with words and music.

After another delicious dinner cooked by Marie, whom I pathetically tried to help, we all converged around the table and the pictures. I brought my drawings down and spread them out. They guys *oooed* and *ahhed* over them and then we sat down to discuss.

"So I'm completely open to whatever you guys are thinking. I could show you some of the memorials I've done before but a lot of them are specific to the person."

"I love the one you did on Daryl's buddies," Mage offered.

Two of Daryl's buddies had come in after losing one of their fellow soldiers to suicide. I incorporated their unit info and symbols into a shield that a soldier was crouched behind, so you only saw his helmet and boots. I tattooed them both in the same day, it was a marathon session, and they told me stories about the guy and the things they'd done together. They cried and laughed. Both ended up loving the tattoos. I thought it was one of my better designs, and I'd enjoyed hearing their war stories. Daryl's friends were a rough bunch but I hadn't met one I didn't like.

Marcus was looking at my spin on the weeping angel. "I love this drawing, Jaylene. I could see this as an album cover. What do you guys think?"

They all got excited and really into the idea, pointing out the different elements.

"Sure, whatever you think. The drawings will be yours anyway. You can do with it what you want."

Marcus frowned. "But I'd want you to do the final drawing and have the final say. Obviously we'd pay you for the use as well."

I shrugged. "Okay, whatever you want. I'm glad you like it."

He was looking at me as if he was making plans—and I didn't like it. I wasn't interested in becoming their artist-in-residence. My work was here.

Thankfully Star got things back on topic. "I'd love for us to come up with something that incorporates the tattoo she gave Maggie. Oh! How about an angel kneeling, cradling a fleur-de-lis in her hands and looking down at it, with wings behind her? Kinda like how you drew this one with some of the feathers coming off?" Star was up and moving around the table.

"I could definitely do that. What do you guys think?"

Mage and Jade were nodding. "I love it, sounds great. Let's do it," Jade said.

He wanted another one already? "Uh, Jade? Your other one isn't finished healing yet, so I'm going to do yours close to the end, all right? You're going to have to be patient this time."

He pouted and whined, "Awww. How come? It's not like it's going in the same spot."

I snickered. He was cute but I can imagine he would have been a trying kid sometimes. "Sweetheart, your body needs to focus on healing the first one. If I tattoo you again, your resistance might get run down and you could get sick. Not going to do it, you're going to have to wait."

He sagged and nodded. "Okay, I guess you're right. Bummer."

Marcus gave him a paternal pat on the head. "You'll be fine, Junior. I promise."

Jade pushed his hand away and socked him. "Oh, you don't want to start that, do you?"

"C'mon, guys, no fighting. I don't want blood all over Mrs. Boudreaux's photo albums."

They all laughed. Except Devon. I noticed he'd been quiet during the discussion.

I walked over to the seat next to him and sat down. "What do you think, Devon?"

He tipped back his water bottle to finish it and then gave me a small smile. "I'm sure I'll love whatever you come up with, chère." He kissed my cheek and stood up to walk outside.

I noticed the cigarette pack was back in his pocket. He hadn't smoked for the past couple of days. I figured something must be on his mind but I was determined to let him have some time to himself. Hopefully he'd talk to me about it later.

I sat around talking with the guys for a while until I felt the yawns coming on. "Hey, guys, I'm going to bed. I'll see you all in the morning, okay? What do you want for breakfast?" They tossed out everything from crepes—which I assured them I couldn't make—to French toast—which I told them would be the safer bet. I waved them all goodnight and climbed the stairs.

Devon hadn't come in, and with Sherry gone, his bed was free. I wondered what he would do. I washed up, put on the lone nightgown I owned and crawled in bed.

I'm not sure how long I was asleep before I heard a sound from next door. Devon was playing his guitar. I debated going in to see him, but thought surely there was no harm in giving him a good-night kiss.

I found him sitting in a chair with his guitar, and paper and pencil next to him on another chair. He was obviously writing and I didn't want to interrupt. I started to back into the bathroom when he looked up. His eyes crinkled with his very sweet smile. He looked tired.

"Hey, chère. Come here."

I hesitated by the door. "I didn't mean to interrupt you."

He put the guitar aside and waved me over.

There was only a lamp on beside him and the shadows it left across his shirtless chest were too much. I walked slowly toward him, squinting a little in the light, hoping I didn't look a mess. He reached for me and pulled me onto his lap, smoothing my hair away from my face.

"When I came back in, they said you were already in bed. I didn't want to wake you so I thought I'd just write for a bit." He was looking into my eyes, searching for something.

"Are you okay? I was worried when you went outside but I wanted to give you space."

He nodded and pulled at his soul patch. This time it concerned me rather than getting me excited.

"I'm okay, it was just getting a little heavy and I guess with this tattoo and everything, it feels like the end...of a lot of things."

Oh. Shit. I stayed quiet, afraid for him to go on but desperately needing him to.

"I mean, getting the tattoo was supposed to be our way of saying goodbye to Maggie and moving on. I guess I'm not sure I'm ready to do that yet."

I nodded. "If you aren't ready, it's not written anywhere that I have to tattoo you now. We could do it whenever you *are* ready."

He smiled gratefully at me. "Thanks. That helps. I was kind of feeling like it was one more thing being pushed on me, and I didn't like the feeling."

"I'm sorry if I was a part of that. I don't want to push anything on you." There was another layer to that statement that I wasn't sure he would pick up on.

He turned me to face him and put his hands on my cheek. "No, Jaylene. You haven't pushed me into anything. You pushed me to talk, and I appreciate that. But that's all. Everything I've told you, everything we've done, is because I wanted to."

I guess he got that deeper layer. I tried a small smile but I still felt unsure.

He rubbed my lip with his thumb. "What is it?" he asked.

I shrugged. "Is part of that end you mentioned because you're going back to L.A.?"

He frowned and looked down at my hands. He took one in his. "Marcus *does* want us to go back to L.A."

I swallowed, but the damn lump in my throat wouldn't go away. I nodded. "You have an album to record. It makes sense. You guys have some fantastic songs."

He squeezed my hand. "Yeah, but I don't *want* to go back to L.A. There's no fucking reason we have to record there. There are some damn good studios here in New Orleans, and I'd just as soon do that than go back there. I don't want to budge on this, and he's going to have a fight on his hands if he keeps fucking pushing me."

I could feel his anger. I smoothed his hair back and he closed his eyes for a minute. Then he looked at me, his eyes imploring.

"Jaylene, I'm not going to lie and say I'll be here always. I do have to travel and play. But as far as I'm concerned, I'm home—and I plan to keep it that way. I want to be with *you*, dammit."

I laughed nervously. "Okay, dammit."

The tension fell from his face and he laughed, too. "Okay. As long as that's settled, let's get you back to bed, shall we?" He picked me up and carried me back to my room and placed me on the bed.

"You're going to hurt yourself carrying me around like that."

He rolled his eyes. "Are you hiding a cow inside you or something? Some scrap metal? Because you weigh nothing and if I can't lift you, I better hit the weights more often." I smacked his arm and he caught my hand in his. He kissed it and knelt down at the side of the bed.

"Are you going to join me?"

He smiled and shook his head. "Not right now. I've still got shit running around in my head. Do you mind if I crawl in here later though? I'd sure like to wake up with you."

I smiled and nodded. "Sounds good. And keep playing, it sounds nice." My eyelids were already heavy and I snuggled down in the bed.

"For you, the world. Good night, beautiful."

I sighed...and was out.

SIXTEEN

Sometime in the night Devon must have crawled into my bed, because all of a sudden I heard him yelling and he started thrashing around next to me.

I grabbed for him and tried to soothe him. Star came flying in the door and found me cradling Devon's head and rocking him gently. I looked up at him, feeling helpless, and he just shrugged.

"It's not as bad as last time," he whispered.

I nodded. "Thanks for checking. I think he's okay now."

He touched my shoulder. "You're his angel, Jaylene."

I smiled weakly just as Devon's arms came around me, crushing me to him. Star snickered and walked out, closing the door gently behind him.

I snuggled closer to Devon; his head was pressed against my chest and he was mumbling in his sleep.

"Jaylene...love you Jaylene. Love you."

I blinked and my heart started pounding. I watched him closely for a long time, memorizing every feature on his beautiful face. Finally, with a smile on my face, I closed my eyes, thinking I felt the same.

. . .

The next time I woke it was barely light out and Devon was snoring softly. I tried to extract myself from his grip without waking him, which took some work, but I succeeded. I threw on sweats and his t-shirt over a sports bra.

I crept downstairs, needing prep time to get my French toast cooking. I stole an iPod and some headphones from the weight room so I could cook with some tunes on. I must have had it up too loud because when Star came in and grabbed me around the waist to scare me, I caught him upside the head with my spatula, getting egg batter in his hair.

"Oh shit, Star. I'm so sorry."

He laughed heartily as he dunked his head under the faucet to wash it out.

"Whoo, that's a wake-up call. Hello!"

I laughed and he threw the towel at me. "You could have slept in, you know."

He shook his head, getting the coffee started. "Nope, you have done this by yourself too many times. Besides, I was *starving* and I could smell the bacon. There's no way I was going to let any of those assholes get to this food first. Mmmmm, delicious," he said around a piece of piping-hot bacon.

"You're terrible. You can take over the bacon; I don't want to screw up the French toast." We laughed and joked for a bit. Then he looked at me seriously.

"He okay after last night?"

I nodded solemnly. "I think so. He's got a lot on his mind and that's how it comes out, I'm afraid. It wasn't as bad as last time, but—"

"What wasn't as bad as last time?" asked Marcus as he came sauntering in. He actually had on a silk robe over his boxers this morning. Whatever.

"Devon had another nightmare last night," Star told him. I turned to Star with a frown and he held up his hands. "Marcus knows. We all know what's been going on. His mom was worried. She thought he was on drugs or something. We had to reassure her that wasn't that."

"Yeah, and what goes on with him is our business, Jaylene."

I turned to him with an eyebrow raised. "I wasn't saying it *isn't* your business, Marcus. Only that he might not appreciate being breakfast discussion."

He moved closer to me, picking up a piece of my hair and winding it around his finger. "You know, just because you're fucking him doesn't mean you have any say over him."

My eyes flew open wide and I had to control my urge to slap him. Instead I slammed down my spatula and clenched my fists at my side.

He stepped back, shocked.

"Marcus," I said in a low voice. "That is the *last* time I allow you to disrespect me. If you speak to me like that again, I will be terminating my contract. I don't have to take this shit from you. Star, do you mind finishing the breakfast?"

He nodded, and I marched out of the kitchen and straight to the weight room, where I hit the treadmill hard. I heard Star yelling at Marcus in the kitchen so I grabbed the other iPod and jammed the earbuds in. I was pleased to see this one had plenty of pissed-off music loaded on it.

A minute or so later, Devon came in and put his hands on the tread-mill gauges. I didn't stop running. He motioned for me to pull the earbuds out and I shook my head.

"I need some space, Devon."

He looked even more pissed and he stormed off.

Flustered, I ripped out the headphones and turned off the treadmill. I figured if I didn't deal with this, those two might go at it.

"How *dare* you talk to her like that, Marcus! What the fuck is wrong with you?" When I entered the bar, Devon was right up in Marcus's face. Marcus at least he was smart enough to look ashamed.

"Look, I just don't want her thinking she's got control of you, Devon. She needed to know her place."

Devon turned and paced away from him. "Her *place*? Her *place* is wherever the fuck she wants to be! As far as I'm concerned, her place is with *me*. If anyone is trying to control me it's *you*, you egotistical bastard."

Marcus narrowed his eyes at Devon and marched over to get in his face. "I'm not trying to control you, asshole. But she comes in here, acting like she knows what's best for you. I've known you my whole life, D. If anyone knows what's best, it's *me*."

Devon just shook his head at him and crossed his arms. "Marcus, the only person you know what's best for is *you*. So stick to what you're good at—looking out for number one. Leave my girlfriend out of this or I swear to fucking god, you'll be looking for a new guitar player."

Marcus just shook his head. "You'd put her before us? *Now* who's being selfish?" He turned around, blanched when he saw me, and walked upstairs, slamming the bedroom door behind him.

Devon yelled, "*FUCK!*" and looked like he wanted to hit something —until he spun around and saw me. His eyes went wide and he stormed toward me, grabbing my hand and dragging me outside with him.

I glanced back and saw the remaining three members of Maggie's Bones, looking at each other like all was lost.

"Devon, I'm sorry, he just pissed me off. I should—"

He stopped me by holding out his hand. "Don't. Don't *ever* apologize for him. He's gone way too far this time. He can bitch all he wants about me but I'll be damned if he *ever* talks to you like that again."

I took a deep breath. "Look, I'm not apologizing for him. But I told you I didn't want to make things difficult for you, and that's exactly what's happened. I'm sorry, Devon. But maybe you guys can work it out if I just go."

His eyes got darker and his brow furrowed. "No." His shoulders tensed and his hands were in fists. He was so angry. I felt helpless to do anything to fix it.

"Devon, please—"

"I said *NO!* Dammit, Jaylene. I love you! I'm not going to let you leave over this."

The shock on my face must have registered with him. It gave him pause for a minute, but he was still angry. "Don't you realize that's what this is? *I love you*. You can't leave."

I stepped forward and put my hands on his chest but he didn't move to hold me. "Devon," I said in a low voice. "I don't want to leave *you*. I just don't want to make things worse."

He started to pace and reached for his pack of cigarettes, cursing under his breath. I wasn't sure if my words were getting through to him. I looked up into his eyes, trying to get him to see me.

"I love you, too." My voice came out smaller than I'd hoped.

His expression changed and his breath caught. He reached for me and his hands gripped my arms hard, pulling me to his chest. "Then don't go." His voice cracked.

"Devon," I pleaded with him.

He squeezed his eyes shut and put his forehead against mine. "Don't leave me," he whispered.

I pulled my arms free and wrapped them around him. His followed and he squeezed me so tight, I could barely breathe. I didn't want him to let go, he was shaking so bad.

"Baby, I'm not leaving. I won't leave you," I whispered to him softly, and I leaned back to kiss him. His hair fell around his face and I brushed it back gently. His blue eyes were so sad and frightened and I hated that I had anything to do with that. "I'm sorry, baby. Please don't be sad."

I wanted to take his pain away. I kissed him with all I had. He kissed me just as hard and we held each other until the shaking stopped.

He took a couple of deep breaths. "I couldn't stand it if you left, especially because of *him*. I get so tired of him sometimes. Maggie was the only one who kept him in check. Well, her and Uncle Daryl. When they weren't around, he tried to boss us all around. To this very day, he believes that if it weren't for him, there'd be no band." He shook his head. "If he's not careful, *because* of him there'll be no band."

I hated this for him. Bad enough they were having problems as a band but they were family, first and foremost. This had to be killing him. "Look, we'll find a way to get you guys through this, okay? Maybe have Daryl come out and talk to you guys? He's good at this kind of stuff."

He smirked. "Yeah, if he doesn't pull Marcus's arms off and beat him with them."

I laughed. I could see Daryl doing that.

"I don't know. I just need to cool down. I haven't been that angry since…"

I knew what he was getting at. "Since the night Maggie died, right?"

He nodded sadly. "I don't know where it comes from, chère. I really wanted to hit him back there, I did. I hit Richard that night. I've never been a violent person. I always talked my way out of fights growing up."

I snickered and he frowned at me. "I'm sure your size had nothing to do with it."

He snorted. "I may have been tall, but I was about a buck sixty soaking wet in high school. I was all arms and legs. It wasn't 'til I went out to L.A. and Maggie refused to let us look like skinny pretty boys that I got any meat on me."

I looked him over and sighed with exaggeration. "And gods bless her for that."

He laughed and grabbed my ass, pulling me into him. He kissed me so sweetly and then stared into my eyes for what seemed like days. "Promise me something?"

I nodded, encouraging him to go on.

"Don't ever *not* tell me when something is wrong. When you wouldn't talk to me back there it about ripped my fucking heart out."

I sighed and shook my head. "I can't promise you I won't need my space, Devon. I didn't know what to say at that moment and I needed time to cool down, too. That doesn't mean I won't talk to you about it, but just like I'll respect *your* need to take a minute, please respect mine. Sometimes talking to someone when you're fuming is a really bad idea. If you take a minute to calm down before you speak, it's likely to be less damaging."

He nodded. "I get it. I'm sorry. I was just afraid you were shutting me out and it hurt."

Shit. "I'm sorry. I didn't mean to hurt you. I just didn't want to make things worse."

He growled. "How much worse could you have made it? He practically called you a whore, that fucking piece of shit."

I slapped a hand against his chest. "Now, no getting all angry again. He did not call me a whore. And I could have made it worse by flinging hot bacon grease all over him or kicking him in his prized possessions. If I didn't let loose, then neither can you."

He pulled me in for another hug. "I really love you, chère. I'm sorry it came out that way, but I meant it."

I smiled up at him. "Good, 'cause I love you, too. Now let's go back in there and figure this mess out."

When we got back inside, Mage, Jade, and Star were sitting at the bar drinking sweet tea. Star jumped up when he saw me. "Jaylene, I'm so sorry. I wanted to kick his ass but Devon came flying in the kitchen as soon as he heard me start yelling, so I didn't get a chance."

I laughed. "It's okay. Thanks for trying to defend my honor but I'm fine."

Jade looked miserable. "I'm sorry, too, Jaylene. I'm sorry my brother is such a dick. He just feels threatened by you, I think. He probably thinks you're going to take Devon away from us." He looked down at his hands.

Devon spoke up. "No one's taking me away from anything. But he's got to quit acting like this, or I'm serious, guys. After this album, if things don't get better with him, I'm out. I'm going to tell him the same thing, but I wanted you to know."

They looked at each other and back at him.

Mage said, "Damn, this is some bad shit. Brother, you can't leave. You belong with us."

Devon nodded. "I know. I don't want to but I can't take his shit anymore. Where the hell is he?" He looked around, glanced toward the stairs, before Star cleared his throat.

"He, uh, said he was going out to Daryl's. He packed a bag and left."

They were all quiet for a minute. Devon finally blew out a breath. "Fine. Maybe this is a good thing. The four of us will work on what we've got, and tomorrow I'll go out there and we'll talk it out."

The other guys looked hopeful.

"You'll come back, D? You promise?" Jade looked heartbroken. Poor guy was torn between his cousin and his brother.

Mage put his arm around him and whispered reassuring words.

"I promise. I'll come back. But he and I need to work some stuff out. And as for what he said about Jaylene..." They all looked like they'd been kicked in the gut. He took in a deep breath and continued, "If anyone else has anything to say, you better say it to me—and say it now. Because I love her, and she's part of my life now."

They smiled and Mage said, "Ain't nobody got anything bad to say about her. We love her, too, man. Marcus was just being an asshole. I don't even think *he* believes the shit he said."

Star stood up. "Whether he believes it or not, he was totally out of line, and I agree with Devon. If he continues to be a dick, I'm out, too. Most of the disharmony we've had since Maggie died has been because of him, and I can't take it anymore. Especially not the way he's disrespected women. I have no tolerance for that."

They all looked lovingly at their friend. This had to be hitting way too close to home for him.

"Shoot, maybe we just all need a break. If you're going to go out to Daryl's, me and Jade will head out to my grandmama's place in Trème. I could use some family time, and he could sure use some of her good cookin'. He's looking too thin," Mage said. I smiled at him.

Jade looked excited. "Really? Aw man, she makes the best crawfish etouffee." They began making plans and Star looked a tad forlorn.

I flicked my gaze to Devon. "I was going to invite you two to come back to my place over the weekend, since Marcus had offered to give you guys the time off. What do you think?"

Devon's eyes flared. His lips twitched, trying to hold back a smirk.

Star, on the other hand, raised his eyebrow. "Both of us, in your tiny place? You sure there's room?"

I walked over and threw my arms around his neck. "Star, there's *always* room for you at my place."

He smiled and looked at Devon, who nodded back.

"And I'll get to see Kenzie?" His voice was a shaky whisper.

I nodded. "Of course. And if I'm not mistaken, she was planning to cook this weekend. She's a damn good cook."

His eyes rolled back. "She can cook, too?"

I grinned. "Like you dream about."

"I'm in. If you're sure you won't mind and that, uh, I won't be intruding." He looked back and forth between Devon and I.

"You're never intruding, Star. You know that." Devon's voice was quiet. It was clear in that moment how much he cared about his friend. I remembered what Star told me about Devon taking him to rehab. It takes a good friend to tell you it's time to take care of yourself.

"You guys want to practice or what?" Mage obviously wanted to get back to work.

Jade jumped up. "I'm in. I want to get these songs tight. Then maybe when Marcus comes back we can get right back to work." There was hope in his voice. I prayed he was right.

"I'll be down in a second." Devon grabbed my hand and led me up to my room. He closed the door behind me and walked me over to sit next to him on the bed. He dropped his head into his hands and sighed. I rubbed small circles on his back.

"I'm tired." He rubbed his hands through his hair roughly.

I moved to rest my back against the wall. "Come here," I told him and held my arms out.

He looked at me with sad, bloodshot eyes and lay down with his head in my lap. He wrapped his arms around my legs, using my thighs as a pillow. He closed his eyes and I kept stroking his hair and his back. I felt him sigh against me.

"What do you need, Devon? What can I do for you?"

He exhaled and said, "What you're doing. Feels nice." His cheek was smashed against my leg so his words came out distorted. It made me giggle.

"Were you really going to ask me over this weekend?" His smushy voice was even cuter now that he was relaxing and it was a little higher pitched.

"Yes, I was. I have to tattoo a couple of people and I thought afterwards, the four of us could have dinner. Then you and I might have some time together. Alone."

He stilled and then rolled over on his back so he could see my face. "Can I hang out while you're working? Seems only fair that I get to watch *you* work since you've been watching me." His eyes looked a little brighter and I smiled down at him.

"If you want. It might get boring."

He closed his eyes and grabbed my hand to move it through his hair some more. "Don't stop, that feels good. How could it ever be boring for me to watch you? I could do that all day." He opened his eyes and smiled at me. "See?"

I laughed softly and drew my finger down to trace along his jaw. "Are you okay?"

He hesitated a minute before answering. "I will be. I *am* for the most part. I'll be better after I talk this thing out with Marcus. I still can't believe he said that to you. I mean, I can believe it because he's an ass, but I don't know what would possess him to, since he knows you're important to me."

I raised my eyebrow at him. "Perhaps he said it because I *am* important to you?"

He closed his eyes again and took a deep breath. "I suppose you're right." He frowned and I ran my finger along the crease between his eyebrows. That made him laugh and then his face relaxed. "I know, I know. Hey listen. I'm going to practice with these guys, and then I think tonight I'm going to run out to my mama's. That okay? I need to do something, and tomorrow I'm going to Daryl's to hash this thing out with Marcus. But then I'm coming to you Saturday, and I'm not leaving until I have to be back here Monday. Is that okay with you?"

I nodded. "Take all the time you need, baby. I'll be here."

He got a big goofy grin on his face. "I really love it when you call me baby. I do." He reached up and cupped my face. I leaned down to kiss him. He groaned and snaked the other hand up through my hair.

"I'm going to miss you so damn much, chère. I wouldn't go but I have something I need to do."

I smiled down at him. "It's okay. Really. I'll hang out tonight and then tomorrow, I'll take Star with me to my place and he can crash on my couch. Or Mackenzie's, whichever he prefers. I can't see her turning him away." We both laughed and he moved to sit up.

"I really like the idea of staying at your place with you. Thank you." He kissed me slowly and ran a hand down my shoulder, giving me chills. "I can't wait."

"Me neither."

He pressed a kiss to my forehead and then he stood up. "I need to call Daryl and Mama and let them know what's going on. Then practice." He put his hands in his back pockets. "You going to be okay? You're sure?"

I nodded and slid down on the bed. "I'll be fine. Promise. I want to work on the drawings and, oh, maybe get a couple of good nights' sleep." I giggled and he blushed. "I'm kidding. It's really nice sleeping next to you. I never thought I would like sharing a bed with someone. I've never even had to share a *room* with someone, so I figured I wouldn't like it. I guess it's just because it's you."

He blushed some more and came over to kiss me one last time. "Holding you makes me sleep like a baby. You make the bad dreams go away."

I frowned. "Not entirely. Do you remember them?"

He stood up and stepped away from the bed. "I remember feeling like my world just ended, pain in my chest, and then that's it. They tell me it's quite a performance." He was trying to joke about it but it was obvious the dreams bothered him.

"It seems to me that these dreams have happened on days when you've been extra agitated. Maybe we can work on that."

He smiled. "I'd like that. Thank you. I'm going to practice. I'll see you before I go." I smiled and said I'd see him later.

I lay my head down on the pillows and closed my eyes for a minute. This morning's events had me exhausted as well. Then my phone buzzed, and I saw it was Daryl.

"Hey, Daryl. What's up?"

I had to hold the phone away from my ear as he let loose a string of profanity with Marcus's name mixed in.

"Hold it, slow down, what is it?"

"Dat peckerhead just about drove me to homicide! Are you all right, chère? He drug hisself over here a little while ago and tole us what he said to you. He's lucky he ain't walking with a limp, I's so pissed at him." I could hear him breathing heavy. "I'm sorry, Jaylene. Real sorry. I never thought he'd treat you like dat or I never would have recommended you go there. But don't you worry; I'm gonna knock some sense into him—"

I cut him off before he made any more threats of bodily harm. "Daryl, relax. No need for you to go into cardiac arrest over this. You know, you need to take care of that ticker of yours."

He grunted and rumbled some more about young people.

"Did you just say 'whippersnapper'? You really are dating yourself." That finally got him to laugh. Good, progress.

"I'm so sorry, chère. What you want me to do wit him? He's a total disaster here."

I told him about the plan. "Devon is going to his mother's tonight and then he wants to see Marcus tomorrow. Will you referee so the two of them can work this out?"

"Of course. Dat's what I do. But dat don't mean I'm forgiving this shithead for the way he talked to you. Fucking numbnuts..."

"Daryl, your ticker! I'm fine. It's not the first time I've ever been insulted and it won't be the last. I'm just glad he came to you. Look, we're all getting out of here tomorrow for a weekend away. I think it will be good for everyone."

"You're right. I'm sending Katie and the girls to her parents for the next couple of days, don't need my babies hearing me put the beatdown on this dipshit."

I couldn't help it. "Why not? They'd learn some colorful language."

He growled at me. "Jaylene Renee, you a naughty one, you. All right. Tell Devon to call me and tell dem boys we'll fix it, okay?"

"I will. Just go easy on them, Daryl. They're so raw from all this, and unfortunately I seem to have gotten in the middle. I think Marcus isn't comfortable with me being involved with Devon."

I heard something crash on the other line and Daryl was breathing heavy again. "I don't give a *fuck* what he's comfortable with. He knows better than to talk to someone in my family like that. And he has no right to get into Devon's affairs. He should be happy for his cousin, not bitching and moaning about not getting his little weenie way!"

I clenched my lips together to keep from bursting out laughing, part out of nervousness because Daryl really could be scary, but also the way he was talking about Marcus was just too much.

"Well, regardless. Take it easy, okay? I'm fine. Devon will be fine. I'll tell him to call you. Now go drink some water and calm yourself down."

He growled and grouched some more and then hung up.

When I stepped out of my room, I heard Devon answering his phone downstairs. "Hey Uncle Daryl, I was just going to ca—"

I peered over the railing to see Devon holding the phone away from his head, and I could just make out Daryl's voice, still yelling from the other hand.

Devon looked up and saw me, and I shrugged my shoulders, saying, "Good luck with that." He smirked and waved at me.

I went back to my room to call Mackenzie and tell her what was going on. She was excited to hear about our plans for the weekend, pissed off about Marcus, and used very descriptive language to vividly explain what she was going to do to his penis if she saw him again. It made *me* squirm, and I'm sure any males in earshot were cupping themselves in fear.

I reassured her everything was okay. She said she'd call me when work was over and we hung up. I took in a huge breath and knew that I needed some rest, but the colors in the corner of my eye caught my attention.

The roses Devon had brought me had opened a little more, and were even more spectacular than they were at first. I grabbed for my sketchbook and drew them from several angles. I took pictures with my iPhone and thought I just might have found the perfect tattoo for the right side of my torso. Maybe. I wasn't going to get carried away but the idea did make me smile.

Later in the afternoon, I wandered downstairs and listened to them play. They really sounded good together but with Marcus gone, the songs were a little empty. The guys were all business as they ran through each one. The list was growing and while they were still playing with arrangements, they were about halfway there.

Marie came to make dinner and walked straight to Devon. He pulled her into a hug and spoke quietly to her. She looked really worried as she spotted Jade, and quickly walked over to him, hugging him tightly. Jade seemed to melt into her and hold on like the little boy that he mostly still was inside.

After a few minutes, the guys all crowded around them and they spoke quietly. Devon looked around and when he saw me, he walked over to join me on the stairs.

"After we eat, I'm going back to Mama's. Then tomorrow I'll go over to Daryl's." He took in a deep breath, feeling around his pockets for his cigarettes.

"You out of smokes?"

He nodded. "It's probably a good thing, but I'm not sure I'm ready."

"Now might not be the time to try to quit, but I know you're worried about it." His blue eyes showed so much conflict. I'd truly never known anyone with such expressive eyes. I figured the good thing about that is, I would always know what his most dominant feeling was at any the moment. I might not be able to tell what he was thinking, but I'd know how he felt.

We sat quietly for just a few minutes, holding hands, before he ran upstairs to pack and I went to help Marie with dinner. When I entered the kitchen, she came over to me and held my hands in hers.

"Jaylene, I am so sorry about my nephew—"

I stopped her. "I'm okay, really. I already talked to Daryl and told him the same thing." But I could talk to her woman to woman about part of this. "Marie, can you think of any other reason why Marcus would feel so threatened by me? He was so protective of Devon, and I just can't help but feel like there's something else going on with him."

She frowned at me. "I don't rightly know, sugar. I know Marcus has never cared much for women who didn't buy into his charms. He was always a tad self-centered with the attention and stuck on himself growing up, but between us, L.A. did terrible things to him. He hasn't been the same loving boy since they left. Maybe he's a little jealous of Devon. I know he was angry when Devon left for college. He thought it meant they'd never be in a band together, and honestly, I don't know if Marcus could have done it without Devon. Marcus might be the mouth of the band, but Devon is its heart."

"I believe it. Your son has so much depth, Marie. He amazes me."

She smiled and pulled me into a hug. "I'm so happy he's found you," she whispered to me.

I squeezed her back. "Me too."

We all ate together, and besides some small chitchat, it was pretty quiet. When we finished, Devon went upstairs for a few minutes and came back with a backpack and a guitar case.

I smiled as he walked toward me. His eyes were sad again and I hated it for him. He pulled me into a hug so tight, my feet were off the ground. "I don't know if I can stand this," he whispered.

He set me back on my feet and my hands came to his face. "We'll make it, because when we're together again, we know it will be that much better."

I'm not sure I was fooling either one of us. I felt sick at the idea of not seeing him for a whole day, and that was very wrong. If this relationship continued after the seventeen days, there would likely be long absences from each other while he was on tour, and I'd have to be willing to deal with that.

Holding him like this made me feel as if it would be worth it.

I pulled back and held his hands. "Take care of you, and I'll see you on Saturday."

He tried to smile but he wasn't there yet. He bent down and pressed a tender kiss to my lips. Then he leaned close to my ear and said, "I love you so much, Jaylene."

The smile on my face felt ridiculously wide.

"Me too, baby," I whispered back, and then he was grinning, too.

I felt someone behind me and looked around to find a chin on each shoulder. Mage and Star cooed, "Us too, baby."

I elbowed them both in the stomachs while they cracked up.

Jade wrapped his arms around my waist from behind and nuzzled my hair. "Yeah, get out of here, Devon. We want to have fun with Jaylene."

If it was anyone other than Jade who said that, I think Devon might have been irked. Instead, he just shook his head and pulled his face into a look of mock consternation. "You kids be safe, now. No throwing a party or any of that loud rock 'n' roll rubbish while I'm gone."

"Loud rock 'n' roll rubbish! Anyone else feeling what I'm feeling?" Jade was hopping back and forth again.

Mage and I looked at each other with big eyes and shouted, *"ROCK AND ROLL HIGH SCHOOL!"*

Star started singing in his best Joey Ramone impression. Jade grabbed his guitar and began playing the riff. Mage and I started moshing and dancing around.

Devon watched all of this with a bemused expression. I caught his eye before he walked out. "Love you," I mouthed to him, and he smiled and headed out the back door.

SEVENTEEN

We finished the song and Jade had the brilliant idea that we should watch the classic cult movie. Star and I made popcorn, still dancing and singing downstairs in the kitchen. We ran back upstairs just as Mage was turning on the film and we all collapsed on the couch together. After the heavy day we'd just had, having some silly guy time sounded like heaven.

We got as far as Eaglebauer Enterprises in the boys' bathroom when Mage hit pause on the remote and the guys all turned toward me. Mage mustered up all the seriousness he could.

"Okay. I don't want this to be weird or anything, but I have to know that you're a good match for our boy."

My face must have turned as red as it felt. Star jumped in for the save.

"Dude, there are better ways to go about this, you know. I don't think a tarot reading is going to really matter. They're in deep, man."

I felt like someone had turned a giant hot spotlight on me. I was even sweating a little.

Jade, who was sitting on my right between me and Mage, just shook his head and threw up his hands. "Guys, why don't we just do Twenty

Questions?" He turned and looked at me. "Are you up to the challenge?"

I blinked. Really?

"I guess. You guys can ask me anything you want and I'll answer if I can. I'm not spilling national secrets though. They told me they'd kill me if I did, and even Devon isn't worth that." Deadpanning outrageous statements had saved me from embarrassing moments before. I was counting on it to work now.

"Do you really? Know like, secret stuff?"

Jade was incredibly gullible. I couldn't believe after all they'd been through, he hadn't been broken of that trait.

"Jade, I am totally kidding. How would I possibly know any national secrets?"

He frowned at me and then got a look of recognition on his face. "How should I know? I get it. You like to tease. Okay, I'm going first, since he's my cousin. Here goes... Are you currently involved in a sexual relationship with anyone other than Devon?"

I balked. "Boy, you don't mess around. But you *do* make assumptions. No, I am currently not in a 'sexual relationship' with anyone. At least not one that actually involves intercourse."

He looked thoroughly confused.

I glanced at Star to my left, and then Mage. They both looked just as confused.

"What? We haven't had sex yet, okay? Do I really have to give you specifics?" I was a little flustered. I didn't mind being honest with them but I wasn't going to give them details.

Star spoke first. "Sorry, Jaylene. We're being rude. I guess we just assumed, like you said."

I shook my head. "Can't you guys even imagine two people spending time behind closed doors without penetration?"

They actually giggled.

"I guess not," Mage answered. "At least no one we know. Look, it's none of our business really, but...why haven't you?"

I laughed. "Wow, invasive much? We haven't because, well...I haven't, like...*ever*. And Devon didn't want it to happen while others might be listening."

They looked shocked.

"You mean... You've never... Oh shit." Jade held his hand to his mouth. "Oh my god. We are *such* assholes. I'm sorry, Jaylene. I can't believe I even brought this up."

I shook my head. "Guys, it's not the first time someone has made assumptions about me. Don't worry about it."

Mage frowned. "But...again, why haven't you? I mean, you're fucking gorgeous. Guys had to have been waiting in line to..." He stopped before he got any more uncouth.

"Bang me? Sadly, no, Mage. I've dated but never found anyone who didn't make assumptions about me and what I might be into." I didn't mean for it to sound like I was upset, but they all scooted closer. Star put his hand on my knee.

"This was a bad idea. I'm so sorry, Jaylene. You don't have to say anything else."

I shook my head. "I don't mind talking to you about this. Really. If nothing else, maybe it will clear up any other misconceptions you have about me—or other women, for that matter."

They all looked down sheepishly, probably afraid to open their mouths again. I confronted them. "Tell me why you assumed I'd had sex before."

They all looked at each other but no one spoke. I blew my bangs out of my face and Star snickered. "Oh, come on. I've worked with guys for years now and not one of them has ever held back on my account. Tell me."

Star rubbed at his hair like he does when he gets flustered and spoke up. "Look, the only chicks we've spent much time around were either the prissy girls from back home who wouldn't give us the time of day, or groupies who wanted to give it to us *any* time of day, you know what I mean? So I guess in our experience, there are only two types of girls: those who do and those who don't. And, well, you're cool, so I just figured even though you obviously aren't a groupie, you'd, you know... had some experience. Plus, you've been, like, to college and stuff and...I don't know. I guess I'm digging myself in deeper here."

"No, I'm glad you said something. At least it wasn't because I have tattoos. And for the most part, you're right. Most women I know have had sex by now. It just hasn't come up for me...so to speak." We all snickered at that one.

"That's what she said," Star coughed loudly.

"Well, it has *now*," Mage sputtered. "Damn, girl, you should have seen Devon working out yesterday morning. I've been working out just like that every morning since we left L.A. Being left high and dry will do that to a guy."

I blushed at that. So they at least knew there was some activity going on. "Yeah, well, he didn't think a cold shower was going to cut it."

They all burst out laughing.

Mage rubbed at his mouth and sent me a heated glance. "No offense, babe, but I'd have to agree with him. Not finishing leaves a man in pain. Especially with someone as fine as you."

"Golly, Mage. You sure know how to make a gal blush," I purred to him and batted my eyelashes. The others laughed and Mage mimicked having to rearrange himself. I didn't want to know whether he was pretending or not.

"What about you guys? Are you all unattached? Or do you have girls in every city just waiting to service you?"

They all blushed and seemed more embarrassed than anything.

"I'm not going to lie, Jay. When we're on tour and when we were in L.A., we all had girls whenever we wanted. We were pretty stupid about it, too. I had a girlfriend for a while but she hated all the other chicks hanging around, didn't trust me. She didn't really have a reason to trust me."

Jade looked a little sad about that, and Mage bumped him. "Dude, you were better off without her anyway. She had 'gold digger' stamped on her ass, for real."

Jade shrugged. "I know. But man, did she give great—Ah...sorry, Jaylene."

I laughed and pushed at his leg. "Okay, new rules. If I'm going to be hanging out with you, you've got to stop being afraid to talk normally in front of me. I'm really okay with it. I'll let you know if I'm not. Just like I did this morning."

They all got serious looks on their faces. Star took my hand in his. "Jaylene, I am still so sorry about that. Even though we might be a little slutty, we try to be respectful. Disgracing girls is never okay. Why Marcus had to go and say that..."

Mage nodded. "Yeah. He's a jackass. Marcus is probably just pissed that Devon will be off the market. The two of them hung out a lot, if you know what I mean, and Marcus probably hates losing his wingman."

I raised an eyebrow at him. "His wingman, eh?" That probably just exposed Devon's second in Amsterdam. Figures. "I guess they'll just have to work that out."

"Jay, I don't want to say anything that will make you think poorly of Devon, that's not my intention," Mage said.

I shook my head. "We talked. I know he's been with women. I'm not so naïve as to think that him being a rock star isn't going to be a challenge. We'll just have to see what happens, right?" I tried to sound confident but I'm sure they saw through that.

"If he does anything stupid, you can be sure we will kick his ass." Jade looked concerned.

I shook my head. "No. Whatever happens is between him and me. I certainly don't want to get in between anyone else in this group. It'll be what it'll be. But let's get back to the questions. You wanted to know whether I was worthy, right?"

Jade's expression was horrified. "That's not it at all. Hell, you're *too* good for us. I already know that. I just wanted to make sure you didn't have a boyfriend or husband hiding in the wings or anything. Now that we have that established— Wait, what about any stalkers or psycho exes?"

"Not a one. Okay, what else you want to know?"

Mage said, "How about religious preference? Are you Catholic?"

I shook my head. "Nope. My father was raised Baptist but had no love for church, so I never went. I did a little reading in college and fell in love with the pagan religions. Somehow worshipping Mother Earth made more sense than some dude with a beard."

Mage was looking at me with that wondrous gaze again.

"What is it *now*, Mage?"

He shook himself. "Nothing. But if you ever decide Devon's not the one, you better watch out, because I'll be all over you."

I rolled my eyes. "I'll keep that in mind."

Jade socked him.

"Ow, what the fuck? I'm not going to do anything about it. I'm just going to have a little crush on her." He leaned over and kissed me on the cheek.

I pinched *his* cheek and the other guys laughed. "I'll keep you in mind, Mage."

He held his hand to his heart and sighed.

Star rubbed his hands together. "What's your favorite tattoo that you have on you, and what's the favorite one you've done? I can't help it, I love your work and all of your tattoos are so awesome."

I smiled and thanked him. "You're so cute, Star. This is an easy one. Favorite tattoo I've done? Probably the one I just did on Daryl of his daughters. They are absolutely the most beautiful little girls, and the innocence and happiness in the picture really came across in the finished piece. Great subject to work with, great finished product." I hoped it was healing well. I wanted to take some professional pictures of it to put on my website. It was such a beautiful tattoo. "Now, my favorite one I have on me? Probably my laughing skull."

I stood up and pulled up the leg of my shorts to expose the back of my thigh. On it, I had designed a tattoo with my favorite quote and a laughing skull.

Star read the words to the other guys, who were craning their necks to get a look. "Whoa, that's really cool. What's that from?"

I tried to look serious. "Only one of the most important composers of our time."

They all looked at each other, confused.

I couldn't take it, afraid they'd never get it. "They're lyrics from the song 'Only Makes Me Laugh'." I waited a beat to see if they'd pick up on it.

Mage threw up his hands. "I have no idea. Who's it by?"

I gasped at them and shook my head. "I am shocked. I thought you guys were thoroughly geeky like me. I'll be right back." I ran to my room, grabbed my iPod and brought it back. There was a docking station with a speaker near the TV, so I found the song and played it for them.

Star snapped his fingers, like he may have recognized something. "Wait, I've heard that voice. Isn't that Danny Elfman?"

I nodded. "Yep. Before he was a big-time composer for the movies he was in an awesome band called Oingo Boingo."

They laughed at the name but they were enjoying the music. We all curled up on the couch and listened to the words.

"Wow, that's kind of cool. I like the vibe. What kind of music is this?"

I shrugged at Jade's question. "They were an alternative band in the eighties. I just really like their stuff."

We finished the song and Star smiled at me. "I like it. Especially the part about hitting the bottom."

He was lying on his back with his head toward me and I patted his head. "I know. It's good, yeah? That's why I had to have it. It was the first one that I designed for myself."

He smiled and closed his eyes.

I wanted some answers, too. "It's my turn now. This question goes out to all of you. What is the best thing and what is the worst thing about being in Maggie's Bones, one of the top-selling, hottest rock bands in the world?"

They scoffed at that. There was some grumbling.

"No, I answered yours, you have to answer mine—and be honest."

They looked at each other like they couldn't decide who should go first. Finally Mage sighed and said, "I'll go. The best thing? Seeing the world. We've been to some amazing places. I never would have been to Germany or France or Japan if I had stayed in Houma. I love traveling."

"I would imagine that would be wonderful. Maybe after, you can tell me what your favorite place to visit has been. I haven't left the country yet."

His eyes bugged out like I'd shocked him with my comment. "There's so much to see. There's still a lot I *haven't* seen, but I'm going to have to travel when we're not on tour. That kind of traveling means hotel rooms, arenas and clubs, maybe a restaurant... Well, except when Maggie made us go to museums and shit. I liked that."

"Me too," said Jade. "I loved the Louvre." They all agreed on that.

"Alright, Mage. The worst part?"

He sighed. "The business part. Having to kiss asses and be at photo shoots, videos, shit like that. I miss the times when it's just us playing and when we get to meet with fans. The music is spiritual for me. I never feel closer to peace than up on that stage, playing with my boys."

I smiled at him. "That's really cool. Thank you." He nodded and stretched out on his end of the couch. "Jade you're next."

His grin was a combo of shy and sly. "I hope this doesn't come out wrong but my favorite part has been the ladies." The other guys rolled their eyes and we all laughed. "I know, that sounds bad. But seriously, women are amazing to me, and I've gotten to meet all shapes, sizes, colors, and they're all beautiful, man. And when they're out there all screaming for us and dancing, that's just a good fuckin' time, am I right?"

"Not to mention the benefits, right?" I couldn't help ribbing him a little.

He blushed. "Yeah, there are perks. I try to be good and just sign autographs and stuff, but when they come to the hotel or are hanging around the bus? It's too tempting. Especially if there's a couple of them and they...well, you know." He licked his lips and grinned.

"Alright, we get the picture. What about the worst thing?"

His face fell and his eyes were suddenly wet. I almost didn't think he was going to answer me but then his voice came out low. "The fighting. I hate fighting, and that's all we've been doing for months. Even before Maggie died. We were fine while we were recording the last album, all excited about touring to support it. But then we started partying all the time, Devon wasn't ever happy with anything and he was on edge. Maggie wasn't happy because of Thomas. Star, you were a mess, and Mage, I don't know. You and I were just doing our thing, right? Until the release party."

Mage nodded. "Yeah, I kept telling everyone I had a bad feeling. Every fiber of my being knew that we were headed for tragedy. I couldn't tell them how or why, and no matter how much I told people they needed to get their shit together, it just spiraled out of control. I was having dreams constantly that I couldn't explain.

"The night before the party, I even talked to Marcus on the phone and told him I thought we should cancel, that something bad was going to happen. He just blew me off and told me about all the pussy that was going to be there, just waiting for me. Unfortunately for Maggie, that night, I was just as wasted as everyone else. I'd even been doing lines with Thomas...so I knew how fucked up he was. I should have stopped her from leaving with him."

Jade hugged him. "C'mon, man. You didn't know that was what the tragedy was going to be. None of us had any clue. And she didn't tell us how bad things were with Thomas." Jade turned to me and said, "We only knew he was an ass to everyone else. We didn't really know how bad he was treating her. I hate what happened. I hate it that we didn't know what to do."

A tear rolled down his face and I hugged him to me. He held on and cried, Mage rubbing his back from the other side. Star was silently crying to my left and I reached over and grabbed his hand. He squeezed back.

I took in a deep breath. "I'll tell you guys what I told Devon. Maggie was going to do what she was going to do. I can tell you from experience that women in those relationships usually don't respond well to pressure from family and friends. They have a tendency to push people away who don't support them. She knew you guys didn't like Thomas, right?"

They nodded. Jade sniffled and rubbed his nose on the back of his arm.

"So if you'd told her that he was no good for her and she should leave, how do you think she'd have responded?"

They shook their heads and were quiet.

"I can tell you—she most likely would have told you to stay out of it, she had it handled. Like she said to you, Star, 'I got this, don't I always got this?'"

He nodded and sobs racked his body. He threw an arm over his eyes and cried. I let my words sink in for a bit and then I said, "She knew you guys loved her. That was the most important thing. If she would have lived, she would have eventually gone to one of you for help. She wouldn't want you to blame yourselves."

I wasn't sure if they were hearing me until Jade said in a whisper, "I miss her so much. I really, really miss her."

The others murmured their agreement and the four of us just sat there holding each other for a while. Then Star said in a shaky voice, "You want to know what my best and worst are?"

"Of course, Star. You go."

He took his arm off his eyes and stared straight at the ceiling. "The drugs."

I waited to see if he'd continue but I had an idea what he meant.

"The drugs were the best when I had them. They were everywhere, they were free, and they were plentiful. I didn't have to feel anything if I didn't want to. I could do whatever I wanted and not worry about the consequences. It was the best. And then it wasn't. It was the worst because I hated who I was. I hated how I felt, how I treated all of you and everyone around me. I hated how much like my father I sounded whenever anyone would try to confront me. And I hate what it did to Maggie."

He was holding my hand tightly and I rubbed my thumb over his knuckles to let him know I was there for him.

Jade said quietly, "I hated what they did to you too, Star. I missed you. I'm glad you're back." They smiled at each other and Star let go of my hand to do a bro handshake with him.

Mage just said, "You are one of the strongest people I know, Star, and I'm so glad you're better. I will do whatever it takes to make sure you stay that way."

Star smiled sadly at him and said, "Thanks, buddy, but it's up to *me* to do whatever it takes to make sure I stay this way. I know you guys are here for me if I need you, but I have to do this by myself."

Mage nodded.

We sat there in silence for a bit in various embraces when Mage cleared his throat. "Uh, guys? I'm glad we had this talk and all but can we finish the movie now? My favorite part is coming up."

We all laughed and untangled ourselves. "Let me take a bathroom break and I'm good to go."

They got up to do the same and to stretch. It was late but I was still wired and I hadn't seen this movie in forever. I hurried to my room to take care of business. I decided to get more comfy, so I changed into my jammies and grabbed a pillow from the bed. I glanced at my phone before running back out the door and decided to check for messages.

Devon had left a voice mail an hour ago.

"Hey, beautiful. I hope you aren't answering because you're having fun with my boys—as long as it's not too much fun. I miss you like crazy already but I'm glad I came to do what I needed to do. Don't worry about calling me back tonight, I just wanted to say I love you and then I'm going to bed. I think I can actually sleep, and maybe my dreams of you will chase the bad dreams away. Good night, chère."

I clutched the phone to my ear and shivers ran through me.

He loves me.

How much more amazing could this man be? I thanked whoever was responsible for this miracle because that's what it was. I came in here thinking I couldn't work miracles, but I'd certainly gotten one.

With a smile on my face, I bounced back over to the couches. The guys had grabbed some blankets and turned the lights out. I went back to my place and the four of us curled up together. Star and I shared my pillow, with our bodies pointing opposite directions. Jade and Mage did the same on the other side of the sectional. The couches were huge, but the guys still had to hang their legs over the ends. Jade was using the ottoman for his, which didn't look comfortable.

Mage turned the movie back on, and in my mind, I was dreaming the shower scene but instead of Dee Dee, it was Devon in the shower playing his guitar for me.

I sighed deeply and the last thing I remembered was being under the hot spray with him, our mouths on each other.

EIGHTEEN

My next conscious thought was that there was an earthquake happening and I was trapped under something heavy. The noises I heard sounded like a chainsaw cutting away at something. It was hot and I was stuck to whatever surface I was on.

When I opened my eyes in the dim morning light, I first recalled that I was in New Orleans and that they didn't have earthquakes here.

The next revelation I had was that the source of the earthquake was Jade, who had somehow managed to swing his legs on top of me and one of them was twitching. The chainsaw noise was Star, snoring away on the floor where he'd rolled off the couch. I noticed he'd pilfered my pillow in the process.

Lastly, the heat and stickiness were because my face was smushed into the leather couch and I was stuck to it with my own sweat and drool. Mage was lying half on, half off the couch, one leg swung over the back and the other hanging off the end.

None of us could have gotten a good night sleep in this mess.

Jade shifted his legs. I could breathe a little easier and the shaking stopped...but then he started scratching himself, and that was it.

"Uh, guys? I seem to have a problem here?"

I heard groaning and Star's snoring stopped. He popped his head up to become face-to-face with me. His eyes grew wide and then he started laughing, loudly.

"Star! What the hell!?" Jade groaned and started to roll over.

"Ow! Jade!" When he moved, he now had me completely pinned, his feet tangled in my hair. My feet were under his back and tangled in *his* hair.

"Ah! I can't move! Who's pulling my hair?" he shouted.

Mage sat up and when he saw our predicament, he rolled off the couch, cracking up on the floor next to Star.

"You guys aren't helping here." I tried to get out but I was quickly losing air. "Jade, I can't move either. Will you two hyenas please give us a hand?"

Finally Mage and Star began the process of untangling feet from hair—none too gently, I'm afraid. Then Jade further pained me by stepping in the middle of my back to get up. I cried out as my spine bowed under his weight.

"Oh no! Jaylene, are you okay? I'm so sorry. I'm really a sound sleeper, I had no idea." Jade tried to help me roll over and the peeling sound of my face becoming unstuck from the couch made them all wince.

"Jesus. This is bad. How the hell are we supposed to tell Devon we all slept on his girlfriend?"

I rolled my eyes as the guys all burst out laughing. "Ha ha, very funny. At least I can tell him you guys all suck." That made the snickering worse. "Okay, not suck—you guys are all hair pullers and face smashers and pillow stealers."

The laughing stopped. "That might not go over too well for us." Jade sounded nervous.

I slowly sat up, knowing I was a wreck. My back was killing me and I felt like the imprint of the leather was never going to come off. My skin hurt like I had an awful sunburn. I held my head in my hands and groaned loudly.

"What can we do, Jaylene? Are you going to be okay?" Star rubbed my back while the other two cleaned up the scene of the crime.

"I'll be fine. I'm going to go do some yoga, maybe a run on the treadmill, and then a shower. When I go home tonight, I'll see if Mackenzie can work on me for a while." I turned to look at Star, whose concern was bleeding off him. "Didn't you know Mackenzie was a massage therapist?"

His eyes flared at that. "Could that woman get any hotter? Really? Damn. Hey, Jaylene? I wanted to bring her something nice when we go tonight...that is, if I'm still invited?"

I elbowed him. "Of course you are. Just because we've slept together doesn't mean we can't be friends."

He slapped his hand against his forehead and fell back against the couch. I couldn't help but giggle. It was obvious they were all nervous about us sleeping together.

"Guys, how about we all go work out together and then I'll make you breakfast? Mage, what time are you and Jade taking off?"

He shrugged. "I was going to call my uncle and have him come pick us up this afternoon sometime. Why? Oh, I bet you need a ride with your stuff, huh? Hey, Jade? Why don't you call Rudy and have him come get us in the Hummer so there's room for Jaylene's stuff?"

He nodded. "I'm on it."

We all headed down to the weight room after quick runs to the bathroom for morning business and teeth brushing. Star and Mage hit the weights, and Jade and I ran alongside each other on the treadmills. Music blared from the speakers and we were all just in our own worlds. I realized I still wasn't completely used to all the skin. The guys were shirt-less, but it didn't feel as weird after our night of bonding. I felt a lot closer to them, even though I still didn't know Mage and Jade as well as Star. They'd all opened up to me and I was grateful for that.

I worked up a good sweat and then went over to an area with mats on the floor to stretch out. I stifled a laugh when I realized how hard they were trying not to watch me. Okay, they didn't look at me like a sister or friend, but they were really trying to. I guess you couldn't take the rock star completely out of them.

Mage took my place on the other treadmill and he and Jade fell into step together. Jade had pulled his long hair back in a tie. Mage's was sweaty and plastered against his back. Star's short hair was sticking out all over.

And while they were all beautiful in their own way, they had *really* won me over with their boyish charms and goofy senses of humor. Part of me was loath to think of them in their real element. As rock stars, they probably weren't this accessible.

"So guys, I have another question." They looked curious but concerned. I laughed. "It's not a huge deal. I'm just wondering how much different you are when you're doing the rock star thing. Because you guys are so much fun to hang out with, I just wonder if when my contract is up and you guys go back to being big time, how different are you going to be?"

They looked at each other, and I thought I detected a note of sadness.

Star shared, "I don't know that we're really that different. We don't try to put on an act, I don't think. But we don't really share our nerdy sides. Makes it rough with the fans when they think we're still nerds."

Jade was smiling now. "And if they want to think we're like what our *music* is about, I guess I don't mind."

I rolled my eyes. I didn't want to know the answer to the next question but I thought I'd better ask. "Do you think you guys will ever settle down with someone or do you still like the chase?"

Mage frowned. "I think what you're *really* wondering is will Devon settle down, or if he's still going to be chasing skirt."

I shook my head. "No, I don't think I'm asking that. I wouldn't want you guys to speak for him. And only time will tell what happens with Devon. No, I'm curious about *you* guys."

He was still frowning but he looked like he was deep in thought.

Star said, "I hope to settle down. I don't need any more empty relationships. I don't want that life anymore."

He seemed determined to stay well—and I was determined to help him in any way that I could. "I think you'll have what you want, Star. And I'll be here however you need me." He smiled and winked at me.

Jade sighed. "If I can find the perfect woman, I'll settle down. I just don't really know what I want. I can't see past getting this album done right now so I don't know what the hell is going to happen to me. Or what's going to happen to *us*."

Mage cut in. "Dude, we're going to be fine. We'll do the album and then we'll figure it out. I don't think we're done yet. We've still got a lot of music left in us, we do. As for settling down?" He got a sly smile on his face. "My woman is out there. She just don't know she's my woman yet. When it's time, I'll grab her up and we'll have about twenty kids together. I can't wait to be a dad."

I giggled. "I can totally see you being a dad. You'll be a good one. But twenty kids is a lot to ask of a woman. I'm assuming you meant *one* woman?"

He laughed. "Yeah, one woman. Okay, maybe ten kids. Is that too much?"

"I don't know, the thought of giving birth scares the shit out of me, so I'm probably not the right person to ask."

Jade raised an eyebrow. "Don't you want to have kids?"

I concentrated on stretching. I wasn't sure how to answer that. "I don't know. It's scary. I'm only just now doing a good job of taking care of myself. I don't know if I'd make a good mom, I wouldn't know what to do with a baby. I love kids...other people's kids."

The truth was, I was terrified of ever having kids. What if I screwed up? My own mother couldn't handle it; how did I know if I'd be any better? And with the upbringing I had? I didn't ever want to put a kid through what I went through, the constant judgments and the pressures. I didn't think I was that kind of person, but I didn't want to gamble a child's life on it.

Jade shook his head. "You'd be a great mom, Jaylene. Just look at how well you take care of us."

I laughed. "Yeah, but you guys are already grownups with healthy egos. A child? I don't know. They're so fragile. I wouldn't want to screw them up."

They all snickered and Jade said, "You've spent over a week with us and you don't think *we're* screwed up? Maybe your counseling skills are a little rusty."

I laughed but it was shallow. He was right about my skills. Before I started wallowing in self-pity, I decided I'd better go shower.

"I'm going to go clean up. What do you want for breakfast?" They all stopped and got starving caveman looks on their faces.

"Aw, Jaylene. Your breakfast is awesome. Can we have French toast again?" Jade was giving me his best pouty face.

I shook my head and laughed. "Of course you can. I'll be down in a few."

They fell into a conversation of grunts and I knew it was time to go. But I couldn't shake this bad feeling I had as a result of our conversation. I turned on the shower and waited for the hot water. Once it was ready, I stepped under the stream...and lost myself in the past.

"Hey, Dad?" I had just gotten my thesis back from my professor and the committee had given me an A, cementing my honors status for graduation.

"What is it, Jaylene?" He was in his study working on some plans for his next trip out of the country. Being a defense contractor meant long trips overseas to sometimes unforgiving locales, and when he came home, he was grouchy and usually sick.

I took a deep breath and handed him my portfolio.

He looked over my professor's comments. I waited impatiently, hoping this time maybe he'd finally be proud of me.

"Well, they gave you good marks, but I still don't understand why this topic has any merit."

I'd chosen to review the effects of divorce on academic achievement in girls. My professor thought it was a great topic, something that schools should be looking at, as well as courts when making decisions about custody. I'd spent two years putting the research and interviews together.

"If a person chooses to be successful, they will be, regardless of their background. I get tired of hearing people make excuses for themselves." He handed the portfolio to me and went back to his work.

I choked back a sob. I nodded and said quietly, "Thanks. Sorry to bother you." I turned and hurried away, hoping I could hold back the tears until I was in the sanctuary of my room.

I wiped at my face, realizing that I'd been crying.

I finished cleaning myself up and tried to chase that memory away. I was glad I was getting away from this place for a couple of days. I needed to be back in my current sanctuary to get ahold of myself.

When I finished and went back to my room, I saw I had two texts. The first one, from Mackenzie, said: *"Hey gorgeous! Just wondered what time you were coming back tonight? I'm cooking tomorrow but I could cook tonight, too, if you want. I just can't wait for you to get back. Troy said he's taking the weekend off since you'll be here, so he's leaving around midnight tonight and won't be back until Monday. So hurry."*

I smiled. I missed her as much as she missed me. It meant so much to me to have a friend like her. She put up with a lot and had been so supportive with this latest venture. I started to think about what Star could bring her and remembered how much she liked the poppet drawings by Clay Davis, down at the French Market. Perhaps he had a disguise good enough to get us in and out of there before we went to the shop.

I answered her: *"Not sure what time I'll be there, I have to check with Star. Wondering if you might be up for sharing some of your massage therapy expertise? I kind of spent the night on the couch with the guys and I'm a mess."*

That was likely to get a lively response from her. The next text was from Devon. I felt my cheeks heat up.

"Hey beautiful. I'm missing you something fierce. I hate it that I won't see you until tomorrow. Everything okay?"

I texted back: *"I woke up a mess, got sweaty, took a shower, now need to feed the cavemen. Missing you too. My pillow still smells like you. Think anyone would notice if I carried it around with me? Looking forward to getting your smell all over my pillows at my flat. Everything okay with you?"*

I grabbed for my clothes and was getting dressed when he texted again: *"Why did you wake up a mess? Sorry I missed the sweaty and the shower. I'll get my smell all over anything you want me to."*

I debated telling him I slept with his band mates last night but I thought perhaps that wasn't information for a text.

"I woke up on the couch. Too much Rock 'n' Roll High School and Twenty Questions. Did you sleep okay?" I hoped he didn't have another nightmare. I went in the bathroom to fix my hair and when I came back, there was another text.

"That couch is not comfortable. I didn't get much sleep but I wrote a

new song. It's a sequel to 'Mystikal Stick'. It's called 'Magic Pole'. I think you'll love it. I don't think I want to know about Twenty Questions, I'm assuming that was Jade's idea? Going to Daryl's now. I'll text when I'm done. Tomorrow can't get here soon enough."

I was beginning to feel the same. Tomorrow seemed forever away.

"Tomorrow actually begins at 12:01 a.m., which is only 13 hours from now. If we were being technical about things. That gives you a window. Hope Daryl's goes okay. Tell him to take care of his ticker."

I had to get back downstairs before the cavemen resorted to cannibalism. When I found them, they were actually quite civilized, sitting at the bar eating fruit and drinking coffee.

"Sorry for the delay, I'll have your French toast out in a jiffy." They all smiled graciously at me and I continued into the kitchen. I made quick work of getting them fed. They were even more gracious when I came back into the bar with the food.

"So Marcus said Sherry has us booked into the studio starting on the second. That only gives us a week to finish writing. I hope we'll be done."

I wordlessly placed the food platters in front of them and tried to process what Jade was telling the guys. I had just over a week. Then Devon would be gone to L.A. Being here with him was a fantasy. Soon, he'd be back in his reality and I'd be back at my shop doing my thing. What did that mean for us?

"Jaylene, did you hear me?" Star was looking at me, concern on his face.

I shook my head and tried to smile. "Sorry, just daydreaming. What did you need?"

He frowned, not buying my smile. "I was asking if you'd thought about what I could bring Mackenzie?" This, I could certainly help out with. My smile was devious this time and he leaned forward on the bar. "You've got a plan, don't you?"

I nodded. "You got any of those disguises Sherry talked about?"

He frowned. "Disguises? Oh. You mean for going out? Yeah, I can work something. What's the plan?"

I told him where we needed to go and for what. He was on board with the plan and he ran upstairs to pack. Rudy was supposed to be over around three to pick us up, so we had time to run out and do a little shopping.

We invited Mage and Jade to come with but they opted to stay and try to write, obviously stressing about their deadline. I was stressing about it, too, but there was nothing I could do. When they left, I'd have to just deal with it and go on. I tried to convince my heart that I could handle getting closer to Devon, knowing he was leaving.

I went into the kitchen to finish cleaning up the mess. Mage helped me carry the dishes in and quietly washed them while I dried.

"Devon's different than us...I know you know that."

His words startled me. I continued drying, not looking at him. "Okay. I know he doesn't share your boy-band fantasy."

Mage laughed. "That's not what I'm talking about, but I see you. I know you like to hide behind jokes, but I see you."

I turned on him with an eyebrow raised. "And just what do you see?" I tried a teasing tone but his look was dead serious.

"I saw how you looked out there when Jade was talking about going back to L.A."

I shrugged and busied my hands with drying the dishes so he wouldn't see them shaking. "And how did I look, Mage?" He kept handing me dishes and I gratefully accepted them. I could feel him watching though, and it wasn't helping me stay calm.

"Just because he's going back to L.A. don't mean this can't work. You can travel and tattoo, right? Things work themselves out."

I scoffed. "My business is here. This bit of time with you guys is an exception. I plan on going back to my shop on May first and it's back to business. Devon's got to do what he's got to do, right?"

He said, "Mmm-hmm. But that doesn't mean it has to be back to old business with him, if you get what I'm saying."

I put down my towel and looked at him. "Just what *are* you trying to say, Mage?"

He put the dishes aside and turned to me, taking a step closer. "I'm saying that just because he's going back to L.A., doesn't mean he'll go back to the L.A. lifestyle, you dig? I see you looking for a way out here. You don't have to do that, you know. He loves you."

I felt my resolve slipping. "He might love me now, but when I'm out of sight, I'll probably be out of mind. I love him, too, but I don't want to hold him back. He's got you guys to worry about."

He crossed his arms over his chest. "So that's how you're going to play it?"

I crossed my arms to mirror his. "I'm not playing anything. I'm just being realistic. We'll see what happens. I'm not fooling myself into thinking that he's going to want to continue things after he leaves. I'm just me, and he's got a whole world out there I know nothing about."

Mage dropped his arms and shook his head, a frustrated sigh escaping. "There's nothing 'just' about you, Jaylene. And if you actually believe all this you're spouting right now? You're just going to push him away. Don't do this."

"Mage, I'm not going to push him away. I couldn't even if I wanted to at this point. So don't worry." I could see that my words weren't going to appease him.

"I *am* worried. We're just getting him back, thanks to you, and I don't want to lose him again—thanks to you. So if you think about running, just remember how he looked the first time he saw you. That's nothing compared to how messed-up he'll be if he loses you."

He turned to walk out of the kitchen and I called out to him. "Mage!"

He turned back around with an eyebrow raised in challenge. "Yeah?"

I blew my bangs out of my face. "I'm not going anywhere, okay?"

He nodded and walked out of the kitchen.

I took a deep breath and turned around to grab the counter for support. I didn't dare get my hopes up, but I knew I couldn't let Devon know how afraid I was. I couldn't let that factor into any decisions he made.

I finished up in the kitchen and was stepping out into the hall when I bumped into a guy I hadn't seen before.

"Hey. What are you doing in here?"

The man turned around and stepped closer to me, backing me toward the wall. "I'm looking for Jaylene Charles. Is that you?"

I freaked out. He stepped closer and I felt my back against the wall. I knew I only had a minute before things went bad. *"STAR! MAGE!"* I screamed.

And the guy started laughing.

He held his stomach and backed up...and something seemed extremely familiar about that movement.

Mage came running in with his fist pulled back. "Hey, what the fuck is going on here?" He grabbed the guy and slammed him against the wall.

The guy never stopped laughing—and soon Mage was laughing too. "That's a great one, dude!"

I took a closer look. Under the black leather jacket, the guy had on a white t-shirt. He was wearing a baseball cap, dark sunglasses, and had a moustache. But I knew that mouth.

"STAR! You sonofabitch!" I pushed him and he held up his hands in surrender.

"I'm sorry, I'm sorry. But it worked."

Sherry had warned me that they were good at wearing disguises. "You scared the shit out of me. You're lucky I didn't use my self-defense training."

Mage punched me in the shoulder. "Yeah, that training really helped you. 'Help me, help me!'"

I punched him back and grabbed a bottle of water off the bar and started tossing it at him. This time *he* was screaming.

"That's cold. That's cold, Jaylene! Help, Jade!"

Jade was at the top of the stairs laughing. "You deserve whatever you guys get. Go, Jaylene."

After chasing Mage around the bar, he tackled me and we fell on the floor in a heap. We caught our breath and then I climbed off of him, we cleaned up the mess, and Star and I took off.

With his mustache and glasses and straight clothes, you couldn't tell it was him. We walked down Ursulines to the French Market and made our way through the tourists and cheap souvenirs to a booth in the back.

"These drawings are Mackenzie's favorites. She discovered Clay Davis a couple of months ago and bought some of his prints. Hey, Clay."

The artist came over to greet us and asked what he could do for us.

"Actually, do you remember my friend Mackenzie? I think she had blue hair when we came to see you? She bought some prints?"

"How could I forget? Does she like them?"

I assured him that she loved Clay's work. "She's wanted to come back and buy some more to hang in our shop. Would you be able to do a custom piece? I was thinking maybe you could make a poppet of her putting a pin into this guy right here."

Clay looked at Star and there was a moment of recognition. "Holy shit. You're Star from Maggie's Bones." Star shushed him with a smile and Clay got the hint. "Absolutely. Can you give me a couple of hours?"

We told him we'd be back and we left to get a few more supplies for the weekend. First stop was the pharmacy to pick up my prescription. There was also a great shop nearby that sold handmade candles and bath products. I knew Mackenzie loved their stuff, and I wanted to get some for my place. I thought I might have a use for candles tomorrow night.

We grabbed some beignets at Cafe Du Monde for a snack. I wiped some powdered sugar off Star's cheek. "You don't get to do this very often, do you? Just sit and people watch?"

He shook his head and wiped some powdered sugar off my shoulder. "Nope. I miss it. That's why we came up with the disguises. We didn't want to give up being able to go out, so we had to dress up."

"What's the worst thing that's ever happened when you guys were out?"

He thought for a minute, taking a long drink of his cafe au lait. "I guess it would have to have been in Florida. Maggie tried to take us to Disney World because we'd never been. We wore hats and tried to cover up with geeky clothes, but it was hard to cover all our tattoos by that point. A group of kids recognized us and before long, we had a crowd of about two hundred people. Park security was getting nervous because there were little kids around, and these fans were all trying to get closer to us to get our autographs. A mom tried to get through the crowd with her little girl when some guys knocked into her, and the little girl fell and got stepped on. She was okay, but we felt awful. We took care of everything but that poor little girl was so scared."

I hadn't thought of how crazy people could be but I knew a thing or two about mob mentality. "Have you guys ever gotten hurt?"

He laughed. "Only Marcus. Outside a club one night, some chicks ran up to him and tried to tear his shirt off him. One of their boyfriends came up and sucker punched him before dragging his girlfriend off. He sported that black eye like a medal though. He wasn't fazed at all. He walked into the club shirtless with a shiner and still went home with three women." He shook his head and finished his beignets.

By that time, we needed to get back to see Clay and head over to meet Rudy to go to my place. The drawing was gorgeous. He definitely remembered Mackenzie, had her poppet all done up in her usual femme fatale dress. She had one hand on her hip and the other holding out a pin. He drew Star's poppet on one knee, holding his shirt open, and the pin was pointing toward his heart.

Star loved it, said it was perfect, and he paid Clay handsomely for it. He even autographed a second copy Clay had done for himself.

Star tucked the drawing under his arm and we hurried back to St. Germaine. When we got there, Rudy was waiting for us, so I ran upstairs and grabbed my duffel and my workbag. I left my table because I had a nicer one at the shop. I packed up my laundry to do as well. I knew I'd have time tonight.

The trip back to the shop only took a few minutes and when we pulled up out front, Mackenzie ran out to greet us. She hugged me tight and gave Star a quick kiss on the cheek, turning him absolutely crimson. I couldn't believe this was the partying, lady-killer, rock star guy. He was so not like that around Mackenzie.

Mage and Jade helped me carry my stuff inside and said their good-byes. "We'll see you Monday, Jaylene," Jade said as he hugged and kissed me.

Mage gave me a pointed look and I made sure to answer, "I promise. Be good. I'll see you both Monday." He nodded and they left, climbing back in the Hummer with Rudy just as a few passersby noticed them, covered their mouths and started to squeal. Luckily Rudy was able to pull away before they climbed onto the running boards of the Hummer.

I shook my head, glad Star was already inside and in disguise. When

I turned around, Mackenzie was playing with his moustache as he tried to keep it from falling off.

I walked over to Troy and we shook hands. The shop was clean and orderly. I had to take a moment to breathe it all in. I'd missed my place. I wanted to get my laundry going, so I told everyone I'd be down in a while and trudged up the back steps.

All I had the energy to do was throw a load in the washer and fall on the bed. I was out in seconds.

Nineteen

I heard knocking on my door hours later. When I rolled over to get up, the stiffness in my back had me held in place and I had to catch my breath for a minute. Damn. That couch had been a bad idea.

"I'll be right there," I called out.

I heard Mackenzie's voice. "JayLENE! If you don't answer this door right now, I am going to use my key!"

I got my feet under me and shuffled over to the door. I opened it to see Mackenzie with her hands on her hips and Star standing shyly behind her.

"What time is it?"

Mackenzie's frown got deeper. "It's after eight. You never came back down so I came to check on you." I opened the door and motioned for them to come in while I hobbled over to a cabinet in my kitchenette that held ibuprofen, and then grabbed a glass of water.

"What the hell happened to you?"

Star cleared his throat. "It's our fault, Mackenzie. We all kind of slept on her last night. Well, not me, I just stole her pillow. It was mostly Jade." He had his hands tucked in his back pockets, looking quite guilty.

When her eyes shot back to mine, I held up my hands. "We fell asleep watching a movie and when we woke up, we were all tangled. My back got a kink in it, and then Jade stepped on me when he was getting up. I'm just a little stiff and sore."

Mackenzie narrowed her eyes at me once more. "Alright. Star, will you be a dear and grab the extra table from downstairs and bring it up? It's in the back room." He nodded and jogged down the stairs. She turned on me next. "You—strip. I'm just going next door to grab my oils and then you're getting some Mackenzie medicine."

I sighed sleepily. "You really are the best friend a girl could ever have."

She rolled her eyes and stomped off. "I know, I know," she called over her shoulder.

I went into the bathroom and took off my clothes and donned a short robe. I went out into the kitchenette and did a laundry switch in my stackable set, and was just folding the last of my clothes when Star came in with the table.

"Where do you want me to set this up?" I pointed to a spot in front of the window. "That's about the only place big enough." It was dark out and I could hear music from across the street. Star set up the table quickly and then peeked through my sheers to look down on Frenchmen Street.

"Man, you guys have a sweet location here. You can listen to the music and watch the people. This is great."

I nodded. "We fell in love with this spot immediately. It was perfect for us. Daryl knew Troy, who needed to get rid of the building quickly, and Mackenzie and I pooled our meager savings together to put a down payment on it. It's been a struggle but we're finally in the black, so all's good."

Mackenzie came back in dressed in yoga pants and a cropped halter with a series of strings holding up the top. Star's eyes bugged when he saw her and he licked his lips. I liked the effect she had on him.

"Alright you, disrobe and get on up here."

Star cleared his throat, a nervous habit I'd discovered. "Uh, you guys want me to get lost?"

I shook my head. "Nah, just avert your eyes for a moment, if you will."

He plopped down on the couch and put a pillow over his face. "This good enough?"

Mackenzie and I both laughed. "Yeah, and no peeking."

He grumbled. "Hell no! I'm not going to peek. You think I want my best friend to kick my ass?"

Mackenzie giggled. "Well, I'll be sure to tell him how good you were, especially considering you had a chance to watch two chicks go at it."

He coughed but kept the pillow over his face. "Aw, chère. Don't say things like that. I'm trying to be good over here."

She moaned a couple of times but still he kept his pillow, just fidgeted a little. By the time she started to pant, I was already on the table with a blanket over me.

Star groaned again. "You gotta be kidding me, Kenzie!"

She giggled and then said, "You can look now, silly."

That pillow dropped in a hurry and he was looking with one eye open. Then he sighed. "Whew. You are a dangerous woman, you know that?"

She purred at him, "You have no idea, baby." He fell sideways on the couch and flung an arm over his eyes. "You are so going to be the death of me."

I turned to face him and rolled my eyes. "Oh, relax over there, Star. You can have her when she's done with me. You want to watch something?"

He laughed. "I *am* watching something. I'm watching how fucking good she is with her hands."

We all laughed at that. I closed my eyes and tried to let Mackenzie's movements loosen all the stiffness I'd built up. I couldn't blame it all on my wacky sleeping arrangements. "This feels great, Kenz. Thank you, I'm sorry you still have to work after being on your feet all day."

She tsked at me. "This is never work for me. I like working on you. Now tell me what has you worked up, other than how you slept last night. Cause I know you, and no matter how many guys slept on you last night, all this? Ain't just from that."

I exhaled a deep breath. "Where should I begin, Dr. McGowan?"

She laughed. "How about with that tall drink of water, Devon? When's he getting here?"

I groaned. "Tomorrow, and I miss him already."

Star laughed. "I'm sure wherever he is, he's feeling the same way. Babe, these two have been inseparable this past week. My boy's got it so bad for her. I ain't never seen him this affected."

I couldn't help it. Star's words had me smiling. I opened my eyes so I could look at him. He was laid out on my couch, tapping his feet in the air along to some up-tempo blues playing across the street.

Just then his phone buzzed and he pulled it out, a sly smile spreading across his face. "Dude. Where the fuck are you? You're missing a great show! Yeah, I'm at her place. She's naked, and you should see Mackenzie going to work on her. It is amaz— Of course she's not, dickhead. She's getting a massage. I guess our little *ménage à quatre* last night had her kinked up... What? She didn't tell you?"

By this time I was trying to cover myself so I could scramble for the phone. Mackenzie walked over, snatched it out of his hands, and gave him a swat on the ass. He was cracking up on the couch as she handed me the cell.

I could hear Devon's deep voice yelling on the other end. "Devon it's me."

He sighed and his voice got really soft. "Hey, beautiful. I miss you."

My cheeks hurt from smiling so wide. I was able to tune out Mackenzie's haranguing of Star just by picturing his delectable lips close to his phone. "I miss you, too. Where are you?"

I heard voices on the other end and he spoke to one for a minute. When he came back on, he said, "Sorry. I'm still at Daryl's. So what's this about a *ménage à quatre*? Was I wrong to leave you alone with my boys?" His voice was playful so I knew he wasn't mad.

"Well, I kind of slept with them all. Is that going to be a problem?"

He sighed again. "If you mean sleeping in the true definition of the word, then no. If you mean the figurative translation, then I might have to kill them all and hide the bodies."

I giggled at that. "It was only sleep—and not very good sleep. We watched *Rock 'n' Roll High School* and the last thing I remembered was you and me in the shower with your guitar. The next thing I know, Jade's feet were tangled in my hair, mine were in his, he was squishing me, and I almost suffocated face down on the couch. I can't even describe what a mess it was. So my bestie here is taking care of my twisted back for me until I can see *you*, and you do that thing where you kiss me and I go boneless."

That soft chuckle of his on the other end almost had me liquid on the table. Mackenzie laughed and called out, "Whatever you just did, Devon, it's making my job easier."

He laughed again and I sighed. "Everything okay over there?" I asked.

He cleared his throat. "Well, it's a start. We've agreed I won't dismember him and he's confessed to being an enormous jackass. He's planning on groveling for your forgiveness. He flew out to L.A. this afternoon to see Sherry and he'll be back Sunday night."

He sounded better but still tense. I hoped they really *had* made progress on healing their relationship. I'm not sure if their friendship could survive another blowup like this one.

"I'm glad you talked and I'm glad everyone is getting away for a bit this weekend. Speaking of..."

He answered, "Mmmm speaking of...I was thinking about that window you mentioned earlier. Just what *is* the likelihood of that window being open around twelve-oh-one?"

A jolt went through me and Mackenzie smacked my ass. "Quit tensing up. Devon, you're doing it wrong. I need *relaxed*."

He laughed and that sent me back on the path to liquid.

"I could agree to that window. I had a long nap this afternoon, so I think I should be *quite* agreeable to that window." I peeked over at Star and he looked confused. I winked at him and he just shook his head.

"Perfect. I'll see you at twelve-oh-one on the nose. I can't wait, chère." His voice was so low and husky, I felt myself getting warm all over.

"Me too. Hurry." I handed the phone to Mackenzie, who threw it to Star. He caught it and stepped outside to continue their dude conversation.

"Wow, there's a lot of physiological response going on here. Shall I assume that he's as good as he sounds?"

I chuckled. "Well, I think I'm about to find out." I was excited and nervous and thrilled all at the same time.

Mackenzie's hands stilled for a moment. "He's your first, isn't he Jaylene."

It wasn't a question. I nodded. "He will be, anyway. I think we kind of planned that it would happen this weekend. He didn't want to go that far while the guys were around. It was difficult agreeing to that once he had his hands on me, but I'm glad. After what happened with Marcus yesterday, I think I would have felt like the whore he made me out to be."

She cursed under her breath. "I cannot believe him. You deserve better than that, Jaylene. I'm glad Devon confronted him but I guess I still wish there was a little bloodshed."

I giggled. "I know, but it was bad enough and I hate to think that I came between them."

She cut me off at that. "No, Marcus's big mouth came between them. Trust me, gorgeous; if he would say something that hurtful to *you*, he probably has lots of ammunition he could use on Devon if he wanted to hurt him. And it's obvious that was his goal. All I have to say is, he's lucky I wasn't there."

"Yeah, I think he's extremely lucky." I could still hear Star talking outside the door. I needed a little advice. "Kenz?"

"Yeah, Jay, what is it?"

I tried to think of the best way to ask. With Kenz, blunt was best. "Kenz, is it going to hurt? Like *really* hurt?"

She had me roll over at that point onto my back so she could work my neck. She shook her head. "It's not supposed to be excruciating but it might be uncomfortable. My first time was terrible, but that had more to do with the fact that it wasn't really my choice."

My eyes flew open. "What?! Oh, Kenzie. What happened?"

She smiled and that vulnerable side of her was on prominent display. "Let's just say my high school boyfriend thought I was his property and he could do with me what he wished. When I didn't go along with the program quick enough for him, he took matters into his own hands. No one believed me because he came from a prominent Garden District family, and my parents basically shunned me for letting go of such a good catch.

"That's why I ran off to New York. My parents wouldn't have

kicked me out, but they made life a living hell for me so I'd leave on my own. Daddy still sent money. I think he felt bad. Mama was in charge, though, and she'd been counting on me marrying Jared. Jesus, he was such a pig. Going to New York was the best thing I ever did. I got to go to beauty school, learned massage...I've never been sorry for any of it."

A tear slipped down my face and when she noticed, she got mad. "Oh, hell. You're not supposed to cry over me. I'm really fine about it, Jay. I got help. I'm good. And you don't have anything to worry about. From the little you've told me and what I've seen, that man adores you and won't do anything to hurt you."

I nodded and wiped at my eyes. Damn, I'd cried more this past week than in the past year. And that was saying something. "I know he would never hurt me. I just want to enjoy it, you know? As much as I've enjoyed everything else up to this point."

Kenzie's eyes flared and she pursed her lips together. "I think it's just the beginning of your enjoyment." She kissed my forehead. "And with that thought, I think *my* enjoyment is about to begin."

Star walked back in then with a smile on his face and fake-pouted when he saw she was finished. "Aw, did I miss the Happy Ending?"

Mackenzie walked over to him, rubbing her oiled hands together, and placed one of them on the side of his neck. I heard her whisper, "Your Happy Ending is about to begin next door."

His knees buckled a little and he grabbed her face and planted a good one on her.

"You kids have fun. I'm just going to lie here in my puddle until I melt away. Nice work, Mackenzie."

She called back, "My pleasure. See you tomorrow morning."

My door shut, hers opened and shut, and I then I heard her bedroom door shut. Thankfully there was a lot of noise outside and her bedroom was across the building from mine. I might have heard her and previous engagements outside her door, but I've never heard things going on inside. It helped keep our living arrangements satisfactory.

I rolled off the table and felt deliciously worked over. My back was a little sore but mostly from the deep-tissue work she did, not from the actual tightness. The oil she put on my skin smelled delightful. I piled my hair on top of my head, rinsed off a little in the shower, then put my robe back on to wait for Devon.

In the meantime, I sat down with a cup of tea and my sketchbooks and looked over the preliminary drawings I'd done for the guys' tattoos. I worked on them a little more, really enjoying whoever was playing across the street. Sometimes the bands were fabulous, like tonight. Other times they played hip hop or garage rock that did nothing for me, so I'd simply close the windows and put in headphones.

I finally did a drawing I thought they all would agree on and I felt pretty good about it, losing track of time until I heard a buzzing sound.

I frantically searched for my phone, which was still in my pants. "Hello?" I answered somewhat breathless.

"It's tomorrow, can I come up?"

Sure enough, my kitchen clock said 12:02.

"Yes. I'll be right down." I hung up, checked myself in the mirror, liked the rosiness to my cheeks and thought the relaxed look in my eyes from the massage would have to do. I scurried down to the back door to let Devon in.

I could see him through the glass. My heart thudded in my chest and I froze. Illuminated in the lights from the back, he stole what was left of my self-preservation. And damn if he didn't look a little nervous, too.

I opened the door for him and he stood there smiling at me, his hands in his back pockets. "It's Saturday," he said in a quiet voice, tinged with excitement.

I nodded. "It is Saturday. Hi."

He let his eyes peruse my attire. They grew more heated with every inch. "Hi yourself."

He wore his usual uniform of frayed Levi's, boots, white t-shirt. He had on his beanie and his sunglasses were tucked in the neckline of his shirt. I don't think Hanes had any idea just how sensual their undergarments could be. They needed to see this apparition on my back step. If they only knew, they could rival Victoria's Secret.

"Did you want to come inside?" I stepped back a few paces, opening the door wide. He smiled and took a step towards me but paused before coming inside. I cocked my head to the side and frowned. "What's wrong, Devon?"

He shook his head and looked down at my feet. "Nothing's wrong, chère. I just...I told myself I only needed to see you, that I could see you and leave to give you your space. But now that I'm here..."

I reached out my hand to him. "I've had space for a very long time. I'd very much like for *you* to be in my space right now."

His blue eyes met mine with an intensity I hadn't expected. It took my breath away. "Letting me in your space might change things, you know. Are you sure you're ready for that?"

I studied him for a minute. Was he worried I didn't want him here? Was he worried my feelings had changed? "Why wouldn't I be ready for that?" I tried to keep my voice low but I couldn't keep the tremor out of it.

He took another step forward and lightly held the hand I'd left out for him. "I just want to be sure *you're* sure. I thought maybe if you had some time away, you might..."

I shook my head. "It only makes the heart grow fonder, don't you know that?"

He smiled and took another step forward. "That was true for me, I just wasn't sure if you'd feel the same."

I closed the distance between us, stood on my tiptoes and pressed a gentle kiss on his bottom lip.

Devon squeezed his eyes shut and pressed his forehead against mine. "Things were so tense back at the St. Germaine. I worried that our feelings were all caught up in that. I know that we said some things..."

Oh no he wasn't. "Devon, if you're getting cold feet, then come in and warm them. If you've changed your mind, well, then still come in. I'll get you a drink and we can talk." I turned around and climbed the steps slowly and prayed very hard to whichever deities were listening that he would follow me.

I got three steps before I heard the door lock and his heavy boots hurrying behind me. Then I was being carried, his warm lips pressed against my neck.

I giggled and relaxed against him. He got us inside my door and closed and locked it. He set me down gently and stepped back.

He stared at me for a long time. I felt a little nervous under his scrutiny. I pulled the sides of my robe tighter together.

Devon shook his head. He stepped forward and tugged on the belt of my robe, pulling it free. The two sides fell open, leaving me exposed to him. I sucked in a breath and stared up at him. His eyes devoured me. He looked as if it pained him. "Devon," I whispered.

His eyes slid up to mine and he fell down on his knees before me. "Jaylene, you are so beautiful. I'm sorry I..." His eyes were full of tears.

I stepped forward and brushed back his hair. "Why?"

He shook his head and pulled me into him. His head rested against my bare chest and I could feel every hair, every eyelash, every bit of stubble from his five-o'clock shadow... Every movement awakened my skin to him. I could feel his sigh heavy against my breast. I took in a deep breath and he pulled me in tighter.

"Because I've never felt so much before in my life. Jaylene, I never thought I would love anyone like this." He laughed breathlessly. "I wrote songs about love but I've never felt *anything* like this. Last night, I couldn't sleep. I was just thinking of everything. My life was a wreck before I met you and now I have meaning. I have inspiration. I've been writing songs like mad and I'm even thinking about a future."

My heart pounded in my chest. I didn't know what to say. I was thinking of those things, too, but my feelings led to fear.

He looked into my eyes, worry on his expression. "Jaylene? You're trembling. What is it?"

I smiled down at him. "Let's just say that you aren't the only one who's a little overcome with emotion."

He reached up and touched my lips, frowning. "I have things to tell you."

I nodded. Then I shrugged out of my robe, letting it hit the floor. I felt him shudder as he caressed me softly. "Can those things wait until morning?"

His eyes left their roaming and met mine. He nodded and I brought my lips down to kiss his. His lips left mine and grazed my neck, my chest, my pierced nipples. My head dropped back and I gasped. His kisses covered my stomach, my hips, his hands pulled me even closer and he ran his tongue along the juncture of my thigh. My knees buckled and he was there to catch me.

He lifted me as he stood and said, "I'm afraid I've missed the tour and therefore I'm not exactly sure where I'm going." I giggled and tilted my head toward the bedroom.

But instead of being playful, he had a very serious look. "The same agreement stands. Nothing needs to happen here that you don't want to happen."

I nodded. "I know. You've been so patient with me. But I want you."

His eyes searched mine and when we moved toward the bedroom, that heat was back in his gaze.

He lay me on my bed and stepped back. I stretched out, drinking in the sight of him watching me. I smiled and asked, "Whatcha looking at?"

He shook his head. When he didn't speak for a moment, I started to sit up but he put his hand out to stop me. "No, please. Stay there. I'm looking at the most beautiful woman I have ever seen, and I cannot for the life of me figure out what I have done to be worthy of you."

At that, I *did* sit up. I looked into his troubled gaze. "Devon, why would you say that? You're perfect. You've been nothing but perfect with me. If anyone is unworthy, it's me."

He sank to his knees in front of me and I ran my hands over his shoulders. "My beautiful girl, I think it's time we *both* do away with this idea that we aren't worthy. I love you. You love me. Let's just love each other...and let all that go." He held my face in his hands, just as he held my heart.

I pulled away and laid back on the bed, waiting for him. "Okay. But I think you're overdressed. Care to remedy that?"

He smirked and blew out a breath. Then he stepped out of his boots and yanked his socks off. Then he pulled his shirt from the back of the collar over his head in one movement and tossed it on the floor, along with his beanie that came off in the process. He stood there breathing heavy for a moment and I sighed.

"You make even the simplest everyday movements seem like art. I could watch you move for hours. Or not move, for that matter."

His hands moved to his hips and he shook his head.

"I'm serious," I said. "Consider me an artist appreciating fine art. Now turn around and let me see the rest."

I could see him blushing but I wanted this reveal. He slowly turned his back to me. I was no longer afraid of the name tattooed across his shoulders. It fit him, it was done beautifully, and I desperately wanted to kiss every letter.

"You know this is a little unnerving," he said over his shoulder.

I laughed. "Why? Don't you trust my artistic judgment? I'm telling you that you're a work of art, and nothing you can say or show me next is going to change that."

Now he was chuckling too. "Okay, you asked for it."

I heard the button pop open and watched him slowly slide his jeans down his hips, letting them fall to the floor. He was standing in his boxer briefs and said, "Can I turn around now?"

"Nope. Lose the drawers, baby." I saw his shoulders drop as he exhaled and shook his head again. With just the tips of his fingers, he slid his boxer briefs down—and I blew out a breath in a whistle.

"Oh, Devon. Truly, they broke the mold when they created you."

He snickered and turned around slowly. I could tell he was uncomfortable with the attention but turnabout is fair play.

He stopped moving and he was there in front of me, bared to me as I was to him. My smile dropped as I took in the magnitude of the moment. I held out my hands to him and he stepped toward the bed and then climbed onto it.

"Devon, you are so beautiful. I can't even find the words..."

He blushed further and stroked my bottom lip with his thumb. "I *feel* beautiful when you look at me like that," he whispered.

"I want to draw you."

His eyebrows rose at that. "Um, I guess, if you want to."

I nodded. "But tonight I'd rather just touch all of you. Is that okay?"

He nodded back. "That would be heaven, chère. I love your hands on me."

I took my time tracing the contours of his torso, my fingers and lips taking turns learning him. The whole time he watched me, he was quiet except for his changing breaths. He kept his hands off me as long as he could but as I neared his hips, he grabbed my shoulders and rolled to cover me with his chest.

"I don't want this over too quickly, and it will be if you linger near..."

"This?" I asked as I grasped his length with my hand.

He groaned and squeezed his eyes shut. "Oh god, yeah, that's what I meant." He groaned as I slowly stroked him from base to tip. The texture was different than I'd expected. He was hard and soft at the same time and I loved the way he felt, the way he trembled as I touched him.

"Is this how you like to be touched, Devon? I don't really know..."

"Oh, yes you do. You know exactly how to touch me, chère. It's too good."

He kissed me all over my neck and chest. I felt my blood pumping into a frenzy. I wanted him everywhere and I wanted to *be* everywhere. Every nerve ending longed to be in contact with him.

I pulled back and stilled him with my hands on his face. "I'm feeling like I can't get enough of you, like I can't get close enough to you."

He smiled my favorite smile and it slowed my heart down just a little. "I know. I feel the same. But I want to make you feel good."

"It *all* feels good. I want more." I was breathless and I didn't know how to ask for what I wanted, didn't *know* what I wanted.

He shifted to my side and looked down at me with an earnest expression on his face. "Jaylene, what do you want from tonight?"

I shook my head. "Everything...I don't know. I can't describe how I'm feeling so I don't know what to ask for."

He smiled and kissed me once sweetly on the lips. "I meant what I said. I want you to want this and to be ready. I really want to make love to you but not unless you're ready."

I raised an eyebrow at him in question and he laughed softly.

"Define ready? I mean, I know I love you. I know I want to be with you. If that's ready to you, then I'm ready."

He still hesitated. "If I make love to you tonight, there's no going back. You've already taken my heart. Making love will only cement the deal. And this will be it for me. I won't be with anyone else. For as long as you'll have me, it will be only you. That's what I mean by ready. And I'm *ready*."

I held on tight to him and tried to get ahold of myself enough to say what I needed to say. "That's what it means to me, too. I'm so happy to hear you say that. But I'd be lying if I didn't tell you I'm afraid of what happens when our time is up. The thought of you leaving scares me so much. I keep thinking that will be it. And I was okay with that before, but now it's too painful to think about."

Devon sat up and ran a hand over his hair. He took a couple of deep breaths and when he turned to me, his eyes were sad. "Why do you keep thinking in terms of 'when our time is up'? I told you before I want to be with you, I want to make this work. I guess I haven't proven to you yet that I'm not going anywhere."

We were both quiet for a minute. I felt so exposed. I turned over onto my stomach, afraid of what I was feeling. This was not at all how I anticipated the night going. I had to tell him everything or he might just walk out the door and decide this wasn't worth it. I rolled over and sat up, facing him. His eyes were still sad but determined. That gave me the strength to say what I needed to say.

"Devon, I'm afraid that it's not anything *you* have to prove to me. It's what I need to accept. Try as I might to be rid of them, I guess deep down, I still have some abandonment issues. Unfortunately, you're suffering from being my first for everything. My first boyfriend, my first love, and I want you to be the first person I make love to.

"You said it before. I don't let people in. That's because I'm always afraid I'll disappoint them and they'll leave. I want to take that step with you, letting you be the first man inside my heart and the first man I trust with my body. It's a lot to ask you to be patient with me, I know. I understand if you can't be."

He smiled at me and took my hand between both of his. "It's too late for that. I'm already in this, chère. I love you. Patient or not, I can't be anywhere else right now but with you. I want you any way I can have you, and if that means I have to wait to be that last first, I'll wait as long as it takes."

I leaned forward and threw my arms around him, pressing my face to his neck. I breathed him in as he pulled me onto his lap and held me tight.

"Devon?"

He kissed my shoulder and said, "Yes, chère?"

I sighed. "Can I ask you a question? About something you said earlier?"

He laughed. "You can ask me anything."

I drew in another deep breath for strength. "When you said before that you were thinking about a future, what does that look like to you? I'm not trying to insert myself into your life, here. I just want to know what you see."

He sighed impatiently. "Like it or not, you're inserted, okay?" He laughed, and I did too. "The future I see has *you* in it. Specifically, I see myself doing music in some form, and you and I together. A family wouldn't be too out there to consider, after we had lots of time to practice." I giggled when he tickled me a little. "Because I assure you, the practice part will be fun." His tickling turned to caressing and I sighed as his lips returned to my neck.

"I know I'm sounding like a total 'fraidy cat but having babies scares me. I just want to put that out there."

He shrugged. "Then we'll deal with it when it comes up. I feel totally open about it. I love kids. There are plenty around to have in my life if I don't have my own. But the thought of you pregnant? I gotta say...you'd be so fucking sexy I wouldn't be able to keep my hands off you."

He pushed me back onto the bed and devoured me as I giggled over his fervor.

"As long as you're okay either way. I just don't know right now. But honestly, I'm saying all that without even having had sex once. I might hate it and never want to have it again. How would you feel about that?" I failed miserably at keeping a straight face with that statement and he saw right through me.

"Oh, you'll hate it alright. You'll hate it when I get you so close to an orgasm and then back off just to prolong the ache for a while. You'll hate it when I finish and you'll want to go again right away. You'll hate it when it's the morning after we've just made love all night and you can barely sit in your damn chair to tattoo that day. You'll hate everything about it...except for loving how it feels for me to be inside of you."

I could feel myself growing hotter and wetter and that need was back with a vengeance. With a very shaky voice, I said, "I don't know, Devon. I might be really hard to convince of that."

He laughed against my earlobe, sending chills down my body, hardening my nipples. Then he ran his hand up the inside of my thigh and stroked me gently from my folds to my clitoris, making me bow off the bed.

"I am so looking forward to convincing you." He looked down at me with a sparkle in his eyes that replaced the sadness.

I stilled him for a moment with my hands on his cheeks. "I love you so much, Devon. I love you and I want to make love with you tonight, fully accepting all the ramifications that go along with it."

He smiled and kissed me deeply, his face tightening up with the passion we shared. "I love you too, chère. And if at any time you want to stop, you just tell me. I want you to trust me, okay?"

"Trusting you has never been an issue. Now why don't you get back to that convincing me part."

He proceeded with a tenacity that was highly commendable. After kissing me into a boneless state, he applied a similar technique to my more sensitive set of lips until I was past boneless to complete liquidity. He did exactly as he'd threatened, bringing me to the brink of orgasm several times so that when it hit, the waves racked my body like the wake of a passing cruise vessel. And with every new experience he gave me, he was tender and generous.

I was lying in a state of bliss but still feeling like I needed him one more place before feeling completely sated. "Baby, it's time. I bought some condoms, they're—"

He chuckled. "Oh, I brought some, too." He reached for his jeans and took out four. I raised my eyebrow at that and he shrugged. "I promised you four, but for your first time, we might not use them all. You might need to work up to a four-time night."

I laughed and barely had the energy left to slap myself in the forehead.

He knelt above me and I watched eagerly as he rolled the condom over his shaft. "That is such an impressive phallus you've got there. The Greeks would have worshipped it, built palaces in its honor."

He rolled his eyes at me and then smacked my ass to get me to roll on my back from my curled-up position.

"Ow! Hey, I'm just being honest. I feel blessed to be experiencing its majesty. Marcus must have been thinking about it when he wrote 'Mystikal Stick'."

He groaned. "Okay, enough," he said, and then kissed me slowly and thoroughly until I was melting. "Now if you're quite finished exalting my cock, I'd like to get to work here."

I kissed him with a big wet smack of my lips. "Sorry. If you hadn't noticed, I kind of make jokes when I'm a little nervous, and seeing as there's nothing *little* about you, I'm largely nervous."

He pressed his forehead against mine. "We can stop, chère. I don't want you to be afraid."

I shook my head fervently. "No. No more stopping. I want you, and by the feel of you, you want this, too. Let me make you feel good, baby."

He smiled. "Everything we've done has been amazing for me. You feel so damn good. I told you, watching you come destroys me."

"Then what are you waiting for? Make me come again."

He shook his head. "It might not work that way your first time, Jaylene. But I promise, we'll keep on practicing until we make it happen, okay?"

I nodded. "Okay. Proceed."

He laughed but his laughter was quickly cut off as he slid slowly into me. We both moaned together and I felt like I was splitting apart. I didn't think I had it in me to tense up, but I did, and he stopped moving.

"Chère, you okay? Am I hurting you?"

My eyes were wide and I was breathing heavy. I smiled. "Doesn't hurt. Just big."

He laughed, dropping his head to my shoulder as he moved his hips back and then forward again. The feeling was *so* invasive. I sucked in a breath as he pushed himself in until our pelvises were almost touching. His eyes found mine, seeking reassurance.

I nodded and leaned up to kiss him, never taking my eyes off his. He stilled for a moment until I could catch my breath. "Are you done or is there still another yard left to go?"

We laughed and my muscles clenched around him. That caused him to wince. "Oh gods, did I hurt you, baby?"

He just laughed again. "Not at all. You feel like heaven, beautiful. Now I'm going to move, and you just hold on, okay?"

And then he was moving, his tip pushing so far into me it took my breath away with every stroke. The friction was so hot, I felt myself tensing and tingling with every thrust, climbing higher until I reached a peak and fell over the edge into those delicious waves again.

He paused as I finished. "That was amazing, chère. You still with me?"

I nodded but felt like I barely had control over my muscles and joints. "I'm with you. I'm useless here, but I'm with you."

He chuckled and then started moving at a quicker pace. He leaned back and hooked an arm under my leg, pushing it towards my chest, and then he *really* started moving.

I watched him above me, covered in a sheen of sweat, his eyelids heavy over those endlessly deep blue eyes, and his lips pursed together as he sucked in harsh breaths. The sensations were even deeper this way, but I was so taken with watching him that my pleasure hinged on witnessing this beautiful man find his release.

When it hit him, he cried out and fell forward, stretching me even farther. He too was being carried on those waves of pleasure, and it was like he crawled farther inside me with every wave that passed him, until he finally collapsed on top of me.

We lay there breathing heavily together and I felt our connection strengthen.

Suddenly, all I could see in my mind was shoelaces... I could see the loops wrapped together and pulled tight, and then a second time. A double knot.

I stroked his back and kissed his neck. He sighed and pulled his hips back slowly. He made eye contact with me and I hoped he saw how much I was feeling in that moment. "I feel like we just knotted."

He raised an eyebrow and leaned down to kiss my nipple, sending shock waves back down below. "Knotted?"

I nodded. "Like shoelaces. I don't know...that's the first thing that came to my mind." I felt a little shy and vulnerable under his gaze. I guess a part of me, smaller now than before, still waited for him to realize that he was a rock star and I was just Jaylene. But what he said next helped to blow that small part to pieces.

"For me, it was like coming home." He smiled, maybe a little unsure as well.

I beamed at him—and then frowned. "I just wondered something. Do you even *have* a home? Like your own? I don't even know where you live."

He chuckled at that and sat up to dispose of the condom. "Uh, the bathroom is where?"

I grinned and pointed. "This place is tiny, Devon. I don't think you can get lost." He stood and walked gloriously naked through my room and I rested my arms behind my head. "Is it okay if I just lie here and watch you?"

He was still laughing as he closed the bathroom door.

I sighed and pulled the covers over me. I was sleepy, pleasantly sore, comfortable and happy. Happier than I'd been in forever.

When he came back in the room and found me smiling like a Cheshire cat, he chuckled. "I'm hoping that is a satisfied smile and not some secret joke going on over there."

My eyes dragged open. "No jokes. I'm just feeling incredibly incredible right now." He pulled back the covers and crawled in next to me. I instantly curved to him and wondered how I'd ever not slept side by side with him.

"I'm incredibly glad. *You're* incredible." He leaned down to kiss me and welcomed the pleasure that Devon brought to my body. I stopped him with a hand to his jaw.

"You didn't answer my question, Mr. Boudreaux."

He rubbed his chin on the top of my head, his arm folded behind his. I rolled over so I could look at him and admired the way his biceps flexed when he lay like that. I did some more admiring, waiting for him to answer. He laughed a little and his smile made me weak.

"I don't really have an answer. I guess I'm kind of between places at the moment. I've been staying with Mama here. We've got the place in Houma. I don't go there very often, but I went there last night."

I woke up a little from my drowsy state at that. "That's where you went?"

He nodded and looked up at my ceiling. I had a dream catcher hanging from the fan above my bed and he studied it for a moment. "I needed to pick something up and, well...I hadn't been back since the guys and I went out there. I felt like I needed to."

I kissed his chest but kept watching his face. "And how did it go?"

He blew out a breath and looked down at me. He had just the slightest double chin when he looked at me like this and I couldn't help but love the way his lips, swollen from kissing me, pursed out just a bit more from this angle.

"It went, I guess. I expected to have that pain in my chest, but truthfully I just went in, got what I needed, looked around a bit and that was that. It didn't hurt as much."

I smiled and his mouth turned up slightly at the corners. "I'm so glad, baby. I don't want you to hurt like that."

He grazed his knuckles along my cheekbone and smiled sweetly. "I'm not hurting so much anymore. And being here with you, I'm more relaxed than I've been since before I left for L.A." He blew out a breath. "I guess that's why I don't want to go back, but it looks like I'm going to have to."

Internally, I'd tried to prepare myself for this conversation, and I silently gave myself a pep talk that I could handle it. "Do you have to go permanently or can you, like, go when you're needed...? I don't know; I'm unfamiliar with your job description and duties required."

He cracked up. "You mean there's a job description for what we do? I'd love to read that. 'Wanted: Dumbass musicians who don't mind being slaves to the label, being packaged and sold, exploited and expected to give sexual favors.'"

"Okay, how much of that is kidding?"

He snorted. "All of it. None of it. I'm just bitter right now, is all. I shouldn't complain. I'm getting paid to play music, and getting paid well. If I play my cards right, I could be set for life, and then get to do what I love."

"I hadn't thought about it like that. I guess you have to put up with the stuff you hate to do what you love, right?"

He nodded. "All except the sexual favors. That part is kind of fun."

I bit his nipple and he sucked in a breath. "Oh shit, Jaylene. I don't know if that hurt or felt fucking great." I ran my tongue over the spot and his eyes rolled back in his head.

I giggled and kissed him some more. But I wanted more answers. "So where do you stay when you're in L.A.?"

His eyes opened. "I know what you're worried about. You're worried you just had hot sex with a homeless guy, aren't you?" I held my teeth over his nipple again and the smile fell from his face. "Okay, okay. We have a house we rented in Hollywood. It's an old mansion built in nineteen twenty-five that's only partially been restored, so it's a little worn, but it's perfect. We've all got rooms there but Marcus has his own apartment closer to L.A." He snickered. "Mage found the mansion. He read about it being haunted and was sold."

I rolled my eyes. "Of course he'd think it was perfect. It sounds great, though. I've always wanted to go to Hollywood. Not that I'm a big celebrity stalker or anything, but there's so much great history there."

His eyes lit up. "There really is. I did some exploring when we first got there. Before things got really crazy..." He trailed off, deep in thought.

I let him have his moment and rested my head on his chest. Listening to his heart beating grounded me.

Sometime later he said, "Jaylene? Would you be willing to come see me in L.A.?"

I turned my head to look at him and smiled. "It could be fun. But I wouldn't want to get in the way."

He frowned. "You would never be in the way. In the way of what?"

I sighed. "The band, your business out there. I don't know. I don't know how I'll fit into your life once you leave here."

The frown still creased his forehead but it looked more pained than frustrated. "Chère, there's no fitting you in. I want you with me." He exhaled and pulled me closer to him. "Look. There's no reason why New Orleans can't be my home. I'll go to L.A., we'll record, then I'll come back here. Eventually we'll go on tour and I'll be gone for a time, but I want this to be my home. I want to be home with you."

I sighed dramatically. "I guess I could clear out a spot in the medicine cabinet for your toothbrush and razor."

I started to giggle but he turned me sharply to face him. "I'm serious, Jaylene. I want *you* to be my home."

My eyes widened as we stared at each other. I couldn't form a coherent sentence, and I knew I shouldn't joke right now. I swallowed the lump in my throat. "You want *me* to be home?"

He nodded, his eyes searching mine. "Yeah, Jaylene. I want you...I want to be with you however I can. Don't you get it? You're home for me."

A tear ran down my face and I brought his hand up to kiss his knuckles. He brushed the tear away, that pained look still on his face.

When I spoke, my voice was so quiet I wasn't sure he could hear me. "I want to be with you however I can, too, Devon. I love the idea of coming to visit you. I *really* love the idea of you being here with me. But my shop is here, my work is here, and I've just gotten things running smoothly. If you're okay with that fact, that I won't give this up, I'll do whatever it takes to be with you."

I would remember the smile that lit up his face right then anytime I ever wondered whether it was worth it, whether I could do this. His hands came up to my face and he pulled me to his waiting lips. His kiss was so tender, and there was a longing there I hadn't felt before. There was hope, joy, fear of the unknown but determination to face it together, all wrapped up in a single touch of his lips to mine.

He pulled me onto his chest and looked deep into me. "I love you so much, Jaylene. Being with you makes me feel like I can face it all, makes me want to be the best man I can. Hell, makes me want to climb mountains and scream at the top of my lungs. Is that too corny?"

I giggled and snuggled closer to him. "Corny is good. I like corny. Bet I can out-corn you though."

His chest rumbled with his laugh, tickling my ear and sending shivers down my back. "Oh, I don't think so. I'm pretty corny."

I looked up at him and thought long and hard. "Well, I would walk five hundred miles and I would walk five hundred more just to be the one who walked a thousand miles for you."

He laughed and rolled me underneath him, kissing me deeply. With his tongue caressing mine, it was hard to focus. I loved getting lost in him.

"Yeah? Well, you might be able to out-corn me with eighties songs but I will annihilate you with cheesy show tunes to profess my love for you."

"Oh yeah?" I was digging this game of one-upping each other. "I will totally slay you with hair metal innuendo."

He scoffed. "Please. Did you forget what it is I do for a living? There's no way you can slay me with innuendo. Remember, I likely contributed lyrics to 'Sin on my Face'."

I was laughing hysterically now. I couldn't help it. He went from being so serious to playful in an instant. "Yeah, well, as long as that innuendo gets me a repeat performance, you can Sin away."

He groaned at that one and I laughed triumphantly. I rolled him over onto his back and straddled him, feeling things warming up again between us.

He stroked my hips with his thumbs and looked up at me, his lids heavy and his breathing sped up. "Was your first time really okay, chère?"

I nodded. "You have to ask?"

He nodded. "I want you to tell me. Did you like it?"

I ran my hands over his perfect abs and pecs, lightly scratching him with my nails. He had just the barest covering of fine hair on him and it was soft as feathers. "It felt really good. I was surprised, actually. So many women I know have said it was terrible their first time. I feel a little guilty that mine was so very good." I moved my hips a little, dragging my core over his waiting erection.

He squeezed my hips and his eyelids got even heavier. "I'm glad it was good, but I'm just not sure if—oh god, that's good—if I got it right. I might have to...hmmmmmm, oh shit...try again. Are you ready for me again, chère?"

I nodded and licked my lips.

Round two was even more amazing since my nerves were gone. There could not be anything better in the human existence than the feel of his body on mine, our most private parts coming together in complete harmony. His eyes held mine, and in them, I saw all the love, hope and promise he'd shared with his words before. He showed me with his touch, his kiss, his penetration. It was just the two of us and I took it all in, knowing that it wouldn't always be this blissful but I'd have these feelings, these memories to get me through.

Our first night in my apartment was full of promises and love, and when I fell asleep nestled against him, my heart was full to capacity.

TWENTY

The next morning when I awoke, and the first thing I saw was his sleepy profile, I couldn't help but giggle. I didn't want to wake him but I was so happy.

He opened one eye and smirked at me. "Why are you laughing?"

I kissed his shoulder as I sat up, ready to face the day, feeling stronger and happier than ever. "Just giggling to myself, thinking that I have Devon Boudreaux lying fabulously naked in my bed, under sheets with puffy clouds and rainbows."

He looked around him and rubbed his hand over his face. "I'm surprised at you, Jaylene. I thought you'd have sheets with skulls on them."

I laughed. "I do, but these were a gift from Mackenzie and they're really soft, so I use them a lot." He ran his hands over them, sliding the sheet down until the bottom of his v-shaped muscles were just showing.

He saw where my eyes were headed and a sly smile broke over his lips. "If you look hard enough, you might find a pot of gold under these rainbows."

I burst out laughing with him and said, "You know, you're probably right about me not being able to out-corn or out-innuendo you. I'm feeling pretty amateurish."

I stood up and walked to my dresser to grab a pair of yoga pants and sports bra. He watched me intently as I went about my morning routine. I wrapped my hair back in a ponytail and moved to my yoga mat in front of the window. I did a few stretches—my back felt much better than it had the previous morning, but it was still a little stiff. I quickly realized that other parts of me were deliciously sore as well.

I bent over to a downward-facing dog pose and then arched up into cobra.

I caught his eye and he was smiling. "I didn't think your body could be any more beautiful, but the way you move... Damn. The only thing that would be more erotic would be if you were naked."

I shook my head and finished running through the basic poses. "Sorry, baby. Not ready to be that exposed in front of you yet. Needed to do that, can't let my back get tight before going to work."

He tugged at his soul patch. I wished I had fewer clothes on. It was nine and I had to be downstairs in an hour. "I have an hour to get showered, dressed, and fed. Any idea how to fit in any extra-curricular activities?"

It turned out Devon had some great ideas, which involved removing my yoga clothes and carrying me into the shower, where he proceeded to wash every inch of me, including my hair, which felt fabulous. He paid particular attention to my sensitive spots and I assured him he was being very thorough. Condom number three was used in the bathroom up against the counter. For being a small apartment, there were sure a lot of creative spaces for us to explore.

By this time, I was feeling satisfied and was having a *really* hard time keeping my hands off of Devon. I loved that my apartment was small and that when we moved around, there were always reasons to touch. He seemed very comfortable here and that made my heart sing. I wanted the chance to get used to this.

We wrapped up our hour by feeding each other fruit and granola for breakfast. About that time, there was a knock on the door.

"Hello, sleeping beauty, are you ready for—work it girl." Mackenzie opened the door as I was straddling Devon's lap, feeding him a grape.

Star was right behind her, rubbing his hair to full spike mode. He laughed. "I wondered what time you were coming over. What the hell did you do? Come at midnight?"

Devon and I laughed and he hugged me close, kissing my neck. "As a matter of fact, I arrived at twelve-oh-two. I was fashionably late." He kissed me one more time before scooting me off his lap. "Had to make sure my girl got up in time for work."

Mackenzie raised her eyebrows high at the possessive nature of Devon's comment and was in full protective mode. "Then I'm also sure you made sure she got enough rest, right?"

We both giggled guiltily, and he turned to her and said sheepishly, "Just how many hours of sleep counts as 'enough rest,' boss?"

She smirked. "Yeah, this is hopeless. All right. Devon, did you need coffee? I know Jaylene doesn't have any but I made some."

He smiled and thanked her. "I'm okay. I'm kind of on a natural high right now." He turned and wrapped his arms around me, hugging me close. I so didn't want to leave this wonderful cocoon. "This is going to be fun. Star, what do you think? A day of watching them work without having to do anything?"

Mackenzie's arms crossed over her chest. "Did you really think you were going to be sitting on your fine asses today? I've got a whole list of chores I need help with."

The guys looked at each other and acted shocked. "You mean no drinking beer and making lewd comments all day?" Star asked.

She rolled her eyes. "You can make all the lewd comments you want, but no beer. Can't risk a run-in with the health department."

Devon threw his arm around Star's neck in a headlock. "We're just messing with you. Star would be happy to do any chores you need him to do."

She looked pointedly at him, and he nodded. "I would do anything for you, Mackenzie. You just say the words."

I loved the way he got all puppy-dog cute with her. Her stern looks gave way to a smoldering gaze. "Good, because I have an idea."

We went downstairs and got ready to open up. Troy had left me a few notes and my station was in great condition. I appreciated him coming and knew I owed him.

My first appointment, Karen, was an old customer from back home who flew out just to see me and get tattooed. She had money to spare and I'd done a lot of work on her, so we knew each other pretty well. I felt honored that she would make this much of a sacrifice to see me, although she explained she should be thanking *me* because she'd always wanted to come visit New Orleans.

She had wanted a phoenix tattoo over a shoulder, biceps and down her back for a few years now, so that's what we were working on today. I'd at least get the outline finished and then she'd come back in a couple of months to get the color done. It was going to be a marathon session. I figured her piece would take at least five to six hours.

My second client, Jonathan, was coming in tonight, driving down from Texas. I'd tattooed him shortly after opening my shop and he wanted more done. He was in the military, so his only opportunity to get work done was at the beginning of a three-week leave.

My drawings were already done and agreed upon. After unpacking my machines and making sure everything was in working order, I took a moment to look around the shop. I snickered as I watched Mackenzie put our two boys to work.

"I've wanted to hang these prints for a long time but we needed someone tall to do it." She'd had the rest of her poppets framed and wanted to hang them in the waiting area. I noticed the new drawing was taking a place of honor.

"I take it you like the drawing?"

She turned to me and gave me a huge hug. "I love it," she whispered. I gave her a squeeze and we watched the boys using a level to make sure the pictures were done right. Devon looked awfully hot with a hammer in his hand.

"So what do you have on the books today?"

Mackenzie looked down at her appointment book. "Hmmm, just three piercing appointments, and Sabrina is coming in for me to strip her hair so we can dye it blue next." I laughed. Those two were always having fun with color. "I was planning to mostly work the counter today and handle any walk-ins we have." Her eyes drifted to Star, who was leaning over the counter, his jeans riding low. I saw her suck in a breath and smile.

"See something you like?" I was teasing her but when she turned to me, her eyes were bright and a little teary.

"I really do," she murmured. "I really like him, Jay."

I knew that was hard for her, and I hoped she didn't run away from him. "I know, and I'm glad. He's a really good guy."

She nodded and bit nervously on one of her nails. "I just hope I don't chase this one away."

I held my hand up to her cheek. "Just go with your heart, dollface. That's the only way to be with him. He's very honest and will know if you aren't. You'll be great."

She nodded again and kissed my cheek. "What about you and your tall drink of water?"

I sighed. "It was perfect, Kenz. He says this is it for him." She must have sensed how surprised I was by that.

"Well, let him prove it to you, baby girl. I think he's a smart man." I squeezed her hand and she said, "How the hell are we supposed to work with them distracting us all day?"

I sighed gravely. "It will be difficult. But we must persevere."

Karen arrived and we hugged tightly. She was a high school administrator and this was the start of her spring break, so she'd have time to heal. I always told her if she'd been my administrator, I might have liked school better.

"Nah, you would have thought I was a bitch like the rest of the kids." We laughed about that. If they only knew that their uptight principal had some very large and very beautiful tattoos.

"You look absolutely stunning, Jaylene. I see the move has been good for you." Her eyes travelled between Devon and I, and her eyebrow rose.

I rolled my eyes. "Karen Browning, this is my boyfriend, Devon Boudreaux." She nodded and extended her hand. He shook it and gave her a low-wattage smile but it still affected her, I could tell.

"Very pleased to meet you, Mrs. Browning." That freakin' Cajun charm of his was unbelievable. She raised the other eyebrow.

"You too, Mr. Boudreaux. I take it you're from these parts?"

He nodded. "From Houma, ma'am."

She rolled her eyes. "Oh, not ma'am, please. I'm on vacation."

He laughed, his eyes crinkling playfully at the edges, and that *really* affected her. I'd told him she was a high school principal and it was interesting to watch him around another woman. Even though Karen was in her late forties, she was very attractive and in great shape. I wondered how he was going to handle her being mostly topless for the next few hours.

"And this is his friend, Star—"

"Stanley Stevenson. Very nice to meet you." He sat back down next to Devon on the couch and tried to ignore Mackenzie and me.

"Stanley?" she mouthed to me. "How Cute." We looked at him and he shrugged, blushing. Mackenzie started fanning herself and he got a sly smile on his face. Devon smacked him in the back of the head and he tried to behave.

"It's nice to meet you both." Karen turned back to us and gave us a very principal-like look and we immediately felt chastised.

Karen and I went over the drawing for a minute and then she went into the dressing room and took off her top. She came out holding the drape to her chest, and I proceeded to wash the tattoo area and apply the stencil. It took a few tries. We were going over the top of her shoulder and down the back, which made the placement a little tricky.

Devon and Star watched with great interest. Mackenzie's first client of the day came in and that kept her occupied for the next hour.

Karen eventually lay down on her stomach on my table and I got to work. She was very easy to work on. With all she'd been through over the past few years, she could handle the pain of a tattoo with ease.

Devon stood and walked around behind me so he could see me work better. Strangely, I didn't feel distracted at all by him. It felt natural for him to be in my space.

"May I ask about the tattoo you're getting?" He was very sweet to ask her. I wondered how he would handle the answer.

"You sure can. It's a phoenix, the symbol of rebirth. After surviving breast cancer, I feel like I'm starting over."

He was quiet for a minute. "It's going to look fantastic. How long have you been cancer-free?"

"Thanks. It's been five years now. I feel good, I feel lucky to be alive. They caught it early so it wasn't so bad. I didn't have to have radiation, just the double mastectomy and several rounds of chemo." Karen had shared her story with me the first time we met. I admired her so very much.

"My aunt died of breast cancer. I'm really glad to hear yours went well."

I sat back and looked up at him, quieting my machine for a moment. His sad smile was back but he looked okay.

"Daryl's first wife, Lila. She was just thirty when she got sick. I was little when it happened but my mom talked about her a lot. I remember her funeral." He cleared his throat and I smiled up at him in support. His half smile was back.

"That explains a little about Daryl." He nodded. Karen looked curious. "Daryl is Devon's uncle. He's also a great friend of mine. He was the man I told you about, who helped Mackenzie and I get our building."

"Ah, the biker dude. Got it."

Devon laughed. "Hey, chère, I'm going to go out back and have a smoke. You need anything?"

I shook my head. "I'm great, thanks though." He kissed the top of my head and headed out the back door. My face must have shown how bad I had it because Karen chuckled to herself.

"Ah to be young and in love. Shit, I'd have killed to be in love with *that*."

I snickered. "He's something, huh?"

She rolled her eyes. "Yeah, something. How did you two meet?"

I could feel myself blushing. "Daryl introduced us and we were kind of working together—him and his cousins and their friends—on a memorial tattoo for his sister. It just sort of happened."

She was smiling at me and then closed her eyes to relax. I was working on her shoulder blade area, which can be quite tender.

"Keep talking, Jay. Helps me forget about the rough spots."

I laughed. "Okay. What else do you want to know?"

Her forehead creased as though she was thinking deeply. "How about what does he do for a living?"

I snorted. "Oh, you'll really like the answer to that one."

She opened an eye and frowned at me. "As long as you don't tell me he's a starving artist."

I couldn't help it. I burst out laughing.

"He is. I knew it. He's got that brooding, intense thing going on."

I shook my head. "Yes, he's an artist, but he's not starving. Not by a long-shot." I paused to clean up the area I'd been working on and inspect the line work I'd finished so far.

"Not starving? Do tell."

I sighed. "He's the guitarist for Maggie's Bones, a metal band."

"I know exactly who Maggie's Bones are. Are you kidding me? That's D? Holy shit, Jay, they are hot. I can't believe your luck. Maybe I should move to New Orleans, too." We both laughed. Karen was very much in love with her husband, so her teasing was just that.

"I can't help but deeply believe that everything happens for a reason. This past week has been good for me."

She snickered. "I bet it has."

"Oh stop it, Karen. It's not what you think. It's just that I wasn't going to take the job. It seemed too overwhelming, out of my comfort zone, you know?"

She turned her head to the side so I could see her raised eyebrow. "Jay, your comfort zone is quite narrow. Besides moving to New Orleans, you don't usually do anything other than work, work, work. I'm glad you did something out of the norm. I see it's paid off."

I shrugged. "I sure hope so. But then, falling in love is *waaaay* outside my comfort zone, so we'll have to see how it goes." I knew my face was red when she looked up at me.

"And it could be the kind of thing that changes your whole life, my dear. Trust me. Don't turn the Fates away when they place something beautiful in front of you. Chances are, it's not likely to be repeated."

I thought about what she said and all she'd been through. I tended to listen when my clients shared their life wisdom with me. I learned as much from them as they got, healing from the process of getting a tattoo.

As I watched Devon walk back into my shop, I knew that I would absolutely embrace what Fate had brought to me.

Devon carried his guitar with him when he returned to the shop. He must have had it in his car. "Jaylene, will it bother you if I play?"

I shook my head. "Not at all. You might want to turn off the stereo though." He laughed at the dirty look Mackenzie shot me. "What? I thought you'd appreciate some live music."

Her eyes lit up. "For that, you can always turn off the stereo."

He sat back down on the couch and dropped a notebook next to him. "I hope this won't bother you, just have some ideas to put down."

I smiled at him and shook my head, hoping he knew just how much I would never mind listening to him play.

"Just warn us if you're going to sing any of the...you know...more colorful songs, so we can be prepared."

He chuckled to himself and I found my heart swelling in my chest. He trusted me. He was here in my space and seemed so relaxed. This was definitely a gift I would never willingly turn away.

About three hours in, Karen needed a food break, so Mackenzie and Star ran down to the deli and grabbed sandwiches. I gave her some juice so she wouldn't shock out on me.

Karen sat up, rolling her head on her shoulders. She was such an easy client to work on. We were a little more than halfway done. I did some stretching as well and I walked over to where Devon was sitting. He'd been playing a very cool song for a while and on his sheet of paper, he had taken many notes.

He looked up at me and smiled then narrowed his eyes and played a few chords from "Sin on my Face." I rolled my eyes and walked over to the front door to get some air. The weather was perfect, a balmy spring day with little humidity.

Karen joined me for some air and she breathed it in deep. "I can smell the magic in this place. I might have to spend a summer break here. Maybe I can finally write my great American novel."

I bumped her with my shoulder. "With all the material you've gathered over the years, I bet you'd have a lot to write about."

She nodded. "Working in schools definitely gives you a lot of material. Some of it I wish I could forget." She'd shared some particularly heartbreaking stories with me before. She knew what I had planned to do with my life before my father died, and I had asked her for her advice. She assured me I would be great but that it would take a toll.

"Hey, how is your stepmom? Do you guys talk much?"

I shrugged. "Every once in a while. They came to see me a week or so ago."

Her eyebrows rose. "And how'd that go?"

"I don't know. It's always hard to be around her. I feel like seeing me makes her melancholy and when she talks about Dad, she's so very sad. She got in a few jabs."

Karen crossed her arms. "And I hope you jabbed right back."

I laughed. Karen was a great corner coach. "Well, I told her I was happy, that I was successful, and she didn't need to worry about me selling my body to support myself. For some reason she didn't find that amusing."

I heard Devon snicker behind us. I hadn't realized he was listening.

"But Grandma called after they left and gave me a great pat on the back. She's always been good at that. I promised them I'd come home around Christmas so I have some time to work on my comebacks."

Karen rolled her eyes. "I love how people try to tell us how to live our lives. Your stepmom certainly never holds back, does she?"

I shook my head, wondering what she would say about Devon. It was mere curiosity, though. I didn't honestly care what she thought.

We headed back inside when Mackenzie and Star returned and we ate quickly so we could get back to work. After lunch, Devon asked if he and Star could go upstairs for a bit to my flat, he wanted to work on something with him.

"Of course." I leaned up to kiss his cheek and whispered, "What's mine is yours, baby."

He looked down at me with that intensity and I shivered. "Thanks, chère. We'll be back in a little while."

"Take your time. I've got another couple hours with Karen and then Jonathan will be here. His shouldn't take me more than a couple of hours."

He frowned. "That's kind of a long day, isn't it?"

I shook my head. "It's about normal. I usually tattoo about seven hours a day at least. Today is different because I normally wouldn't do another after a big one like Karen's, but I needed to put them together to only be gone one day."

He shook his head, looking bitter. "You mean because of us?"

I nodded and grabbed his biceps. "Yes, but it's fine, really. I feel great."

He smiled down at me and kissed me before leaning to whisper in my ear, "Me too. I love being here with you. I hope it's okay?"

I beamed up at him. "It's more than okay. Now go on, we need to have girl-talk time and you won't want to hear what we talk about."

Star pouted. "I want to hear girl talk. No fair. You got to hear dude talk all week."

Mackenzie threw a pen at him and he ducked.

"Alright, geesh. I guess girl talk is more violent than dude talk." The two guys went up the back steps and we giggled conspiratorially.

Mackenzie had been busy for most of the morning so far with piercing appointments but after we ate, Sabrina came in and they got to work on her hair. As she sat in the chair getting processed, she called out to me, "Hey Jay, how'd the clothes work out for you?"

Mackenzie spoke before I had a chance. "Sabrina, our little girl has finally gone and done it. She let a boy touch her feminine side!"

I groaned. I knew it was a bad idea to let these two gang up on me. "Kenz! Seriously? Do you have to?"

She nodded. "Oh, baby girl, we've been waiting forever to see you find happiness with a boy. Of course, being the overachiever you are, you find it with a bona fide rock god."

Sabrina gasped and I quirked my eyebrow at Mackenzie.

"WHO IS IT? Omigoddess you have to tell me, Jaylene."

I sighed. I guess she'd find out sooner or later, especially if he came down while she was still here. "His name is Devon and he's from Houma and he happens to be a musician."

I waited a beat while her eyes got bigger. "You can't mean Devon *Boudreaux*?! I'm going to faint over here." She fanned herself vigorously. I rolled my eyes, trying to concentrate on Karen's lines, but Karen was laughing so hard it made it difficult.

"Would you stop? I'm going to make your phoenix look like Wavy Gravy." She apologized.

I got back to work and Karen sighed. "Is it going to be weird knowing that millions of women want a piece of your boyfriend?"

I paused the machine for a minute and cleared my throat. When I spoke, it was in a low voice. "It's scary as hell. I'm so far out of my league here I don't even know the sport."

Sabrina laughed but Mackenzie got pissed. "I better not hear you talking like that. He is just a man, Jaylene Renee, and he is lucky to have you. Remember that or I'll kick your ass."

"Yes, Mom," I said.

Karen laughed but then she said, "She's right, you know. And I can tell by the way he looks at you that you have nothing to worry about. But I know you'll worry anyway."

"You *are* worried, aren't you Jay?" Mackenzie and Sabrina stood behind me, looking over my shoulder at my progress.

I shrugged, a little uncomfortable discussing my fears with these strong women. "I am, a bit. He's my first boyfriend, what do I know about making things work? And other women? All I can do is trust that he'll be honest with me. I know temptation will be all around him but I have no control over that."

Sabrina pulled up a stool and sat across from me. "Look, Jaylene, I know it's on a much smaller scale, but Kurt's band has its share of groupies, even for a local band. I worried like hell in the beginning. One night we got in a huge fight about it and he said, 'Babe, if I wanted all that, I wouldn't be with you. You're what I want, and I'm not going to fuck that up for all the pussy in the world.'"

We all burst out laughing.

She continued, "I never said he wasn't crass. But I had to take him at his word, right? And we've been together for five years now. I believe him. He's shown me over and over that I'm important to him, so I still take him at his word."

Sabrina was so confident; I wished I had that kind of confidence in myself. I hoped I could be as confident in Devon as she was in Kurt.

The ladies continued to talk boys and I focused on finishing up Karen's phoenix. The lines moved gracefully along her shoulder blade and onto her arm. When she lifted her arm, it would appear the bird was spreading its wing.

"I think we're done with the outline, Karen. Take a look." She stood up, a little shaky, so I handed her some Gatorade and she walked over to our huge three-way mirror.

"Oh, Jaylene. You've outdone yourself this time. It's perfect! I can't wait to come back and get the color done. I can't wait for summer." She hugged me and I was careful not to touch her new ink.

"Thanks for coming all this way, Karen. I hope you like it."

When she pulled back she had tears in her eyes. "It's exactly what I needed."

I handed her a tissue and looked up to see Devon and Star coming in from the back. "Did you guys want to look before she wraps it up?"

The guys walked over and whistled appreciatively at her tattoo as I cleaned up all the excess ink and started applying the antibiotic ointment.

"You know the drill, keep this bandage on until maybe right before bed and then gently wash with antibio soap. Keep applying bacitracin after that."

She nodded. "Yeah, yeah, I know. I promise I'll take good care of it 'til I come back."

Once I had the bandage on, she went into the dressing room to change. I started to clean up my station, but Star had already donned some gloves and was wrapping up all the plastic.

"Since when do we have a shop boy, Kenz?"

She looked up at him and laughed. "I was wondering about that. But he's a looker; he'll probably help bring in more chicks who want to get pierced."

Speaking of chicks, Sabrina stared wide-eyed at the guys. She cleared her throat and elbowed Mackenzie. "Aren't you going to introduce me to your friends, friend?" I would have been mortified to meet these guys with my head wrapped in plastic, but she thought nothing of it.

"Devon and Star, this is our friend Sabrina. She owns a vintage clothing shop here in the Quarter." They both shook hands with her and she barely contained her eyelash flutters.

Jeez, if even one of my best friends got that flustered meeting Devon, what would it be like for all the women he met while on tour? I had to stop thinking about that. It was unproductive and I refused to let it impose on the time I had with him.

"It's very nice to meet you guys. My boyfriend and I are big fans." They both said thank you graciously but blushed a little, like maybe after all this time, they were still a little uncomfortable with the fame.

I listened to them chat while I got my station set up for Jonathan, who was due in a half hour. "Guys, I'm going to run upstairs and grab a snack before my next appointment comes in." They waved at me and Devon followed.

His arms came around my waist. "I could use a snack, too." He bit my neck. I squealed and broke away, running up the stairs, Devon chasing me.

TWENTY-ONE

We burst through my door and he caught me up against the wall just inside. His kisses were hungry and I was so happy to have my hands back on him. I kissed him with matching enthusiasm. When he pulled away, we were both breathless.

"I know you really need a snack, I just had to do that. I'm sorry."

I shook my head and slid my hands around his waist, pulling him closer to me. "Don't ever be sorry for kissing me like that. I love it." I reached up and bit his neck and he groaned. As I pulled him closer still, I could feel that this was more than just playing for him. I looked up and he gave me a sexy half smile.

"I kiss you like that because I'm like a starved man around you. I can't get enough. Watching you work today was nice but I couldn't focus too much on your hands because it made me think of last night, and just how good your hands felt on me."

I rested my cheek against his chest and he enveloped me in his strong arms. We stood like that for a few moments and I drank it in. I knew what he meant about starving. Now that I'd allowed myself to care about him, to let myself want him, it was all I could do not to tear his clothes off and keep him naked in my apartment forever.

That thought made me giggle and he rubbed his chin on top of my head. "What're you thinking down there, beautiful? That sounded wicked."

I looked up and he kissed my nose. "Hmmm, I was thinking about how I could explain your disappearance to the guys. 'See, he was here Saturday and then he just left. I have no idea where he went.' And meantime, I'd have you naked and tied to my bed, where I could look at you and touch you whenever I wanted."

His eyes flashed at me and he reached down to cup my ass, pulling me in tight. "Oh, chère. I like how your mind works. I'd like nothing better than to be naked in your bed with you." His eyes searched mine and then looked over my shoulder at the clock. He let out a little breath with an impatient whine mixed in. "How much longer are you going to be?"

I knew what he meant but I had to stand my ground. "I'll probably be another two and a half or three hours. Then Mackenzie is going to cook for us. We have to behave until then."

He smiled down at me. "I know, I was just checking. And I promise, me and my phallus will do our best not to distract you while you're working."

I burst out laughing and swatted at his arm. "Great, now that's all I'll be thinking about. I really do think it's amazing."

He rolled his eyes and groaned. "I love you, chère."

Those words would never cease to warm my heart. "I love you too, you big, sexy man. Now this working girl needs to eat something." I pulled away from him and opened a cabinet to grab a protein bar. I offered him one and he accepted. I grabbed a Diet Coke from the fridge and turned to ask him what he wanted.

"I'll just have a water, thank you. So speaking of working girls, were you serious about your stepmom thinking that?" He was frowning so deep he was almost scowling.

I shrugged. "I doubt she would think I'd go that far, but yeah. She really doesn't think I'll be able to support myself with my art. I told you she was quite unhappy with my decision to leave my internship."

He shook his head. "Yeah, but how could she not support you? How could she not see how amazing you are?"

"I don't know. It's just not something in her frame of reference so therefore it's not possible, I guess. It's fine though. I know I'm doing well and that's what counts, right?"

His frown lessened but was still there. "Sure, but I wish she would be more supportive of your dreams. I guess we were just lucky that our whole family was behind us when we started out, and they've stuck with us ever since. I want the same for you."

It made me feel warm inside to hear him speak so kindly to me. "Thanks, but I had to accept a long time ago that she and my father weren't going to agree with my life choices. I could either do what they wanted me to do and not feel satisfied, or follow my heart and be happy. So I chose happy."

He wrapped his arms around me again. I would never get tired of being in the safety of him. "Happy is good. I want you to be happy. It's going to be my mission to show you all kinds of happy."

I felt like such a sap but the waterworks were threatening again. "You already have," I whispered. "You mean there's more?"

He laughed, dropping his head back and accentuating his gorgeous neck. I couldn't resist kissing him at the base of his throat. That got a sigh out of him.

"There's so much more. But for now, you have work to do, woman." He smacked my ass playfully and I scooted away from him.

"I know. I'll be out in a minute." I took a moment for a bathroom break. I looked at myself in the mirror before heading back out and was pleased to see that my smile and my proximity to Devon had left a glow on my face.

When I went back downstairs, Mackenzie was chatting with Jonathan and Sabrina, who was now blonder than me.

"Hey, Jaylene. Long time no see." Jonathan greeted me with a hug and then stepped back quickly. He was looking *way* up so I figured he'd noticed Devon.

"Glad you could make it, Jonathan. This is my boyfriend, Devon, and this is my friend Star."

Again with the wide-eyed stare. He stuck out his hand but seemed unable to speak.

"Pleased to meet you, Jonathan," Devon said quietly.

Jonathan nodded back and then looked at me and whispered, "Do you know who they are?"

I quirked my head at him and deadpanned, "Well, as much as I can. We met in an online dating forum this past week. You think there's something I should know?"

He looked startled and the others were doing a poor job of keeping it together. "Jaylene, they're in that metal band Maggie's Bones! Haven't you ever heard of them?"

I frowned and turned on Devon. "How could you keep something like that from me? How could you?!"

He threw up his hands and said, "Don't blame me. 'Rock star' wasn't one of the options on the employment section."

I turned back to Jonathan and his expression was priceless. "Guess I'll have to get my money back."

His eyes went wider and I couldn't, in good conscience, keep up the shenanigans. I laughed. "I'm sorry, Jonathan, that was mean. Yes, I am fully aware of what this man does for a living."

He looked confused for a minute and then laughed as well. "Damn, Jaylene. You are too good at that."

I smiled guiltily and the others just shook their heads. "Couldn't resist. Alright, shall we get started?"

I brought out the drawing for his tattoo. He wanted to get a traditional-style American eagle tattoo on his forearm. It was good sized so it took me some time to shrink it down on the copier until it would fit. Jonathan was busy talking to the guys and didn't mind the wait a bit.

"I'm a huge fan. Me and my buddies from the base saw you play two years ago before we deployed to Iraq. What a great show."

Devon and Star thanked him and asked about his military service. Jonathan told them he'd already served two tours in Iraq and now he was back stateside for the time being. He'd made it through relatively unscathed, physically at least. But the last time we met, he'd shared with me some of the not-so-visible scars. He'd still been having night terrors at that point, but was getting counseling on base and was able to do his job.

Devon was playing guitar again and Star and Mackenzie had disappeared behind her privacy curtain. Sabrina walked over to check out what I was working on before she took off for the day. She admired the stencil on his arm and my pencil drawing I'd left out on the counter.

"That's going to be a great tattoo, Jonathan."

He smiled in appreciation. "Thank you. Jaylene has done most of my tattoos. Been waiting to come back and see her again."

Sabrina bent down to whisper in my ear, "If I'm not mistaken, I think Mackenzie is piercing that poor boy back there."

I giggled and peered over at the curtain. I could hear them talking softly and laughing. I looked at Devon and he shook his head, looking in the same direction. Sabrina gave a wave and shouted her goodbye to Mackenzie before heading out the front door.

Then we heard Star shouting. "Ow, shit, honey! That fucking smarts!"

I heard Mackenzie's voice down low and then the unmistakable sounds of smooching.

"Hey Kenz? I don't think that's sanitary to be doing back there."

She pulled back the curtain just a bit. "It's sanitary. He's fine."

I distinctly heard him say, "I'll be fine when you're done. Ow!" More smoochy sounds and grunts of pain. "Sugar Honey Iced Tea! That hurts like a bitch."

Devon looked back at me with his eyebrow raised.

"You want to make sure she's not impairing your drummer?"

He shook his head. "Uh-uh. If I look, I might be scarred for life. He's my best friend, but I don't need to see what she's piercing right now."

"I heard that, fucker." Star hollered, and I heard Mackenzie giggling and more kissing. I went back to working on Jonathan, anxious all of a sudden to be done so I might be able to do some smooching of my own.

Jonathan caught me up on how his therapy was going. I told him I was glad he continued to go, that he seemed much better.

"You're just about done here, Jonathan. Let me just put in the last bit of shading." It had taken me just under two hours and it looked pretty damn good.

He smiled from ear to ear. "Thanks so much, Jaylene, for fitting me in. I really wanted to get this done at the beginning of my leave. I'm meeting up with buddies later on Bourbon Street. We decided to spend the weekend here."

We shared with Jonathan our local knowledge of where to go and where to avoid and he appreciated the advice. After I cleaned him up and let him take a look, he was very pleased with his new ink. I wrapped his arm and gave him the instructions. He pulled me into a hug before he left.

Then he sheepishly looked over at Devon and cleared his throat. "Hey man, if it isn't too weird, could I have your autograph?"

Devon told him no problem and I showed him where some of my shop postcards were. He signed one for Jonathan, and one for one of his buddies. Jonathan shook his hand and thanked him. "Hey, you take care of this lovely lady, now. She's the best."

Devon smiled back and looked over at me. "She is that. Enjoy your tattoo."

Jonathan nodded. "I'll probably see you in six months or so. Hey, let me know if you're ever in Texas, I'll come see you."

I waved at him as he left and turned to look back at the state of my shop.

Devon was still playing softly in the corner, and he seemed so comfortable it made me feel all warm and squishy inside. I was getting a lot of that feeling around him, and it was nice.

Mackenzie pulled back the curtain, and out came Star with two very angry-looking nipples, now pierced with silver hoops.

"What the hell did you do to him?" I asked Mackenzie.

She beamed and he smiled right back at her. "He wanted them. I just did my thing. You know how it is." She winked at me and I felt my cheeks redden.

Star frowned at me and sputtered, "You? Really?"

I shrugged. "I can't turn down a dare, Star. Ever."

He laughed at that and Devon just shook his head. He stood up and took a pained glance at his friend's chest. "You really should have considered that these could be an occupational hazard."

Star frowned. "What, these? Nah. I won't catch them on anything."

I laughed, thinking about how crazy he was when he was drumming. "Well, you might want to make sure you keep your shirt on, just in case." I laughed again and Mackenzie agreed with me.

"I think that's a great idea, honey. If you rip one of these out, you will *not* be a happy man." I'm sure she had no problem with him keeping his shirt on around all those screaming women.

"Alright, time to close up?"

I locked the door and Mackenzie shut down the computer. "It is definitely time. I've got dinner to make for you guys."

We all headed upstairs and into Mackenzie's flat. She and Star got busy with the dinner preparations, and she handed Devon and I each a bottle of water and shooed us into the living room.

We flopped down on the couch together and he took a hold of my hands and started massaging them. I let my head fall back on the couch. "Hmmmmm, that feels so nice. Thank you, but you don't have to do that."

He smiled. "Sure I do. You worked hard today. I can't believe how much you got done on those two and you barely seem tired at all."

I laughed. "I'm a little tired but it was worth it. I'm glad I got to fit them in." He moved his way up one forearm and then the other, working the tension out of each of my fingers, and then he spun me around so he could work on my shoulders.

"If you keep that up, I'm going to be Jell-O in your hands."

He leaned close to my neck and whispered, "That's what I'm aiming for, chère." I turned to face him and he kissed me softly, so sweet.

I pulled back. "I really liked having you in my shop today. Was it too boring?"

He smiled and shook his head, bringing my hands up and kissing each one. "Not boring at all. Number one, I'm rarely bored. Number two, I was watching you. That's all the entertainment I need. And number three, it was relaxing. No one bothered me, no one bossed me around. It was awesome."

I thought about the pressure he'd been under and thought perhaps this kind of a day was exactly what he'd needed. He looked down at me with a serious expression on his face. "What's wrong, baby?"

He smiled faintly. "Nothing's wrong. But remember last night when I told you I had things to tell you?"

I nodded and braced myself for whatever it was that had him so serious. "I do. What is it?"

He held my hands in his and looked down at them when he talked. "I talked with Marcus yesterday, as we planned. We agreed to a truce. He apologized for how he treated you and plans to make amends. I agreed to his terms as well."

I frowned and scooted a little closer to him. "What are his terms?"

He blew out a breath and shook his head. "He and Sherry found us a new producer, a guy we've been wanting to work with for a while named Scott Cross. He's agreed to produce our album, but the only way we can work with him is if we head back to L.A. in a week." He looked up hesitantly.

"Okay. Jade mentioned something about that and you said this was probably going to happen. How do you feel about going back?"

A pained expression crossed his face. "The same. I don't want to fucking go there but it's what's best for the band. The good news—or bad news, whichever way you look at it—is that Scott is intense. He works his bands hard and usually has an album recorded quickly. That means we'll be done sooner, but it means practically twenty-four-seven in the studio. And since we're not where we should be, this next week is going to mean crunch time."

I nodded and put my arms around his neck, forcing him to look at me. "Are you going to be okay with this? I hate the idea of you being stressed while trying to create."

He smiled weakly. "I'll be fine. I guess. But dammit, I thought I'd have more time..." He trailed off. He looked so worried.

"Devon, what is it?"

He searched my eyes. "I don't want to be away from you," he said in a broken voice.

I wrapped my arms around him, crawling onto his lap. "I know, baby, I don't want that either. But we knew this was coming, right?"

That didn't appease him at all. He took my arms from around him and grabbed for my hands. "I'm coming back though, you know that, right? I'm coming back as soon as we're done. This isn't it."

Oh gods. He was worried about me. My eyes welled up and I shook my head. "Of course you're coming back. We'll be fine, baby. I don't want you to worry about *us*. You're going to have enough on your plate dealing with Marcus. You don't need to worry about me. I'll be here. I'll be here waiting for you, okay?"

He squeezed his eyes shut, and a tear escaped. When he opened them and saw me smiling, he smiled tentatively. "You promise? I don't want to go, thinking you're convinced we're done. I won't."

I shook my head. "I'm your home, remember? You told me last night what I needed to hear. I'm home for you, so I'm not going anywhere. Can't have you being homeless anymore."

His mouth found mine and he kissed me again like that starved man. I kissed him back with as much emotion, and before too long we were both out of breath, crying and laughing with happiness.

When Mackenzie and Star found us, they just stood there speechless. "Okay, who's pregnant?"

My eyes jerked up to them in shock and they both laughed.

"What's that supposed to mean?" I sputtered.

Mackenzie huffed and crossed her arms over her chest. "You tell *me*. You guys are in here crying and laughing all over each other. That usually means someone is knocked up." I tossed a pillow at her and she threw up her hands. "I'm just saying. Dinner's ready, you sick fucks."

We both laughed and took a moment to collect ourselves. I held his face in my hands. "Are you okay?"

He nodded. "I think I am. For the first time in a long time, I feel okay. It's going to suck, but I'll be on the phone with you every spare second and the minute we're done, I'm on a plane back to you."

I smiled and kissed him softly. "Good. Now let's go eat."

We spent the rest of the evening eating and laughing with our friends, sharing a delicious dinner and conversation. About ten o'clock, Mackenzie started nibbling on Star's ear and we knew it was time for us to go next door.

"Hey, dude. I was going to take Jaylene out tomorrow. You cool here or you want me to drop you somewhere?"

Mackenzie hopped onto Star's lap and wrapped her arms around him, possessively. "He's going nowhere. I've got plans for him."

Star moaned and said, "I like your plans, honey."

They started kissing so we said our goodbyes, which were waved off, and made it out *almost* before their clothes started coming off.

TWENTY-TWO

When we got inside my place and Devon shut the door behind him, we just stood and looked at each other for a long time.

"So," I said to break the silence.

He grinned back at me. "So."

He walked towards me and wrapped his hands around my waist, pulling me into his chest. My head tilted back to look up at him and he kissed my forehead. "So," I whispered. "We have a little over twenty-four hours 'til we have to go back."

He nodded and started nibbling my neck, my knees almost giving way. "Yes we do. I'm taking you somewhere tomorrow, but tonight I just want to relax with you. Just hang out. So what do you do when you're just hanging out?"

"You mean what do I do when I'm not working? Hmmm... Typically after a long day like today, I might turn on some tunes, take a hot bath, paint my toenails...maybe read or watch a movie. I got news for you: that's the extent of an exciting evening for me. Occasionally Mackenzie and I will go listen to music somewhere but that's it. I'm really boring."

He was looking down at me with the dreamiest expression. "That sounds perfect. Can we do that?"

I laughed. "Which part?"

He shrugged. "All of it?"

"I would love to. But first, since I was a poor hostess last night, let me give you a quick tour." He grinned as I took his hand for what would likely be a short tour. He looked around as we walked, admiring my dishes and selection of flatware. He commented on my color scheme for the living room.

"If you're going to tease, you can forget that spot I promised you for your toothbrush."

He smirked and kissed me on the back of the neck, momentarily distracting me from being irritated by his comments.

"I'm not teasing. I love your place, I do. It's giving me a little more insight into you."

I frowned at him. "What can you tell about me that you didn't already know?"

He looked around. "Well, for instance, I can tell that you at least have some affinity for purple, since there seems to be a lot of it."

I had a purple rug and throw pillows in the living room and the bathroom was done in lavender. "Okay, I guess besides black, it's my next favorite. What else?"

He walked over to look at some pictures on my wall. "You like birds?"

I chuckled. "My father took those. It was his hobby, photography. Mostly wild birds." He glanced at me to check my reaction. I smiled weakly. "Keep going. I never knew my place was so reflective of me."

He laughed gently. He looked over the book titles on my shelves. They were equally covered by psychology texts and vampire literature. "I take it Anne Rice may have had something to do with your move here?"

I blushed. "I love her writing. I read *Interview With The Vampire* when I was a junior in high school and then proceeded to devour the rest of her works. Guess I have a thing for the supernatural."

He looked at my tattoos of the classic monsters and said, "I kind of figured that." We both laughed. "Your place is just like you, comfortable, fun and sexy."

I burst out laughing. He had my iPod off the dock and turned on my blues playlist. "Sexy? How is my place sexy?"

He walked slowly towards me. "It smells like you, like vanilla and sugar. So sweet it lingers, you know?" He drew his finger along the neckline of my shirt. "Everything is soft, from your sheets to your towels to the fabric on your couch. You do that intentionally, don't you?"

I shrugged. "I kind of shop by touch."

His voice dropped down an octave. "See, even the way you shop is sexy."

I giggled and he took my hand and brushed his lips over my knuckles and fingertips. "You're just making that up."

He shook his head and walked me towards the bathroom. "Nope. You even buy sexy candles for your bathroom."

I looked in and noticed at some point he'd set out the candles I'd bought on my shopping trip with Star. He took out his lighter and lit a row of them then looked appraisingly at my tub.

"One of the selling points for me with this place was that, even though the flats were dinky, the bathrooms were large and included these massive claw-foot tubs."

He nodded and turned my cheek up to kiss it gently. "It does look massive. Big enough for both of us."

I smiled knowingly up at him. He grasped the hem of my tank and pulled it over my head and did the same with his shirt. He easily unclasped my bra and let it drop.

"I guess we should test that theory. Are you ready to start relaxing?"

He nodded. We removed the rest of each other's clothes and he grabbed a hairband from my stash. He motioned for me to turn around and then oh so gently gathered my hair up into a half-pulled ponytail. He turned the water on and got the temp just right.

I stepped next to him and held out a bottle of lemon oil. "This okay?" He looked up at me and that devastating smile was back. I squirted in a couple of drops and then he stepped in and held out his hand to me. I took it and we lowered into the tub, my back to his chest.

We sat in silence for the longest time, just enjoying the feel of the water and the proximity of each other's bodies. He was breathing steady behind me. I turned around to peek at him and his head was resting on the back of the tub, his eyes closed.

"This is a great playlist," he said, keeping his eyes closed. "Didn't know you liked the blues, too."

I kissed his chin and he wrapped his arms around me for a squeeze. "I've really gotten into it more since I came here. I guess the metal is sometimes about being angry for me, and I'm not so angry anymore. I heard Tab Benoit after I moved here, and then Dr. John. I spent some time looking into their influences and just loved it all. It's relaxing for me after a day at the shop."

He smiled his half smile, and I traced my fingers along his arms, feeling him sigh beneath me. "I've played with Tab before. He's amazing."

"Really?"

He murmured, "Mmmm-hmmm. He lived in Houma at one point. My daddy knew him. Every once in a while he'd come to town and play at a club, and when I was fourteen, I guess, my daddy took me to see him. He invited folks up to play with him and my daddy made me go. It was unnerving, to say the least, but I'll never forget it. I learned to play slide watching him."

"That's so cool. I wondered when you started playing."

He smiled. "About the time I got my first boner."

Shocked, I splashed him and he grabbed me tighter.

"What? It was. I was like eleven years old. I went to my daddy because I thought something was wrong. He shook his head, handed me his guitar, and said, 'Son, that ain't gonna bring you nothin' but heartache. Learn to play this; it'll help with the pain.' I had no fucking clue what he meant for a long time, but the first time I got one around a girl, I knew what he meant *then*. For the longest time, girls were nothing but trouble. Playing guitar kept me occupied so I wouldn't dwell on unproductive feelings."

"Or boners," I laughed.

He snorted. "Exactly. My daddy was a pretty smart guy."

I kissed him on his neck and he moaned softly. I loved how responsive he was to my every touch. But I wondered... "Do you miss him?"

He nodded. "A lot more since Maggie died. She kind of filled a guiding role for me. Even though she wasn't a man, she kind of thought like one sometimes, and she would talk about anything with me. But my daddy was just as infectious as she was, and I felt like if he would have been around, things definitely would have been different." He opened his eyes and studied me. "How 'bout you? Do you miss your daddy?"

I thought about his question for a minute. "Not in the way you would think." I was worried about how he would take my answer.

"What is it, chère?"

I frowned and then gave it a shot. "It's hard to explain. You've probably gathered from the little we've talked about it that my family life was very different than yours." He nodded. "Well...I don't miss him like you miss yours, or how you miss Maggie. It's more like I have to remind myself that he's not here anymore. He's not going to criticize me anymore. He's not going to make demands of me. He can't hurt me anymore."

Devon's eyes grew dark with anger. Then concern took over. "I can't even imagine how you made it out of that, how you became the incredible woman you are in spite of how you were raised."

His words touched me, deep down where that woman he knew me to be was still an insecure little girl just wishing for once her father would be happy with something she did.

"Well, I didn't make it out unscathed, I guess. *You've* probably experienced the effects more than anyone else has."

"You mean how you were worried about letting us down."

I nodded. "And other things. Look, I hate how he died, I hate how miserable he was the last few years of his life, and I hate that the only way I ever felt strong enough to tell him how I felt was when he was in a coma in the hospital. But that's how it went with us. My stepmother isn't as bad, but the judgment is still there sometimes, so I'm usually on guard around her. It's easier to tell her how I feel. I pretty much did when she was here. But hey, this soak in the tub was supposed to be about relaxing. I'm sorry."

Devon turned me to face him. "No, *I'm* sorry. I just wanted to know a little bit more about what makes you tick. I'm sorry I brought it up."

I smiled up at him. "It's okay. I don't mind talking about it. I'm really okay. I've had plenty of time to think about it...and now I have more important things to think about."

He raised an eyebrow. "Such as?"

I sighed and batted my eyelashes. "Such as what color I'm going to have you paint my toenails."

His eyes flared. "Are you serious? That sounds really fucking sexy. Do I get to choose?" I kissed his bottom lip, giving it a little nibble, and stood up slowly in front of him. He watched me and moved to stand, but I stopped him. "No, you stay there."

I reached for a towel and stepped gently and as gracefully as possible from the tub and patted myself dry. His eyes tracked my every movement.

I wrapped the towel around me and peered on the top shelf of my cabinet for my nail polish collection. What can I say? I like colors on my body. "What's your favorite color, Devon?"

He said, "Hmmm, on you? Something dramatic. How about a dark red?"

I smiled at him and said, "Whatever you like, baby." I made quick work of removing my black polish and dipped my toes back in the tub to rinse. He was still watching me with wonder.

"You know, I've never been privy to this level of feminine beauty practices before. I kind of feel like I joined a secret club, learned the secret handshake or something."

I handed him the bottle of blood-red polish and he smiled approvingly.

"Any advice for a first timer?"

I shook my head. "I trust you, you've got skilled hands."

He smirked. I sat on the toilet and placed my toes on the edge of the tub. He got to work and applied himself to doing the neatest paint job my toes had ever seen.

"Mmmm, you are so hired. You sure you've never done this before?"

He shook his head as he applied top coat to the last toe. Then he blew across my toes to help them dry and desire pooled in my belly, watching his lips purse like that.

"I am so in love with your lips, Devon. Do you have any idea how sensual they are?"

He blushed a little and shook his head. "Honestly, I've never really paid any attention to what I look like. I feel a little self-conscious around you, like I've never felt before."

I reached out and touched his arm. "Oh no. I'm sorry. Is it something I said?"

He laughed and kissed my hand. "No, it's nothing bad. It's just, I feel like you're the first person to really see me. Not just my body, but the real me. People so often project onto me what they want me to be, but you *see* me."

I knew what he was saying because I felt the same about him. "I do. I mean, I'm trying. It was hard at first because there were so many sides to you. I love that about you. But did I make you feel uncomfortable?"

He laughed. "No, not really. Just never saw myself as anything but that skinny, awkward kid. I mean, I know I look different now, but I haven't really paid attention to how I've changed. And when *you* look at me, it's with love, not because you want a piece of me. I guess it's a little unnerving."

"I don't want you to feel uncomfortable. I just can't help it. You're so beautiful. Not just because you have a great ass—"

"Or a majestic phallus," he interrupted.

I huffed at him "Devon. I'm being serious. You're beautiful because you're you, because you wear your emotions for everyone to see. Your eyes are so expressive. Your expressions, the way you carry yourself, all of it. You are beautiful to me on the inside, and your body is just another representation of it."

He stood up from the bath and reached out a hand to me. His vulnerability only made him that much more beautiful. I grabbed a towel and held it up.

"I've never had anyone say something so heartfelt and so loving to me. I'm just kind of feeling stunned right now."

He kissed the top of my head and moved to step out of the tub. I took the towel from him and dried him off. He watched me with heavy lids.

I paused in drying him to look up at his expression. I smiled gratefully and continued up his thigh with the towel and stepped behind to get his back. When I came around to his front, he took the towel from me and hung it on the rack, then he pulled mine off and did the same. He brought his hands up to caress my cheeks and I relaxed into his grip.

"We okay?" he asked softly.

I nodded, "Yeah. We're good. I think?"

He laughed and kissed me tenderly. "Yeah, we're good." He looked down at our bodies touching each other and he blew out a breath. His hands floated down to caress my breasts lightly and he said, "So let's see: We took a bath, listened to music, painted toenails. What's next?"

I giggled and said, "Movie or reading would be the usual follow-up activity, but right now, I can think of some *other* activities that would be pretty fantastic as well."

"I like how you think, beautiful girl."

I took his hand and led him to the bedroom. We fell in a heap of limbs, touching, kissing, caressing and then biting, sucking, squeezing, until we'd worked ourselves into a state of need.

This time when he made love to me, it was frantic. Once he'd rolled on the condom, he fell on me and took me fast and hard. He pulled out and flipped me over, raising my hips off the bed, and he entered me from behind, taking my pleasure to new heights. I came harder than I had yet, and when he found his release, he cried out against the back of my neck and continued to push into me until he was completely spent.

"Baby, I don't think you can crawl up inside of me. It's just not possible but I don't mind if you keep trying."

He burst out laughing, his weight falling on me until I thought I just might have had too much of a good thing. I tapped his hip with my arm that was trapped at my side. "Um, need oxygen here."

"Oh shit, I'm sorry." He moved hurriedly to let me up and went to dispose of the condom. I fell on my back and tried to catch my breath. I heard him use the sink in the bathroom and then he changed the music on my iPod. A playlist '90s metal came on, starting with Pantera.

He came back in and climbed onto the bed next to me, kissing my stomach and ribs, and taking his time with my very sensitive nipples. "I didn't hurt you, did I? I'm sorry; I think I got a little carried away."

I ran my fingers through his hair and sighed. "I had a feeling that if you were to ever let loose the hold you had on your passion, it would be nothing short of mind-boggling."

He laughed shyly. "Yeah, well, you are just so... Fuck Jaylene, you are so goddamn sexy. I just can't keep my hands off you—or *any* part of me, for that matter."

I couldn't believe he still had energy after that performance but he was ready for round two already. He sat up on his knees and looked down at me with that fiery gaze and I knew I was in trouble. I reached out to stroke him and his eyes closed tight. I'd been dying to taste him, so I leaned forward to sample the merchandise.

His groan let me know he was enjoying it, too. I took my time, running my fingers, lips, tongue, and teeth over every ridge and swell of him. His fingers grabbed for my hair, quickly smoothing it back so he could watch me. He was so large I couldn't take him all in, but I touched him. I could feel him straining.

"God, Jaylene, I'm...I, I can't...*oh, goooooooooood!*" He came in a rush, but not before pulling me up by my shoulders and kissing me hard, whimpering and covering my belly with his release. "Now, chère, you can't do that. I can't—"

I cut him off. "Oh yes, you very well can. That was *amazing*. Did I do alright?"

He gripped my arms tight and his blue eyes were blazing as he smiled at me. "It was incredible," he whispered, sounding awestruck. "I just didn't want to finish like that. I kind of made a mess."

I smiled up at him and took his bottom lip between my teeth, bringing another groan from him. "I like your mess. That was fun." My eyes flashed at him.

"When I said you were fun earlier, I had no idea *how* much fun."

"So does that mean it was okay? I'm serious. Tell me what you like; I want to make you feel good."

He shook his head. "You already do. The way you touched me while you were using your... Fuck me, that was intense." He ran his hand back over his hair and shook his head at me. "I love you so much, Jaylene. I love being with you like this."

I grabbed some tissue and cleaned us up. Then we collapsed together on the bed. I curled up with my back to him, and he kissed my shoulder and pulled me in close.

"You know something? I am so glad I waited for you."

He chuckled and rubbed his chin in my hair. "I am too, chère, but why do you say that?"

I wiggled my hips closer to his and he responded by squeezing my thigh. "I just feel really comfortable with you, I trust you. It's made this so much better. It feels natural, not forced, you know what I mean? I'm not spending the whole time worrying, 'should I be doing this, will he think I'm weird if I ask him to do this.'"

He murmured, "I'm glad I can be that for you. And you can ask me anything. I'd do anything you want me to do. I'm just loving learning your body and what you like, what makes you pant, what makes you gasp, what makes you scream."

I giggled. "I kinda did scream that last time. It feels really intense when you're behind me like that. It's deeper."

"Hmmm, I know. I love it all. I just love watching you move."

I closed my eyes and relaxed into him. I felt so safe in his arms, so cherished. It was the best feeling. The years I'd wondered and waited were absolutely worth it to be here with this man right now.

"Devon, I wanted to tell you... I'm going to start taking the pill in a week or so. By the time you come back from L.A., if you feel okay about it, we won't have to..."

He sat up and leaned over me. "You are? You'd do that?"

I nodded, smiling at him. "I did it for us, baby. I just thought it would make things better, less worry, you know?"

He nodded, resting his chin on my shoulder. "I appreciate it but I don't mind using condoms. I haven't ever *not* used them, so it's no big deal."

I turned over to face him, kissing his chest. "You mean that could be a first for you?"

His eyes flared and he nodded. "Yeah. I mean, if you're sure. And if anything happened, I would be absolutely okay with it. I told you, I think you'll be sexy as hell pregnant." I rolled my eyes and bit him. "Ooooh, what you do with those teeth. I love it when you bite me."

I giggled. "I appreciate you saying that. I *am* scared though, about being pregnant. I'm really not ready for that."

He held me close and sighed. "Then we'll make sure it doesn't happen 'til you're ready, okay? But I don't want you to be worried about *me* if it does. I'm not like some guys who don't get it that one and one makes two, you know what I mean? I take it seriously."

"Thank you. That means a lot. But before you have me barefoot and pregnant in the kitchen, let's just see if we can work up to that fourth time first."

He laughed and kissed me and I heard his stomach rumbling. "I guess I worked up an appetite. Can I get you anything?"

I shook my head. "Just some more water. I need to replenish."

He squeezed my ass and hopped out of bed. Watching him move through the shadows cast by the streetlights that filtered in through my windows was the last thing I remembered seeing before sleep overtook me.

Twenty-Three

The sun was shining when I woke up the next morning to the sounds of Led Zeppelin and the smell of bacon frying.

I rolled over and stretched thoroughly before sitting up. Devon's jeans, shirt and boots were in a neat pile next to a duffel he must have brought in last night or this morning. His beanie and sunglasses sat on top of my dresser.

Seeing his things in my room made me feel warm inside. The fact that he was cooking me breakfast was even more enticing. I said a silent prayer of thanks for this man and the wonderful way in which he was becoming an integral part of my life.

I stumbled out to the kitchen in his shirt and found a precious sight.

He was barefoot, in just his boxer briefs, and he was singing along to "Ramble On." But the *piece de resistance*? He was wearing my naked lady apron to avoid grease splatters.

I watched as long as I could before the giggles slipped out.

He turned around and without missing a lyric, walked over and put a piece of bacon in my mouth and then kissed me.

I sighed happily and stepped into the bathroom. Things were certainly tender. I noticed I had fingertip bruises on my hips from where he'd gripped me the night before. I knew it would bother him, but it gave me a rush.

When I came out, he had a plate of bacon, eggs and fruit waiting for me at my tiny table. I walked up behind him and wrapped my arms around his waist, whispering, "It's kind of like feeling myself up."

He looked down and saw my hands on the breasts on the apron. He chuckled. "I guess I *do* have a nice rack."

When he turned to kiss me good morning, he was radiating joy. "I didn't want to wake you. I tried to be quiet but I just needed to be up this morning. I feel too good."

I smiled up at him. "I slept great. Sorry I crashed on you last night. You *did* sleep, right?"

He nodded and shooed me over to the table. "Don't let that get cold. Yes, I did sleep some. I was wired, I guess. I wrote a new song."

I narrowed my eyes at him over my juice glass as I took a sip. "You seem awfully chipper for someone who's barely gotten any sleep lately. Here I am, crashing all over the place, and you look refreshed on just a couple of hours. How is that possible?"

He took a bite of bacon and smirked. "Good genes? I don't know. I usually get around five hours a night. I do okay with that."

I shook my head. "But that's not healthy."

He smiled. "I'm fine, Jaylene. I feel better than I have in a long time."

I shrugged. I didn't know that I wanted to have this fight with him. "Okay, but tonight we turn in early."

He leaned over and kissed my cheek. "Whatever you say, chère. Now, eat up. I'm going to take a shower and then when you're ready, I want to take you somewhere."

I smiled at him. "Like a surprise somewhere?"

He nodded, finished his breakfast, and took off my apron. He hung it back next to the refrigerator and walked toward me. I stopped him with one hand and wrapped my arms around his waist. He smiled, brushing my hair away from my face. When I kissed his belly and rubbed my face against his velvet skin, his hands gripped my arms and I felt him shudder.

I looked up at him and he shook his head at me. "I can't stop to cuddle or we'll never get out of here, and I'm already fighting the Viking urge to carry you back to bed and claim you."

I giggled and kissed him once more before letting go.

"I'll be out in a minute, chère." He sauntered into the bathroom and I sighed.

The food was delicious, my aches were delicious, and *he* looked delicious. I couldn't think of a more wonderful Sunday.

When he finished, I took my turn in the shower. I did a quick French braid and stepped out of the bathroom in my robe. He was already dressed, pulling on his boots at the table.

"You'll probably want long pants and shoes you don't mind getting a little dirty." I gave him a quizzical look and he raised his eyebrows at me. "C'mon, beautiful. We need to get a move on."

Suddenly quite anxious to get some time outdoors on a beautiful day, I hurriedly dressed in jeans, Keens and a red tank with a skull on it. I rubbed on some sunscreen and put on some eyeliner. I packed my sketchbook and pencils in my backpack.

"I'm assuming we have some mode of transport? You do know I don't have a car?"

He nodded and a fiendish grin graced his gorgeous mug. "I have a vehicle parked right outside, milady. You ready yet?"

I grabbed a couple of waters from the fridge and asked, "Do I need to pack us some snacks or anything?"

He shook his head. "Just your pretty little self. Now let's get a move on."

He grabbed his guitar and took my hand, leading me out. I decided to text Mackenzie later to check on her. I figured they might want to sleep in. Who knew what they'd been up to last night?

We stepped out the back door and I had to squint in the bright sunlight. "You know, I kind of feel like a vampire. We've been inside so much lately. The sun feels great but man, does it sting the eyes."

He chuckled and said, "I've got an extra pair of shades if you need them."

I smiled up at him, using a hand to shade my eyes...

And that's when I saw it.

"You brought it," I breathed in wonderment.

I felt his kiss on top of my head as I was drawn to the black and chrome beauty before us. "I told you I needed to get something from Houma. I needed my other girl."

I was speechless. Gods, the car was perfection. A 1972 Dodge Challenger convertible. Black on black with chrome finish. I turned to him with stars in my eyes and said, "This is a fantastic piece of machinery."

He chuckled and threw his arm over my shoulders. "This is Rose. My daddy bought her when I was a kid and taught me how to work on her. The paint and interior we had done by someone else, but he and I rebuilt the engine ourselves. You up for a ride, chère?"

I was bouncing on the balls of my feet. "Absolutely."

We climbed in and he placed his guitar and my backpack in the backseat. He cranked the engine and the roar that sounded was loud and furious. I grinned at him maniacally, impressed by his cool exterior. In his white t-shirt and jeans, black hair loose and hanging in pieces around his face, and silver hoops reflecting in the sun, he was that bad boy personified again.

He drew on his shades and handed me another pair from the glove box. When I didn't take them right away, he looked over at me.

"What is it, beautiful?"

I had the shades clutched to my chest and all I could do was stare at him. He laughed at me and I just settled farther into the seat and sighed. "Just enjoying the view."

He pursed his lips together, put the car in reverse and backed out of my small driveway. Only about four cars could fit in the back of our building. Mackenzie had an old truck back there and the other spots were reserved for customers. I hadn't wanted or needed a car when I arrived, and Mackenzie lent me her truck whenever I needed it.

Devon pulled out onto Frenchmen Street and headed away from the Quarter. "I've not done much exploring of your glorious state. Where are you taking me?"

He smiled at me. "No? I'm glad I get to show you around then. I thought we'd head over to Houma if that's okay with you?"

This date was getting better and better. "I would love that."

He reached over and grasped my hand. "Well then, sit back and enjoy the ride, chère."

I rested my head against the seat and pulled my legs up under me. Devon navigated the streets with ease and when he pulled onto the interstate, he gave the engine a kick and we flew down the road.

The car was pristine. The interior was polished and lovingly tended to. Devon switched on the radio and we listened to Cajun music and just enjoyed being out and about. I pulled our hands up and kissed his knuckles. "This could be all we do today and I would think it was a perfect date."

He laughed softly, glancing over at me, and squeezed my hand. "I'm glad to hear you say that, but it's not all we're going to do. I just felt like being outside, and Rose has been neglected for too long. I had to have Daryl give her a jump last night. I haven't had her out since I've been home."

We rode for a long time without speaking. I stroked his hand with my fingers and he had a peaceful smile on his face. I realized in that moment how much he really had relaxed since I'd met him. I didn't know how he was with others before, but I know he wasn't smiling, and the thought that his feelings for me helped get him to this point made my heart swell.

We'd driven for a little over an hour through the gorgeous land of southern Louisiana. I hadn't been out this way and the view was breathtaking. We pulled off Highway 90 and took Main Street through town. Devon turned into the parking lot of Magnolia Cemetery and turned off the car.

He sat for a moment, staring out the windshield, his face expressionless behind his shades. I waited for him to speak. When he took a deep breath and smiled weakly, I knew why we were here.

"I wanted to come see Maggie and introduce you. I hope that's okay."

I scooted over next to him on the seat and cupped his face in my hands. "I'd be honored, Devon." I couldn't see his eyes through the shades but I knew what they would tell me. Deep sadness would be there, and maybe a little uncertainty about how I would feel about this. But I meant what I said. I knew how hard this was, and I was so proud of him for facing his fears.

We stepped out of the car and he grabbed his guitar case and a backpack. I followed him through the gates and down the path through the rows of tombs. I found the cemeteries of New Orleans fascinating. However, it was a more somber occasion this time as I was about to see a tomb for a real person, someone I'd met. The tombs seemed so old, like from another time. I knew they still buried people that way. I guess it hadn't occurred to me that Maggie would be in a similar one.

He led me to an older tomb with the name Boudreaux elegantly carved into the stone. He took out a blanket and laid it on the path for us. The weather was warm and the sun was high in the sky. I could hear the buzzing of cicadas in the trees surrounding the cemetery.

We sat next to each other and he was quiet for a while. He held my hand loosely against his thigh and stared up at this resting place of his ancestors. I thought about what that must be like, to have such a family history, to know where they ended up, and to have a connection to your past. I envied him for that. There were dates going back to 1861 on the tomb.

I didn't know anything about my family, other than my paternal grandparents were from Colorado originally, and that my father moved to California when he joined the service.

"The last person we buried here before Maggie was my daddy, and before that was my great-grandmother." He winced. "I didn't think I'd be back here so soon after my daddy."

I squeezed his hand and he took a couple of shaky breaths.

"I've been wanting to come out here since we came back, but I didn't feel strong enough. I'm still not sure I am." He laughed nervously. "When we buried Daddy, Maggie held my hand and gave me tissues when I cried. She helped me pick out one of Daddy's old suits and a nice red tie for the service. The pants were a little short and too big in the waist. The sleeves rode up on the jacket. But she assured me I looked handsome. She didn't leave my side the whole day. She didn't even cry until we got home and she could go to her room and be alone."

I wanted to soothe him but I could tell he needed to continue, that he needed to get this out.

"When it was time to get ready for *her* funeral, I thought about my daddy's suit and how I felt like he was with me when I wore it.

There was no way it was going to fit, though. I had some Armani bullshit suit Maggie made me get, so I wore that. I did find the red tie."

He turned and kissed me on top of my head and then reached for his guitar case. He brought out a beat-up Marshall acoustic and strummed it a few times, getting the tuning right.

"When I went home the other night, I planned on just grabbing the keys to Rose, but I walked around a bit and ended up in my room. I found that damned tie in the closet along with this, my first guitar. I wrote a song that night, and I want to play it for you."

I smiled at him and said, "I would love to hear it."

He smiled back sadly, but I still couldn't see his eyes.

The melody he played was achingly tender, and when he started to sing, I didn't need to see his eyes to know how much pain he was in.

She held my hand through my darkest days
She dried my tears and kept me moving
She dressed me up and gave me strength
She made me stand and kept on proving

And when I thought life would tear me down
She was there to help me turn it around

Love will be with you through all the pain
Love will comfort and always remain
Love will keep you always sane
Love will shelter you through the rain

She left me here in darker days
She left me and I gave up moving
She dressed me up and left me hollow
She made me stand and left me so low

. . .

And when I thought her death would end me
  Her words were there haunting me

Love will be with you through all the pain
  Love will comfort and always remain
  Love will keep you always sane
  Love will shelter you through the rain

You pulled me out of the darkest days
  You dried my tears and got me moving
  You undressed me and gave me strength
  You helped me stand and keep on proving

And when I thought I was forever broken
  She sent me an angel, her words again spoken

Love will be with you through all the pain
  Love will comfort and always remain
  Love will keep you always sane
  Love will shelter you through the rain

He played a few more notes and then stopped, his arms resting on top of the guitar.

I reached over and pulled off his shades to find his eyes on mine, unsure of what my reaction would be. His words were still reverberating in my head. The depth of his emotions fascinated me.

"I really want to kiss you right now, Devon. Can I kiss you?"

He smirked and set down his guitar, then pulled me onto his lap. His eyes searched my face for my reaction, but words couldn't express to him how his song moved me. I hoped my kiss would be enough to show him how much I wanted to do those things, to be that angel for him.

I pulled back and held his face in my hands. "I want to be that love for you, Devon. I'm so glad you're letting me."

He smiled and held me tight in his arms. From far off we heard children laughing, and I thought it might not be appropriate for someone to come across us in this position, so I slipped off his lap and sat in front of him.

"So, are you going to introduce me to the Boudreaux clan?"

He held my hands and motioned for me to turn and face the tomb. He cleared his throat and then leaned over my shoulder. "Daddy? Maggie? I'd like for you to meet a very special person, Jaylene Charles. She's my girlfriend, and I would very much like for her to be part of the family. Jaylene, this is my sister Maggie and my daddy, David Boudreaux."

I turned my head towards him to see if he was finished. He was smiling nervously. I gave him a quick kiss and turned back towards the tomb.

"I'm very pleased to meet you both. Devon has told me so much about you. I'm grateful he brought me here to see you today." I glanced at him before I continued.

"I wanted to take this opportunity to tell you how wonderful a man you both helped to raise. He is unbelievably brave, kind, and generous. You should be so proud of how hard he has been working to put his life back together. He misses you both so very much, and he's doing his best to honor you by being a great friend, son and cousin. I hope that you know your words have helped him deal with his loss, but he could still use a little more help. So if you don't mind sending him some peace, that would go a long way in helping him move forward and meet his obligations to the band.

"I'm so grateful to be a part of his life, and I will be here to hold his hand through whatever else life decides to throw his way, you can count on that. Thanks for listening."

Devon shook his head and laughed. "Leave it to you to find conversing with my dead relatives perfectly understandable. You're incredible, you know that?"

He wrapped his arms around my waist from behind and at that very moment, two white butterflies flew out from behind the tomb, circled each other, flew around us while doing their dance upon the breeze, and then fluttered off into the trees.

We looked at each other, both shaken by the experience. We knew something important had just happened.

"I'm kind of looking for Mage to be hiding behind a tomb or something," Devon said nervously.

"I think it's beautiful. You know they supposedly symbolize death and the spirits of those we've lost. They're meant to comfort the loved ones left behind."

He shook his head. "I didn't know that. Do you believe they're really still with us?"

I thought about it for a minute. "I'm not actually sure. I'd like to think they're watching us and sending us hope and love when we need it. But I also want to think of them as beyond pain, and I would think it would pain them to see us suffering. So I don't know."

Devon nuzzled my neck and inhaled a few deep breaths. "How about we go get some lunch?"

I looked to him and smiled. "Sure, unless you need more time?"

He shook his head. "Nope. I did what I came to do."

We stood and I made quick work of folding the blanket and putting it into the backpack. Devon stepped over to the wall of the tomb and he ran his fingers lightly over David's and Maggie's names. When he turned to look at me, his half smile gave me hope. He looked better. Much of the sadness had left his gaze.

As he took my hand and led me to the cemetery gates, I said a silent prayer that he would be able to keep this peace in the coming weeks.

We drove back down Main Street and stopped at the Houma Grill. "Isn't this your family's place?"

He nodded. "Haven't been here for a while, thought maybe you could meet more of the family. The living ones." He laughed and kissed me lightly before we entered.

The restaurant was very much a seafood shack kind of place. There were wooden picnic tables with red-and-white checkered tablecloths. Wood beams hung low, and there were family pictures all over the walls, along with some of local celebrities. I quickly noticed pictures of the band and smiled at the thought of how proud these folks must be of the boys' success.

There were also several pictures of Maggie at various ages. I particularly liked the one of her and Devon hugging that must have been taken not too long ago. He looked as he did now. Maybe his hair was a little longer.

As we approached the hostess stand, a girl in her late teens ran forward screaming, "MAMA! Devon's here!" She hurled herself at Devon and he caught her and swung her around in his arms.

Three other women came forward and hugged him as well. He kissed them all on the cheek. "Ladies, I would like you to meet my girlfriend, Jaylene Charles. Jaylene, this is my Aunt Claudine, and my cousins Deborah, Ada and Jeanette."

The women looked at me in shock, and barely caught themselves in time to avoid a look of scorn from Devon before hugging me warmly.

"It's very nice to meet you," I said nervously, Devon's hand at my back keeping me from completely freaking out.

They all exclaimed how happy they were to see us and seated us at a table near the back of the restaurant. Jeanette was the young girl, and she took our drink orders while the older ladies, in their thirties and forties maybe, asked after Devon's mama and the rest of the gang.

"Jaylene, these ladies are cousins on the Boudreaux side. Aunt Claudine was Daddy's sister, and Jeanette is her daughter. Deborah and Ada are my second cousins."

The ladies continued to gaze at me curiously. Claudine saw my confusion and spoke. "So Devon, what brings you home?"

He smiled and said, "Uncle Daryl helped us rent the St. Germaine House in the Quarter so we could work on songs for the next album. Jaylene and I had a day off, so we came on out. We went by the cemetery first."

They all nodded in understanding. Deborah reached out and touched his shoulder and he smiled sadly.

Claudine said, "We haven't seen Daryl much lately, how's he doing?"

Devon told her he was good, that he'd spent some time with the guys recently. They asked about Marcus and Jade, and Devon said they were fine, leaving out the part where Marcus behaved like a jackass.

When Jeanette came back with our drinks, Devon's cell phone rang. "It's Marcus; I need to take this, chère." I waved to him to go ahead. He leaned forward to kiss me on the cheek and then stepped outside, leaving me with his four gaping relatives. I looked up at them, and they must have sensed my growing discomfort.

Claudine sat across from me and smiled. "Darlin', I apologize if we was bein' rude when y'all first came in, but we've just never met any girl-friend of Devon's before. I think we were all a bit shocked."

I laughed and the others relaxed a bit. "I've been getting that a lot."

They all smiled, obviously relieved, and Deborah said, "We were were worried." Ada elbowed her and she said, "What? We were. We hated him bein' all alone. He's never brought any girls around before and you know what it's like out there in Los Angeles. We thought maybe he just hadn't met the right, you know, *guy* yet."

I stifled a laugh. I wonder if he knew what his family thought...

I glanced out the window to see him pacing with his phone to his ear and a cigarette dangling from his lips. That didn't look good.

"So if you don't mind my askin', how did y'all meet?" Claudine seemed very friendly, and I didn't think it would hurt to at least tell them the basics.

"I met him a couple of weeks ago. Daryl brought the band into my shop."

They were staring as if they expected more. Deborah asked, "What kind of shop do you have, chère?"

I smiled and thought to myself that if Devon brought me to meet them, I guess he was prepared for their reaction to me. "I run a tattoo shop in the Quarter called Pins and Needles. My girlfriend Mackenzie does piercing and hair there as well."

They were trying desperately to not be intrusive or discourteous but I could tell this was surprising for them. "Well, that sounds interesting. Where ya from originally?" Claudine was obviously the most diplomatic of the group.

"I'm from the Bay Area, Northern California. I moved here a year and a half ago. We opened the shop almost a year ago. Daryl knew the guy who was selling and helped us get set up. I'd tattooed him and a bunch of his friends already, so I sort of had a built-in clientele."

A few other customers came in, so Deborah and Ada went back to the kitchen and Jeanette went to take care of them. Claudine smiled at me. "And how do you like living in New Orleans?"

"I love it. I've met some great people and my business is doing very well."

She smiled and looked out the window, to where Devon was still pacing. "Well, I'm glad Devon has met someone. That poor man has been through so much heartache."

I nodded. "He has. I'm grateful we met, too."

She winked at me and I took a drink of my Diet Coke as Devon came back in. He sat on the bench, his body turned toward mine, with one leg still behind me. He placed his hand on my lower back and let out a frustrated sigh.

"Everything okay?" I asked.

He took a drink of his sweet tea and nodded. "Yeah, he was just calling from the airport to tell me that Rudy is picking him up because Daryl's not feeling well." He was scowling.

"Shall I assume the call didn't go well?"

He grunted and took another drink of his tea.

"I'll leave you two be now. Do you know what y'all would like to eat?"

I turned to Devon and said, "Order whatever for me."

He perked up a little and ordered the alligator boudin, biscuits, and red beans and rice. Claudine said she'd have it out right quick and we thanked her.

"I'm sorry about that. Marcus just wanted to go over the details of the studio time with Scott. I don't even want to think about that yet."

I placed my hand against his cheek and said, "And you don't have to. Let yourself have the rest of the day to not think about it."

He melted into my hand and then leaned forward and kissed me sweetly.

"Instead, you can think about whatever it is your cousins will be saying to each other in the back about your new tattooed girlfriend."

He laughed. "Funny. I'm sure they're just glad to learn I'm not gay."

I had been taking a drink when he said this and it went down the wrong pipe. I started coughing and sputtering.

He rubbed my back, concerned. "Sorry, chère. You alright?"

I nodded and as soon as I could catch my breath, I said, "They *really* thought that?"

He pulled me into him, resting his chin on my head. "Probably. The last time I was here, they were asking questions about whether I was seeing anyone, trying to find out without asking outright. I was probably not too forthcoming and might have let them think otherwise, just to see them squirm."

I slapped lightly at his thigh. "That wasn't nice, Devon."

He laughed again. "Well, served them right for being nosy. I'm just picky. I hadn't found you yet. And seems I was right to be picky."

I leaned into him and enjoyed the warmth of his embrace. "Can't say I'm sorry you waited." I grinned up at him and he kissed my forehead.

Jeanette came out with our food and asked me, "Is it true you're a tattoo artist?"

I nodded, and Devon said, "Yes she is, and she's amazing."

Jeanette's eyes flared and she looked behind her to make sure none of the ladies were listening. "I have wanted to get a tattoo forever. Can I come see you sometime?"

I told her, "That would be great. I can get you one of my cards. I think I have one in my bag out in the car. I need to use the restroom anyway." She pointed towards the restroom, which was near the front of the restaurant, so I told Devon I'd be right back and he winked at me.

I took a second to look at him before I left. He seemed weary but happy. I figured I should get him back to my place and let him rest after this, although I had no idea what else he had planned for the day.

I walked out to the car and looked through my backpack. I found one of our shop cards at the bottom of the last pocket. I also checked my phone and saw a text from Mackenzie. I quickly answered her that we'd gone out to Houma and that I would check in with her when we got back tonight.

When I went back in the restaurant, I saw that Claudine and Jeanette were back talking to Devon, so I used the restroom to give them some time to grill him about me. I was nervous about what they thought, sure, but I knew I had the blessing of Daryl and Marie. I figured that counted for something.

I washed up and took a minute to collect myself. When I came back to the table, they smiled widely. I sat down next to Devon, who turned again to face me and pull me into him.

"We'll let you two eat in peace. Thanks for coming in, darlin', and tell your mama we miss her."

"I will, Aunt Claudine. And thank you for lunch." They all smiled knowingly at me and walked back to their duties.

I turned to Devon and raised an eyebrow at him. "So?"

He looked back innocently and took a bite of his sausage while I buttered a biscuit. "So? So what?"

I narrowed my eyes. "*So?* Did they lecture you about being involved with a woman of ill repute?"

It was his turn to almost choke. "No, Jaylene, they most certainly did not lecture me about you. There is nothing ill about you; would you quit? Why? Did they say anything to you?"

I shook my head, taking a bite of the sausage and closing my eyes, overcome with the taste of the delicious meal. "Oh, that's divine." I chewed and swallowed. He never took his eyes off of me.

Then he frowned. "Did they say something negative to you, chère?" he asked softly.

I didn't want him to worry, so I said, "No, they didn't say anything to me. They were perfectly nice. But it's obvious they love you and they probably think my line of work is a little scandalous."

He shook his head at me. "Jaylene, there's nothing scandalous about your work, and to be honest, Claudine was telling me how glad she was to see me finally happy. She also said you were beautiful and wondered when the wedding would be."

My eyes flew open wide and I turned to him to find him grinning.

"What? Would that be a bad thing?"

"She did not just ask you that!"

He was laughing soundlessly at my reaction. I could feel my cheeks flushing. "She did too. Chère, we Boudreauxs don't mess around when it comes to love. When we find someone we want, we usually snatch them up quick. My daddy asked Mama to marry him just two weeks after their first date—so you'd better be ready."

He was teasing, but part of me felt like he was testing me as well. "Well, what did you tell her?"

He stopped laughing and he turned serious. "I told her as soon as I could convince you, I would marry you."

He grinned sheepishly and I just sat there in shock. I had no comeback for that.

"Does that scare you?" he asked quietly.

I took a drink and just stared back at him. "Probably not as much as it should. It's crazy though…isn't it crazy?"

He shook his head. "It's not crazy. I'd ask you right now if I didn't think you'd run screaming from me."

I laughed nervously. "I don't know if I'd run screaming but I—"

He kissed me firmly on the lips, taking away what was left of my thoughts, and then shook his head. "Don't answer me now. I'm not asking…yet. But that's where my head's at." He smiled and kissed me again.

We finished our lunch and Devon walked up to the counter to pay. Claudine kissed him on the cheek and tried to wave away his money. I stood next to him and heard her say, "You don't have to do that, Devon."

"I know, but I want to. You ladies take care and thanks for lunch." Jeanette gave him a hug and the others waved.

"Thank you so much, it was nice to meet you."

They all hugged me again. Claudine lingered and whispered to me, "Take care of him, darlin'."

She kissed me on the cheek and I whispered back, "I will."

We waved goodbye and walked out to the Challenger. Devon opened my door for me. As we pulled away, he said, "I'm glad it's still in family hands but I'm more glad Mama's not killing herself there anymore."

"I bet," I said. "I would think running a restaurant is very hard work."

He nodded. "Especially after Daddy passed. And now she can do whatever she likes, she's near Uncle Daryl, and soon I'll be back too." He took my hand and kissed it as we turned onto the highway.

Devon hummed to himself on the way back to New Orleans. I couldn't help but watch him. He had his left arm rested on the window ledge, his long legs taking up so much of the room under the dash. His hair was pushed back and he'd left the beanie at home. I loved his hair however he wore it. His lips were a darker red today than usual, which drew my attention. He held my hand in between shifting and absently stroked my wrist with his thumb.

I must have sighed louder than I thought because he looked over at me. "You still with me, chère?"

I smiled, loving the term of endearment he used with me. For the most part, his accent was very slight, but today it was back, perhaps thanks to the visit home.

"I'm with you. Just admiring the view. If I didn't think I'd get car sick, I'd have my sketchbook out right now."

He smirked. "Thanks for coming with me today. I *wanted* to take you out somewhere to forget about everything, but since I'm probably leaving after next week, I needed to do this today."

"I understand. I'm glad you took me with you. Just being outside for a while made it perfect. Well, that and being with *you*."

He squeezed my hand and brought it up to his lips to press gentle kisses against my knuckles.

"So what's next?" I increasingly believed that getting back to my flat would be the perfect way to end the day, but I didn't want to ruin any plans he had.

He glanced over at me. "Well, I had thought about taking you to a movie or something, but I kind of just want to take you to bed. Is that presumptuous of me?"

I laughed and scooted closer to him so I could whisper in his ear, "I like presumptuous. I was just thinking the same thing." I kissed his ear, tugging lightly on his hoop, and he let go of my hand to steady the wheel.

His voice came out gravelly. He was too damn sexy when his voice got like that. "You're going to have to stop that if you want us to make it back to your place."

I laughed softly and kissed his neck before resting my head on his shoulder. "Sorry, couldn't be helped. And I really like this bench seat up here. Way to go, Dodge."

He laughed and put his hand on my thigh, stroking it gently. "I like it, too, if it means you're sitting close to me."

I smiled. I loved that he had his hands on me as much as possible. I wanted to tell him as much, since I really had no idea what I was doing with this whole boyfriend thing. "Devon, I really love that you're affectionate with me when we're alone and when we're with others. It's new for me, but I like it. It's just one of the many things you do that makes me feel loved."

His hand stopped moving for a moment and I heard him take in a breath. "My daddy and mama were always touching when they were together. It was like their bodies were connected, even if they weren't physically touching. After he died, I think that was one of the hardest things for Mama to get used to. Maggie said to me once that physical expressions of love were often more important than words, because you can't fake a touch. Your intentions are clear. Even if you're having sex with someone, it's clear whether it's fucking or making love. It's the truest way you can express yourself."

I smiled and shook my head. "Man, Maggie was a smart lady. I knew that, but the more you tell me about her, the more I think she was one of those people that you maybe come across once in a lifetime. I'm glad I met her. I really wish she was still here."

He nodded soberly. "I do, too. I feel like she is. I know what you said in the cemetery, about hoping they aren't in pain anymore, but I don't think Maggie would be in pain watching us. She might get pissed if we screw up, but I feel like every action I take, I can still hear her words to me from growing up, guiding me. I don't know how she got so damn smart. She was always wise beyond her years. But I'll take it. If that's all I have left of her, I'm not forgetting her wisdom."

We drove in silence the rest of the way back to my flat. I thought a lot about what he said and it was so right. I was a failure with words in so many ways but my drawings expressed my feelings clearly, and I could never hide how I was feeling about something in a drawing. Words could certainly be false.

What worried me was that when Devon left in a week or so, all we'd have would be each other's words, whether it would be phone calls, texts, etc. That's all we'd have of each other for a while. Maybe that was what I was afraid of. With him here, touching me, smiling at me, I knew where I stood.

When we got back to my flat, we could hear loud music and banging next door. Mackenzie's door was open so I peeked inside. "Hello? Are you decent?"

I shouted a couple of times before opening the door all the way. When I did, I found Mackenzie in a sheer bra and underwear set, her hair piled up high on her head. She was pummeling a piece of meat on the counter. Star was beside her in his boxer briefs, mashing potatoes.

The music was blaring so loud they didn't hear us come in, so we stood there watching them for a moment before Mackenzie looked up and saw me. The mallet she was using flew out of her hand, hit Star in the eye, and caused him to fling potato all over Mackenzie and the cabinets.

"Ow! What the hell is it with you women in the kitchen?" He was holding his eye.

Mackenzie grabbed the steak she was tenderizing and slapped it against his face. "Oh, baby, are you alright?" She kissed the non-steak-covered side of his face. He smiled broadly and cupped her ass with his hands and lifted her onto the counter.

Devon cleared his throat and they only sort of looked over.

"We're back but, ah, we'll just be going. Didn't mean to interrupt," I said.

Mackenzie wrapped her legs around Star's waist. "No problem. You guys want to join us for steak?"

Devon laughed. "Not anymore."

Star whispered something to Mackenzie and she sighed loudly, his mouth moving down her neck.

I called out, "Thanks, but I think we'll just let you guys continue whatever it is you're doing." Star was starting to pull Mackenzie's bra straps down as Devon turned, and I followed him out the door.

"I guess we know what *they* were up to today." He laughed, pulling at his soul patch.

I grinned. "Yes...and I think I like that plan myself."

He closed my door behind us and pulled me in for a kiss that quickly got serious. We moved together to the bedroom, our lips never leaving each other's, and in our wake, a trail of clothes landed on several surfaces.

But just as we fell on the bed together, he stilled. We lay like that for a long time, just looking into each other's eyes. "Today was a great day, Devon. Thank you for taking me to meet your family."

He smiled and kissed my shoulder. "Today was great because you were with me, beautiful girl. I feel like I could spend all day, every day with you and *still* not ever get enough of you."

I giggled. "I wouldn't go that far. You've seen many sides of me, Devon, and not cringed in sheer horror. You've seen me when I wake in the morning, even smelled my morning breath and lived to tell about it. But there are things you still don't know, and you might not be able to handle them, pretty boy."

Devon burst out laughing and pulled me on top of him. "You are too much, chère. What could I possibly not be able to handle about you?"

I thought long and hard. I needed to do my best to gross him out, or at least prepare him. "I don't shave every day."

He raised an eyebrow. "Please, Jaylene—"

I held up a hand. "You have to let me finish. I talk in movies. Well, *at* movies, actually. I yell and scream and laugh embarrassingly loud."

He was trying very hard to listen without commentary.

"I have horrible gas in the mornings after eating green vegetables. I'm prone to adult acne. I've only been so drunk that I threw up one time, but I did it spectacularly."

He let a laugh escape. "Aw, chère you gotta tell me that one at least."

I shook my head. "Will you please let me finish?"

He pulled his face into the most serious expression he could, which was extremely silly.

"I'm afraid of enclosed spaces and zombies, and especially a combination of the two." I figured I'd done a good job of getting the highlights of my neuroses out. "I think that's it. You already know I'm afraid of disappointing people, I have to draw all the time, and that I'm a little afraid of you leaving...not because I don't trust you or trust how you feel about me."

He nodded and his serious look was really serious now. "I know. I'm afraid too. Not of your ridiculous list though. Those things just make me love you more."

I rolled my eyes. "Alright, you've been warned."

He bit me hard on the shoulder and I gasped at the pleasure of it. When his eyes found mine, he said, "You didn't say you were afraid of vampires or werewolves."

I shook my head. "Not afraid of them at all. Actually, I thought you already knew I was a vampire."

He chuckled. "You do have really cold hands sometimes, and you do like to bite me."

At that, I demonstrated how much I liked to bite him...all the way down his torso.

"If you truly are a vampire, I've died and gone to vampire heaven. Fuck, that feels good."

I bit him on the insides of his thighs and he jolted under me. When I grazed his most sensitive flesh with my teeth, his hands flew to my hair and he moaned loudly. I couldn't help but smile wickedly at him when his eyes landed on me. I took him as far in as I could.

His eyes rolled back in his head and he lost himself to the pleasure.

I tried to touch him, kiss him and lick him everywhere, but soon he started to squirm and his legs were shaking. He gently lifted me off him and grabbed frantically for a condom.

Once it was on, he lifted me effortlessly by my hips and brought me down hard on him.

Crying out in a mixture of pleasure and a little bit of pain, I wrapped my arms around his shoulders. We were so close, with me on his lap like this. It quickly became my very favorite way to make love with him. I was just above his eye level and he gazed at me with such emotion in his deep blue eyes.

We moved against each other as his hands gripped my hips. He took one nipple and then the other between his lips. His teeth pulled on my piercings lightly and my head fell back in ecstasy. I didn't think I could take much more—until I felt his touch on my clitoris. I quivered uncontrollably.

I screamed out his name as I came the hardest I have yet.

But he wasn't finished. He gripped me by my shoulders, bringing me down harder and faster onto him. I leaned back and rested my hands on his thighs. He was so deep inside me I was overwhelmed. His gaze was so intense as we clung to each other. We exploded, our bodies singing with passion for each other. Sweating, shaking and still crying softly, we held onto each other like that for what seemed like days. I never wanted his body to *not* be connected to mine like this.

"I keep thinking about what you told me Maggie said, about not trusting words like you can trust touch."

He opened his eyes and looked up at me. "Yeah?" was all he could say.

"Yeah," I answered. "I agree with her. And I wish we could be like this always."

He smiled and kissed me deeply. When we came up for air, he chuckled. "I don't know how to tell you this, but I think being like this forever would definitely interfere with both of our careers. I don't think I could fit a guitar between us, and I *know* you couldn't tattoo anyone naked with my cock inside you."

I burst out laughing and it became evident that I needed to move. He gently lifted me off him and went to clean up. "Although," he said over his shoulder, "it just might fit with the whole rock god persona. If we could be having sex, and I could be hitting an amazing solo at the same time? I might just make the rock 'n' roll hall of fame."

I groaned loudly in response. I loved how his sense of humor came out at the most interesting times.

"I think I need an ice pack," I hollered to him. I heard him laughing and then I heard a knock at the door. "Tell Mackenzie I'm sorry if we disturbed them." Then I started cracking up, because I knew her answer would be that she was happy to be disturbed by those sounds.

Devon came back in a minute later with a towel wrapped around his hips and shut the bedroom door behind him. "Chère, it's not Mackenzie. It's Marcus."

I frowned, standing up quickly to grab a sports bra and a shirt. "What is he doing here?"

He was looking at me. "He wants to talk to you."

I pulled the shirt on and then grabbed for some shorts. "Why?"

He pulled on his boxer briefs and shook his head. "I guess he wants to make amends. Although I wish he would have told me he was coming here."

I looked closely at him and giggled, covering my mouth. "Shit, I wish he would have too. Devon, I left marks on you."

He looked down at his chest—at the faint trail of teeth marks I'd left behind. He laughed a happy and satisfied male laugh and pulled me to him for a kiss. "Chère, don't ever be worried about that. I'll wear your bite marks with pride." He looked at himself in the mirror and ran his fingers over one of the marks. "God, that's just fucking sexy. I told you that you were fucking sexy."

I elbowed him and looked in the mirror. "Yeah, well, I look like a disaster. Can you bring me a brush from the bathroom? No sense in being *completely* obvious about what we were up to. You can tell him I was taking a nap."

He smacked my ass. "Really? A nap? How does that explain the bite marks?"

I looked at him as innocently as possible. "I was dreaming you were chocolate cake?"

He licked his lips at me. "Hmmm, that gives me ideas. You got any frosting?"

"Go get my hairbrush, bad boy."

He winked and then stepped out, closing the door.

I looked again at myself in the mirror. When Marcus made his comments to me the other morning, I hadn't slept with Devon. I was still a virgin. Tonight, he'd shown up just after I'd been thoroughly made love to by his cousin.

In a way, I felt it made what he said to me true. I *did* feel like I had a say over Devon, but not in the way he meant. I'd never try to use that say to control him. To protect him, I'd have my say in a heartbeat. Because he was mine, my love, and I hoped Marcus could see that for what it was. I wasn't some groupie or Yoko Ono-type. I loved Devon, but I also loved the rest of the guys and deeply cared what happened to them.

They'd brought me into this. Marcus couldn't expect me to just sit back and not care.

Devon walked in while I was giving myself this mental pep talk and he must have seen the determination mixed with a little fear on my face, because he turned me to him and held my face in his hands. "You don't have to do this if you don't want to. I know what he said bothered you, and I know why. But he was wrong—*very* wrong. You had every right to stand up for me and I appreciate that you did. I love you, chère."

I smiled and kissed his bottom lip. Oh, how I loved that lip. "I love you, too, baby. And yes, I have to do this. He is a huge part of your life, and he and I need to come to an understanding."

He just held me and looked down at me for a moment before pressing his forehead to mine. "Whatever I did to deserve you, I'll never know. But I'll thank God every day that you're in my life."

"Yeah, well, just remember that when you reach down and discover it's one of those days I didn't shave, or a morning after I've had vegetables."

I turned to walk out the door, and he said, "And when I take you to the movies, I'll love you and be thankful the whole time."

I turned back to give him one more smile before taking a deep breath and stepping out into the living room.

TWENTY-FOUR

Marcus stood from the couch when I walked in. He was smiling but looked haggard, like he hadn't slept all weekend. He also looked admonished, guilty, and terribly sad.

I walked over to him and he stepped forward to take my hand and kiss me on the cheek. "Thanks for seeing me, Jaylene. Sorry if I'm imposing."

I shook my head and motioned for him to sit back down on the couch. I took the other end and sat with my legs up under me. I didn't say anything. I let him work out what *he* needed to say.

"Before I apologize, let me just say that I'm here tonight because I wanted to talk to you before everyone was around, and I wanted you to know that I came on my own, not because of what Daryl or Devon said. Not even because of what Sherry said to me when I got to L.A. She kicked me out, by the way. Wouldn't see me. Said I was a complete jackass."

I figured that might have caused some of his current state of distress. "I'm sorry, Marcus. I know you care about Sherry a lot." He looked up at me, surprised. "I can tell. You might try to act like you and she just have a casual thing, nothing serious, but I know she means more to you than that."

He looked down at his hands and shook his head. He looked like he'd slept in his clothes and his usually perfect hair was a perfect mess. "Yeah, well...it doesn't really matter how I feel, because she's made it clear that we are strictly business from now on." He shrugged and smiled sadly.

"Can I get you some tea or something else to drink?"

He nodded. "That'd be real sweet, Jaylene. Thank you."

I started the kettle and Devon came out of my room, dressed and with his boots on. "I'm going out for a smoke. You need anything just holler, okay?"

I nodded and he kissed me on the cheek. He gave Marcus a hard look before he walked out the door.

In a minute, the kettle whistled and I poured for both of us. "Do you take honey, Marcus?"

"I do, thank you."

I brought the mugs into the living room and handed him one. "It's chamomile, I hope that's okay."

He nodded. "You're too kind." I waved off his compliment and took a sip of the tea along with him.

He set his mug down and leaned forward, clasping his hands between his knees. "What I said to you, back at the St. Germaine that morning, was an awful thing for me to say in so many ways, I don't even know where to begin. I can't say anything in my defense, and I wouldn't disrespect you by trying. It wasn't until I heard a ration from Daryl, and then tried to talk to Devon, that I realized just *how* awful it was."

I didn't know what to say to him. He obviously had more to share, so I let him.

"Devon was right, you know, when he said I only looked out for myself. In this case, he was right. See, Devon has been my best friend since we were kids. I looked up to him and he put up with my shit more than anyone else. He also believed in me, and gave up his own dreams to join me on this roller coaster. I know he wanted to finish college. I know he wants to make more serious music. And I hate it that I'm holding him back. Then Maggie died, and I'm left plugging the whole dam together with my fucking finger. Thing is...I can't do it. I'm not strong enough. Only Devon is strong enough to hold us all together.

"When you came along, and he started speaking up and asserting himself, it was easier to blame you—and his feelings for you—than it was to face the fact that I was losing him. And I am; I'm not stupid. I know that when this album is finished, he's going to quit. And I understand it, I do. He's better than all of this."

I was completely floored. I'd known there was something deeper at play with Marcus and his hurtful words, but I'd had no idea.

He took a shaky breath and glanced up at me. His hazel eyes were wet with unshed tears. "The thing is, Jaylene, I want him to be happy even more than I want it for myself. He deserves a hell of a lot of happy. And I'm so fucking glad he found you. He's been miserable for so long, and the moment he laid eyes on you, he lit up like a damn Christmas tree. He's so in love with you, Jaylene. I envy him tremendously."

I could feel this poor man in front of me crumbling, and that just wouldn't do. "Marcus, whether you believe it or not, *your* strength is what kept you guys together through all this. If you hadn't stepped up, I think things would have been a lot worse. You've been limping along, sure, but everyone was functioning for the most part. Think about how out of control things were before Maggie died. If it weren't for you staying on these guys, do you really think they'd be where they are now? Do you think Star would have gone to rehab? Or would you have had to attend at least one more funeral?"

He stared up at me with dead eyes, and when he spoke again, his voice was trembling. "I was so afraid of that. I thought if I kept pushing them and pushing them, they wouldn't have time to fall apart. So I did. And they hate me for it. But I didn't know what else to do, Jaylene. I couldn't let them fall apart. I love those guys more than life."

He dropped his head in his hands. His level of pain came close to the first time I talked to Devon about Maggie. "Marcus, they don't hate you. I know Devon doesn't hate you. He loves you and he worries about you. But he's angry. I don't need to tell you that."

He laughed. "Oh no, you don't need to tell me that. I really don't know how I made it out of Daryl's place alive. Between the two of them, I thought my ticket had finally been punched. And I've pissed off people bigger and scarier than them before." We both laughed.

"I think you did the best you could with what you had, Marcus. I think they all appreciate you for that, even if they don't show it. But at some point, you need to let go of your need to control everything or it's going to kill you."

He nodded. "I know that. I'm exhausted. I haven't been able to sleep. My blood pressure is ridiculously high right now." He leaned back against the couch.

"You need to take care of yourself. Do you even know how to do that?"

He laughed. "I guess." He looked at me for a long moment. "I can't believe I hurt someone as precious as you. Can you ever forgive me?"

I smiled at him and reached over to take his hand. "I forgave you the minute I walked out of that room. I knew exactly why you said what you did, maybe not just how deep it went. I knew you were just scared of losing him. You won't lose him, you know."

He shook his head. "No, I guess not. He's too good of a friend and cousin." He paused and looked over at me with that devilish grin of his. "Did he tell you I crashed Rose once?"

I blanched. "What?! He let you drive her?"

He shook his head. "Not exactly. I kind of took her without asking. He was pissed enough about *that*. But when he saw the damage a fence post did to the rear quarter panel, I thought I was done for. But you know, he never said anything to me. He banged around outside in the garage, cursing my name in colorful ways, but he never yelled at *me*. He didn't talk to me for a couple of months. Then one day he came over to pick me up, Rose was completely restored, and we went out to hear some music. I think it was a year or so after his daddy died." He shook his head. "He's always been too good for me."

I could feel his sadness, but I had to speak my mind. "I'm not going to lie. I was really hurt by what you said." A pained look crossed his face and he met my gaze, looking like a kid waiting for his punishment after disappointing his parents. "I was mostly hurt because I was afraid you guys would actually think that little of me."

He looked horrified and sat up. "No. No, Jaylene, I never thought badly of you. It had nothing to do with you. I'm so sorry. Jade told me what you shared with them after I'd left, and I swear, if I could have kicked myself any harder..."

I laughed. "Yeah, they were all pretty surprised. But you didn't know."

"It doesn't matter if I knew or not, I was way out of line. I'm sorry, Jaylene, and I swear, I will never, ever disrespect you ever again. I am so fucking grateful for all you have done for us, especially for Devon. I know I'll have to earn back your trust. I just hope you'll let me."

"It's okay, Marcus. We're good."

Marcus rested his hand over his heart and closed his eyes, taking a deep breath before he grabbed me into a hug and squeezed. He was shaking and I just held on to him for a moment.

I heard the door open then Devon's boots as he came in. He walked into the room and Marcus quickly let go. Devon crossed his arms and said in a stern voice, "She must have gone a helluva lot easier on you than she should have, by the looks of it."

I rolled my eyes and motioned him over to join us on the couch. He sat behind me, putting me between them.

"I know. I'm feeling even shittier now."

I pushed at his shoulder. "Oh, quit. Both of you. Marcus, where are you staying tonight?"

He shrugged. "Thought I'd go back over to the St. Germaine."

I looked at Devon with an eyebrow raised, warning him not to argue with me. "No, that's not acceptable. This pullout couch isn't the most comfortable thing in the world, but I'd feel better if you stayed here tonight."

He looked up at me and one tear escaped his eye. Then he looked over at Devon, who shrugged and said, "She's the boss. If she wants your sorry ass on her couch, I'm not telling her no."

I smacked Devon's thigh and he jumped. "You be nice. Grab him an extra pillow and blanket from the closet, would you please?"

He rolled his eyes and went into my room. I motioned for Marcus to stand so I could pull out the couch.

"Jaylene, I appreciate this. Everything."

I hugged him and kissed him on the cheek. "I know. Now get some rest, okay?"

He nodded. He helped me move the table and pull out the couch.

Devon threw the pillow and blanket on the bed and said, "Good night, asshole."

Marcus laughed. "Love you too, cousin." He winked at me and I just rolled my eyes at the two of them.

I went in to use the bathroom and when I came back to bed, Devon was under the covers with his bare chest visible. He watched me as I took my clothes off and I crawled over him to get into the bed. He groaned, and as soon as I got under the covers, he pulled me into him and kissed me thoroughly.

"You are so fucking beautiful, Jaylene. You're a beautiful person. Thank you. He doesn't deserve it, but thank you."

I smiled up at him and ran my tongue over his lip, producing another groan. "He does too deserve it. He loves you, Devon. And you love him. Once you're done being mad at him, you'll be glad I let him stay. He's a mess, baby."

He nodded soberly. "I know he is. He's just been too busy being a jackass to take care of himself." He ran his hands over my ass and cupped me there, letting his fingers wander.

I gave him a wicked grin and purred, "Hmmmm, at least he didn't wipe out *my* rear quarter panel."

He chuckled and took extra care caressing said rear. "I'll break him in half if he so much as looks at your rear quarter panel."

I sighed dramatically. "How romantic."

He did something with his tongue then that had me breathless. I at least had the presence of mind to stop him before I got loud again.

"Devon, he's right on the other side of the wall! I know you guys have been witness to each other's exploits before, but I'd rather he not be witness tonight."

He looked up from what he was doing and said, "The guys tell you?"

I nodded. "Well, they said you were his wingman. I just put two and two together."

He sighed and rolled me over on top of his chest again. "I knew it was a bad idea to leave you with them." He tried to sound mad but he was smirking.

"They made sure not to ruin your upstanding reputation." I giggled and he tickled me a little, making me squirm in all the right places.

"I think I'm doing pretty good with my upstanding, thank you very much."

I reached down and grabbed his upstanding reputation and wished I wasn't so determined to do the right thing. "I really wish I could explore that reputation right about now."

He laughed again and his chest rumbled. I loved that sound. "We'll have plenty of time for exploration, beautiful. Let's get some rest."

We kissed for a long time before falling asleep in each other's arms.

TWENTY-FIVE

My phone buzzed at five a.m.

"Hello?" I mumbled.

I heard sobbing on the other end. I checked the number and saw it was Daryl's wife, Katie. I was immediately sick to my stomach.

"Jaylene, god...I need you guys right now!" I got the information from her and then hung up.

I dropped the phone on the bed, ran for the bathroom—and heaved up what little was left in my stomach.

Marcus and Devon called after me, and Devon burst into the bathroom to find me in the corner next to the toilet, my arms wrapped around my knees. He sank down beside me.

"Chère, what is it? What happened?"

I looked up into his blue eyes and I had to be sick again. He held my hair back and yelled for Marcus. "Grab her phone and see who just called."

I held up my hand and, once I was finished, I caught my breath and told them. "It was Katie. We need to meet her at the hospital. Daryl had a heart attack."

Devon fell back on his heels, looking at me in shock. I stood shakily and brushed my teeth and then moved past him to the bedroom to put on my clothes, too out of it to care that Marcus had just seen me naked.

The two of them dressed hurriedly and Marcus went next door to tell Star. I heard Star tell him that he and Mackenzie would meet us at the hospital.

Devon kept trying to talk to me, but it was all I could do to put one foot in front of the other. We went out to his car, Marcus crawled into the backseat, and Devon drove fast but safely to Tulane Medical Center. When we parked, he turned towards me, reaching for me, but I was already out of the car.

The three of us burst into the waiting room and found Katie there with the girls curled up next to her.

She looked worried but was holding it together. "Thank you guys for coming. Jaylene? Do you think you could take the girls to get something to eat?"

I stared at her, frozen. I couldn't make my mouth form any words. My feet were cemented to the ground.

Marcus finally saved me by saying, "I've got it, Katie. C'mon, girls. Let's go raid the vending machines and see if they've got any of those yummy donuts." The two little angels were still in their pajamas, and bounced up and into Marcus's waiting arms. He nodded to Devon and stepped out towards the cafeteria.

Katie filled us in. Daryl had woken her up and said he didn't feel good. When she turned on the light and saw him rubbing his left arm, she immediately called 9-1-1. He hadn't lost consciousness at the house, which was good, and once he was loaded into the ambulance, she'd followed behind with the girls.

The paramedics told her that luckily they'd caught it early and he'd probably be fine. She was just waiting for the doctor to come out.

"I'm so sorry, Katie. But he'll be okay. This is Uncle Daryl we're talking about. I doubt even a heart attack could slow him down for long." They both laughed and she hugged Devon. Then they looked over at me.

"I'm sorry, Katie. I... I'll be right back."

I turned and practically ran for the nearest bathroom, and continued to dry heave until I heard Devon calling from the door. "I'm fine, Devon," I yelled to him. "I'll be out in a minute." I flushed the toilet and splashed cold water on my face. My heart pounded out of control and when I looked in the mirror, I saw that my face was completely pale. My hands shook and my breathing was shallow. I couldn't seem to focus on anything...

"Baby! Oh my god. *Someone help me!*"

I could hear Devon screaming but I couldn't see him. My head hurt and I was cold all of a sudden. I felt myself being lifted. I tried to speak but nothing would come out...and then everything was black.

When I woke up, I was in a bed under fluorescent lights. My head felt smashed and my mouth was dry. It took me a minute to get my senses online.

"Jaylene? Chère? Can you hear me?"

Devon's face came into view and I blinked in confusion. "Of course I can hear you. What happened?" He looked so worried—and there was blood on his shirt. "Oh my god, Devon, what happened? Who hurt you? What..."

He squeezed my hand and kissed it. He looked so concerned. I tried to sit up to touch him and pain hit me so hard, the lights dimmed again.

"Chère, you're in the emergency room. We came for Daryl and we were talking to Katie. Then you ran to the bathroom and said you'd be right out. When you didn't come out, I opened the door in time to see you faint on your feet and fall over, bashing your head on the sink before hitting the floor."

I reached up and found a bandage wrapped around my head and blood caked in my hair. "I'm so sorry. Is Katie okay? Is *Daryl* okay? Gods, what a mess I've made. I'm so sorry, Devon."

He shook his head and moved to sit on the bed next to me. "Stop it, chère! Don't apologize. I don't know what happened to you. I was so worried."

"Don't worry about *me*, I'm fine. I'm just sorry I'm keeping you from your family. How is Daryl? Where is he?"

Now he looked downright pissed. "What the fuck, Jaylene? You almost killed yourself hitting your head! You are not *fine*. The doctor said you have a serious concussion and they fucking had to stitch your head up, so don't tell me you are *fine*!"

I shrank back from him and he looked horrified.

"Jaylene, I'm sorry. But you're scaring me, chère. What happened to you?" His voice cracked and his hands were shaking. He was having a hard time getting close to me and not hurting me.

I reached my hand up to touch his face and he held onto my arm like a drowning man. I tried to calm down, as crying was really not a good idea with a concussion. When I spoke, my voice was a whisper. "I'm sorry, baby. I'm sorry I scared you."

He wiped angrily at the tears on his face with one hand and took a deep breath. He looked away for a minute and I could see the strain on his face, in his shoulders. When he looked back at me, he tried his best to control his tone of voice. "Uncle Daryl is going to be fine. They had to do surgery to put stents in. The doctor said it was a mild heart attack and he believes Uncle Daryl will make a full recovery. Katie has been in to see him, and she said he's already hitting on the nurses. Star and Mackenzie took the girls back to her place. Marcus is with Uncle Daryl now."

I frowned, but even that hurt. "What time is it?"

The thin layer of control he had on his emotions was being pulled dangerously thin. "For fuck's sake, Jaylene, it's noon! You've been out for six fucking hours. Now will you talk to me please? I'm freaking out over here."

I pulled back from him. His anger and frustration scared me. I felt so guilty for causing a scene when he needed to be there for his family. "I'm awake now. Why don't you see if you can go visit Daryl?"

He jolted up and paced away from the bed. I saw him take in a deep breath, his hands on his hips. The curtain pulled aside and a nurse came in.

"There you are, Miss Charles. Glad to see you're awake. How's the pain?"

"About as to be expected, I guess. May I have some water, please?"

She nodded. "Of course, darlin', and I'll send the doctor in to see you."

I thanked her, and she gave Devon a stern look as she passed him.

"I'm keeping you from your family, Devon. I'm sorry. I'm okay now. Why don't you go and I'll wait for the doctor."

He turned back around and shook his head. His voice was low when he spoke. "What the hell part of 'I love you' and 'you're home for me' did you not understand? What part of 'I'd ask you to marry me right now' did you not get? Or did you hit your head so hard that you forgot all that? They've assured me that the only thing I need to worry about with Uncle Daryl is the sexual harassment suit we'll have to settle when he gets out of here. Now will you *please* talk to me, chère? You're not getting rid of me, okay?"

I covered my face with my hands and tried to turn onto my side.

He walked back over to the bed and said, "Move over." He scooted me over and spooned up against me. I cried softly and he held me as patiently as he could. I knew he was scared, but my head hurt so bad, I couldn't get the words out.

After a while, I turned over and curled into his side. He kissed my forehead. "Whatever it is, chère, I'm here, okay?" I nodded and closed my eyes.

Just then the doctor came in and frowned when he saw Devon on the bed with me. "Miss Charles, I'm Dr. Franklin. Do you know where you are?"

I nodded. "The Tulane Medical Center."

He smiled. "Good. Now do you remember what happened?"

My stomach lurched and I covered my mouth with my hand. Dr. Franklin hurried to my side, grabbing a pan on the way, and handed it to me while my stomach decided that for the second act it would try to purge my soul.

Devon got up off of the bed and said, "She keeps throwing up, Doctor. Is that normal?"

Dr. Franklin nodded. "Nausea often accompanies a concussion. But you said she'd vomited before she hit her head. Can you tell me what happened?"

Devon started pacing and said, "We got a call early this morning from my uncle's wife, saying he'd been admitted here. He had a heart attack. As soon as Jaylene hung up the phone, she ran to the bathroom and started throwing up. Then when we got here, we saw Katie, and she ran for the bathroom again. When she didn't come out right away, I opened the door and saw her fall."

Dr. Franklin nodded and took the pan away from me. The nurse was back and she offered me a cup of ice chips that I was so very grateful for.

"Thank you," I whispered to her, and she smiled, patting me on the arm.

"Miss Charles, do you remember any of what Mr. Boudreaux has said?"

I nodded, which was a tremendously bad idea. "Yes. I remember."

He stepped over to the bed and had his penlight out. "May I check your eyes?" I nodded again and winced. "Hurts, doesn't it? Don't nod."

I smirked. At least he had a sense of humor. His penlight exam was no picnic either.

He said, "Well, you've given yourself a helluva concussion, young lady. I want to keep you overnight for observation and if all goes okay, you can go home tomorrow."

My eyes flew open wide at that. "No, please. Can't I just go home?"

He raised an eyebrow at me. "I would strongly discourage that. I'm not happy about how long you were out, and I want to keep you here. We need to make sure there's no swelling."

Devon spoke up. "Then she'll stay."

Dr. Franklin smiled at him. "Smart man. Okay. The nurses will have to wake you up every hour. I suggest you try to get some rest. They'll be moving you to a room in a little while."

I was stunned, and so not happy with this plan. Devon thanked the doctor, who assured us he'd be back in to check on me.

Stuck here with no way out, I sank back into the pillow and closed my eyes. I felt Devon lie down and wrap his arms around me. I inhaled his scent deeply.

"Rest, chère. I'm not going anywhere, and when you feel up to it, I hope you'll tell me what's really going on."

"I'm sorry," I said, and I heard him curse before I slipped back into sleep.

The next time I woke up, I heard whispered arguing and Devon's body wasn't next to me. I opened one eye to see Devon and Marcus in a heated conversation.

"Can't you guys quit arguing even in a hospital? Good grief."

My voice sounded raspy and Devon swung around to the bed just as a nurse came in to check my vitals.

"Mr. Boudreaux, can you please wait outside while I examine Miss Charles?"

He practically growled at her.

Marcus grabbed him and physically showed him the door. "Yes, ma'am. Jaylene, we'll be right back, okay?"

I nodded and my head felt a little less heavy this time.

"Sweetheart, is that man bothering you?"

I shook my head vigorously, another really bad idea. "Ow, why does that hurt so bad?"

She laughed. "Honey, you got a bad knock on the head. It ain't gonna feel good for a day or two." She motioned with her head. "Is he a problem, dear?"

"No. Absolutely not. I'm the only problem here."

She quirked her eyebrow at me. "You're hurt, honey, how is that a problem? Did you fall down on purpose?"

I laughed. "No, although I am quite a klutz. No, I think I was just having a good old fashioned panic attack."

I smiled weakly at her and she nodded. "I thought that might be the case. We get folks in here a lot passing out because of stress, although it's usually new fathers." She laughed and I felt some of the weight lifting off my chest.

"Do you think you could do me a favor?"

"Sure, honey. What do you need?" She was a beautiful woman, probably in her forties, and her name badge said Sylvia.

"Sylvia, do you know if my boyfriend has been to see his uncle?"

She shook her head. "No, I don't think he's left your side since you were brought in."

"I was afraid of that. Listen, is there any way I could be allowed to go and see his uncle with him? I think I would feel a lot better if I could see with my own eyes that Mr. Doucette is okay."

She smiled knowingly. "I'm sure you would. Let me check with Dr. Franklin." I thanked her and she finished taking my vitals.

"Oh and Miss Charles?" I looked up at her as she was leaving the room. "Give the poor guy a break. He's been a wreck, worried about you all day."

That made me wince, and she walked back towards the bed. "What's the matter?"

I took a deep breath for courage. "I just feel horrible. He should have been with his family today, and instead I go and make a scene. I'm just not great at hospitals. This was a little too close to home, you know?"

She nodded gravely and patted my hand. "I understand, but it's obvious that he wanted to be here. I'll be right back."

I smiled and thanked her again.

After she left, I rested my head back against the pillow. Apparently they'd moved me while I was asleep because now that I looked around, I realized I wasn't in the ER anymore. And by looking out the window, I could see it was late afternoon.

I heard a knock at the door and I opened my eyes to see Marcus. "Is it alright if I come in?"

I nodded. He smiled warmly at me, and I noticed that he looked much better than he did last night. It even looked like he'd showered and put on clean clothes.

"I sent him to get some coffee and something to eat. I promised him I'd stay with you until he got back." He pulled up a chair and sat down next to the bed, his hand reaching out to grasp mine.

"Is he okay, Marcus?"

He shrugged. "Not really. He will be as soon as you tell him what's wrong."

He had a bemused expression on his face and I rolled my eyes at him. "Jeez, that hurts too." My hand came up to my head and he looked alarmed.

"Do you need me to call the nurse?"

I shook my head and winced again. "Do you have any idea how many forms of basic communication require moving parts of your head?"

He burst out laughing. "I do, chère, but I think other forms of communication would hurt just as much right now."

He was still laughing, and I was trapped. "Gods, I can't even roll my eyes at you or anything. How else am I supposed to express my disgust with this whole situation?"

His laughter stopped and he said, "How about just saying a few words? Starting with, 'I am here because...'"

"That easy, huh?"

He grinned. "Yeah, it's that easy. Start with 'When the phone rang, it was like—'"

The door opened then and Devon came in, his face gaunt and his hair hanging down on the sides. His blue eyes were so haunted, I thought to myself that here we were, back at square one. *Way to go, Jaylene.*

He walked over to the other side of the bed and took my other hand. I looked up at him but it was too painful, both because of my head and because of the knowledge that once again, I'd put the pain back in his gaze.

I took a deep breath and closed my eyes, gathering the strength I would need to tell them where I'd gone that morning.

"January fifth last year, at five a.m., I got the call from my grandmother that my father had had a massive heart attack. I drove frantically to the San Ramon Regional Medical Center from my apartment in Hayward, and went into the ICU. My stepmother greeted me, and told me she'd woken up because my father was snoring really loudly, and then she heard him gasp for air and stop...just stop breathing. She called nine-one-one and started CPR immediately. When the paramedics arrived, they were able to get his heart going again, but they had no idea how long he'd been without oxygen."

Devon sank to his knees on the floor next to the bed and both men leaned in, holding tightly to my hands.

"They put him on ice for thirty-six hours to try to keep the swelling down and he was placed in a medically induced coma. The doctors had no idea if he would come out of it, but said that was his best chance of survival."

A tear slipped down and Devon wiped it away with a tissue. I opened my eyes and smiled at him. I could see the gratitude in his gaze that I was finally talking to him. I closed my eyes again so I could get the rest out.

"Shannon and I took turns sitting next to his bed for the next seven days. He'd have moments of progress, moving his legs, opening his eyes when his name was spoken, but then his lungs filled with fluid and he had to be suctioned frequently. When the nurses would suction him, his eyes would open and his face would scrunch up like he was crying. But that was it. That was all we got.

"Brain scans finally showed extensive damage, and the pneumonia in his lungs was getting worse. The doctors suggested that we provide him with comfort care, and said taking him off life support was our best option. It was the eighth day when we did that.

"My grandmother and stepmother and I held hands and sat with him for seven hours while he drowned in his own lungs and died."

I had to stop for a few moments and catch my breath. Just that little bit had made me tired. Devon rested his forehead against my hand and I touched his hair.

"When the phone rang this morning...I guess my body just reacted. I'm assuming I had a panic attack in the bathroom. I haven't been in a hospital since that day, a year ago last January. After the nurses came in to tell us he was dead, we hugged, and then the two of them got in their car and drove home. I went back to my apartment alone.

"The next day I called the therapist I was doing my internship with and told him I was quitting, that I needed to leave. He was furious, told me I'd never get my license in California, that he'd personally see to it. I packed up my shit, put it in storage and made arrangements to come here. I stayed in a boarding house, doing some guest tattooing at local shops. I met Daryl and Mackenzie, and then I moved to the building six months later with her.

"I haven't been back to California since. And I obviously still have some lingering issues around death and dying." I chuckled at that and felt Devon rise up next to the bed and place a kiss on my forehead.

I opened my eyes and his beautiful blues were looking down on me with so much compassion. And love.

He brushed my cheek with his knuckles and smiled sadly. "I'm so sorry, chère. I knew it was bad, but..."

Marcus cleared his throat. "Jaylene, I'm sorry you had to go through that alone."

I couldn't look at them. My heart hurt in my chest, along with my head killing me. I was so tired. I needed to finish so I could rest. I closed my eyes again.

"Daryl's been so good to me, almost like the dad my father could never be. When I heard Katie this morning, it was…"

I couldn't hold back the sobs then. Devon pulled me into an embrace and held me.

I don't know how long I cried, but when he moved to lay me back against the pillow, I must have gone back to sleep.

The next time I woke up, I was curled next to Devon again and Marcus was gone. I rolled over and found Devon sleeping. I tried to sit up but he was gripping me so tightly, I had to wake him.

"Baby? I'm sorry to wake you but I really need to pee."

His eyes opened and he sat up, dazed. He stood and put the side rail down on the bed. He gently grasped my ankles and pulled them off the edge of the bed, then bent down and, before I could protest, lifted me from the bed and carried me effortlessly to the bathroom.

Once inside he stood me carefully in front of the toilet. I looked up at him and his eyes were bleeding concern and fatigue.

"I'll wait right outside the door. Hold on to the rails."

I nodded and he turned from me. Boy, I'd really fucked things up. I sat down and did my business. When I was finished, I stood slowly, feeling a little dizzy. I turned to wash my hands and caught sight of my multi-hued face.

I gasped and Devon was immediately at my side.

"Oh, shit. How horrifically colorful is my face right now?" Both of my eyes had deep purple around them and my jaw had an equally purple bruise forming on it. My hair looked completely disgusting. Blood was still caked in it on one side. From the looks of the bandage, I hit the left side of my forehead and must have bounced off and to the side, because the bruise was along the right jawline.

I suddenly became aware of an ache on my right shoulder, and pulled the hospital gown aside to see a lovely purple bruise there as well.

When I looked up again, I caught Devon's eye in the mirror. I looked down and made quick work of washing my hands.

"Miss Charles?" Sylvia, the nurse, had entered the room, and I saw her step behind Devon. "Are you feeling okay?"

I smiled. "Nature called. Devon helped me."

She laughed. "Well, that's a good sign. I talked to Dr. Franklin and he said if you were able to get up out of bed, you could go and see Mr. Doucette. Are you still up for it?"

I looked up at Devon and he just looked exhausted.

"I brought a wheelchair. Mr. Boudreaux, would you like to take her over?"

He nodded and put his arm around me to lead me out of the bathroom. He sat me down in the wheelchair and looked to the nurse.

"He's just down the hall. Follow me?" She walked out ahead of us and Devon pushed the wheelchair. As soon as we left the room, I saw Mage and Jade and Marcus sitting together on a bench in the hall.

"Jaylene!" They rushed over and fussed about me and my bruises and bandage. They'd already heard what happened and Marcus must have told them what I'd said, because they didn't ask questions. They each kissed me on the cheek and then Devon wordlessly led me down the hall to Daryl's room.

I could hear laughing all the way outside the door. It stopped immediately when we entered the room. They both gasped and Katie sputtered, "Holy God in heaven, look at you!"

Devon wheeled me over to the side of Daryl's bed and Katie jumped up to come around to hug me.

"How are you feeling?" I asked Daryl in a small voice.

He frowned. "Sure as shit better'n you. Are you alright?"

I shrugged. "I guess. I'm sorry I wasn't here earlier. And Katie, I'm sorry I took Devon away from you when you needed him."

They all just looked at me like I'd told them I was really Liberace. Devon cursed behind me and walked over to the door, his hands shoved in his pockets. I watched him take a few deep breaths and then I slowly turned back around, trying to disappear into my seat.

Katie kissed Daryl on the cheek. "I'll be right back, sweetie. Devon, will you walk me out to my car? I want to call and check on the girls." She gave me an understanding smile and walked out with Devon.

I couldn't look up at Daryl, so I just stared down at my hands. "I can sure clear a room, can't I?"

Daryl blew out a breath and leaned back against his pillow. Alarmed, I looked up to make sure he was okay—and I was met with Daryl's most stern "you are gonna get it" look. *Oh shit.*

"Jaylene Renee, if I hear the words 'I'm sorry' out of your mouth one more time, I will make good on my threat to put you over my knee. Now you better talk, and talk right now. Something is wrong with you, and neither of us can fucking go anywhere, so you got no choice but to spill."

I laughed and winced from the pain. Even in a hospital gown, Daryl was intimidating.

Daryl's look got downright dangerous at that point.

"I'm so—" I started, and then thought better of it. "It's just, Daryl, you're a very important person in my life, and when Katie called this morning so upset, I thought..." Tears pooled in my eyes and I grabbed my aching head. "Grrrr. This fucking hurts and I can't stop crying."

Daryl held out his hand and I took it in mine. When I looked up again, his eyes were watery too.

I took a deep breath and said, "I thought I'd lost you, and it hurt even more than when I lost my own father. You've been there for me more than he ever was, and I've only known you for a year and half. And how do I show my thanks? I keel over in the damn bathroom, get this amazing makeover, and piss off your too-good-for-me nephew."

I let go of his hand and my head fell forward. I tried to just breathe and will the pain to go away. I didn't look up until I heard Daryl's voice, softer than I'd ever heard it.

"Dollface, you need to stop feeling guilty and blaming yourself right now. If anyone is to blame for this clusterfuck, it's me for not taking care of myself like you and Katie have been after me to do. Dat's all. It's not your fault you had an asshole family dat don't appreciate you, and made you feel like shit for needin' anyone. Dat's not us, chère. We all need each other. And you been there for my family and friends more times than I can count. You're one of us! Dat means you don't ever feel sorry when you knock da shit outta yourself in a hospital bathroom, for fuck's sake."

He started getting loud and I looked up, worried. "Daryl, you better stop or you'll get us both in trouble."

He cursed again and I couldn't help the giggle that slipped out. "Now dat's better," he said haughtily. "And as for my nephew, you better get it through dat thick skull a yours dat he loves you, and he ain't goin' nowhere. If I'd a found out dat he left your side to come check on my sorry ass, I woulda kicked him in *his* when I got outta dis place. He don't leave your side, dat's how we do. Tell me you would'na done the same thing in reverse."

"Of course, but Daryl—"

He shook his head. "No 'but Daryl,' Jaylene. Dammit, girl! You deserve his love, and you deserve it from all of us. So take it, and quit trying to do everything by your damn self."

He started coughing and the nurse came in. "Mr. Doucette, you need to take it easy."

He waved her away. "Now, now, you'll have to come back and do my sponge bath later, honey. I need to talk to my girl here."

She rolled her eyes and said, "You ain't gettin' no damn sponge bath, you dirty old man."

I couldn't help but laugh. "Didn't take them long to get *you* pegged." He smirked at me and gave me a wink.

I took a deep breath. "I love Devon so much, Daryl. I love him and I keep screwing up. I promised him I would never cause him to have that heartbreaking sadness in his eyes again, and I did it today. I don't want him to hurt anymore, and I'm afraid I'm going to keep screwing up because I don't know what I'm doing. I've been alone for so long. You and Mackenzie are the best friends I've ever had, and now Devon comes into my life and all I do is disappoint him."

A mixture of anger and sadness flittered across his face and I flinched when he ground his teeth together before speaking. "Jaylene, girl, you need to learn the difference between disappointment and concern. Sure, he's goin' ta get frustrated with you. What man in this world ain't been frustrated by the woman he loves? I can tell you, women are a frustrating lot by nature. But *disappointed* he's not.

"Hurt? Now dat may be. He ain't used to being around someone who is so damn closed off. And you do a helluva job of dat sometimes. I know you ain't used to letting people in, but you betta learn and you betta learn quick. Don't you push him away for any of your bullshit reasoning. He's a big boy now, a grown-ass man, so let him fucking take care of you." He coughed once again and then settled back down in his bed, glaring at me.

"Daryl! Your face is all red. I told you to take it easy," said Katie as she hurried back over to his side. He smiled when he saw her and his whole face relaxed.

I used to watch the two of them together and wonder what it would be like to be loved like that.

Devon loved me like that. I was grateful for his love, and I needed to figure out how to quit frustrating him.

"You both look like shit, so I'm taking you back to your room, Jaylene. I'll be right back, honey."

Daryl made a lewd comment that got a blush from Katie. She sashayed back over to him and whispered something in his ear that made him groan. She laughed and started to turn my chair around to push me out.

"Hey, Jaylene, you think about what I said. Now I love you, girl, and I ain't goin' anywhere either, so go rest your pretty little head."

I smiled back at him and said, "You better not go anywhere. I love you, too."

He smiled approvingly at me and then closed his eyes to rest. He didn't look like my father had, yellow and gray and old. Daryl was still full of life, and I felt that he probably *would* be around for a lot longer. Especially if he started taking better care of himself.

Katie wheeled me down the hall and back to my room. She helped me into bed and said, "Honey, would you like me to try to wash that out of your hair?"

"I'll do it," said Mackenzie as she stomped into the room.

Oh boy. Another pissed-off person. "Maybe I should just go to sleep," I whispered.

Mackenzie just plopped on the bed next to me. "Uh-uh. No fucking way. You're going to talk to me, dammit." In the dim light, I could see that Mackenzie wasn't wearing makeup and looked like she'd been crying.

"Katie? Where's Devon?"

She smiled at me. "I sent him back to your place to take a shower and get you some clean clothes. I think he needed a break, even though he argued with me the whole way out to the car. I'm going to go check on Daryl. Thanks again, Mackenzie, for watching the girls."

"No problem at all," she said. "We played makeup studio and they got to practice on Star. Don't worry, I got pictures."

I laughed, but it hurt so I had to try to stop. Katie kissed me on the cheek and said, "You stop trying to take care of everyone else, okay? Take care of you."

I smiled weakly at her and said, "Thanks for everything, Katie." She nodded and left the room.

"I'm not going to yell at you because I'm sure Daryl just did. I'm going to wash this gunk out of your hair and then you're going to sleep until Devon gets back."

I nodded, "Yes, Mom."

She harrumphed at me like a satisfied mama bear and went to the bathroom to get a wet washcloth and a bowl of warm water. I closed my eyes and tried to relax while she gently washed the dried blood from my hair. She was very quiet for Mackenzie, and I opened one eye to peek up at her. She had a very serene smile on her face and her touch was so tender.

"Thank you for coming, Mackenzie. I'm happy you're here."

She smiled. "Anything for you, dollface. Now just close your eyes and rest. You're going to need it, because I'm kicking your ass tomorrow."

I chuckled, winced, and promptly fell asleep.

I heard Devon's guitar and thought I was dreaming, but I was being poked and prodded, so I figured if I *was* dreaming, it was a horrific nightmare full of pain and suffering. I felt like my skin was being ripped off and I cried out.

"Sorry, Miss Charles. I needed to change your bandage and check your sutures." It was a different nurse. The guitar strumming stopped so I thought maybe I *was* imagining it, until I felt a familiar weight settle onto the bed next to me. I smiled and turned in his direction.

"I thought I was dreaming. You really are here."

He laughed softly and kissed the unbandaged side of my forehead. "I'm here. Do you need anything?"

I grinned and said, "I probably need to add a few things to my list of gross-outs. Top of the list has to be that I'm a terrible patient and have the worst after-puking breath in history."

He laughed again and rubbed his hand across my stomach. It was a little tender but the warmth from his hand felt great. I held it there against me and he stilled. "Does that hurt?"

I shook my head. "No, your hand feels nice. Stomach's a little tender. But I think I'm making progress because my head only feels like it weighs fifty pounds, not a hundred."

He kissed my cheek. "Okay, beautiful girl, why don't you try to rest some more. If you're feeling better in the morning, the doctor said I can take you home."

I snuggled up to him. But then I jumped and my eyes flew open. "Oh my gods, Devon! It's Monday. We're supposed to be back at the St. Germaine. You guys should be practicing."

He pulled me back down and shushed me. "Actually, it's Tuesday and it's about three a.m., so we wouldn't be practicing. You don't need to worry about anything."

But they had so much work to do. How could he be so calm about it? "But Devon, you guys lost a whole day and—"

He shook his head on the pillow next to mine and closed his eyes. "No more worrying. It's all taken care of. Now go back to sleep." He must *really* have been tired if he wasn't worrying.

I turned over and pulled his arm close around me.

Nurses came back twice more after that and woke me to ask my name and birthday. Devon stirred when they came in, but he'd made it very clear that he wasn't leaving, so they didn't even bother to ask.

The sun woke me the next time. That, and the pitiful sounds coming from my stomach. My mouth felt like the Sahara and ice chips weren't going to cut it anymore. A new nurse came in and laughed a little at poor Devon's huge body hanging off the side of the bed. I motioned her over to my side, and with her help, I was able to get up without disturbing him.

The dizziness had lessened and I felt more human. She led me to the bathroom, where I found the most amazing prize. Someone had brought me my toothbrush and paste and even my hairbrush.

I sighed and the nurse said she'd stand guard while I took care of personal needs. It was the greatest teeth brushing ever experienced by womankind.

When I stepped out of the bathroom, I smiled at the sight of my beautiful man, sleeping ridiculously sound for being in what must be a totally uncomfortable position.

The nurse giggled and said, "I wanted to ask for his autograph but I didn't want to disturb y'all. Watching him sleep is just as amazing."

I took a closer look at the nurse. She was probably a couple of years younger than me and she obviously recognized Devon. I smiled at her. "He is pretty amazing when he sleeps."

She put her hand over her mouth. "I'm sorry, I shouldn't have said that. But you are *so* lucky."

I laughed and that caused him to stir. "I am unbelievably lucky," I said to her, and I gave her a wink.

"Are you ready for some breakfast?" she asked me from the doorway.

"I would kill for something to eat right now. I'd literally kill something to eat, if it would make my stomach stop growling."

She laughed and left the room as Devon opened an eye.

"Wow, chère. The colors on your face are even more fascinating today."

I rolled my eyes at him, which hurt considerably less than yesterday, and crawled back into bed next to him. I looked into his eyes, trying to determine where things stood. "I'd really like to be doing this in my own bed with you. And with fewer clothes."

He smiled and tried to stretch a little. "The sooner the better. My back is killing me right now."

I felt so bad. "Oh, baby. You didn't need to—"

His eyes flew open, daring me to finish that sentence.

"I only meant I hate it that you didn't sleep well. Am I allowed to say that?"

He frowned. "At least you didn't say sorry again."

We looked at each other for a really long time without speaking, until throat clearing at the door broke apart our gaze.

"I brought your breakfast, Miss Charles. Doctor said only toast and juice first. Your stomach needs to rest a bit more."

I nodded. "This is great, thank you."

The nurse nodded, her eyes bugged out at Devon, and then she hurried out of the room.

"You're going to need to leave an autograph for her. The poor girl has been beside herself all morning."

He shook his head and sat up. He ran his hands through his hair and I envied how easily he achieved his look in the morning.

"I also really, *really* want to take a shower and wash my hair. Think maybe you might want to help with that?" I was only sort of teasing. I knew I needed help but I didn't know what he was feeling right now. "I understand if you need to go, though."

He stood up and stretched and I heard his back pop and crack. Then he sat back down next to me and reached to roll the tray with my lame breakfast on it closer to me.

Devon broke a piece of toast off and held it up to my lips. I raised an eyebrow at him and took the food. He watched me closely as I took another bite from his fingers. The third bite, his fingers lingered over my lips. By the fourth bite, he was caressing my face, and by the fifth, he was kissing my neck in between.

"As soon as they give you clearance, I am going to drive you home and caretake you like nobody's business. I am going to bathe you, wash your hair, feed you, watch over you, maybe even paint your toenails again. I am not leaving your side."

I looked up at him and the love in his eyes was so powerful, it took my breath away.

"That would be pretty damn wonderful. But what about..."

He shook his head. "Marcus and I had a long talk yesterday and he called Scott, the producer. We told Scott we weren't able to come out to L.A. right now, and he was fine with it. He actually had another band that was ready this week, so they're taking our time with him. That gives us another month or so to fine-tune what we've got and come up with some better stuff. So I'm not going anywhere. I even told the guys I'd be staying with you until you were better—and they were pissed because they *all* want to come take care of you, too."

I laughed at that and he held more toast up for me. I pointed at the juice and he gave me a sip. I was a little over-attentive to the bendy straw on my juice box, causing Devon's eyes to narrow and a growl to sound in his chest.

He pulled the juice box away and kissed me deeply, his tongue gliding along mine, stroking and caressing. I moaned softly and he pulled me to him, crushing me against his chest.

A soft tapping at the door interrupted us and we both looked over to find Dr. Franklin smiling.

"Well, I see things are progressing in here. How do you feel this morning, Miss Charles?"

I smiled at Devon. "Better. Much better."

Dr. Franklin chuckled. "I can see why. Mr. Boudreaux? Would you mind if I examine Miss Charles? It will mean getting her home that much quicker."

Devon smiled his devastating smile, my favorite of his smiles, and I felt like things just might be going right in the world.

Epilogue

The guys' reprieve lasted two more months. During that time, I was in and out of the St. Germaine, tattooing them and just hanging out. They decided on the drawing of the angel cradling a fleur-de-lis, just like Star described. When I finished the drawing, Jade just *had* to have it done first.

I worked on each them over a couple of weeks and learned even more about them during that time. Mage was insanely ticklish and his tattoo took the longest, since he wanted it on his rib cage.

I tattooed Devon last, when he was ready, and it was a moving experience for both of us. He decided to have it placed on his back under his last name. It was a perfect fit.

I made sure I spent plenty of time hanging out with the other guys as well. We watched more cult classics together, played more Trivial Pursuit, and we finally made it out to their old paintball stomping grounds in Houma. I was victorious. Most importantly, they wrote some amazing music together. Much of it was very different from where they had started, and a huge departure from their earlier albums. All of it related to losing Maggie, and finding their way back to life, wherever that journey led them.

The guys went back to L.A. in early July to go into the studio with

Scott Cross, and wrapped recording in mid-August. They returned to New Orleans for a couple of weeks in September and Devon and I spent almost every single minute together. He hung out at my shop, we went out to listen to music, and we spent lots of time with Marie, Daryl, and the rest of the family. Daryl fully recovered from his heart attack and started working with a personal trainer. By late fall he'd lost fifty pounds and looked even scarier, now that he was starting to tone and build muscle.

Business was booming at the shop. Mackenzie and I decided to hire another tattoo artist and a shop girl, so that she and I would be able to travel from time to time together to see the guys. She and Star hit a few bumpy patches, including the night he knocked on my door in his birthday suit because Mackenzie had gotten angry and kicked him out.

All he could figure out was that she went to use the bathroom and he'd left the toilet seat up. The next thing he knew, she was hitting him with a pillow and screaming at him to get out. Devon gladly lent him a pair of shorts and he crashed on the couch after we ate a pint of ice cream together.

When Devon and I awoke the next day, Mackenzie was curled up next to Star on my couch and he was snoring happily.

October was filled with a series of shows in major cities. They played more intimate venues than usual, and Devon loved it. He called me every day from the road, sometimes twice or three times, and he said he felt like the new stuff they'd written had invigorated him. It was hard with him gone, but the extra time we'd had together further solidified our feelings. My confidence in us was growing.

The short tour ended in New Orleans for VooDoo Experience the week of Halloween. It was my first time seeing them perform in a regular setting, and I was completely awestruck. They had a stage built, pyrotechnics, film running on three screens, and they performed with such aggression and power it blew me away.

They played a few songs from the new album, which they'd titled *Haunted*. As Marcus had suggested, they used my original drawing for the cover. Rock radio stations everywhere picked up "Heavy" as the first single. It immediately went to number one on the charts and stayed there through November.

The album release was set for December and, in poor taste, the label planned a release party the same week as the anniversary of Maggie's death. This time it was held at the Key Club on Sunset in Hollywood. Devon and I talked a lot about it ahead of time, and by the time the night arrived, he was feeling more comfortable with the idea.

Things were very different this time. The guys were all sober, Sherry did her best to be sure any bad influences wouldn't be around them, and Devon felt like he could do it if he was holding my hand. The plan was for them to play three or four songs from the album, we would toast—with Martinelli's—and that would be that.

But Devon had something else in mind. After they played their set, they lingered on stage and Devon stepped up to the mic.

"Before we finish up here, I have one more song to sing. I would like to dedicate this to my beautiful Jaylene."

Devon played and sang "Branded"...

I feel your needle on my skin, marking me as you've marked my soul
The buzz like the feeling I get whenever you are near to me
The lines and colors you etch into me like the memories of holding you close
The moment you touched me you branded me
You branded me
And I'll never be the same
My life before you left marks and scars I never thought would heal
My life before you was an endless drone that left me numb and cold
My life before you was broken lines and muted colors
But the moment you touched me, you branded me
You branded me
And I'm forever changed

From now on I'll share my soul with you
From now on I'll hold you close whether near or far
From now on we'll make the lines and colors more vivid than ever before
Now that you've branded me
You've branded me, a part of me you'll always be.

. . .

When the song finished, he gestured for me to join him onstage. Mackenzie elbowed me and Sherry pushed from the other side. I walked up to the stage, careful not to stumble in the gorgeous deep red gown Devon had bought for me and on the heels I was so not used to wearing.

Marcus took my hand and helped me up the steps to Devon, who took me in his arms and kissed me. He got down on his knee and my world tilted on its side. He still held the mic in his hand.

"Beautiful girl, you've held my hand through these many months and made me the happiest man alive. I told you shortly after we met that I was going to ask you to marry me, and, well...I've wanted to do this since that day. Jaylene Renee Charles, would you do me the most incredible honor of becoming my wife?"

He held out a breathtakingly beautiful platinum ring with a large black diamond in the center, surrounded by smaller white diamonds.

I was shaky and had some trouble breathing. He looked concerned but the smile never left his eyes. After all we'd been through, I didn't ever want that smile to leave his eyes again. I said a silent prayer of thanks that those eyes *continued* to smile.

When I didn't answer right away, he cleared his throat and said, "I dare you." His devastating smile almost did me in.

When I answered, I had never been so sure of anything in my life.

"Yes, Devon. I would love to be your wife. You don't even have to dare me."

The guys in the band sarcastically played the wedding march and the applause from our friends and family in the club was heartwarming. I wasn't just marrying my best friend. I was marrying into the family who had already adopted me.

I felt safe, I felt cherished, and I felt loved. And though we would always be haunted by those we'd lost and by the tragedies of the past, we were all closer than ever. Maggie's Bones were about to reconquer the world.

Devon slipped the ring on my finger and made sure it was snug before rising to his full height and cradling my face in his hands. "I love you desperately, chère. I can't wait to be married to you."

I shook my head. "I can't wait to be Mrs. Boudreaux." We both laughed and he pulled me into a tight embrace. I barely heard the congratulations that were given by all the partygoers.

Her eyes our lens
  Her smile our light
  Her laugh our applause
  Her memory our hope

Stay Tuned for more Rock 'n' Romance featuring Maggie's Bones!

Acknowledgments

Haunted was my first published novel. It's a story incredibly close to my heart as I wrote it to process the death of my father, David Charles Merrill, in 2012. Everything I've written since Haunted has roots in the process; from the confidence and love I derived from this story, to the readers who love "dem boys," and to the wonderful people I've met on my journey. I'd like to think my writing has come a long way since I published this labor of love in 2014, so when I decided to put my books in print, I held this one back. I owe a huge debt of gratitude to my editor Kelli Collins for taking on the ginormous task of helping me make this beast the best it can be! Thank you, Kelli, for your infinite patience.

I am also incredibly fortunate to have the friendship and support of Ellay Branton and Kimberlie L. Faye, both of whom were with me since the very beginning.

To my beloved Kelli Smith, I love your kick-ass self and cannot thank you enough for always giving me a shoulder, ear, or eye... Basically any body part I require to support the process!

And now... A definitive guide to Maggie's Bones...

Haunted Reading List (in order):
Haunted
Bated: A Haunted Story
Fated: A Haunted Story
Minded: A Paranormal Haunted Story
Blossomed: A Minded Story
Father F'in Christmas: A Minded Prequel
Shifted: Magic and Mayhem Universe

Ghoul Me Once: Magic and Mayhem Universe
Gator Me Twice: Magic and Mayhem Universe
A Peculiar Prom Night
Feuds and Interludes: Road to Rocktoberfest 2024

Coming Up Next:
Jaded

About the Author

Whether she's writing contemporary romance featuring quirky and relatable characters or diving deep into the paranormal and supernatural to give readers a shiver, R.L. Merrill loves creating compelling, diverse, and inclusive stories that will stay with readers long after. Winner of the Kathryn Hayes "When Sparks Fly" Best Contemporary award for *Hurricane Reese*, Paranormal Romance Guild's Best Rockstar Romance for *You Can Do Magic*, and Daphne DuMaurier finalist for *Connection*, Ro spends every spare moment improving her writing craft and striving to find that perfect balance between real-life and happily ever after. You can find her connecting with readers on social media, advocating for America's youth, cruising around town with Great Dane Velma, cuddling with twin black cat familiars Frankenstein and Dracula, or headbanging at a rock show near her home in the San Francisco Bay Area! ***Stay Tuned for more...***

Newsletter: www.rlmerrillauthor.com/all-the-links

ALSO BY R.L. MERRILL

Haunted Series: (Contemporary Romance)

Haunted

Fated

Bated

Jaded – (Coming Soon)

Minded Series: (Paranormal Spinoff of Haunted Series)

Minded

Blossomed

Father F'in' Christmas

A Peculiar Prom Night

Magic and Mayhem Universe: (Funny Paranormal Romance in the universe created by Robyn Peterman)

Shifted

Ghoul Me Once

Gator Me Twice

Magic and Mayhem/Shifted Collection

Fang Me Three Times

Fangtastic Four

Five Fanger Witch Punch

Hollywood Rock 'n' Romance Trilogy: (Contemporary Romance)

Teacher

Teacher: Act Two

Teacher: The Final Act

Contemporary Romance Series:

The Rock Season

Road Trip

You Fell First

The Heart Knows (Re-Releasing Soon)

A Match Made in Spain

LGBTQ Romance

Pinups and Puppies (Originally in Love Is All Vol. 2)

I Want, More – Bolder Breed Studios #1 (Originally in Love Is All Vol. 3)

Love and Pride – Bolder Breed Studios #2 (Originally in Love Is All Vol. 4)

Everything's Better With You: An MM Sports Romance

All I Wanna Do — Bolder Breed Studios #3 (Email Ro for your copy)

Under His Sheets: Accidentally Undercover – Out April 9, 2024

Feuds and Interludes: Road To Rocktoberfest 2024 - November 2024

The Banes of Lake's Crossing (Historical Horror Romance)

The Fourth Man (The Banes of Lake's Crossing) (Historical Horror Romance)

The Redemption of Nathaniel Bane

The Absolution of Jonah Bane

The Gifted Series: (Supernatural Suspense/Paranormal Romance)

Healer

Connection

Protector

Sundowners (M/M Paranormal Romance

Sundowners Book One

Sundowners Book Two (February 13, 2025)

Forces of Nature Series: (Gay Contemporary Romance)

Hurricane Reese

Typhoon Toby

Summer of Hush Series: (Gay Contemporary Romance)

Summer of Hush

Brains and Brawn

You Can Do Magic: Carnival Of Mysteries (A Summer of Hush Tie-In)

You Can Save Me: Carnival of Mysteries (Season Two, Book Two)

Anthologies:

Thanksgiving Day Parade From Hell (Worst Holiday Ever) (Gay Contemporary Romance

Valentine's Day From Hell (Worst Valentine's Day Ever) (Gay Contemporary Romance)

Salty and Sweet (Summer Fair) (Lesbian Contemporary Romance)

The Fourth Man (The Banes of Lake's Crossing) (Historical Horror Romance)

A Piece of Him (Gone With The Dead) (Horror)

Breaking Bread—Dark Divinations from HorrorAddicts.net Press (Horror)

Exchange (Renewal) (Science Fiction)

Tap-Tap-Tap (Impact) (Horror)

Human Sacrifice (Innovation) (Horror)

The Sitter (Clarity) (Horror)

Joy Is A Phone Call Away – A More Perfect Union (Lesbian Contemporary Romance)

The House Must Fall – Haunts and Hellions from HorrorAddicts.net Press – May 2021 (Horror)

A Kept Woman – BAQWA Presents: Horror Show 2021(Lesbian Horror Romance)

Gods of Rock 'n' Roll (Free on Wattpad)

How Bittersweet is Karma? Free on Wattpad)

Let Me Stand Next To Your Fire (Queer Cheer)

Midnight in the Renaissance Elevator

Holiday Romance

A Peace Offering (Re-release)

Love and Pride – Bolder Breed Studios #2

Once Upon A Holiday Story 2024 (December 2024)

Audiobooks

The Rock Season (Kiss App)

Brains and Brawn (Kiss App)

Teacher (Kiss App)

Hurricane Reese (Kiss App)

A Match Made in Spain (Audible)

Healer: Gifted Book One (Audible)

Under His Sheets (Audible Coming Soon)

You Can Do Magic: Carnival of Mysteries (Coming Soon)

Road Trip: A Rock Season Novel (Coming Soon)

Non-Fiction

Horror Addicts Guide To Life Volume 2 - Edited by Emerian Rich

Death's Garden Revisited - Edited by Loren Rhoads (Out Fall 2022)

www.ingramcontent.com/pod-product-compliance
Lightning Source LLC
Chambersburg PA
CBHW021842010726
47493CB00005B/1519